FATEPLAY

BY DUNCAN MCGEARY

PROLOGUE

Notre Dame rose above the city like heaven itself, strong and eternal, a reminder to the crowds below of mortality and the afterlife. On this day, two men would join the angels—or the demons. Even now, with the time of execution almost upon them, no one was sure which way the citizens of Paris would turn. Scorn and pity warred in their hearts. Some threw rotted fruits and vegetables upon the prisoners, while others—despite King Philip the Fair's spies in the crowd—shouted defiance at the executioners.

Eight of us had survived to reach Paris, a disparate crew of experienced fighters. We had decided to attack the procession as it neared the Bridge of Notre Dame.

The central nave of the great cathedral had been finished only eleven years before, in 1303. Scaffolds still covered the exterior as skilled artisans carved gargoyles and chimera, and painted façades of saints and sinners. The flying buttresses and rose-colored windows floated above earthbound Paris, looking down upon the condemned.

We pushed our way through the surging crowd from the direction of the Avenue of Tanners. We tried to blend in, our swords still sheathed, bows slung upon our backs. My body vibrated from the intoxicating tension filling the air. The flaring emotion of the throng was impossible to resist. This was to be my day of deliverance as well, one way or another.

At my side, Marie of Poitiers retched at the smell of urine and dung. "Never mind the guards," she muttered, "we'll die from the smell."

The cart clattered up the steep arch of the bridge. Those of us who still survived were to meet at the far end, a concerted attack at the narrowest point of the route. Marie and I reached the nexus. No one else had made it.

I saw fear in Marie's eyes, and I'm sure my eyes reflected the same fear. It was down to just the two of us.

The old farmer's cart was encrusted with hay and manure and was so rickety that the prisoners struggled to keep their footing, weighed down by irons and chains. The guilty were not to be afforded any luxury, nor given any sign of respect.

The condemned were old men now, these bent figures who'd once been as powerful as kings: Jacques de Molay, Grand Master of the Order of Knights Templar, and Geoffrey de Charney, Preceptor of Normandy. It was clear from their postures that they had given up all hope of rescue. Most of the Templars who'd survived the slaughter had disappeared into the countryside. No doubt there were a few in the crowd watching, unable to help.

That was our task, to rescue the Grand Master and the Preceptor, though they were guarded by dozens of men-at-arms on horseback and archers on foot. I drew my sword and turned to nod at Marie, but iron gloves fell upon her shoulders from behind and she fell backward with a cry.

I leapt upon the cart and bounded toward the two prisoners. Up close, they looked even older, their eyes dull with the knowledge that they were about to die.

Now what? I wondered. I didn't have the keys to their locks or the tools to break their irons. It had never occurred to me that I might actually make it this far or that I would be alone. There was no way to remove the prisoners from the cart—therefore, I had to take the cart itself.

I pushed past the astonished Jacques de Molay. The driver, cloaked in a gray-hooded robe, stood and turned, casting off her disguise.

It was the Blue Queen, the host of the Jubilee Games, owner and designer of the scenario we were playing out.

The Blue Queen wasn't supposed to be there, of course. At the time, Paris was packed with princesses and queens, but Maureen O'Rourke's character wasn't one of them. She was dressed in blue leggings and a blue jerkin, which while bejeweled was modest for her. Her red hair was loose; her green eyes shone mischievously.

She winked at me. As always, her beauty stunned me, and as always, I wondered if she looked that way in real life.

I was distracted just long enough for a guard on horseback to rush me. The guard's lance went through my belly and out my back, slicing my spine in two. I dropped to the ground like a sack of grain, my bones liquefied by the red flashing badge on my chest.

Notre Dame and its vicinity disappeared. My heart skipped a beat as it always did when I was thrown back into reality. Instead of being beneath the gargoyles and frescos of the cathedral, we were inside the cavernous interior of the largest tent in the world. The Eiger was vast and seemingly solid though frayed around the edges; stains marbled the canvas, tears and rents, as if it had existed for a thousand years.

No one had ever come close to winning this Hyper-reality scenario. Jacques de Molay and Geoffrey de Charney always met their fate in the bonfires of the Island of Jews. Most Hyper-reality players considered "The Rescue of Jacques de Molay" the least winnable of scenarios. Which was the appeal, of course.

But damn. We'd almost made it.

People hustled about, dressed in costumes of every era and from every fictional universe ever created. They were already preparing for the next game, tearing down the bare façades of the streets and castles of medieval Paris. Someone was waving at me from the sidelines.

I'd left my phone with John Hansen, who'd planned on joining the game but was hobbled from an injury from his Indiana Jones LARP the day before. Electronics weren't allowed inside the Eiger during the Queen's Jubilee while a game was in progress.

John handed me the phone, a worried look on his face. "It's your mom. I think it's an emergency."

CHRPTER ONE

When Joseph Cambermire first hired me to run Pegasus Corp, most LARPers and cosplayers emulated current pop culture. But the more Hyper-reality took over the world, the more people reached into the past for inspiration. You were just as likely to meet a Humphrey Bogart as you were some newer star like Hall Canfield.

It made sense in a way. The whole world was becoming one big time machine, where everyone was connected to every pop culture moment of the past, so that it all blurred together, and walking arm in arm among us was a 1960s-era Elizabeth Taylor Cleopatra and the boy-throb of the current moment, Shogun Markel. Where an "I Am Legend" marathon could attract cosplayers of Vincent Price, Charlton Heston, Will Smith, and the newest incarnation, Jeremy Reid. Where Theda Bara and Madonna vamped together.

Diary of Roger Ackroyd

I hadn't checked the mailbox in days, so I expected it to be filled with junk mail. Instead, a single envelope sat in the middle of the corrugated metal box. Sunlight outlined the familiar square shape of a ticket, red color bleeding through thin paper.

My morning laziness vanished. The nerves in my fingertips tingled in anticipation as I reached in. Right there on the sidewalk, I tore the envelope open. The all-venue Red Pass fell into my palm, so lightweight that when I closed my eyes I couldn't feel it. But it was real, all right.

A door slammed across the way. John Simmons nodded to me as he walked to his car, which this week he had holosleeved as the 1964 Aston Martin DBS from the movie *Goldfinger*. He wore a dapper three-piece suit, his fedora tilted rakishly. "Sorry about your mom," he said.

I nodded back. I wasn't sure Mom and Mr. Simmons had ever exchanged more than two words.

I was suddenly conscious that I was in my bathrobe, my black hair a wild halo. I hadn't shaved in days—I was thinking about growing a Lincolnesque beard, because I couldn't quite get a full mustache. I was pretty sure my breath could be smelled from across the street.

I lived in a little tan house with a yellow lawn and a broken sidewalk, remarkable only in how dreary it looked compared to its neighbors. It was the only unsleeved house on the block, the irony of which was not lost on me. Next door, the Sandersons had chosen a replica of Fallingwater, complete with a creek running under it, while on the other side, the political junkie, Burt Bryson, had sleeved his home as a mini-White House. Across the way, Mary Swenson went to Las Vegas as often as possible and lived in a little mini-casino, with neon lights glowing day and night.

Just about everyone could afford to live in a holographic castle these days if they chose to.

But Mom had always been different from everyone else. She lived a simple life, with her garden and her journals. She wanted peace and quiet. Her bedroom probably would have felt austere to a Buddhist monk. An unobtrusive tan house, a small yellowing lawn, and a broken sidewalk. It was what it was...real.

It's strange, looking back, that Mom let me get involved in Hyper-reality at all, because it was clear she didn't approve of it. Not that she'd ever tell me what to do. In fact, she'd given me my first ticket to a Pegasus Convention—and every ticket thereafter.

"Where do they come from?" I'd asked. They were always Red Passes, way too expensive for Mom to have bought them.

She'd waved her hand in the air as if summoning a genie. "An old boyfriend. I forget his name, even."

Strangely, I didn't doubt it. Mom had been a free spirit, born in the wrong decade, the last of the hippies and age hadn't changed her. We lived in harmony in that little house, despite living completely different lives. I had to quit college to take care of her those last couple of years, but she'd insisted that I continue to go to the Pegasus Conventions, no matter what.

It was only luck that I was home when she died quietly in her sleep. It was a blessing in the end. She'd refused all medications except her usual weed, her will stronger than the pain and fear. I was holding her hand when she passed, and I was forever grateful that I was there.

Since her passing, I'd barely budged from the house, reading my way through her library, as if I could keep her if I read what she'd read. Her free spirit floated in the air, in death as in life. She was still there somehow, in the threadbare rugs, the tattered rock 'n' roll posters on the walls, the flowers that bloomed in her garden.

Problem was...I was broke. Mom had been generous to me—apparently at the cost of taking out a second mortgage on our humble abode. Pathetic, really: a grown man, living in his dead mom's about-to-be-repossessed house.

The envelope with the Red Pass had no return address. Whoever the mysterious benefactor was, there was no way to inform them that Mom was gone.

I went back into the house sensing that this day was different. I felt my blood quickening. My Civil War re-enactors group met every Friday afternoon down at Pioneer Park. How long had it been since I'd attended?

I tracked down my phone, which was buried under a pile of dirty laundry. It was dead. I hadn't used it in weeks.

It was time to join the real world, I thought. And yes, I was aware of the irony. The tan house with the yellowed lawn and a broken sidewalk *was* the real world. What I was really doing was rejoining the fantasy.

I put on my long blue coat and headed out, my scrunched-down Union cap in one pocket, my glasses in my other pocket.

For the first time since Mom died, I felt the urge to play. I was pretty sure my friends would be surprised to see me.

A Union picket challenged me at the gate, which consisted of a couple of ribbons strung between trees. I put on my virtual reality (VR) glasses.

Instead of ribbons, a massive barricade blocked the way. Instead of a riverfront park, a vast military camp spread out in front of me, hundreds of tents, thousands of soldiers milling about bonfires, cooking, cleaning, and drinking.

Jerry Opie waved a bayonet in my face. The blade nicked my chin. The soft plastic boffer tip bent, breaking the illusion. I took off my round rose-colored glasses, which owed more to John Lennon than to the Civil War.

"Watch it!" I said.

"Sorry, Zach," Jerry said. "Caught some guys earlier trying to sneak in without paying."

"No problem... and that's Major Dundee, *Private*." Major Dundee was my character's name, based on an old Charlton Heston Western.

"Yes, sir!" Jerry saluted lazily.

I held up my six-pack of beer. "Will this do?"

"My hero," Jerry said, extracting a bottle. "The others are down by the river. Some damn Middle Earthers snagged the picnic tables."

My crew was sitting down by the banks, a dozen guys and Marie McGraw, who was sort of our den mother and made sure we got fed. The grass was covered in goose poop. Someone— probably Marie—had brought a couple of blankets, but there was barely enough room for everyone to fit. Stephen Steward and Glenn Halligan scooted over far enough for me to squeeze in. I handed them each a beer.

The Buellers were my favorite group of players, wayward Civil War re-enactors infected by steampunk. (We called our- selves "Buellers" after General Buell, the worst Union com- mander of the Civil War—with a nod to Ferris Bueller.)

We weren't strict constructionist live-action role-players. There was no game master, no organized play. We were in it for the fun. There was usually at least one other Hyper-reality group in the park, of some variety or another. It was the rare public space now that wasn't taken over by people in costumes, playing arcane games, speaking in jargon only their fellow genre players understood. Most people came directly from their jobs, having worn their costumes to work.

At twenty-five years of age, I was old enough to remember when dressing in costume was considered weird. I'd never thought Hyper-reality would get this far. It seemed that everyone was pretending to be someone else these days, whether at home, at work, at school, or at play.

In fact, it was rarer to see someone out of costume than in—except for the Thentics, of course, those stick-in-the-mud types who thought it was all nonsense. Unlike most of my fellow players, I didn't look down on these people, maybe because of my Mom, who, while not a Thentic, had been happy to live alone with her own thoughts without all the stimuli and hoopla.

"You all right?" Stephen asked. I realized from his tone that my friends had been worried, because they'd had no way of getting ahold of me.

"Yeah," I said. I held up the Red Pass.

"You lucky bastard!" Glenn shouted. "Is that to the Portland Con?" He hesitated, then said in a softer voice, "You going?"

"I think I will," I affirmed. It was time. Mom was gone and she wouldn't have wanted me to stay in a funk forever. Nothing had ever brought her down. She wouldn't have wanted me to mourn forever.

Glenn patted me on the back companionably. My friends had never acted envious of me, maybe because I'd given them Red Passes to conventions whenever Mom was especially sick and I couldn't go myself.

We sat drinking desultorily. For some reason, everyone was a little down that day. Across the grass, the hobbits and elves and dwarves were having a great time, laughing and whooping it up. They were Filking, singing some dirty little ditties about nasty elves.

The one bad thing about Civil War re-enacting is that so few women join up as soldiers, or nurses, or even camp followers, now that I think of it. The Middle Earthers had no such problem.

"I don't understand it," Glenn said. "The furry-footed bastards get all the girls."

Stephen's voice was formal, like it got when he was drunk. "I believe that they are laughing at us. I do not think we should stand for that."

"You're right!" Glenn shouted, standing up. "This means war! Bring on The General!"

The cannon was the centerpiece of our group. Without it, I doubt we'd even have existed. We quickly formed up in ranks and started marching toward the picnic tables.

The Middle Earthers saw us coming and formed lines opposite us, brandishing swords and axes. "Not this day!" one of them shouted.

"Halt!" Glenn ordered. He was our commander when we bothered to have one. Stephen and a couple of others positioned The General.

Glenn raised his sword above his head. "Ready! … Aim! … Fire!"

Stephen lit the fuse. The cannon exploded with an extraordinarily loud *Boom!* Every time I heard it, I imagined the carnage of a battery of these monsters firing into the ranks of gray-uniformed Confederates.

Red, white, and blue confetti almost reached the Middle Earthers. With my rose-colored VR glasses on, I saw cannonballs and slaughter.

With a roar, our opponents charged. We managed to fire off a few blanks, and a couple of halflings obligingly rolled into the dirt, and then it was a melee. I had forgotten to bring my sword, so I stayed out of the way until Mark Dupless fell to the ground next to me mortally wounded. I reached down for his sword.

"You don't mind, do you?" I whispered.

"Be my guest," he said, his breath blowing up the dust.

As always happened, my heart raced, fear mixed with excitement. It always felt real to me, all of it. I was in the moment, at war. I fought off a huge goblin, finally stabbing him in the throat.

"I suppose you got me," the goblin said, resignedly. He took his time lying down, then put his hands behind his head as if he was stargazing.

The melee was turning to single combat; bodies littered the

ground. I turned in time to see someone dressed as Mr. Zander striding toward me.

What's he *doing here?*

There couldn't have been a character more removed from Middle Earth than Mr. Zander, the only game character who'd ever scared me. In the video game, he was tall and gangly, with a sharp goatee and a twirled mustache, knee-high shiny black boots, and a crumpled top hat. In the movies, Hall Canfield portrayed him, though the famous actor was a foot too short for the role. At least he got the nasty attitude down right.

Mr. Zander's long frock coat clattered as he sped toward me, the row of knives lining the inside flashing. He was carrying a long stiletto.

My vision narrowed, as if I was looking through a telescope. The ground shook; he loomed over me, impossibly tall. To the east, jagged mountains lined the sky. The smell of death filled the air, and the screams of dying men. The trees looked taller, yet unhealthy. It was suddenly twilight, as if the sun had never existed.

All of which was impossible. In reality, to the east of Bend was the high desert. And it was still early enough that the sun should have been in my eyes.

The blade in Mr. Zander's spindly hand looked sharp and real. I looked down at my sword, which gleamed in the twilight. There were runes etched into the metal, runes that hadn't been there before.

I raised the sword just in time. Mr. Zander's stiletto shattered, and he howled. Without thinking, I thrust the sword into his stomach.

And then the sun was in my eyes again. I stood there, stunned. My imagination had never taken me that far before. I looked around for my opponent, intending to congratulate him on the authenticity of his costume, but there was no one there.

I felt a sharp point in my back. "You're dead," a small voice said.

I turned to find a young boy dressed as a halfling. He was waving a replica of Sting, and it was a real blade, if dull. He stabbed me again.

I grabbed my belly, yelled theatrically, and collapsed. The kid giggled and put his furry foot triumphantly on my chest. I opened my eyes a slit, just to make sure that the twilight realm hadn't returned. It had felt so real that I was still trembling.

Half an hour later, the two groups were mingling, exchanging parts of their costumes, drunk enough to consider a Civil War/Middle Earth crossover. We sat and drank beer among the pine trees, the Deschutes River meandering nearby.

"You all right, Zach?" Stephen asked for the second time. "I mean, you look freaked out."

"Mr. Zander freaked me out," I said.

"Mr. Zander? What are you talking about?"

I hesitated, but I needed to know. "Did you guys notice anything strange during the battle? Like it got really dark for a minute?"

"Are you feeling OK?" Glenn asked.

"What? I'm fine."

"I mean, I'm sorry about your mom."

I felt a pang. For a few moments I'd almost forgotten. "Mom was sick a long time," I said quietly. "I knew it was going to happen."

"Is that blood on your coat?" Stephen asked.

I looked down. A wet splotch covered my chest. How did that get there? The memory of Mr. Zander's gushing wound came back to me.

Stephen and Glenn exchanged worried glances.

"Never mind...I think I must have landed in some duck poop," I said, not even trying to explain the stain's red color. I hadn't been out of the house in weeks. I was still depressed about Mom. I had just gotten a little overexcited and overstimulated. That's all.

In the distance, from the highway that ran by the park, someone shouted, "Grow up, you wankers!"

Everyone pretended to ignore it, but it broke the mood. The players started to drift off. Stephen and Glenn got up, both ruffling my hair. "Glad you're back, man," Stephen said.

I lay back in the grass, putting my arm over my eyes. The

bright red behind my eyelids turned into a dark blue, then faded to black. I sensed a shadow looming over me and sat up with a shout.

I was alone.

I finished my beer and walked to my Toyota, an old car with a steampunk locomotive sleeve, and drove home. I was too tired to drop by one of the bigger grocery stores and pulled into Marko's to get a loaf of bread and some sandwich meat.

My heart fell when I saw Marko behind the counter, sneering through the window at my steampunk car. I'd hoped his wife Norma, who was a sweetheart, would be behind the register. I grabbed the food and brought it up. Marko ignored me for a few awkward moments, talking to some guy dressed in camouflage fatigues. The guy was probably a hunter, not in costume. That was the crowd Marko's attracted.

Marko looked exactly like Jeebs, the wall-eyed character Tony Shalhoub portrayed in *Men in Black*. But he wasn't a Hyperreality player. In fact, he'd made it more than clear to me that he despised anyone who dressed up in costume—especially me. He was more redneck than most of the locals, even though he had a thick Eastern European accent.

I handed him a twenty-dollar bill and he held out a five-dollar bill in change. I reached for it, and he drew back. The camouflage guy laughed, which unfortunately only encouraged Marko. I reached out a second time. He pulled the bill back again.

I thought about walking away and never coming back. Marko wasn't even really a Thentic, who at least had beliefs they stood by. He was just a jerk.

"Marko, I'm really too tired for this." The light dimmed and I swayed. I reached out to steady myself. It seemed to me that Marko's face opened into a row of clashing teeth.

I must have stood there with my mouth open, because I heard Marko laughing. "Wake up, buddy. You want your money?"

The door behind the counter opened and Norma stepped beside her husband, short and chubby. She snatched the money out of Marko's hand and gave it to me. "Sorry about Marko. He's in a mood."

I walked outside, red-faced. As I stood there for a moment trying to gather myself, a coyote trotted toward me.

A coyote...in the middle of town. I watched him approach, somehow not surprised. I'd seen coyotes in the wild before, trotting nonchalantly as if they didn't have a care in the world. This coyote had the same insolent attitude. It stopped in front of me and sat down on its haunches. Its disturbingly intelligent yellow eyes examined me.

"Cambermire," the coyote said. Then it shook its head as if disappointed and trotted away.

I got in my steampunk-sleeved car and drove home to the little tan house with the yellow lawn and the broken sidewalk.

Cambermire, the coyote had said. *Cambermire.* Why would it mention the founder of Pegasus Corp?

I laughed out loud.

Why am I trying to make sense of what a coyote said?

A touch of heatstroke, that had to be it.

The moment I walked into Mom's threadbare house, I was exhausted. For the first time since Mom died, the house felt truly empty. I stumbled to my bed.

When I woke up, I wondered if I'd dreamed the whole thing. But there on the bed stand was a five-dollar bill. There on the chair was my Union coat with a red splotch that still felt tacky when I reached over and rubbed it.

I pulled the Red Pass out of my pocket and checked the date.

It was time I started living my life again.

CHAPTER TWO

I admit it surprised me when the LARPers and cosplayers adapted the newest technologies onto their costumes. In some ways, the current affordability of holograms and virtual reality is due to the wholesale adoption of such tech by the Hyper-reality community.

It is hard to know, nowadays, where the physical costumes leave off and the digital trickery begins. Almost anyone can use VR; sometimes, if their makeup is elaborate enough, even a mask isn't necessary. Holograms can be used with or without VR.

There are extreme users who live in a complete VR/holo world, though that is usually only possible for the very rich.

There are others who refuse to use technology at all. Who feel it is but a cheat. Certainly, their costumes are no less elaborate—indeed, sometimes the real makeup and costuming is even more impressive.

But everyone mingles together without judgment. That is something Joseph Cambermire has insisted upon from the very beginning. No one is better than anyone else. If you show up at a Pegasus Convention wearing only a hat, you will probably get some odd looks, but no one will say anything.

After all, everyone has to start somewhere.

Diary of Roger Ackroyd

It wasn't until I was driving past Mt. Hood that I realized I'd forgotten to pack a costume.

I never missed the Portland Con since it was only a few hours' drive over the Cascade Mountains—the only Pegasus-sponsored convention in my home state. Red Passes arrived in the mail every year. I got tickets for most conventions, along with plane tickets and motel reservations. But Portland was my favorite.

Whoever Mom's old boyfriend was, he was rich.

I knew from the set of Mom's mouth and the tone of her voice that she'd never tell me who my benefactor was. But now that she was gone, I wondered why I'd never followed up on it. I'd just taken the tickets gratefully and used them as often as I could. I didn't make it to every convention, but I was certainly a regular. People knew who I was—people who at first assumed I was as wealthy as they were. When they discovered different, I became a curiosity. I got a lot of free meals out of that notoriety.

Strangely, I was always glad to get back to our simple home, which had none of the VR and holosleeve technology, no A.I. or robots, or costumes or games. Hell, Mom didn't even have a TV, much less the Internet. I went from one extreme to the other, and somehow it felt right.

I hadn't worked for the last couple of years while I was taking care of Mom. I didn't know she was paying me with borrowed money...and what little I'd saved up was rapidly diminishing. I was going to have to get a job and soon. But first, one last convention—since I was all but certain the Red Passes would go the way of the Social Security checks.

The Portland Con always coincided with the first Saturday of May, otherwise known as Free Comic Book Day. I figured I'd visit a couple of "Things From Another World" stores in the morning, then hit the Pegasus Convention in the afternoon.

I got my free comics and headed over to the convention hall, but I felt naked without a costume. I looked around and realized that no one else was out of character. I ran into a few friends who razzed me about being a civilian.

Of course, I could have bought a costume. The hall was filled with wonderful creations, imaginations free of everyday life. But what I could afford would have been more embarrassing than no costume at all.

Even though I'm not a particularly *out*-there Hyper-reality player. I mean...I like to think I'm original, but I'm not especially flamboyant. I am wowed by what other Hyper-reality players create at Pegasus Conventions, the amount of inventive-ness, sometimes done on a threadbare budget.

I checked my wallet. I had just about enough to money to buy a meal from the Dollar Menu at McD's and gas to make it home. Not enough to buy any costume I'd want to be seen in.

"Turning into a Thentic?" someone asked from behind me.

Marty Hampton was standing a few feet away at the end of a long line that didn't seem to lead anywhere but a bare table with one person behind it. Marty was short and round and eager to please; he checked to make sure I wasn't offended. He was also one of the first people I'd ever befriended at a Pegasus Convention. But my attention was drawn to the bare table, which was unheard of, especially in a prime location near the entrance. The convention hall was full of color and sound, an overwhelming sensory overload.

At the next table over were two Leeloos, with bright orange hair and white strips of cloth barely covering their privates, sell-ing replicas of *The Fifth Element*'s Four Stones. On the other side were people on stilts, juggling and singing in a made-up lan-guage, no doubt amusing themselves if no one else. Everyone in the convention center had to shout and move and splash the air with color in order to be noticed.

An empty table was completely incongruous and therefore the most noticeable thing of all.

"What are you waiting in line for?" I asked.

"I'm getting tested," Marty answered. "They're still looking for Que. I'm pretty sure my mom wouldn't cheat on Dad but, well…it can't hurt to make sure."

"What?" I asked.

Marty turned to me confused.

"Que is the word for 'what' in Spanish," I explained.

Marty laughed. "That works. In legal filings, he's called John Q…Joseph Cambermire's long-lost son? Everyone's started calling him Que. Where you been, man?"

"Out of touch," I said. This was the first I'd heard of it.

And yet, suddenly my head was filled with the knowledge of the long search for Que, the million-dollar reward, the specu-lation in the news. I hadn't been to a convention in months and

I had consumed very little media. Had I overheard something while at the same time not paying much attention to it? And what did it have to do with me?

"Screw this," Marty said. "They're only paying twenty bucks, and it's taking too long. Come on, there's a steampunk game starting in a few minutes. You got your VR glasses?"

I pointed to my nose and my rose lenses. He laughed. "Come with me, I'll loan you a hat."

He whipped a railroad conductor's cap from his bag, blue-striped with a long bill, and handed it to me.

"Yeah, a *hat* will make all the difference," I said. Still, I'd always liked steampunk scenarios involving trains.

I showed my Red Pass at the door, though the guy barely looked at it. It was clear they were short of players and weren't asking for an admission fee. No one wanted to host a game where no one showed up to play.

The locomotive was spectacularly ornate, with curved fins, a shiny red enamel surface, extra lights and horns, and a cabin that looked like it belonged in a hotel. "You're my assistant conductor," Marty said. "The object of the game is to survive a journey through Marauder territory."

Seemed straightforward enough. I tipped my hat and started up the steps, but the steps just kept going. As I looked upward, I could see that the locomotive had expanded in size and shape, and was no longer red but a grimy black, as if layered with centuries of smoke. The chimney extended into the sky, obscured by mist. It was as if someone had dimmed the convention's LED lights. I looked around for Marty, but he was gone. There seemed to be no one on the platform, which now extended into the distance. I pushed my glasses up onto my forehead, but the scene didn't change.

I entered the locomotive. The floors were pine planks and the stove was open, lighting the room with a red glow. A tall thin man with a top hat and a long black cloak grinned at me.

Mr. Zander stood before me, knife in hand.

Someone pinioned me from behind. I looked down. Tentacles were wrapped around my arms, though I couldn't see who or what they belonged to.

"Hold him still," Mr. Zander said. "Personally, I don't see why we don't just kill him, but Tom wants to make sure. I need to take his blood."

"All of it?" said a small voice behind me. It seemed to originate around my knees.

"I suppose if I cut off a finger or something, that ought to be enough."

"Let me do it," the smaller voice said. Another tentacle whipped around me from behind brandishing a dagger. I started to cry out, but the scene began to waver.

"Hurry!" the tall man said. "We need proof!"

The tentacles squeezed tighter. I couldn't breathe. I realized that I had been holding my breath and still had one last chance to make a sound. I shouted as loud as I could. "Heellllppp!"

The tentacles waved in the air as if in distress and then let me go. My gut dropped as the steampunk train suddenly shrank beneath me. The glasses fell down onto my nose again, but even with the VR, the cab was still smaller, the platform behind me a small raised dais.

I was on my knees. Marty crouched next to me.

"What happened?" I asked.

Marty looked scared. "You froze and shouted, then started to fall. It was freaky, man. Your eyes rolled back in your head, like in the movies."

I turned and stumbled down the steps to the train platform.

"You OK?" Marty shouted out behind me, but I kept going.

I slowed as I reached the exit then sat down hard on a chair near the trash cans. *Wha...just...happened?*

What was surprising was that I wasn't even more freaked out. Maybe all the role-playing had prepared me for the day when reality started sliding sideways.

I removed the Red Pass from the plastic sleeve of the lanyard around my neck, and stared down at it.

I'd always wondered about my good fortune. Nothing is free. I should have known there would be a price to pay eventually. Who would have the authority or the resources to send me all those plane tickets and hotel reservations? And why?

Maybe I was part of some experiment, assessing new technology. Maybe they were dosing the Red Pass with some kind of drug. Maybe this was some kind of advanced VR or hologram they were testing.

Either that, or I was going crazy...and I didn't feel crazy. So if I wasn't crazy, there had to be some other explanation.

I should just return to the tan house with the yellow lawn and broken sidewalk.

I had a feeling if I did that, I'd never see a talking coyote or a homicidal Mr. Zander again.

And then what? Apply for a job at Walmart?

No...something was happening. I needed answers.

The Emerald Tower loomed over downtown Portland, half again taller than any other building in the city: Pegasus Corporation's national headquarters.

I'd once caught a glimpse of the tower from the other side of Portland, with its green glow against the white snows of Mt. Hood, and it seemed like it was out of some fantasy—a real Oz, an Orthanc, a Dark Tower...a Barad-dûr.

It was as if Sauron's eye was fixed on me, pulling on me.

I turned toward the Emerald Tower, clutching the Red Pass in my hand.

CHAPTER THREE

Just as reality itself has become difficult to discern in the flow of creativity that is Hyper-reality, so too has history blurred, melding with fiction, creating a hybrid that is in some ways closer in spirit to what really happened than the bare facts.

Re-creation has discovered new facets to events that had become fusty and boring in the history books, giving vitality to events that had been reduced to cliché by repetition—no matter how inconsequential or grandiose they were when they happened. Hyper-reality is, in a sense, living history, and all time is now open to new interpretations.

I leave it to others to decide if this is a good thing or a bad thing. All I know is that I have seen the sacking of Troy, the signing of the Declaration of Independence, and the bombing of Pearl Harbor enacted by real people, giving such scenes a thrill and an immediacy that once was lacking.

Diary of Roger Ackroyd

Within a few blocks, my head began throbbing. Every wall and every post were filled with flickering advertisements. At home I could wear my glasses in peace; Bend had outlawed the holographic bombardment.

I took off my glasses and the buildings turned into plain brick-and-mortar structures, bare walls ready to be sleeved.

Even so, I could barely cross the street, as I was forced to dodge a parade of costumed and holographically enhanced cosplayers. Weirdly enough, my street clothes made me the most unusual person on the block.

Madame Minisquel sat on a curb, her chubby hands out-stretched for offerings. She was a goddess, sculptural in shape, and had probably had some very expensive surgery to make her waist that thin, her butt and breasts that large.

"Good sir, my Marshall is in need of live prey," she said.

The little creature cawed at me from her shoulder, and I barely restrained a surprised yelp. I hadn't noticed the Marshall nestled in the feathered gown the goddess was wearing. It looked like someone had crossed a parrot and a lizard, pretty close to the Marshall in the *Minisquel* comic book, a secondary character who'd taken over the story.

I pulled out a twenty-dollar bill, handed it to her, and kept going.

I hadn't gone three steps before Mr. Zander came out of the shadows, holding out an elegantly gloved hand, tipping his broad hat to me.

I couldn't help myself. I shouted out a visceral warning, though I wasn't sure what I could do if he drew one of his blades.

"Take it easy, buddy!" the tall man said, sounding alarmed.

I looked closer. It was decent cosplay, but the hat was a little too tall, the coat a little too short. His coat opened in a gust of wind and revealed the rows of gleaming knives sheathed there, but as he bent over, one of the long blades bowed in the middle and I knew it was boffered.

"I'm sorry," I said. "That was my last twenty."

He loomed over me, and again I quailed; but no, his knives remained sheathed, and the only thing he pointed at me was his long, bony finger.

He looked me over from head to toe, and apparently decided I was telling the truth. He swirled his cape and somehow sig-naled to the rest of the characters that I wasn't worth the trou-ble, and they left me alone.

The doors of the Emerald Tower opened wide as I approached I was almost surprised that would they let the likes of me in, especially since I wasn't in costume. This was the center of the Hyper-reality world, and here I was looking about as Mundane as possible.

I went to the main desk and was ignored for five or ten

minutes. I showed them my Red Pass and demanded to know who had bought it. The Disney princess at the desk gave me a dubious look and directed me to sit in the lobby until someone could speak with me.

The lobby was massive and mostly empty. The few chairs and tables in the vast expanse seemed as if they'd floated in on a tide of granite. The ceiling was so far above that I was pretty sure that Mom's house could have fit comfortably within the space.

I heard the click and echo of her high heels before I saw her emerge from the swirl of costumes. She was dressed in a severe, if tight, black suit, her long legs in striped steampunk trousers, buckled shoes descending in needle-thin spikes. It was a costume of sorts, but not of any character I'd ever seen.

I liked that. I always liked original creations.

"Zach Spence?" She stared down at me curiously. She was very tall and very black, her skin lustrous like obsidian. Her hair was short, her makeup minimal. She didn't need it. These days, anyone can be beautiful if they want to be and can afford it, so beauty has lost a little of its cachet. When you're in the presence of natural beauty instead of manufactured beauty, it can still be startling.

"I'm Numera," she said, extending her hand. She appeared reluctant to touch me.

I stood and clasped her thin fingers gently. I was suddenly conscious of how ordinary I looked—jeans, T-shirt, disheveled hair.

"Mr. Ackroyd sent me to fetch you," she said.

"Mr. Ackroyd?" I froze at the name. Other than the founder, Joseph Cambermire, there was no one more important in the Pegasus world. "Are you sure?"

"Quite," she said, managing to keep most of the mystified tone out of her voice, though there was a wisp of puzzlement. "He asked for you specifically."

She led me past a bank of beautifully etched elevator doors depicting scenes from Homer as painted by Frazetta, then turned down a narrow hallway toward a glass door that I expected to lead to an alley and my expulsion. Instead, she turned left into a niche that was unnoticeable from the lobby. Beyond was a plain elevator door, already open.

The elevator shot upward, leaving my stomach on the floor. Numera placed an elegant hand on my arm when I stumbled. "Sometimes I forget how fast this thing is," she murmured.

The door flashed open.

The room beyond looked like a library in the aftermath of a tornado. Books were piled on the floor and stacked against the walls. It was a small room for such an important person, with wooden floors and throw rugs. Behind a flat, wide table a man was nearly buried behind further stacks of books and papers, his ruby-red beret poking over the top. The famous beret was Roger Ackroyd's one bit of flamboyance, his one concession to his domain of role-players. His hair under the beret was as white as his mustache, contrasting with his dark skin.

He stood up, pushing aside enough of the papers to create a line of sight to us. "Thank you for coming, Mr. Spence."

Numera shot her boss a confused look, and then glanced at me as if reappraising me.

"Will you please find a chair for him, Numera?"

"A chair?" she asked, as if the request was the most unusual thing she'd ever heard. Then she got busy. From under a pile of books emerged a plastic chair, the kind you find in a high school cafeteria. She brushed it off and waved me into it, then stood at attention to one side.

"I think there's been a mistake," I said. "I just wanted to know who's been sending my mom these Red Passes all these years. I assume you have a record of who buys them."

"You could say that." Ackroyd stared at me as if I was an apparition. "You know, you look just like him."

"Like who?"

Ackroyd turned to Numera. "Doesn't he? Can you see resemblance? Imagine Joseph forty years younger…"

She looked at me curiously, and then her eyes widened. "Maybe…" she said, then seemed to catch herself. "Then again, he's also just some guy in off the street."

Ackroyd waved away her doubt. "We've been trying to pry Que's name from the DNA ancestry company for some time now, but they are holding out for a larger payoff. Joseph refused to give in, so we've been investigating by other means—quite unsuccessfully. The last thing I expected was that the heir apparent would walk in off the street. We'll have to test you, of course, but I have no doubt that you are Joseph Cambermire's progeny."

I heard the words he was saying, but they seemed to vanish from my brain the moment they arrived. I couldn't think of a thing to say.

I vaguely remembered taking a DNA test with my mom. She'd been hoping she was English or Irish, and when it turned out we were a weird jumble of Eastern European, she'd never brought the subject up again.

Mr. Ackroyd stared at me speculatively. "We've been sending Janice Spence free Red Passes for years. I thought it was weird, but Joseph insisted. 'She's the one that got away,' he said. 'She hates me *because* I'm rich.' I suppose we should have realized... I mean, we knew someone was using the passes, but when we investigated, it seemed like Janice was giving them away to random people. We tested a few of the pass holders, just to make certain, but nothing came of it."

Little by little, my brain started to function again. Apparently, when they'd checked out the Red Pass users, they'd stumbled across Glenn or Stephen or one of my other friends instead of me.

Ackroyd continued. "Joseph was rather...let's say *active* when he was a young man. We figured his son was the fruit of an anonymous one-night stand and whoever the mother was didn't know."

"But Mrs. Spence *must* have known," Numera said. She had none of the enthusiasm in her voice that her boss did. "Why wouldn't she say anything?"

Ackroyd didn't answer, but turned expectantly to me.

"Mom wouldn't have wanted anything to do with someone like Joseph Cambermire," I said. It was a simple truth.

This is your father you're talking about, came the thought. But still...there couldn't have been two people more opposite—Joseph Cambermire, the playboy billionaire, and my mom, the stoic Buddhist hermit nun.

"You talk about her in the past tense," Roger said softly.

"She died a few months ago," I heard myself saying.

"I'm sorry," Roger said.

The room was silent for a moment. Numera's expression softened, and it was that little bit of sympathy that brought tears to my eyes. I stood up abruptly.

"I have to go." I don't know where I was planning to go or why, but I just knew I couldn't stay there.

"Sit down, Zach." Ackroyd's voice was firm. "It's time you met your father."

My father? I have *no father,* I thought. Yet I said, "He's here?"

Numera and Ackroyd exchanged a look. He reached under his desk and toggled something.

From behind me came a voice.

"Hello, son."

CHAPTER FOUR

Joseph Cambermire has a son! If true, it's a bloody miracle.

He admits that he played around a lot when he was younger. He thought he was being careful. Most of these women didn't know who he really was, didn't know about his wealth. It was casual, he insists, without meaning: "Maybe I should be ashamed of myself—but I don't remember their names."

Somewhere out there, a woman gave birth to his son. And not knowing who Joseph was, she never sought him out.

The discovery of his offspring was quite accidental.

As Joseph's illness progressed, I insisted he undergo a genetic profile, comparing it to other DNA samples in the files. (So far, the doctors are calling it an "unusual strain of ALS that defies all current treatments.")

DNA databases are held in confidentiality. Of course, it would be a simple matter to use Joseph's wealth to bribe the appropriate officials or politicians.

"Do you want me to do that?" I asked him.

He knew what I was really asking. From the beginning, Joseph Cambermire had vowed to never use illegal or unethical means to get his way. What I was really asking was, "Do you want to throw away a lifetime of integrity at the last moment?"

"I have so little time left," he said, sighing.

"I assure you, we will find him," I said. "We'll use every means possible."

"Do that," he answered. He searched my face, as if wondering if I'd be willing to bend the rules for him without being told. But of course, if he'd thought the answer was yes, I'd no longer be trusted with his legacy.

Diary of Roger Ackroyd

I didn't recognize the old man in the corner at first. I'd never seen Joseph Cambermire without the iconic white beard that reached his waist. It had always been his trademark—a young face and sparkling eyes and the contrasting white beard.

The beard was gone and the face was no longer young. But even without the facial hair, I recognized him. It was the same face, plus twenty or thirty years' worth of wrinkles, that I saw in the mirror every morning.

I scrambled to my feet, not sure if I was supposed to bow, or shake his hand, or...hug him? Hug Joseph Cambermire?

"Ah, I see that Roger has finally found you," he said. "What is your name, young man?"

"Zach...Zach Spence."

"Spence?" His eyes lit up, and he looked young for a moment. "I should have known. So Janice hid you from me all these years? Of course she did."

"I doubt she thought of it that way," I said. "She didn't much care for ostentatious wealth."

My...my father?...laughed. "Janice didn't approve of anything about me. Yet I think she loved me for a time. Does she still talk of me?"

"She died," I said.

The old man seemed to lose his footing for a moment. "Roger...for God's sakes, find me a chair."

Roger frowned. He reached under the desk. The image of my father froze.

Roger leaned back in his chair and looked over at me. "The database is almost to the level of artificial intelligence, especially the way it captures Joseph's orneriness. We dumped every bit of information we had into the program. Joseph spent many of his last precious days interacting with it. But he...it...is not quite there. I can still tell the difference. It's a little disturbing, frankly. It's my boss, and yet it isn't. Personally, I'm going to stick to an old-fashioned diary."

I plopped down in my chair staring at my father, who looked perfectly lifelike, his frown just starting to form. "He's gone?"

"Missing. Took his yacht out alone about six months ago.

They found it drifting near Hawaii. He was deathly ill, so I think he simply ended it. But yes, there can't be much doubt that he's gone. Since then, everything you've seen in the media about Joseph Cambermire has been this hologram—with his beard, of course. I chose to show you how he looked in those last months, which was also how he presented himself when he didn't want people to know who he was."

"Why keep his death a secret?" I asked.

Numera answered. "Pegasus Corporation is having some difficulties right now. We needed to find his heir—if there really was one—before we announced his death. Without a line of succession, we're not sure the company can survive."

Succession...as if I was some kind of prince. *The king is dead, long live the king?*

"I wouldn't know how to even begin to run a place like this," I said.

"That's for sure," Numera muttered.

Roger seemed unperturbed. "That's why I'm here, young man. I can help you, if you'll let me. But of course, you need to trust me. Your father and I have set up a little presentation."

The hologram flickered and then my father was standing straight again, as if he'd forgotten that he'd ever wanted a chair. "I'm sorry I'm not there to greet you, Zach, but it is important that you trust Roger. If Pegasus Corp is to survive, I need to tell you how it all began."

My father's appearance shifted again; now I was seeing the public face of Joseph Cambermire, the voluminous bushy beard, the dark flashing eyes. His voice was strong.

"When I first met Roger, he wasn't the shrunken gnome he is now, but a tall black man, wearing a sweater instead of suit. He didn't even have a secretary. Makes me laugh to think about it. I immediately felt comfortable in his presence.

"Hiring him was the best decision I ever made. He is responsible for what Pegasus has become while I played around."

"Untrue," Roger murmured. He turned to me. "Pegasus was your father's creation, I just facilitated his ideas."

My father's hologram kept speaking as if Roger hadn't interrupted.

"I'm proud that Pegasus has done a lot of good in the world. From the beginning I made sure that ten percent of all gross profits went to charities—gross, not net, because as much as I trusted Roger, I wanted to make sure the real money was paid out.

"People think I'm a genius when the only really smart thing I ever did was hire Roger. I've always tried to stay in the background, let Roger run things. I lived large, spending my money. What people didn't know was that the beard was my disguise. I had another life.

"I have attended just about every Pegasus Convention. I go dressed as any number of characters, but I'm just one of the crowd, even when I wear my own face. I'm just Joe, a familiar presence but no one special. And I like it that way. Chances are, Zach, if you've been using Janice's Red Pass, that we've interacted, perhaps more than once.

"I'm asking you to take the same leap of faith I did, Zach, and trust Roger in everything. What we've built is in jeopardy. As you know, Pegasus Corp is a privately held company, but over the years we've sold shares to trusted friends. We were probably a little too generous, because we no longer have enough shares to securely control the company. For a long time, it didn't matter because no one challenged us.

"But we recently learned that someone's been buying up enough shares to take control."

The image flickered, and a rueful look came over my father's face. "That's what wanted to tell you, Zach. I'll leave the rest for Roger to explain.

"But before I leave, I want you to know, Zach, that until recently, I had no idea you were alive, otherwise I would have found you. I wish I could be there, but if you're seeing this hologram it means I'm not around anymore. I am so sorry. Goodbye."

He blinked out of existence.

I started to turn to Roger.

And then the lights dimmed and a dark figure began to coalesce in front of me.

CHAPTER FIVE

To this day, Mr. Cambermire swears I didn't bat an eye when he presented me with his winning lottery ticket. That's not how I remember it. I remember the jolt that went through me, the certainty that I'd found my life's calling.

I doubt Joseph knows just how lucky he was that he came to me first. Not because I'm such a genius, but because I'd recently split from a law partner who had defrauded our clients, and I'd sworn that I would have the utmost integrity in my dealings from that moment on.

Joseph was so young and naïve, I'm not sure that any other lawyer could have resisted the temptation to take advantage of him. Of course, by being honest, I have probably reaped more riches than I ever could have managed to steal. I watched Joseph grow up, then grow old, just like me; the fifteen-year age difference seems like nothing now. I've protected him as best I could.

I went along with his funding of the Pegasus Cons, though I didn't understand that world much.

Now it appears that I may have to start all over again with his son, if we can find him.

If I am given enough time.

Diary of Roger Ackroyd

I jumped to my feet, certain Mr. Zander was back for his pound of flesh.

Instead, the image of my father once again materialized—but now he shone brightly, as if from within. I glanced at Numera and Roger. They were carrying on an intense conversation, their heads bent toward each other. They didn't seem to notice this new incarnation of my father.

Joseph Cambermire smiled at me. There was no hint of the Uncanny Valley that the previous hologram had given me. This was my real father, I realized...either that or as my crazy brain imagined him to be.

"Listen to me, son," he said. "You are in danger. Everyone in this reality is in danger. I don't have time to explain, but you must do as Roger says. There are things he doesn't know, but they will be revealed if you follow the plan. Remember, not all your friends are friends and not all your enemies are enemies."

"I don't understand," I said.

"Trust your instincts, Zach. You will be given the task of saving the company, but remember, it is the people you'll meet who really count. You must save them, and they must save you. I have left what hints I can. A guide will be sent to you. Do as he says. Please be careful..."

He began to fade.

I was suddenly certain I'd never see him again. "Wait!" I blurted. "What happened to you? Where are you?"

The apparition of my father closed his eyes. With what appeared to be a great effort, his image coalesced again.

"I'm sorry, son. I have been given this one chance to speak to you." His voice seemed to come from a vast distance, as if from across universes. Tears formed in his eyes, and he reached out as if to touch me. His hand passed through mine. "I wish I could have been there for you, Zach, but I didn't even know you existed until it was too late. Forgive me."

"There is nothing to forgive," I said. An unexpected sadness washed over me. I'd wondered about who my father was sometimes, but told myself you can't miss what you never had. "You didn't know."

"Thank you, son," he whispered. His tears shone as they flowed down his cheeks.

He blinked out of existence. The lights returned to normal.

"Did you say something?" Roger's question lingered in the air.

Roger and Numera were looking at me strangely. It was

clear to me that they hadn't witnessed the second appearance of Joseph Cambermire.

I fought my impulse to blurt out what I'd just seen.

If I'd just met someone and they told me that they were talking to their dead father, what would I think? Roger and Numera didn't know me. I could only imagine their response. So the long-lost son of Joseph Cambermire shows up and he's damaged goods? Numera, for one, would instantly dismiss me as a nut. She already doubted I was legit. I didn't want that. I wanted her to like me.

But in my own mind, I had no doubt. That had been my real father.

"I...I'm just in shock," I managed to say, certain they see right through me. "I wasn't prepared."

"I'm sorry, Zach," Roger said softly. "To lose both parents in such a short time. Joseph wanted so much to meet you."

I cleared my throat. I remembered what my father—or the illusion of my father—had said. "What kind of *danger* are we in?"

Roger gave me odd look, as if hearing the alarmed tone in my voice. "Danger? There's a chance we could lose the company, but it's not too late."

I didn't say anything. I sensed that Roger was hiding something.

Roger leaned forward. "Are you all right, Zach? Has this all been too much to absorb?"

I shook my head. "I'm fine."

I felt a hand on my shoulder. Numera had moved to my side and was looking down at me with a newly sympathetic look in her eyes. "No, you aren't," she said firmly. "And who would be, finding all this out?"

Roger looked startled. "Of course, how thoughtless of me. Why don't we meet tomorrow when we've had time to sleep on it? Our plans will need to change anyway, now that you're here, Zach. If you'll take my first bit of advice, we'll keep your arrival a secret for now. And if you'll accept a second piece of advice," he nodded toward Numera, "I'm going to ask you to let my daughter show you around."

His daughter?

Of course, I should have realized it, as much as it was hard to envision this shrunken old man as the father of such a tall, elegant woman. I had every intention of doing whatever Roger told me, even if was putting me into the hands of this woman who seemed to have little faith in me.

"I think there may be a few things you can teach Numera about Hyper-reality as well, Zach," Roger continued. "Meanwhile, we'll need a cover story for you to be following Numera around. We're currently running a Harvey Bowman lookalike contest, the winner to be an intern for Pegasus Corp for a month. Luckily, you kind of look like this Bowman character."

I frowned. Harvey Bowman was a gunslinger, a time traveler to the Old West from the twenty-third century, a cool-looking character with a wide-brimmed hat, a long black duster, and two Colt revolvers that never ran out of bullets.

Me? A Harvey Bowman lookalike? Not likely.

Roger said, "I'm going to do something I've never done before and rig the outcome. It would be better, of course, if it were also plausible. Try to make sure you have something that wows the judges so much you can't help but win."

Numera stared at me speculatively and nodded. "I can arrange that. That's my old department."

"Is that all right with you, Zach?" Roger asked.

I nodded. It still felt more than a little weird that he was asking my permission. This was the legendary Roger Ackroyd, who, along with Joseph Cambermire (I still couldn't think of him as my father), was the creator of our Hyper-reality–dominated pop culture.

Roger stood up and extended his hand. I scrambled to my feet. I saw the look in his eye and a shock went through my arm as I realized that the handshake signified acceptance of my fate. None of it seemed real.

Refuse the DNA test. Tell them it was all a big mistake. But, I doubted Roger would let it go so easily, and unlike Numera, I was pretty sure Joseph Cambermire really was my father, if only because of the way my mom had thoroughly expunged him from our lives.

"Is there anything else you need, Zach? Anything need to be taken care of back in Bend?" Roger asked.

I winced at the thought of the little tan house with its yellow lawn and broken sidewalk, now empty and abandoned. I realized at that moment that I'd finally moved on, that I was willing to let go.

"I'm fine, though...could I bother you for twenty bucks for dinner?"

Roger stared at me with a straight face for a few long moments, then burst out laughing. Even Numera joined in, while I sat there with a stupid grin on my face.

He pulled out a wallet and handed me a fifty. "Keep it. I won't even charge you interest."

Numera stood. "The contest starts in two hours. Let's get you a killer costume, Zach."

CHAPTER SIX

I named my daughter Numera because of my love of numbers. My dear departed wife, Carol, didn't fight it, but started calling her Mera from her first day home from the hospital.

It was only as she entered her professional life that my daughter decided to accept the name she was given—because it distinguishes her, I suppose, from everyone else, but also because she has shown the same proficiency for numbers that her Daddy has, if not an even greater proficiency. I still use the calculator for most things. She does the same calculations in her head. It's a bit scary.

My job has been not to teach her the numbers but to help her look beyond the numbers. She hadn't been here a week before she started pointing out inefficiencies.

"Why do you suppose that is?" I asked.

She stopped in midcalculation. "I don't know. I suppose it's slightly easier on the convention goers. But they'd get used to it."

"Perhaps. But my orders from Mr. Cambermire are not to maximize profits but to make the convention experience as pleasant as possible."

She stared at me thoughtfully, then nodded. "Someday I'd like to have a talk with this Mr. Cambermire."

I smiled to myself. It was inevitable that they would meet.

I planned to be there when that happened.

Diary of Roger Ackroyd

The flagship store of the Merlin's Costumes chain was just down the street, in the middle of the Emerald Block, which made sense as it catered to the explosion of cosplay generated by the success of the Pegasus Cons.

Every convention had a huge Merlin's booth and almost every metro area in the country had a store. I almost never missed at least a visit whenever I came to Portland, even if I couldn't afford most of the colorful offerings.

The store was multilevel. The bottom floor was devoted to games and gameplay, with tables and booths and arcades. To one side was an old-fashioned 1950s-style diner. The second floor was devoted to technology—the latest in holographic and virtual reality devices. But it was the third floor that really enchanted me. It was all costumes, without the tech, just good old-fashioned role-playing.

Along one entire wall were the detailed and elaborate masks of dragons and ogres and wizards and unicorns and every other kind of fantasy creature you could imagine, as if they'd been slain in battle and their heads mounted. Another wall was full of weapons, both boffered and harmless and realistic and dangerously sharpened. It was bad form to show up for a game with a real weapon, but it was equally unusual for pure cosplayers to exhibit fake ones. On the floor itself was rack after rack of costumes, ranging from fully authentic, to the type of costume that were mostly Disneyfied polyester. (There's no accounting for taste.)

Numera stopped within ten feet of the entrance. "Oh, wow. I always forget what a sensory overload this place is. If you don't mind, I'm going to scoot into the diner and wait."

She reached into her pocket and handed me a credit card.

I was a little disappointed she wasn't going with me, but I understood. Even I sometimes felt overwhelmed by the sight of so much Hyper-reality. The colors and shapes, the sights and sounds of the arcades, could be too much stimuli for even a seasoned player.

I made way alone to the third floor and started looking through the Western section. There were tons of duster coats and cowboy hats and boots, but I couldn't decide. It was the very nature of the overwhelming choice that stumped me. How to choose?

As I worked my way through the rows, I came near the cash register stand at the back. A big man with a white beard and wizard's blue pointed hat was manning the table. He saw me coming and his smile broadened. "Zach! Get in here!" he said, hurrying to set aside the stanchion blocking the way.

As far as I knew, I'd never seen this man before. But then again, I'd learned that anyone could be anyone at a Pegasus Convention. Just because I didn't recognize this guy in his current guise didn't mean I didn't know him.

He opened a curtain to a storeroom behind the counter, packed with costumes as well as every manner of weapon hanging from hooks. A small card table was set in the middle of the crowded space, and a single chair, which the wizard motioned me into. He loomed over me. I suppose I expected him to remove his beard and introduce himself.

On closer inspection, I saw the beard was real—and I still didn't recognize him.

"Things have gotten worse since we talked last," the man said. He dropped his smile. In fact, he looked scared. "You need to talk to Roger."

"I sorry, I don't remember meeting you before. Who's Roger?"

He stared at me for a long moment.

Then, with a shock, I realized who he was: Merlin himself, with his wizard's hat and his loud Hawaiian shirts, Birkenstocks, and white socks (Birkensocks?).

"Not knowing Roger is a big problem," he said. "You're the only one who can do anything about this, Zach. You're the only one with the money and the power."

"You've mistaken me for someone else."

"I'm Merlin," he prompted. "You know—owner of Merlin's Costumes? Oh, dear. Not knowing me is an even bigger problem."

I started looking for a way out, but the big man blocked the only exit. As far as I knew, Merlin never appeared in public...and if he did, he wouldn't have anything to do with the likes of me. There was a Merlin's store in every city and at every convention.

And there were few people with less money and power than me.

Merlin threw up his arms in exasperation. "You really don't remember? The guy we hired, Carter, has disappeared, and nobody seems to know where he's gone. No one seems to remember him at all."

"I'm sorry," I said.

"So it's true...you've shifted again...or I have. Apparently you haven't been discovered yet in this reality," Merlin said. He looked around, then reached up and took down a wizard's staff from one of the hooks. He swung it a few times in the confined space. I nearly ducked under the table.

"This is bad," he said. "The universe won't allow two of me in the same reality for long, and if this isn't *my* reality, I'm the one who'll get the boot."

"*This* reality?" I said. Every once in a while, you ran into someone who took Hyper-reality a little too seriously.

He laughed. "Hard to tell anymore, isn't it? Everyone pretending to be someone else, to live somewhere they don't. How would they know that things have changed? Someone doesn't remember an event or a place, or even a person? Old friends not recognizing each other? Understandable, with everything that's going on. But it's only a matter of time before what's happening to us starts happening to everyone else. He started on the important people first, trying to get rid of us."

"He?" I asked. I tried to keep the alarm out of my voice.

"Maybe this is a good thing. If he hasn't found you yet, you still have a chance. Be prepared, Zach. You're the only one who can stop this."

Then Merlin froze, his eyes growing big.

"Behind you!" he shouted, seeming to swing the staff toward my head. I ducked and tumbled sideways off the chair. There was a *thud* above me, and an ear-splitting screech, but from under the table all I could see was the wizard's white socks and Birkenstocks and facing them, two shiny black boots. I heard Mr. Zander's sinister snicker.

The table flipped, and I tried to rise, but flew backward through the air. I heard a shout, Merlin shouting an incantation from some earlier time, then a flash of light and heat.

I closed my eyes and shook my head. When I opened them again, the Birkenstocked feet and the black boots were gone. The room was empty. I reached up and grabbed a sword from one of the hooks, even though I knew it was too dull to do any real damage.

"What are you doing here, buddy?" came a voice from the entrance. A young man poked his head in, but kept his distance.

"Where's Merlin?" I asked.

"Look, I don't want no trouble. Just leave and I won't call the security guards, all right?"

I felt myself blush. I put down the sword, dusted myself off, and left, trying to act harmless. The young man kept his distance.

I stumbled down the stairs, passing the second floor without being truly conscious of it. I was out the front door and on the sidewalk before I remembered that Numera was in the diner. I turned to look into the window, only to find her staring back at me from a table, looking astonished. I motioned urgently for her to come out.

"What happened?" she asked, as she hurried to my side. "You look like you've seen a ghost."

"Have you ever met Merlin?" I asked. I started walking, not really caring which direction I went, as long as it was away.

"Sure—we have meetings with him in all the time. We've been contemplating buying him out."

"Is he always so eccentric? He doesn't seem quite...stable."

Look whc's talking.

"You met him upstairs? How odd." She reached out and grabbed my arm, stopping my panicked retreat. "Quit kidding around. And where's your costume?"

"I couldn't find anything I liked," I muttered.

"Hmmm," she said, giving me a puzzled look. "Well, I have an idea. I know someone in the Emerald Tower who can probably help us."

Numera led the way back into the tower and to the same elevator we'd used to reach Roger's office.

The elevator dropped under us, taking my stomach with it. I counted the seconds and figured we'd zipped past the ground floor and kept going down. It surged to a stop, bending my knees.

The door opened onto a white space so glaring and uniform I had to shield my eyes. As my sight adjusted, I saw that we were in a lab of some kind. It looked abandoned and yet pristine. Numera led the way between the benches into a back room.

The room looked like a cave, down to the rock walls and pool of water in a grotto a few steps down. Lights under the water lit the rock walls with a shimmer. At an ancient desk sat a woman dressed in white. I thought for a moment it was an older woman with white hair, but when she turned I saw that not only was she not old, she looked more like a high schooler. Her hair was dyed white, but her eyebrows were still dark. She must have been wearing tinted contacts, because her eyes appeared purple.

"Agate," Numera said. "I need some help with a costume."

Agate stood, a blue cape over her shoulders, and waved airily. "I don't do costumes," she intoned.

"Don't put on airs, Agatha. I need for Zach here to look exactly like Harvey Bowman."

Agate's arms dropped to her sides and suddenly she was all business. "Isn't that cheating? I've never known you to cut corners, Numie."

"This is a special case."

"Special, huh?" Agate examined me and didn't seem impressed. "He's got the basic bone structure, and I can do the rest. But I ain't doing nothin' until you tell me what's going on."

I was starting to feel like I was merely a holographic projection, so I stepped forward, extending my hand. "I'm Zach Spence. Otherwise known as Que."

"Holy..." Agate stepped back, then fell into her chair, her mouth open. It wasn't the reaction I expected, and it was somehow thrillingly satisfying.

Numera whirled on me. "Why'd you tell her?"

"Sorry. But you seem to trust her."

"Trust her?" Numera scoffed. "Agatha's been a nutcase since we were in grade school. I warn you, don't believe half of what she says." Then she shrugged. "But...in this...I guess I do trust her."

"Oh, man. Oh, man. Oh, man." Agatha/Agate said. She hopped up from her chair and rushed me. I didn't have time to react before she wrapped her arms around my waist. Her head barely reached my chin. "Glad to meet you, Que. Welcome to Pegasus. This place saved my nerdy little life."

"Let's not get melodramatic," Numera said.

"What?" Agate turned to me. "Numie has no idea. She was always smart and popular. It was ridiculously unfair. But also a stick in the mud."

Numera rolled her eyes and checked her phone. "The contest is in an hour. Let's get busy."

For some reason, at the moment it all came home. I felt completely overwhelmed.

Man up. I told myself. *This isn't a game.*

But why think of it that way? came a wisp of thought. I tracked the thought down and pinned it to the ground. Why *not* treat it like another game, maybe one of those small convention games where the game master is in complete control of every element?

Somehow, the idea that there were no real stakes involved made me relax. "Let's do it," I said.

CHAPTER SEVEN

When Joseph created the term "Hyper-reality," I had my doubts.
I wondered if Joseph understood the Orwellian doublethink nature of the word. But the more it was used, the more I realized how apt it really was. The term eventually covered every kind of pretend: from LARPers (live-action role-players), to cosplayers (costume players), to history re-enactors, to The Society for Creative Anachronism (though they might object to being included), to just about anyone who pretended to be someone else.

At first, Hyper-reality players were mostly in the genres of science fiction and fantasy. But as Hyper-reality became more and more popular, just about every genre and time period that could be imagined started to be played. "Little subcultures everywhere," as Joseph put it.

VR and holographic technology had become so cheap by then that almost anyone could afford to be anyone or anything they wanted to be—at least on the surface.

Diary of Roger Ackroyd

I won the Harvey Bowman lookalike contest going away. I would have won with or without the fix, or so I'd like to think.

I'd never had a get-up like that. Professional down to the last detail. Agate led me to a room beyond the holo of the grotto that was full of costumes. She picked out a black duster, knee-high boots, a hat and a bolo tie, and a belt with a turquoise buckle. Next I was outfitted with a couple of revolvers, a wicked-looking Bowie knife, and a Winchester rifle.

When it came time to pose for the judges, I remembered a

McFarlane toy I'd had in high school of Billy the Kid, his posture of putting a boot up on a casket, rifle propped on his knee, head down, peering up from under the hat brim. It was a killer pose, which I copied when it came time for pictures. It made all the news sites, helping convince everyone that it wasn't so weird that this particular contest winner would be trailing the COO of the Pegasus Corporation around for the next few weeks.

I recognized three of the other finalists. After I was crowned, Cameron Bose moseyed up to me. He was always in character, always a Western hero. He'd tried to adapt his usual white hat cosplay into a Harvey Bowman look and it was pretty close, but in the end, he'd come in second.

"Damn, Zach. You took it ace high. How'd you do that?" He reached out and fingered my duster.

"Just lucky, I guess."

"Bullshit, you cleaned my plow. Well, I always reckoned if you ever hankered to win you'd be a formidable opponent. I mean, I don't think there is anyone who goes to as many shows as you do. You must know more players than anyone."

The glow of victory vanished. I felt kind of embarrassed. I mean...none of this was my doing. Agate had been the one to dress me up. I'd cheated.

"Don't worry, Cameron. It won't happen again," I assured him.

He slapped me on the back. "Hell, pilgrim. I'm proud of you." He walked away shaking his head.

"I have to admit, you do look a little like him," Numera said as she led the way out of the Emerald Tower.

"Huh?"

"You're the very image of Harvey Bowman. I think you've found your alter ego, Zach."

I doffed my black hat. "Why, thank you, ma'am," I said in my best John Wayne voice, hoping to get a smile out of her.

She continued to stare at me and I started getting uncomfortable. Then she seemed to catch herself and turned away.

Numera is way out of your league, came the voice of my high school loner sprite on one shoulder. *Besides, you just met her. Besides, she doesn't even seem to like you.*

What a minute, came the ego sprite on my other shoulder. *You're the richest man in the world, and as Que, the most famous—that is, famous for being unknown, but that's pretty much the same thing, isn't it?*

"Where did you work before this?" Numera asked.

"Odd jobs. I was taking community college classes before Mom got sick."

"You must have worked somewhere."

"Well…my longest job was probably at the local comic book store."

She stared at me, then burst out laughing. "That's perfect. I should've known."

I started to flush, but she was shaking her head. "I suppose it's possible Father is right, there are a few things you can teach me about nerd culture. I've never felt completely comfortable where numbers aren't involved."

"I can do that. Prince of Nerds, that's me."

"Where do you want to go for dinner?" she asked.

"Do you mind if we just go to a drive-thru somewhere?" I was peopled out. Most days, if I talked to more than a dozen people, that was a lot.

"Good idea. Then we'll head home. I've booked you a room in my condo complex—part of the prize for the Harvey Bowman contest. It's just a couple of floors down from my place."

We snagged some fast food. I hid my amusement at Numera's attempt to negotiate the ordering and the pickup. For one thing, the Jaguar (real) she was driving was so low to the ground that she had to talk upward into the speakers. Finally, I leaned over her and placed the order for both of us. As I got within a few inches of her, I became hyperaware of her mouth and lips. She was wearing a subtle fragrance that I could only smell when I was that close.

Who is she wearing that for? I wondered. *Does she have a boyfriend?*

As the bags of fast food were handed over, she said, "I think maybe you have some things to teach me about everyday life, too."

That didn't sound like a compliment. "Oh, sure...the fine art of fast-food dining, grocery coupons, and budget rent-a-cars. It's a bewildering maze, I tell you."

"I'm just out of practice," she said.

Was that defensiveness I heard?

She dumped the bags of food into my lap and pulled away from the restaurant. "I wasn't always this way," she commented.

Which way was that? Beautiful, sophisticated, and accomplished?

"I'm just going to follow you around, Numera. This is a whole new world for me."

"Don't worry about it," she said. "I'll take care of the business end of things."

The garage door under the condo was invisible from the street. There were private parking spots for each unit. Numera pulled up to the last two spaces, which were walled off from the others. A VW bug was in the other space.

A private doorway was hidden a few feet away, and behind it was a narrow spiral staircase that led up to a fourth-floor landing. Apparently, she rated the entire fourth floor.

The condo door opened before we reached it. Agate stood there, her zombie-white hair tied in a bun, sans makeup, dressed in a floppy housedress.

"Great," she said to Numera when she saw me. "You couldn't warn me? At least tell me you brought me a hamburger."

We'd forgotten—well, Numera had forgotten, I hadn't ever known—but I'd ordered two for myself, so I quickly spoke up. "Of course."

The kitchen looked bigger than my mom's house but looked like it had never been used. The only habitable, comfortable part was a marble-topped island as wide as a table, with stools surrounding it. It was piled with papers and books. As I set the bags of food down, I caught glimpses of drawings of creatures and costumes before Agate scooped them up and stacked them to one side.

"All we've got is water and red wine," Numera said, looking

into a refrigerator that seemed to take up an entire wall and that was so shiny it could've served as a mirror.

"Oh, red wine, of course," I said. "I never eat McDonald's without it."

As we dug in, I tried to figure out how to broach the subject that was running through my mind. "So you two...are you...a couple?"

"A couple?" Agate laughed. "I've thought about it, but Numera is such a prig."

Numera blushed. "I like men. So sue me."

The weirdest thing was that it felt like I'd known them both forever. I could almost anticipate what they were going to say. After a couple of glasses of wine, I lost my self-consciousness and joined the flow of conversation. Numera seemed to lighten up a little too, even laughing at a couple of my jokes.

Much later, I found myself laughing at something I'd already forgotten. There were two empty bottles of wine on the island. I looked up at the clock and saw that it was after midnight. Numera was staring at me stone faced, while Agate was smiling. *How long have I been babbling?*

"I'm knackered," I said. "Which way to my room?"

Numera pulled a key out of her purse and handed it over. "Two floors down, the second condo over."

I headed for the door. Either the wine or exhaustion made me stumble a little. I felt Agate's hand on my elbow. "Get some sleep, boss."

As she closed the door behind me, I felt completely deflated.

Boss. Damn, that wasn't quite the way I'd hoped she'd see me.

I took the stairs instead of the elevator. When the lights started flickering, I knew instantly that I was having one of my delusions. The stairs turned into a steep hill ringed with rocks, at the bottom of which was a small dell. A weathered stone pillar rose out of the middle of the clearing. The grass grew high around it as if the creatures were afraid to eat it.

A dark figure crouched there. She turned her head toward me, and I could sense her surprise. She stood, seeming to rise higher and higher, as if she was a giant. Her hair was decorated with red stones, which were also wrapped around her neck and arms. She was wearing nothing else.

I flushed when I saw her face, for I'd been imagining just such a vision. Numera the Goddess.

She approached me, shrinking to human size, though still regal in my eyes. There was a strange conspiratorial smile on her face. "The enemy has crossed over, my love. We must be wary."

She'd appeared to be reaching out for me as if to take me in her arms, but now she stepped back. I saw doubt form in her dark eyes.

"You are not *my* Zach," she murmured, with a hard K sound. "But it matters not. You belong to me in all worlds, and you are in danger in all worlds. You must beware, my love, of this world and time."

"Beware of what?" I managed to ask.

"The enemy. You will know him, for we have faced him before. My Zach has already defeated him more than once."

I closed my eyes. The earth shifted under my feet, and when I opened my eyes again, I was tripping down the last three stairs. I managed to stop myself from landing headfirst. I sat down, still reeling.

When my racing heart slowed enough that I could actually make out individual heartbeats, I staggered to my feet and found the apartment. I didn't look around, but headed straight for the bed.

I lay there, my head whirling, trying to make sense of it all. The funny thing was, no matter how strange these imagined fantasy worlds were, they weren't as strange or frightening as the one I was in, where I was the great Joseph Cambermire's son and richer than sin.

No, I decided, *that's not real.* I was Janice Spence's son, from Bend, Oregon, who lived in a tan house with a yellowed lawn and a broken sidewalk and had a small circle of friends. That was reality.

It was everything else that was a fantasy.

CHAPTER EIGHT

Just as nerd culture moved from being a shunned minority in the middle part of the twentieth century to the dominant form of entertainment by the end of the century, so too did Hyper-reality move from a strange subculture to a mainstream phenomenon.

I'm proud of the fact that Pegasus Corporation had much to do with that. When there is an event every weekend in a city nearby, it becomes routine to dress up and go. When small subcultures pop up in every little town in America, no matter how isolated, then what was once strange becomes the norm.

At first it was considered a fad, and I must admit even I had my doubts. But I'm also old enough to remember that the Beatles were supposed to be a flash in the pan. (To this day, the annual Beatles festival in Liverpool is one of my favorite Pegasus-sponsored events.) Just as rock 'n' roll and hip-hop continued on their merry way, so too did Hyper-reality.

It shows no signs of disappearing anytime soon.
Diary of Roger Ackroyd

Dad was in the backyard, weeding, wearing a sombrero. His long white beard was catching twigs and grass as he bent over. Mom handed me a glass of lemonade to take to him. That's all Dad drank, except for a couple of cups of coffee first thing in the morning. It was a lazy day, the kind that seemed unreal, as if it was the wrong time and place.

I was home from an emotionally traumatic term at college, and the normalcy of my parents, the humble comfort of the tan house, was reassuring, instead of irritating me as it had before I left for school.

Dad got up. "Creeeeeeck," he vocalized as he straightened his back. "I swore I would keep up with the weeds this year."

"It's been over ninety degrees every day this month," I said.

He plopped down on a lawn chair in the shade of the patio and removed his sombrero. His hair was dripping with sweat.

"I'm sorry we're so boring, son," he said. "Sometimes I wonder if I just settled for comfortable instead of challenging myself. But I found your mom, and we had you, and that's all I ever wanted."

When I was little, our next-door neighbor, Mr. Simmons, had won the lottery. I still read about him in the papers sometimes. He went on to produce some movies and date movie stars. What would have happened if it had been Dad and Mom who'd won? How would life be different?

I took a sip of my own lemonade.

The sun dimmed as if smothered by a dark cloud. I turned to Dad, but he was gone. The garden was gone; instead there was a yellowed and dying lawn. Mom was humming inside the house.

I went inside. The house was cool. Mom was bent over the dishwasher. She looked healthy.

This is wrong, I thought. *This isn't reality.*

Heavy footsteps came from the hallway, and Mr. Zander came in, without his frock coat and hat, but as tall and spindly as ever. I saw that without his hat, his hair was thin and graying on top, but his mustache and goatee were as black as ever. He walked right up to Mom and slapped her in the face. "I told you to get me a drink!" he shouted.

I stood stunned for a moment, then launched myself at him. My fist went right through him, and I followed. A sickening sense of pain and anger washed through me.

Mr. Zander merely frowned. "Did you feel something?"

Mom cowered, her hand on her face. She didn't answer. But it wasn't Mr. Zander she was afraid of. Instead, she was looking at me.

"Who are you?" she whispered.

A hand gripped my arm, squeezing.

I woke up shouting, rolling off the bed to get away from the painful grip.

"Careful!" a feminine voice shouted as I slammed to the floor.

I poked my head up over the bed. For a moment I couldn't remember the white-haired girl's name. Agatha...Agate. I felt a little sick to my stomach and only then remembered the red wine from the night before. I wasn't much of a drinker. I must have overdone it and had the bad dreams I always seemed to get.

I reached up, snatched the bedspread, and covered myself.

"Sorry, Que," Agate said. "I didn't mean to alarm you, man. You weren't answering the door, so Numera went off to get another key. It wasn't until she was gone that I realized your door was unlocked."

I crawled back onto the bed, still wrapped in the blanket, and flopped face first into the pillow with a groan.

"You gotta get up, Que. Your meeting with Mr. Ackroyd is in one hour and the Emerald Tower is a thirty-minute drive."

"Screw it," I muttered into the pillow. "We'll be late."

"That's your prerogative," Agate said. "You're the boss... though it's kinda rude."

Numera came into the bedroom carrying a big cup of coffee. "Thought you might need this," she said. "Get dressed. We'll be waiting in the hallway."

We were fifteen minutes late and I was still groggy.

I sat in the chair in front of Roger's desk, trying to follow his conversation with Numera, but quickly realized it was about everyday corporate matters that had nothing to do with the meeting and I tuned them out, grateful to have a few more moments with my thoughts.

I couldn't shake the dream...or rather, dreams. They had both felt so real, as if they were the true reality and it was my memories that were false.

Numera had found another chair beneath all the books and sat down next to me. She looked as prim and put-together as she had the day before, as if the wine hadn't affected her in the slightest. She gave me a measuring look, as if trying to gauge whether I was going to throw up all over the carpet.

Roger didn't seem to notice. "Are you ready, Zach? I'm going to try to include you in all the important decisions from now on. If you have any thoughts, please feel free to contribute."

I sat up straight in my chair. "Yes, sir...I mean, yes."

"We think we have found out who is buying up the shares." He paused as if he couldn't believe he was going to say what he was going to say. "As crazy as it sounds, it's Billy Box."

I knew who Billy Box was, of course. He was the newest media star—a crude troll, with a squarish head and body, thin arms and legs, his hair cut like a North Korean dictator's. I couldn't stand the character, who had his own show on multiple platforms. I think maybe I'd watched five minutes of his stuff in total—mostly pratfalls and crude practical jokes.

"Why would he do that?" I asked.

Numera answered. "We believe he's a front for someone else. He's been buying up Pegasus stock at a rapid rate. By the time we noticed, he had a head start on us. We've been matching him dollar for dollar ever since, but he seems to have an uncanny sense of who's vulnerable."

Roger broke in. "My mistake, Zach. I underestimated him. I fell for his blockhead persona. I should have made sure we had protections in place, but it never occurred to me that anyone could match our buying power. Especially Billy Box. But it turns out he has a backer."

"Unicorn Industries," I said.

"Very good, you got the implications immediately," Roger nodded. "Yes, they are the only ones who could pull off an operation of this size."

A few years after Pegasus Corporation started their conventions, Unicorn Industries popped up as a rival. They were always a distant second, usually having to place their conventions in the off-season or in towns too small or out of the way for Pegasus. Pegasus was already spread thin, so they let Unicorn have the leftovers.

But it turned out there was a lot of money in out-of-the-way places and off-seasons, maybe because everyone else ignored them. Unicorn Industries wasn't weighed down by charitable contributions, and they charged more and provided less, and seemed to get away with it.

"So we fight them," I said.

"Indeed we do," Roger said, "but not just because we want to keep the company to ourselves. There's a bigger problem."

"Something worse?" I asked. The idea of Unicorn Industries taking over the Hyper-reality world was terrifying in so many ways.

"What do you know about the Copyright and Trademark Fair Use Act?"

"Only that it's ridiculous and unenforceable."

From the beginning, there had been the problem of people dressing up as, doing art as, or posting videos as famous characters. The general rule of thumb was that as long as people weren't making money using Marvel or DC or Star Wars or Middle Earth characters, or any other commercially licensed character, then it was OK.

But of course it wasn't that easy. If you dress up as Deadpool for every convention, and make sure you are filmed, and then post the video on sites where you get paid for every view, are you an amateur or a professional?

So it has always been a gray area. As Justice Potter Stewart said about porn: "I know it when I see it." It used to be pretty clear when someone stepped over the line, but with the whole world dressing up as trademarked characters, how do you police that?

I expected Roger to shrug it off, but to my surprise, he seemed serious. "Unicorn Industries is lobbying for it—they're telling Congress that they can enforce it by asking for micropayments at the door. Pay to play, so to speak."

"Ridiculous," I repeated.

"Not really," Roger said. He turned to Numera.

"It's possible to do," she said. "It would be like the way music is paid for, by keeping track of whenever and wherever a licensed song is played. A lot would fall between the cracks, of course, but in general, it's feasible—especially if the two biggest

Hyper-reality corporations are the ones who enforce it."

It still made no sense to me. The "C & T," as the act was called in the Hyper-reality world, was usually ridiculed, though there had always been doom and gloomsters who'd pointed out that no one had ever thought Net Neutrality would be curtailed either. "What's in it for Unicorn besides a huge hassle?"

"Charging a small fee for each transaction."

I sat there calculating how many people came to conventions, how many showed up for work, how many went about their daily business dressed up as licensed characters. The numbers were staggering. Even micropayments would add up quick.

"So people will just go off and do their own thing," I said.

"No, they won't," Numera said. "They come to Pegasus or Unicorn conventions because they want to be seen. In fact, our surveys show that it would result in even fewer small events because no one will have the infrastructure to deal with the C & T effectively but us."

Roger broke in. "Micropayments have a habit of becoming not so micro. I foresee enforcers on every street corner. You are correct, Zach, that the C & T will never pass as long as Pegasus Corp is fighting it. We have enough influence over politicians to make sure it never comes to the floor of Congress. But if Pegasus is taken over by Unicorn, it will become inevitable."

I don't know how long I sat there stewing it over before I realized that both Roger and Numera were staring at me.

"What do we do?" I asked.

"Numera, do you have that list I asked you to assemble?" Roger asked.

She nodded, standing up as if she was in a corporate boardroom. "Yes, sir. There are five people we need to be concerned about. If Unicorn can manage to buy out any three of these five individuals, they will gain majority control."

"I think I know who they are, but go ahead," Roger said. "Gentry Partridge, of course."

"Yes, sir. He's the most vulnerable. Since his show was cancelled, his ratings on all social media platforms have dropped precipitously. He hasn't slowed down his spending a wit, so he's starting to run out of cash."

I almost spoke up, amazed that I knew one of the people on the list. But then, I attended a lot of Pegasus Conventions with my Red Passes, so maybe it wasn't all that surprising.

Numera continued. "After Gentry, I'd guess that Maureen O'Rourke is next. Of course, since no one has seen The Blue Queen in several years, it's hard to know exactly. But she isn't even popping up on the boards anymore. She appears to have lost interest in Hyper-reality. There are rumors that she's sick."

Maureen wouldn't sell. Not the Maureen I knew. I wondered again if I should say anything or wait until Numera's presentation was done.

"Who's next?" Roger said, twirling his hand.

"Coventree," she said.

Coventree was at the height of her fame, though most people weren't quite sure if she was a she or a he or some other gender. Her costumes were so elaborate, it was sometimes hard to tell if she was human at all. Her voice wasn't anything special, her costumes limited her movement, and her songs were unmemorable. But the shows she put on were so elaborate, they were unforgettable.

I knew her as Kate Williams, a Phoenix girl who, right out of high school, had come to her first Pegasus Convention dressed as a little-known manga character, a teenage witch called Coventree.

What were the odds I would know three out of the five people we needed to sell to us? I decided to let Numera finish, because I had a funny feeling.

Numera consulted her list. "Then there is Pretty, Pretty."

"Who's not so pretty anymore," Roger said. "No worse fate in the world than to be an aging ingénue."

"She was pretty good in *Djinn*," I objected. The horror movie had been her comeback and she'd exhibited some acting chops that had won over the critics. She was far from the heights of fame she'd once achieved, but mostly I spoke up because I wanted to defend her. I liked Debbie Johnson, and I'd liked her for a long time before she became famous.

"The last person we need to convince to sell to us is Stallo," Numera continued.

"Do we have to?" I asked.

Both Numera and Roger turned to me in surprise.

"I know Stallo," I said. "He's a complete jerk."

"You know him?" Numera repeated dubiously.

I nodded. "In fact, I know all five of them...pretty well, actually."

There was a long moment of silence. Numera obviously didn't believe me, and Roger was looking at me as if really seeing me for the first time. These were famous people and I was—or had been until yesterday—a nobody.

Funny, that, because I was still the same person. Except for the visions. Those were new.

"The Red Pass," Roger said, nodding thoughtfully.

"It gave me certain privileges," I agreed. "At most events, I was allowed to go backstage. But that's not how I got to know most of them. When I met these people, they weren't famous yet. We just sort of became friends."

"What are the odds of that?" Numera said, as if she was going to whip out a calculator and figure it out on the spot.

Without meaning to, I said what I was thinking. "I wonder if it was just somehow meant to be."

"What do you mean by that?" Roger said sharply.

"Just that...well, it seems like I'm in sort of movie right now, as if everything is preordained, as if whatever my reality is, that is the reality of the world."

Numera was frowning, but Roger nodded. "It can feel that way sometimes when things move fast. Anything happen in particular?"

Here was my chance to tell them what I'd been seeing, but the uncertain look on Numera's face dissuaded me. They still didn't know me. They'd just think I was nuts and cast me aside. Oh, I'd still be owner of the company and still rich, but I figured they'd find a way to isolate me. Better to keep my mouth shut and see what happened. The vision of my father had told me to go along with Roger's plans. That sounded like good advice.

"Zach knowing them may be the advantage we need," Roger said. "Zach can appeal to them personally."

"I don't understand," I objected. "Why don't we just pay them whatever they want?"

"Because we can't outbid Unicorn," Numera said. "It's your father's fault. He ran Pegasus almost as a charity."

"But I thought he was a trillionaire...the richest person in the world!"

"No, Zach," Numera said. "*You* are now the richest person in the world. But only on paper. We are cash poor, Zach, because most of the excess profits have been given away to charity. The Pegasus Conventions have been overspending for years, while Unicorn has been hoarding money. So you see, the only way to make enough money to buy shares is to sell some of your shares...and that doesn't make much sense, does it?"

"Can't we borrow the money?" I asked, "I mean, if the company is really worth so much, it should be good for collateral, right?"

Numera shook her head. "Again, if we borrow the money from other corporations, hedge funds, or banks, we give them too much control. You'll have to appoint them to your board of directors, and believe me, they won't want to run things the same way your father did. It would defeat the very purpose. We'd be destroying the company to save the company."

I turned to Roger helplessly, but he was staring at his daughter in amazement. "I didn't think you understood," the old man said.

Numera threw up her hands. "I get it, Father. I always did. But I also knew that if we didn't run our company efficiently, it would eventually put us in jeopardy. As it has. If we get in a bidding war—if it's only about how much we can pay per share—we'll lose."

"How did these five get so many shares in the first place?" I asked. "I thought we were a private company."

"That's my fault," Roger said. "When we started, I thought it would be smart to pay the talent with shares instead of cash. I also put a minority share up for sale. It seemed smart at the time. To be honest, I thought Pegasus Corporation was a lark and that we wouldn't succeed. I wanted to protect your father's money as much as I could. Lots of lottery winners lose it all on bad investments."

Numera said. "We have to assume that Unicorn Industries knows about these five individuals and may even now be approaching them. So...Zach. Now you know the truth. We have to convince at least three of these five to either sell to us or to not sell to anyone at all."

And then I said the unluckiest thing I could have said. "Shouldn't be too hard."

Roger winced at my words. "When it comes to money, nothing is easy."

Numera said, "So, Zach. Which one these people should we approach first?"

"I can't imagine any of them picking Unicorn over Pegasus," I said. "Except...well, Stallo would. If for no other reason than spite. So if we are in a hurry to lock down these shares, I'd go after him first. I have to tell you, I hate the idea that he got rich off of us."

"Then it's decided," Roger said, getting up. "You two will leave first thing."

Numera didn't budge. "Both of us? Are you sure that's a good idea? No one knows that Zach is Que. But it won't be a secret for long if he's in the same room when negotiations are going on."

"Can't be helped," Roger said. "The world is going to find out soon enough. You are in charge of negotiations, Numera. But remember, Zach knows these people."

I didn't speak, even though I thought my going along to see Stallo might be more of a negative than a positive. But there was no way I was being left behind.

Numera stood up slowly, then turned to me. She held out her hand. I was confused for a moment. "Shake my hand, Zach. I'd like us to start fresh."

Confused, I took her hand.

"Before we left my condo this morning," she continued. "I got your DNA results back. You are a Cambermire, without a doubt."

CHAPTER NINE

If people dressing up as characters had been all there was to it, Pegasus Corp would have never turned into the megalith it is today. Even when it spread to people wearing costumes at home and to work, it might not have taken off. It might even have been a fad, strong for a few years and then gone.

I remember the day Cambermire emailed me wondering why, if he could dress as Batman to go to work, he couldn't also drive a Batmobile. That was the true beginning of the growth of our technology division.

And of course, there was no reason at all. Cars quickly became blanks that could be sleeved as any conceit.

From there it was a short leap to being able to live anywhere you wanted. Wear a Batman costume, drive the Batmobile, and live in Gracie Mansion (or the Bat Cave).

That was something almost no one could resist. A man's home truly became a man's castle, or safari tent, or cabin in the woods. It was this development that really pulled the magic carpet out from under the Thentics. From that moment, they became a sliver movement, little more than cranks.

But of course, they became all the more militant because of it.

Diary of Roger Ackroyd

Numera led the way out of her father's office through the front door instead of through the small elevator in back. Beyond was a room bigger than Roger's where a small, matronly woman sat behind an orderly desk, writing on a yellow notepad.

"Take care of Father while I'm gone, Joan," Numera said as we passed.

"I always do," the woman said in a surprisingly deep, raspy voice.

The hallway beyond bustled with people, who tried but couldn't quite pull off not staring at Numera. It was clear she was the big boss who ran the day-to-day operations of Pegasus Corp. The workers gave me only a cursory glance.

As we entered the larger, more ornate public elevator, she turned to me. "Why do you think we should start with Stallo?"

"He's the most venal, the most likely to sell out for a high enough price."

"Which makes him the most likely target for Unicorn too. I wonder why they haven't approached him yet," she mused.

"They probably have. I'll bet he wants more than they're willing to pay. So they'll go after the others first."

"So how high do you think we should go?" Numera asked.

"I think we'll have to blow whatever budget you got. I'm pretty sure the others would much rather sell to us. But Stallo won't give a damn. No matter what, we can't let Unicorn Industries win."

"You'd best let me do the negotiations then. You're too eager." I snorted. "I'm just an intern, remember?"

She frowned, and opened her mouth as if to object.

"Look, Numera," I said before she could say anything. "Nothing's changed. I may be the heir, but I still don't know what I'm doing. You were right to be skeptical of me. I'd rather you kept being skeptical."

She stared at me. "You need to give me final approval on how much to spend. We'll have to work out some signals."

I was shaking my head before she finished. "Just do what you do best, Numera. I'm along for the ride."

"Do you need anything back at the condo?" she asked. "We'll head out for Phoenix right away."

"That's a hell of a long drive."

She laughed. "You still don't get it, do you? You own a corporate jet, Zach. Hell, you own a fleet of corporate jets. You need to start throwing your weight around."

"You think so?"

She didn't answer for a moment. Then she frowned and said, "Maybe not."

I wasn't sure what she meant by that. She no longer seemed angry at me, but that wasn't the same thing as accepting me. I thought about telling her about how I'd met Stallo the Ogre but decided that it was too embarrassing.

The first time I saw Stallo, he was cosplaying Shrek, painted a dark green that seemed to make everyone who came in contact with it sick, except Stallo. Nothing stopped Stallo.

It is said that Andre the Giant could drink a hundred beers in a single session. I suspect that Stallo had him beat. The man is almost seven foot tall, and over five hundred pounds. After that first convention, Stallo realized he didn't have to paint himself green to look like an ogre. All he had to do was open his mouth, show his jumble of teeth, and growl.

He was an instant hit. His name on the marquee brought in thousands of paying conventioneers.

Drunk or not, he was obnoxious and a bully.

I should know. I was walking through an early Seattle convention in my leprechaun costume when he suddenly picked me up and started mimicking Gargamel from the Smurfs.

"Oh sweet ambrosia! I shall eat the happy blue essence and become infallible!"

"I'm not a damn Smurf!" I shouted as the crowd laughed.

"Yeah, he's green!" someone shouted.

"Green?" Stallo roared, and dropped me to the ground. I was totally caught by surprise and landed on my ass much to the amusement of everyone there.

Have I mentioned I don't like being the center of attention?

I figured that eventually Stallo would step over the line and be banished by someone other than me but he seemed to have an uncanny sense of just how far he could go.

I wasn't looking forward to our next meeting, but if it meant buying his Pegasus shares and hopefully never seeing him again, I was willing.

Stallo lived in a cave. Not a nice holo of a grotto like Agate's office, but a real cave, carved out of a mountainside in Arizona by some poor man who couldn't afford a house. Stallo had bought him out, outfitted it with every convenience imaginable, used dynamite to create some bigger rooms, and installed an indoor Olympic-sized swimming pool and regulation basketball court.

He was a true monster. I hoped the hill would collapse on top of him. But not before we pried the Pegasus shares out of his beefy hands.

He was as polite as could be to Numera, which was a side of him I'd never seen. He looked me over—I in my Bowman gear—and nodded as if not quite sure if I was important enough to pay attention to or not.

Not, I sensed him decide.

It was clear he didn't recognize me, though we'd interacted many times—never pleasantly, but at close quarters. I remembered what Merlin had told me about old friends who didn't recognize each other. Apparently, neither did old enemies.

Despite the heat outside, the cave's interior was cool and humid. "I save a buttload on air conditioning," Stallo laughed.

Numera gave me a disgusted look that was very gratifying.

Stallo handed us a couple of bottles of beer. Numera set hers aside with a grimace. The ogre sat back in a chair he must have had specially built. It was twice as big as a normal chair, more like a throne. It was constructed of skulls, most of them animal, with a few human skulls mixed in. I had the sense that the skulls were real. Again, Numera gave me a look.

Frazetta paintings covered the walls, which was a shame, because he was one of my favorite artists. I half expected Stallo to begin the negotiations by saying, "I'm here to crush my enemies, to see them driven before me, and to hear the lamentations of their women."

"As we mentioned over the phone, Mr. Stallo..." Numera began.

"Just Stallo. Ogres don't have two names."

"Right. Well, as we talked about, Pegasus Corp is in the

process of buying back as many shares of the company as we can get. We are prepared to be generous."

"Unicorn offered me six thousand a share."

I wanted to laugh—but I was just the intern. That was almost twenty percent higher than the going rate. If Stallo was telling the truth—and there was no guarantee of that—then it was no wonder Unicorn was managing to buy up so much stock.

I laid my right hand flat on my thigh, the signal we'd arranged to match whatever Unicorn offered.

"We will match whatever Unicorn offers, of course... if you'll provide proof," Numera said.

Stallo flushed, and I realized Numera had made a mistake. But the mistake was probably due to the advice I'd given her. I told her that Stallo was crass and imperturbable. I wouldn't have thought he could be insulted.

"Match, hell. I turned them down. I was expecting you to come crawling. I want what I told them, $7500 a share."

Numera couldn't hide her shock. She looked ready to stand up and leave. I laid my left hand on my left thigh and moved it down my leg, the signal to pay the price.

"We'll be willing to pay you $6500 a share, Stallo. That's a full twenty-five percent more than what we can purchase stock for on the open market."

"Go for it," Stallo said. "What's stopping you? Oh, there isn't any stock to be had, is there? Not without buying little scraps here and there that don't add up to what you need. You see, I don't give a shit whether you or Unicorn win. Either way, you'll pay my rate."

No, we won't, I thought. I looked at Numera and nodded. Pay whatever it took; we were through with this man.

"Seven thousand," Numera said, going against my instructions.

Stallo reared back and laughed. "You people must be desperate! Very well, I'll do it. Transfer the funds to this account." He reached into a voluminous pocket and pulled out a scrunched-up piece of paper and threw it at Numera. She pulled out a phone and entered the numbers. Stallo did some scrolling on his own phone, and Numera turned and nodded stonily at me.

It was done.

I rose from my chair and marched up to Stallo. My head barely reached his chest, but I looked up into his face defiantly.

"You got a problem, buddy?" Stallo said.

I could tell he was taken aback by my aggressiveness. What the hell was I doing? He could squash me like a bug. "Yeah, I do. You're a creep, Stallo. You're never going to work at Pegasus again. When we drive Unicorn out of business, you'll have nowhere to go."

He pushed me. It didn't take much. I flew backward over the chair. I looked up to see Numera charging the giant, grabbing a lamp off a table that she tried to smash over his head. She got only as high as his shoulder.

He backhanded her, and she went down without a sound. I got up and attacked, slamming my fists into his belly. He grunted, then I felt a sledgehammer hit the side of my head, and I was on the floor looking up. He stomped over to me and raised a huge booted foot over my head.

Without thinking, I drew one of my six-guns and pointed it at his head.

He laughed. "Oh dear, a prop."

I squeezed the trigger.

Fortunately—or unfortunately—the bullet whizzed over his head and smashed into the overhead chandelier, spraying glass down over both of us. I'd call it luck, except… it was as if, in that last moment, my vision splintered into a dozen vectors and my mind calculated precisely where, in each vector the bullet would land. I chose the one that would just barely miss Stallo's head, which had taken some last-minute willpower.

I got to my feet, my gun now pointed directly at the center of his chest. "My name is Que. Maybe you've heard of me. When I say you aren't working in this town again, I mean it."

Stallo shrugged. "You've just made me so rich, I could start my own studio."

Numera got up, looking surprisingly calm. A bruise was already showing on her cheekbone, but she seemed okay other than that.

"You want to call the cops?" I asked.

"I want nothing more to do with this man," she said, and left the room. I shrugged at Stallo. "Goodbye, Mr. Ogre. Good luck trying to get any of your movies shown. I hope to never see your face again."

He stood there in the middle of the room looking like the stupid beast he pretended to be at conventions. It was clear that the implications of my revelation were just starting to sink in.

CHAPTER TEN

My daughter has come to work for me. Despite getting the best grades at the best schools, it didn't seem that she could find a job to match her talents. So she reluctantly came to me. I am not above a little nepotism, if she is up to the job, which she is more than capable of doing.

She started out as my assistant and has picked things up so fast that it's astonishing.

It's especially surprising in that as a child, she not only didn't show an interest in the Hyper-reality world but actively avoided it. Probably because it's what her daddy did. She was surrounded by costumed and strangely acting people whether she wanted to be or not.

Nevertheless, as I said, she has picked things up fast and I'm grooming her to take over when I'm gone—which may be sooner than I'd like.

Diary of Roger Ackroyd

A gate opened the door to the condo before we could put the key in.

"You put *live rounds* in my revolvers?" I blurted.

Agate shrugged. "I told you, I don't do *costumes*. That coat you're wearing? It's a hundred fifty years old. That cool hat? Belonged to a bank robber named Hank Hymes. Those boots? They were removed from a hanged man by the name of James Best."

I was wearing a hanged man's boots? All ten toes seemed to tingle at the thought, as if they wanted to escape their confines. "I thought everything was boffered," I said.

"Good thing they weren't," Numera said.

I couldn't argue. Back when the first Pegasus Con was

announced, most fighting was boffer-designed—that is, done with cushioned or dull blades or blanks; boffer swords and boffer axes and boffer guns. But sometime in the last few years, the players had started getting serious. Half the cost of attending an event was paying for the insurance that covered it. Everyone signed away their lives, basically. But even that ironclad contract didn't keep Pegasus from being sued every other weekend.

But live rounds? That was another whole level of reality that I didn't think I liked much—even if it did just save my life.

Numera went to the kitchen and poured us all a glass of wine. We sat at the island, saluting our first success.

"Who's next?" Numera asked.

I'd been puzzling over that question all the way back on the corporate jet. If I had to guess—and I guess I did have to guess—the next target most likely to sell was Pretty, Pretty. By all accounts she was on the downside of her career but still living a megastar lifestyle.

Besides, I hadn't seen her in years. Oh, I'd seen her from a distance, surrounded by her entourage, but I hadn't been close to her in a long time. I doubted she would remember me. But with Numera, I had access. I could look Pretty, Pretty in the eye and explain what was happening.

I envisioned that conversation in my head, and what came back was a blank look from Pretty, Pretty. Talking about copyright and trademark licensing would only confuse her.

Stick to the money.

"I'd say we should approach Pretty, Pretty," I said.

Agate barked out a laugh and turned to Numera. "Told you, Numie."

Numera sighed, reached into her pocket, and extracted a twenty dollar bill, which she handed over to her friend

"That's unfair," I objected. "It's not because she's...pretty. I mean, by those lights, why did I pick Stallo first?"

"Because you were spoiling for a fight?" Numera said. She raised one eyebrow and took a sip of wine.

"Oh, so now you guys think you know me."

Agate leaned over and touched my hand. "Do you have any idea how many nights we've spent speculating on who you were and what you were like? Have you read the stuff people have been writing about you? I particularly enjoy the slash fiction."

I blushed. I had once gone to look at the stuff, and it had been embarrassing as hell.

Agate said, "We've all had ideas about what you'd be like, anywhere from a five-hundred pound schlub who never leaves his mother's basement to a Martin Conley lookalike, of *Ocean's Twenty* vintage."

"Great. How am I ever going to measure up to that?" I said. It scared the hell out of me—disappointing people. I mean, I am just an average guy. No way could I live up to either extreme. They wanted someone who stood out and my whole ambition was to blend in.

"Stallo sure wasn't expecting you," Numera said, laughing.

"Tell me! Tell me!" Agate got up from where she was sitting next to me and moved her chair so that she could look into our faces. Numera gave a short version of events, which I had to admit made me sound like a man of action instead of a frightened little nerd who resorted to a gun the first time he was challenged.

"How long do think it'll be before Stallo tells people about Que?" Agate asked.

"I suspect he's pretty embarrassed by the whole thing. But... he'll get over it. I mean, this is just too good to keep quiet," Numera said.

The two women looked over at me. "Oh, dear," Agate said.

Yeah, my face was drooping. I mean, I could feel the skin sagging. Since I'd found out who I really was, I'd let a few daydreams invade my consciousness: the fantasies usually started out as Roman Triumphs, me riding onto the stage in a chariot with roses spread before my progress. But then I'd remember that part of the triumph was a slave standing behind the victorious commander whispering, "You too shall die."

Then the daydreams would inevitably turn bad. Me hounded like Elvis in Graceland, like John Lennon at the Dakota, like Barry Manning nearly torn apart at the Gates of Elysium.

"We didn't tell Stallo my name," I said, but even as I said it, I knew it was a thin cover.

Agate gave me a pitying look. "Yeah, he'll never figure out who the Harvey Bowman lookalike is."

It had been all over the news about how a nobody named Zachary Spence had come out of nowhere to win a major contest. Yeah, Stallo would never think to look that up.

"We may still have time before it becomes general knowledge," Numera said. She set down her wine glass. "Let's get some sleep. Pretty, Pretty is attending a Pegasus event in Seattle tomorrow. We'll head up first thing in the morning."

"Can I come along?" Agate asked.

Numera looked at me.

"I don't see why not," I said.

"Thank you, my man," Agate smiled. "Thank you."

Neither Agate nor I had arisen from our seats. "I'm going to get a buzz on," I said, taking another sip of wine. "Don't worry, Mom, I'll be in bed by midnight."

Numera gave the two of us a last speculative look. "Be good." She left the kitchen and went to her room.

Agate grinned at me. I wasn't really sure what was happening, I just knew that I wanted to talk to her.

"I like you, Zach," she said abruptly.

I smiled back uncertainly.

"What? Is that such a surprise? I'll tell you what, Mr. John Q. I was prepared to think you were a dick. I mean, why the hell would somebody who was about to inherit the world hide unless there was something wrong with them? But now I see it—you just wanted to be normal. I can understand that."

I poured myself some more wine, telling myself that it would be my last glass. "I actually didn't know. My mom was sick. I was out of the loop. I wasn't being coy. Even now, I don't feel like I did anything to deserve it."

"Didn't your Mom tell you..."

"...that life is unfair? Yeah, I get that. But... I look around and I see people struggling and striving and getting nowhere and all I feel is guilt."

"Oh, you poor boy."

I stared at Agate, wondering if she was mocking me. She put her hand on my arm. She leaned a tiny bit my way.

I leaned a tiny bit toward her. She leaned a little more and…
we were kissing. It was the best kiss I'd ever had—not too dry,
not too sloppy, just right. Soft lips and sweet breath, her smell
warm and suffusing, her hair tickling my cheeks.

I broke off and stood up, my chair making a squeaking
sound as I pushed it back.

"Everything all right out there?" Numera's voice drifted to
us from behind her bedroom door.

Agate flushed, and she also got up, looking flustered. "Do
you two have a thing going?"

"No, no." I said. Of course, I'd been thinking about it.
Numera was the most beautiful woman I'd ever seen up close.
Agate…she was a surprise.

A hugely nice surprise.

"I'd better get some sleep," I said.

Agate followed me to the door. I leaned down and kissed
her briefly on the lips. "That was one of the nicest things ever,"
I murmured.

She grabbed my arm before I could leave. "You know, Zach,
every woman in the world is going to be throwing herself at
you. I just want you to know…I forgot who you were there for a
moment. I mean, it was real…"

"I know," I said, in my best Han Solo voice.

I floated off to my room, fell into my bed still dressed, and
dreamed sweet dreams, until sometime in the middle of the
night, the wine wore off and I popped wide-awake with dread,
staring up at the ceiling remembering every doom-ending
Hyper-reality scenario I'd ever played.

CHAPTER ELEVEN

How is one to know what is real and what isn't anymore? I mean, those of us who are old enough to remember the mundane world before holograms and VR can tell when something isn't quite right—we know that animals don't talk, that there are no such things as dragons—but how are the younger generations to tell?

Children are being born into a world where—on the surface at least—anything is possible. How will they be able to know what is achievable and what isn't? Or even what is important and what isn't? If everyone can be a prince or a princess, then why strive to attain anything?

I brought this up with Joseph once and he laughed and said, "Don't worry, the kids will be all right. They'll be able to tell the difference, maybe better than we can."

I wish I had his confidence.

Diary of Roger Ackroyd

I must have fallen back to sleep, finally.

Suddenly, I was on the street in front of the Emerald Tower, facing Mr. Zander again, only this time it was twilight and the tall man was drawing one of his blades. When his bony hand grabbed my arm, I woke up with a shout.

"Quiet," Numera said. She sat on the edge of my bed, fully dressed. "You'll wake Agatha and she's not used to drinking wine. She needs to sleep it off."

"What is it? What's going on?"

"Father called. Something's wrong. We need to go check on him."

"Now?" I stumbled out of bed, reached for my shoes, and

realized I'd gotten under the covers with my clothes on, which I had never done before. With Numera only inches away, I remembered kissing Agate and felt embarrassed. I started to get to my feet, felt lightheaded, and sat back down.

"Come on, Zach. Hurry!" Numera urged.

She loomed over me, impossibly tall and elegant. Even though it was only a couple of hours before dawn, she was immaculate, her short hair neatly combed, wearing high heels and a tight skirt with a blue satin blouse.

"Where is he?" I rubbed my eyes, trying to kick-start my brain.

"He never leaves the Emerald Tower." This time, I heard the panic in her voice.

"Did you call security?"

"We send them home at night. No one can get into the tower who shouldn't be there."

"What did he say?" I asked, finally making it to my feet and following her to the door.

"He said my name, twice. Then he said, 'Mera,' which he never does because it reminds him of my mother. Then we were disconnected. When I called back, he didn't answer."

Numera drove the Jaguar down the empty streets of Portland at twice the speed limit. I held on for dear life, expecting we'd be pulled over by the cops at any moment. All the lights were green, thankfully, because I don't think Numera would have slowed down for anything. Downtown appeared deserted, no one on the streets. Even the bars and restaurants were quiet. I began to wonder if I was dreaming or seeing one of my visions again. How would I know?

Numera drove into a small garage behind the tower that wasn't visible from the street, and practically ran for the elevator. It was the same tiny elevator she'd used the first time we'd visited her father's office. Its acceleration left me even woozier this time.

The light was on in the office, and Roger's red beret bobbed behind a stack of books. He was humming tunelessly to himself.

"Father?" Numera said.

He stood up. "What are you two doing here?"

"You called me!" Numera said, her voice rising. I couldn't tell if she was relieved or outraged.

"Yes, I did," Roger said. He looked faintly apologetic. "I was feeling unaccountably sentimental, remembering your mother. I'm sorry. I don't know why we got disconnected, but I decided I'd best not disturb you."

"Disturb me!" Numera cried. "I was worried sick!" She stomped toward the desk. I'm not sure whether she intended to slap him or hug him, but she suddenly stopped and made the strangest little strangled sound. Her hand went to her mouth and her eyes opened wide.

"What is it?" Roger and I asked at almost the same moment.

"Nothing," she said. "It's just...I...I was so scared." She swayed, looking as if she was going to faint. I stepped to her side and put my arm around her waist. I was almost surprised when she didn't shrug me off.

"I'm going back to my apartment, Father," she said tiredly. "Please never do that to me again." She turned abruptly and re-entered the elevator. I shrugged helplessly at Roger and followed.

The elevator doors closed, and suddenly Numera was in my arms. "You're really here, aren't you, Zach? I'm not dreaming this?"

"I'm here," I said. "What's wrong?"

She stepped back, and composed herself. "Let's get out of here." When the elevator door opened, she brought out her keys and unlocked her car.

The car that emitted the beep wasn't a Jaguar, but a humble Toyota sedan. I started to say something to Numera and stopped in my tracks. She was wearing a pantsuit instead of a dress, with sensible shoes instead of high heels. Her hair was long and uncombed. She stopped at the same moment, looked back at me, and gasped.

"What is it?" I asked.

"You have a beard!"

And then it struck both of us that the air around us was suffused with a reddish gleam. We both turned and looked up at the lights of the tower. They were bright red.

"Are you seeing that?" she asked. "It's red instead of blue?"

I answered. "Instead of green, you mean. The Emerald Tower?"

She ran to the car, and was already pulling away before I was fully in the front seat. She drove down the street even faster than she had in the Jaguar.

"Pull over, dammit!" I said. "We need to talk about this."

She drove another block before veering into the parking lot of a Wendy's. The girl on the sign had raven-black hair.

Numera leaned over the steering wheel and put her hands over her face. The eerie red light of the tower saturated the air, and I could see her fear.

"What did you see?" I asked.

She sat up straight and was still for a moment, her eyes closed. "I saw Father at first," she said quietly. "But there was a shadow behind him. It moved. Something long and snakelike was attached to the back of his neck. I could see it spasm as my father talked, as if he was a puppet. That wasn't him, Zach. Am I going crazy?"

Weirdly, I felt almost relieved, if bad for her. "No. The same thing's been happening to me." I told her about my visions, one by one, up to and including the tower's change of color and the changes in our appearances. As I was talking, the red light turned green. I looked at Numera and her hair was short again, and she was again wearing a dress. We were sitting in a Jaguar. I reached up and rubbed my bare chin.

"What's happening?" she breathed.

I couldn't help it. I laughed shakily. "This has been unreal for me since I got the Red Pass in the mail. To be honest, the delusions haven't been any stranger than the idea that I'm Que, the richest man in the world."

"They aren't delusions," came a third voice from the little jump seat behind us. Numera looked behind her and then looked at me calmly. Apparently, she was all out of shocks.

"Tell me you see a coyote," she said.

"A talking coyote," I answered.

The coyote said, "I've decided that I need to choose a single form that is recognizable to you so that you will know it is me and no one else will think it strange."

"Because no one will think a talking coyote strange," Numera said.

"That's good of you," I said. "But who are you?"

"I can't tell you," said the coyote. "I am limited in what I can say. I'm allowed to give you some guidance, to keep you on track. I don't know how long this reality will hold, so listen carefully. My advice is that you continue with your plans. Everything will become clear as you progress."

"How reassuring," Numera said. "Look, are you some sort of new holo projection?"

"I'm real, I assure you—for now. And as such, I shall see you again." It was clear that the coyote was going to disappear on us.

"Wait!" Numera cried. "What about my father? Is he all right?"

The coyote's yellow eyes softened. "I'm sorry," it said, and vanished.

CHAPTER TWELVE

The Legend of Que has gathered steam over the last few months. Some intrepid reporter tracked down the fact that a John Q. would be the heir to Pegasus Corp. He elongated that into Johnny Que, and finally, it became just Que, which apparently was exotic enough to catch on.

From then on, it was like looking for Bigfoot. The longer the mystery continued, the more bizarre the rumors. Every famous person in the world was suspected at first.

Then people figured out that Que was a nobody, which only seemed to double the interest. How could that be? How could the richest man in the world not know it?

The only thing that everyone could be sure about was that Que probably attended Pegasus Conventions, which didn't help much. So did pretty much everyone else.

Diary of Roger Ackroyd

In the basement of the condo, Numera turned off the car and sat quietly for a moment. Neither of us had spoken on the way back. Now she turned to me and put her hand on mine.

"Would you stay in my room for the rest of the night?" she asked.

"Your room?" I repeated, sounding stupid to my own ears.

"I not asking for...you know. I just don't want to be alone."

"Sure," I said.

We walked to her apartment in silence. It was the quietest time of a very quiet night, with dawn not far away. I doubted

either of us would sleep. What would we do? I had no sense that
Numera wanted anything but company.

When we got to her room, she lay on the bed, still clothed. I
sat in the corner chair. She tried to keep her crying from being
audible, but wasn't able to hide her sniffles. I'd never in my life
wanted so much to hug someone. I closed my eyes, and in my
mind's eye I saw the shadow behind Roger exactly the way
Numera described it. Maybe my subconscious had seen it all
along.

"What did that coyote mean by 'I'm sorry?'" she asked.

Despite sitting upright, despite everything, I'd almost fallen
asleep and almost didn't hear her. "I don't know. We can call
your father in the morning."

"I can't," she said. "I can't bear it."

I didn't have an answer for that. I wasn't sure I would be
able to talk to Roger without giving away my suspicions either.

Sounds of someone trying to be quiet while making coffee
emanated from the kitchen. Numera swung herself off the bed
and went to the bedroom door, and I followed.

I don't suppose either one of us thought about how it would
look when we emerged from the bedroom. We hadn't done anything, after all. Agate's mouth dropped open. Her coffee mug
drooped to one side, and a few drips landed on the counter.

Just a few hours before, I'd been feeling guilty in Numera's
presence about kissing Agate; now I felt even guiltier, even
though nothing had happened.

"Coffee's brewed," Agate managed to say, turning her back
on us and walking to the kitchen island. Numera walked to the
chair next to her friend and sat, putting her head in her hands
and groaning.

"You all right?" Agate said.

"I've been better. I couldn't sleep, so I asked Zach if he'd
keep me company. We've been up all night talking."

Agate looked toward me for confirmation. It was a lie, but it
was such a good lie that I nodded and made it seem believable.
The lie was the truth, as least as far as what Agate was thinking. Her expression was hard to read: Doubt? Disappointment?
Relief? I really couldn't tell.

We drank our coffee and talked about our coming trip to Seattle. "Would you call my father and confirm that the plane is ready?" Numera asked.

Agate looked surprised. "You want *me* to call him?"

"He was getting all maudlin about my mother the last time I saw him. It's been ten years this Saturday since she died. I don't want to talk to him about that right now."

"Sure," Agate answered. "Do you think he's awake yet?"

Numera assured her that he was, so Agate went off to her own room, and we could hear her having a casual conversation on her phone. She came back into the kitchen and nodded. "All set up."

"How did he sound?" I asked.

"Same as always. Maybe a little cheery for this early in the morning, but then I've never talked to him this early in the morning."

Numera looked over at me and I could tell she wasn't reassured. Agate was quiet, examining us, as if realizing that something had happened between us, something that she'd been left out of.

"I'm going to take a shower and change clothes," Numera said. "We'll leave in an hour."

The first reporter picked us up at the Portland airport. Fortunately, he couldn't follow us into Pegasus Corp's private hangar, but that didn't keep him from trying. He shouted out a question as the doors closed in his face. I didn't catch all of it, but I did hear the distinct cadence of the letter Q.

"They're still trying to track down the story," Numera assured me. "Reputable news orgs still require at least two collaborating sources and they only have Stallo."

"What about disreputable news orgs?" I asked rhetorically.

The flight to Seattle was basically one steep climb up and one deep dive down. It seemed to take only moments. But things were so awkward between Numera and Agate and me that even that seemed too long. Agate seemed a little embarrassed and wouldn't look me in the eye. It probably didn't help that I didn't leave Numera's side, giving her what support I could.

A limo was waiting for us, and it whisked us off to the Seattle convention center.

We walked in with management tags, but no one gave us a second glance. I'd half expected to be mobbed. Instead, I got friendly nods from cosplayers I'd met at other venues. A couple of closer friends came over and chatted me up, looking Numera over as they did. They winked at me as if they thought maybe I'd finally gotten lucky.

Pretty, Pretty still rated her own room, but it wasn't exactly crowded. She sat at a table, looking bored, occasionally glancing up and turning on the charm. Agate rushed toward her, exclaiming her delight. Pretty, Pretty could see that Agate was genuinely excited, and her old glow suddenly suffused the room.

Numera started toward her.

"Hold back a second," I said.

I remembered the first time I'd met Pretty, Pretty.

When she'd first shown up at the Pegasus shows she'd been a Marilyn Monroe lookalike. I'd thought she was perfect and went up to tell her so.

She'd looked at me, confused. "Who?"

"Marilyn," I said, thinking she hadn't heard me.

"No, I'm Madonna."

I laughed, then realized she was serious. "Come over here a second," I said. I pulled up Marilyn Monroe singing, "Diamonds are a Girl's Best Friend" on my phone and showed it to her.

"I don't understand," she said.

"Madonna was doing Marilyn in her 'Gentlemen Prefer Blondes' phase," I explained. "What's your name?"

"Debbie Johnson."

"That won't do at all. So what do you think your best skill is?"

"I'm pretty?"

"Besides that," I urged. "One other skill."

"I'm really, really pretty," she said, without the slightest bit of irony.

So, you could say that she did the "dumb blonde" bit really well. She savvied up quickly, though, and soon gained a large following. But if anyone wondered what Marilyn would have looked like after the age of forty, they could examine Pretty, Pretty. Years of drinking and eating had made her figure even more voluptuous. She was still hired for commercials, but they put plenty of Vaseline on the lenses or whatever CGI they did these days.

Apparently, Roger had seen her potential early and paid her with some early stock in Pegasus. That stock had been split again and again over the years and had turned into a fortune. But as far I knew, she'd never sold out.

The sign on the door read, "Debra Cromartie, 'Pretty, Pretty,' star of the hit movie *Djinn*." I remembered that she'd had a brief marriage to the actor Martin Cromartie. Better than the last name Johnson I supposed. Just as Debra was a little sharper than Debbie. When you're a star, I guess, these things counted.

What shocked me was how stunning she still was. I'd expected her to appear wasted, from all the rumors I'd heard. Oh, she wasn't pretty anymore in the conventional sense. She'd lost weight since the last time I'd seen her and she was no longer trying to look like Madonna or Marilyn or anyone but herself. Her face was almost sculptural, though it didn't appear to be the result of plastic surgery.

Stress and age had added contours to her face, and her body, and...from the looks of it, her personality. She didn't have that vacuous bimbo gleam in her eye anymore; instead she looked almost...wise.

Wise. Not a word I ever thought would apply to Pretty, Pretty.

I finally approached her. She smiled brightly when she saw me, and it wasn't all fake. She seemed happy to have another fan. She looked at my hands, and I realized I hadn't brought anything for her to sign.

"Can I have a picture taken with you?" I asked.

"Of course! It would be my honor."

I stood with my arm around her as Numera took our picture with her phone. Then I let Debra go and stepped back.

"I know you from somewhere, don't I?" she asked.

"I met you at your first convention. Zach Spence."

Her face lit up and she let out a small squeal. She still had some of the old coquettishness in her, after all. "You know, I always wanted to thank you, Zach. I had no idea what I was doing. I was so bewildered by it all. I must have seemed a complete idiot. I went home and looked up Marilyn, and then I read some more on Madonna and I found Bettie Page and so on, and then I started getting a clue."

Her smile fell away and she fixed me with a fierce look.

"However, I wish you hadn't fixed me with that Pretty, Pretty moniker. Turns out, it wasn't easy to grow out of."

"Sorry," I muttered. Truthfully, I'd never expected her to have a career at all.

She laughed. "I'm just teasing you, Zach. I had a good run. This will probably be my last convention."

"I'm sorry to hear that. Why?"

"I've been disinvited," she said, shrugging. "I don't pull in the paying customers anymore, apparently. It's all right. I'm hoping to concentrate on my acting career anyway."

I shot a look at Numera, who appeared sheepish. "She's right, Zach. It's what happens. Surely you knew that."

Well, no. I hadn't known that. I had seen stars rise and fall, but it had never occurred to me that Pegasus had something to do with that.

"You've got a spot anytime you want one, Pretty," I said. "In fact, next show you get top billing. 'Debra Cromartie.' That's all it needs to say, after all."

She smiled tiredly. "That's nice of you to imagine, Zach, but my lawyer says I'll be arrested for trespassing if I show up."

"No, you don't understand, Debbie. I'm Que."

She looked at me, expecting me to keep talking I guess. Because no sentence she'd ever expected to hear ended with "I'm Que."

"You're...Que," she said, finally.

"I'm Que, the one and only. What I say goes."

Pretty, Pretty looked toward Agate for confirmation. Agate nodded, her expression serious.

Damned if Pretty, Pretty didn't burst into tears. She threw herself into my arms and bawled her eyes out onto my chest. I felt helpless to do anything but hold her. Numera had taken a step back and was hovering, as if uncertain what to do. Debbie finally let go of me, wiping her face.

Numera spoke up. "We do have something we need from you, Miss...Pretty."

"Anything," Debbie said.

"We are in a battle with Unicorn Industries for control of Pegasus."

"Those bastards. They tried to lure me away from Pegasus and when I refused, they blackballed me. That was before..." Her voice trailed off.

Great. Not only had we been on the verge of banishing Pretty, Pretty from our conventions, we'd somehow convinced her before that to turn away her only other prospect. Of course, I shouldn't forget that Pegasus stocks had made little Debbie Johnson a very rich person, but this just showed me again, as if I needed any reminders, that money wasn't everything.

I said, "We are hoping you'll sell your shares to us, Debbie... or if you wish to hold onto them, we'd ask that you not sell to anyone else. That means no one, because anyone could be a stalking horse for Unicorn, if you don't mind the pun."

"I'll talk to my lawyer tonight and sign whatever you want me to sign tomorrow," she reassured me.

"I'll call my father," Numera said, holding up her phone. "We can do it right now."

Pretty, Pretty smiled gently. "Yeah, well. I've learned the hard way, never, ever, ever make a major career decision without sleeping on it. Don't worry. I'm not going to change my mind—it's more that I want to ask David, my lawyer, if I'd be better off selling or holding."

Numera looked as if she was ready to object again. I broke in, "That's fine, Debbie. Tell us where to meet you."

"Room 127 at the Deluxe," she said.

We headed out of the convention center. The crowds were thick by now and we were going against the flow.

Numera stopped so abruptly, I almost ran into her.

"What's wrong? Did you forget something?"

"It's Billy Box," she hissed.

"Box?" Agate exclaimed.

I saw a wedge of burly men moving through the convention floor, the crowd parting before them as if from the prow of a ship. Box led the way, beaming at what he imagined to be his admirers, though most people turned away. He saw Numera and nearly hopped over.

"I'm buying your company, baby. It's all going to be all mine," he said.

"We'll see about that," Numera said.

"Already a done deal," Box said. He was twice as broad but a head shorter than Numera. He still managed to get up in her face. She glared down at him as if ready to slap him.

"That's enough, Billy," someone said.

Out of the scrum came the small, slender shape of Jordan Shipman. He was dressed in a gray suit, his thin blond hair combed neatly.

Billy Box looked bewildered for a second, then red-faced. One of Shipman's security men pushed him to the side.

"So, Jordan, you've finally decided to drop the pretense," Numera said. "You're too late. Debra has already agreed to sell to us."

"Ah, but the papers aren't signed?" he said, his voice surprising deep for such a compact man. He was not much over five feet tall, and until you saw the wrinkles on his face, you might have thought he was a boy.

"We have a verbal agreement," Numera said.

I was surprised that she was so cool and collected. She was polite in a way I was pretty sure I couldn't be.

"Which is worth the paper it is printed on," Jordan said. "You don't mind if I make my offer, do you?"

"Won't do you any good," I said.

Jordan turned slowly toward me, his eyes seeming to cut right through me. I was only playing at being a billionaire; this guy knew how to inhabit the persona all the way down to his elevator shoes. "So it's true. Que has emerged."

Neither Numera nor I spoke.

"Doesn't matter," Jordan shrugged. "I don't see how that's going to change anything."

"You'd be surprised," Agate said, glancing at me. "Thank goodness you've dropped Billy Box as your proxy. I was tired of seeing his face."

Jordan shrugged. "As soon as you got to Stallo I knew that you were on to us."

"Good," Numera said. "I hate all that deviousness."

Jordan smiled, as if to say, *That's your problem.* "Well, no doubt I'll see you in Nashville soon," he said. He motioned for his bodyguards to slice through the crowd again and disappeared.

"Debra won't change her mind," Numera said, but it was almost a question.

"She won't," I answered.

"Then the minute we get her signature, we fly straight to Nashville. We'll just have to hope the Shipman doesn't get to Gentry Partridge before we do."

CHAPTER THIRTEEN

Hyper-reality has become a major component of the economy, and of people's lives. I have always let others try to figure out if this is a good thing or a bad thing. I personally find it liberating and interesting. I make friends I wouldn't otherwise make; I have fun. But the arguments by the Thentics are pretty persuasive. Living in fantasy, according to them, is an elitist activity that only those who can afford it can indulge in.

I don't think that's quite true. I mean, plenty of workaday people are Hyper-reality players. It is no more expensive to outfit yourself with your chosen gear than it is to, say, buy a boat and fishing gear, or a four-wheeler, or whatever hobby one might want to pursue.

But I've also personally seen some players get so caught up in the fantasy that they lose their jobs, their savings, their family.

"All things in moderation" is one of the only things I remember my father saying.

It wasn't as if we were all out there growing or hunting our own food, sewing our own clothing, living in Mother Nature. Most of us woke up in square rooms, got into self-driving cars to go to work, spent most of the day in another square room, and if we weren't too tired or too broke, ate dinner in another square room.

How can a little fantasy be wrong?

Diary of Roger Ackroyd

We'd had a hard time finding a hotel room that night. Turned out the Pegasus crowd had taken almost every vacancy in town and the Unicorn people had booked the rest.

"Shipman did it on purpose," Agate said. "Just to mess with us."

"That's a little paranoid, don't you think?" I said.

Numera gave me an "I'm an adult and you're a child" look. "And you're not paranoid enough, Zach. It won't happen again. I didn't have my head in the game yesterday."

Unicorn's people had bought up all the rooms in the mid-to-luxury hotel and motel range, but we finally found accommodations at a low-end two-star-motel chain. It was just as miserable an experience as I remembered from when I was kid and couldn't afford anything else.

As the others headed wearily for their rooms, I stayed by Numera's side as she handed her credit card over to the motel clerk.

"Would you have really called your fa—Roger?" I asked her.

Numera didn't look at me. I knew that even hearing her father's name was painful.

"I have full authority to make the deal," she answered as she put the credit card back in her pocket. "But I've found that using my father's name has a salutary effect. People think I'm too young to have that kind of power."

Our rooms were right next to each other, on the ground floor. I followed her into her room and closed the door behind me. She turned in surprise.

"What are we going to do about your father?" I asked.

Numera sat on the edge of her bed, removed her shoes, and rubbed her feet tiredly. "I don't understand any of this, Zach. If you hadn't been with me I would have thought it all a delusion."

"Maybe I'm deluded too."

"No...I trust my own senses. That *thing* wasn't my father."

"Then what happened to him?"

She stood up abruptly. "What do you want me to do, Zach? Call the police? Tell them there's a monster where my father used to be? I'm screaming inside."

I moved to her side and tried to take her in my arms, but she pushed me away—gently, but firmly.

"Every part of me wants to go back and confront that thing," she said. "To demand that it tell me where my father is. But my father's last wish was that Pegasus be saved. Nothing has changed. We still need to beat Unicorn."

"That's what I don't understand," I said. "Both the coyote and the doppelganger told us to continue—but I'm certain they aren't on the same side."

She sat down again, her long body folding in on itself. She didn't answer for a long moment. Then she looked up at me with tears in her eyes.

"He's gone, Zach. I can feel it."

I sat down next to her and this time she let me put my arms around her. She put her hand under my chin, turned my face toward hers, and kissed me hard. The world opened with that kiss.

And it was a promise.

I pulled back, reluctantly. If I took this any farther, I'd always wonder if I'd taken advantage of her grief. I got up before I could change my mind and headed for my room.

Thankfully, she didn't try to stop me, because I wasn't sure I could resist a second time.

As compensation for the lousy motel, Numera steered us to a swanky restaurant for breakfast.

I was ready to brace Pretty, Pretty at first light. To my surprise, it was Numera who counseled patience. "Either she's afor' us or agin' us. It was all decided yesterday, against my better judgment, one way or the other."

She gave me a fierce look that told me that I'd interfered with negotiations and had let Pretty, Pretty off the hook. But she couldn't keep up the pretense of being angry and broke into a smile. We stared into each other's eyes for a long moment.

"Ahem," Agate said, looking at the two of us curiously.

"Don't worry," I repeated for what felt like the tenth time. "Debbie's afor' us."

"I agree," Agate said. "She seemed genuinely grateful. I like her."

"You like everyone," Numera groused.

"I like almost everyone," Agate said. "But those I don't like, I really, really don't like."

The restaurant was everything Numera had promised. I'd always thought pancakes were pancakes were pancakes, but I was proven wrong. The blueberries popped in my mouth, and the dough melted. It was better than any dessert I'd ever had.

We finally got to the Deluxe Hotel at around ten o'clock in the morning.

"We gave Ms. Cromartie a wakeup call at eight o'clock," the clerk said. "She didn't answer. Our policy is to wait two hours before trying again."

"Never mind," Agate said. "We're heading that way."

Numera and I exchanged a look. She turned back to the deskman. "Do you mind coming with us?"

He stared at her for a moment and saw something in her expression that convinced him. He motioned a bellboy over. "Accompany these folks to Room 127, Sal."

We went up in the elevator in silence. I didn't question Numera because I'd felt the same twinge of worry.

Numera knocked on the door. When there was no answer, Agate smashed her little fists against the hardwood and yelled, "You in there, Debra?"

We stepped back and the bellboy, with great reluctance, unlocked the door. He let us enter but didn't follow.

It was staged, I could tell that right away.

I'd seen pictures of Marilyn Monroe lying dead and naked on her bed, and Debbie had been placed in the exact same position. Upturned pill bottles were strewn about, and pills had rolled out on the floor. There was a half-empty glass of amber liquid by the bed. I couldn't see Debbie's face from where I stood, and I decided I didn't want to.

I heard a click from behind me and saw the bellboy turn and hurry away. The picture he took showed up online within the hour, and was on the front page of every surviving newspaper the next morning. You could just see Debbie's blonde hair, half off the pillow, and a glimpse of her nicely rounded white rump.

"The bastards," Agate said.

Part of me wanted to move Debbie, to cover her up. I hated the idea that her killers had posed her this way. It seemed wrong to let them get away with it.

And yet…another part of me knew that Debbie would want this. I don't mean she wanted to die, but if she was going to die, she'd want it to look like this.

The police showed up not long after, interviewed us, and took our names. Unknowingly, the bellboy took a second picture as we left the hotel. It clearly showed the faces of Numera, Agate…and me. When this photo was published, along with our names, it didn't take long for everyone to figure out who I was.

As we fought our way through the crowd waiting for us at the airport, Numera said, "Things just got a lot more difficult."

"Who do you think is in her will?" Agate asked, once we were in the air. "She doesn't—didn't have any kids."

"I'll be willing to bet that Shipman knows exactly who is in her will and has already talked to them," Numera said.

"We can't let them get away with this!" Agate said, pounding the seat in front of her.

Numera and I looked at each other. If not for the coyote, both of us would have suspected Unicorn Industries too.

"Then we have to beat them, whatever it takes," I said, not sure who "them" was.

We flew to Nashville that night. Numera bribed a desk clerk at the best hotel in town for the three best rooms.

It was time, as Numera said, "to start throwing our weight around."

CHAPTER FOURTEEN

Of course, it didn't take long for those in the show business world to catch on to Hyper-reality. In some ways, movies, TV, and the internet had to compete with what their customers were doing. But they had the money and the expertise to do it bigger, if not better.

Most people in the Hyper-reality world have adopted characters who were created by someone else. It is the minority who come up with completely new creations. However, everyone puts their own spin on things.

Some parts of show business were slower to adapt than others. Country-western music tried to stay "authentic," until that crowd became such a minority that they had to give in.

Gentry Partridge was an early adopter. He'd always been flashier than others in his genre, always a bit of a character. He reaped the benefits.

Diary of Roger Ackroyd

When we got up the next morning, there was a man sitting on the hallway carpet outside my hotel room. As he rose to his feet, my eyes kept following him upward, as if he was a balloon rising into the sky. He was so well proportioned that his height wasn't noticeable until you had something to compare it with.

"My name is Burke," he said. "Mr. Ackroyd sent me."

"What for?" I asked.

Burke stared at me with his flat eyes as if willing me to figure it out. Of course I had, and it was a silly question, but it was rude of him to rub it in. Then again, if the fake Roger Ackroyd had been responsible for Debbie's death, why would he send a bodyguard? Unless…unless it was an excuse to keep tabs on us.

"Just don't get in our way," I said.

"You won't even know I'm around."

I snorted. "Yeah, you're a little mouse."

But damned if he wasn't right. Within hours, I started to forget he was there. He stayed just a little out of my eyesight but was instantly in front of me when we had to push our way through the crowds that now surrounded us wherever we went.

When Agate saw him, she marched right up to him, put her hand flat on the top of her head, and then extended it to where it hit Burke. "Two ribs from the top," she pronounced.

Numera, on the other hand, took him in stride when she joined us in my room. "Burke," she said when she first saw him, nodding as if she'd expected him.

Agate went downstairs and returned juggling three Styrofoam cups and a plate of donuts.

"Almost tripped over a mangy dog in the hallway," she grumbled.

Numera got up immediately and poked her head outside. She turned and shook her head at me.

Agate had apparently also stopped in the lobby and grabbed the morning paper, which she'd put under her arm. Liberated from the coffee cups, she threw the newspaper on the bed.

There the three of us were, our shining faces labeled with our names, me looking like a sinister Western villain. "Que?" said the headline.

We checked online and the same picture headed every news site.

"Maybe I should change my clothes," I said.

"Don't you dare," Agate said. "It wouldn't help anyway, unless you ditch Numera and me, yin and yang. And you won't be doing that."

There were two competing headlines, and it was a contest which was more important. I got the lead story on the left, but the bigger headline was for the death of Pretty, Pretty.

It was amazing how important she'd become overnight. Crowds were gathering wherever she'd had a significant career event, flowers piling up before the gates of her Hollywood mansion, an impromptu shrine appearing on her Hollywood star, her old music videos showing twenty-four/seven on all the music channels.

Suddenly she was no longer on the downside of her career, but a promising actress dying in her prime. It was somewhat ludicrous to me that people who couldn't be bothered to walk into the signing room at a Pegasus Convention to see her now acted like she was the most significant person in their lives.

Ludicrous and slightly embarrassing, because to me it seemed so inauthentic.

But what was clear was that she was heading for icon status, alongside Marilyn, Diana, Madonna, and all the rest. Soon young girls would be cosplaying her, showing up at conventions unaware that they looked like Pretty, Pretty, who looked like Madonna, who looked like Marilyn Monroe.

We got ready to leave. I caught a flash of something brown at the end of the corridor.

"I'll catch up with you in a minute," I told Numera.

"Don't wait too long," Agate said. "The Uber guy sounded impatient on the phone."

While the others took the elevator, I went to the stairwell.

The coyote was sitting on the landing, looking at the door.

"Did you know Debbie was going to be killed?" I demanded. "Could you have stopped it?"

"We don't know anything," the coyote answered. "Everything is possible right now. Do you have the myth of Pandora's Box in this world?"

"In *this* world?"

"I'll assume you do. Well, someone has opened Pandora's Box and Schrodinger's cat has jumped out. Jumped out and got hit by a car. Or had kittens, who knows? We are trying to gauge probabilities here. Right now, the safest course is to continue with your plans."

"So that's when you show up? When someone dies?"

It stared back at me for a long time, then sighed in an almost human way. "It is only through death that doors open. Two of the same consciousness cannot exist in the same reality. But take comfort, for consciousness continues on—if not here, then somewhere else."

"You're a big help," I said. "Why are you even here?"

"When your mother died of cancer, did you ask why? Wait...of course you did. But did you expect an answer? Then you shouldn't expect an answer from me either. You are being shown more than most."

"Shown what?" My voice echoed in the stairwell.

"You mustn't give up, Zach. Keep on course. No matter what happens, you must pretend everything is normal. Only that way is there a chance it will be."

The coyote rose and started down the steps. I followed, but it scampered ahead, and by the time I reached the street, it was gone.

I wondered if Gentry Partridge would remember me.

Of all the famous Hyper-reality stars, Gentry Partridge was the most unlikely in my opinion. He was what he was—a silly country-western star with a spangled hat and garish costumes, a sort of hick Elvis with a silky voice. Like Elvis, he was getting older and fatter, and though he still had a huge following among middle-aged women, he was—if you will—old hat to everyone else.

Like Johnny Cash before him, Gentry crossed over to all kinds of music genres. I'd once asked Dudley MacKenzie at my local comic shop why he never played country-western music in his store and he'd shaken his head and said, "I can play anything to my people—jazz, folk, classical, rock, hip-hop...I've even played opera and gotten indulgent grimaces. But damned if I can play country without someone complaining."

Well, I liked me some country rock, and I'd stood in line to meet Gentry once. He'd been gracious, signing my first-edition record album while saying, "You sure you want to ruin this with a signature?"

"Yes, sir. I have another one at home."

"Do you now," he'd said, looking at me with his dark brown eyes that all the women swooned over. His record sales had started off small, with extremely limited print runs, so they were incredibly rare. For me to have two of them marked me as an early fan.

He had whipped out a concert ticket and invited me to his show that night.

He was at his peak then, his voice easily ranging over three octaves, his movements smooth and mesmerizing. I was in a crowd of women, and I think they were so turned on that I probably could have gotten lucky if I'd made the effort.

I went back to his dressing room. He was drenched in sweat, but greeted me like an old friend. As he wiped off the makeup, he looked at me in the mirror.

"You're young," he said. "You've got time to get your act together."

I blushed, wondering if my insecurity was that apparent.

"Yep," he said. "Sometimes I wish I could start all over again. I never had more fun than when I was on the road in a single van with a few of my bandmates, playing in small towns. What's your name?"

"Zach Spence, from Bend, Oregon."

"I played there once. Kind of a cowboy town?"

"I suppose...overlaid by a layer of sophistication."

"So stay there and enjoy your life, my man. But in the meantime, how would you like to meet some of the most gorgeous women you've ever seen? They're waiting outside that dressing room door, right now. I put my hand on your shoulder and you can have your pick."

"No thanks," I said, getting up.

"Good man. It's cheap sex, but damned if I can resist. Stay humble, friend."

He shook my hand and I left.

For a couple of years after, I got mailers and tickets through the mail, and when Gentry was on the West Coast, I went to his concerts. He got puffier and more tired every time I saw him, his voice limited to his lower octave, his movements still smooth but a little too practiced. He was, I had to admit, a good object lesson about fame. His career was flaming out faster than most.

Which meant he'd probably be willing to sell his shares.

The gates to Gentry Partridge's estate opened as we drove up.

"We're expected," Numera said.

"So?" Agate said.

"I didn't call him."

"Shipman has had plenty of time to get here before us," I said. "Maybe we should split up after this, approach the other two separately."

"Why don't we just Skype them?" Agate said.

"Our secret weapon is that Zach knows all these people," Numera answered. "You saw the effect he had on Debra Cromartie."

We fell silent at that for a few moments as the truth of her death impacted us again. Which only reminded me of my mom, and Numera of both her father and mother. When my mom had died, it had seemed to hit me every ten minutes. Eventually, so people told me, it would hit a little less hard, and then a little less hard than that, until it became but a sad memory.

That thought didn't help, and I felt tears well up.

"See what I mean?" Numera said, pointing at my tears. "He's our one advantage, our best hope of swaying these people, if for no other reason that he means well and he damn well means it."

Gentry waited on the porch at the top of the steps. I turned to Burke. "Stay in the car. You'll scare him."

Burke looked to Numera who hesitated, then nodded.

I took the lead and trotted up the steps, extending my hand.

Gentry shook it enthusiastically. "Well, I'll be. If it isn't little Zachary Spence."

"Hello, sir. I'm glad you remember me."

He shook his head. "I admit, it didn't come to me at first. I saw your picture in the paper this morning and thought, 'I know that guy.' And I read your name and thought, 'I've heard of this guy.' Then I remembered, 'The guy who owned two of my debut album.'"

I tipped my hat.

"Still the only guy who's ever told me that," Gentry said.

"I like your music," I said.

"Too bad Pegasus Corp doesn't feel the same way."

"What do you mean?"

He searched my face as if trying to decide if I was really that uninformed. Apparently I was, because I had no clue what he was talking about.

"Best come inside so we can talk about it," he said. "Though...I feel like I should tell you now, you're too late. I've already sold my shares."

In the corner of my eye, I saw Numera slump a little. She motioned for us to leave.

"We've got to go," she said. "We can still get to Louisville tonight."

Gentry looked at me expectantly.

"I want to know why," I said. "An hour won't make that much difference."

He led us into a cavernous living room. Filling one wall were dozens of gold records. I started to count them, but they were arranged in such a way that I kept losing count.

"Sit down," he said, motioning to the huge, overstuffed couches. "My new record just came out. Have your heard it?"

Silence.

"Of course you haven't. No one has, because no one is buying it."

He put it on and stood in front of the record player staring at us. I put an expectant smile on my face. I'm afraid it might have slipped a little as I listened.

Gentry had obviously gone the route Johnny Cash went, in the last years of his life: American standards, good, strong songs of all genres, done in Johnny's own deep-boned style. Every fading star since had tried the same gambit, though none of them had succeeded like Johnny, because it was obvious that's exactly what it was—a gambit.

Gentry had been country's Elvis—you know, if Elvis wasn't

already country's Elvis—but he'd never quite managed to do ballads the way his predecessor had. Upbeat was the Gentry signature tune. "Balls Out"; "Motorin'"; "Beat Me To It"; that kind of thing. His voice didn't have the depth for the kind of songs on this album.

"Another flop," Gentry said. "Good thing I have a gig next week at the Unicorn Convention in Oklahoma City."

"Is that why?" Numera said. "Because they hired you and we wouldn't?"

Gentry said it straight. "Of course that's why."

"Wait," I said. "What do you mean, 'we wouldn't?'"

"When do you think the last time was that I played at a Pegasus event?" Gentry asked me.

I wracked my brains and realized I didn't have the slightest idea, and with that realization, I knew that it must have been a very long time, because I knew that kind of thing.

"Yeah, exactly," Gentry said. "It's been over five years, Zachary Que. Five...long...years."

"So you sold to Unicorn out of spite?" Agate said, getting up from the couch and marching toward him.

"No, I did it because I want to play my music. I don't give a damn about the money. Unicorn has been booking me steadily this whole time and you know what? It's been profitable for them, because I've got a solid fan base. But apparently, not quite solid enough."

I looked at Numera, who avoided looking back. "I didn't know, Gentry," I said. "I wasn't making the decisions."

"Well, boy. That's a shame."

Apparently, Pegasus wasn't what I thought it was. First Debbie telling me that she'd been dropped because of a lack of response, and now Gentry. That's not the way I'd imagined it.

I stood up. "Thank you, Mr. Partridge. You've been a big help to me. No hard feelings. Don't be surprised if you get some booking from us in the near future...if you're still willing."

"Well, damn. I'm a little bit sorry I was so hasty. But you give me hope, Zach. Time for you to get involved, son. Turn this ship around."

"Yes, sir," I said.

I walked out alone, not caring if the others followed me. I didn't speak all the way back to the airport, and after a few attempts at conversation, Agate and Numera left me alone.

I had some thinking to do.

CHAPTER FIFTEEN

At first I was amazed that Unicorn Industries dared to compete with us. We laughed at them at first, but once Jordan Shipman became CEO, we stopped laughing. He was diligent about sweeping up the dregs that we'd overlooked. Thing was, the dregs began to cohere into something more substantial.

The competition was probably good for us. It made us more efficient. I consulted with Joseph and he reluctantly let me tighten up some of the less efficient practices. He wouldn't budge on the ten percent charity offerings, but he let me tinker with the conventions themselves. I turned to Numera for help. We cut loose some of the celebrities who weren't pulling people in.

She might have been a little more severe than I knew.

Diary of Roger Ackroyd

We were halfway across the country flying toward the darkness of the East Coast when I finally came out of my fugue. I'd been half-listening to the others talking, but something finally penetrated.

"We've lost two out of three," Numera was saying. "We lose one more and we're beaten."

"Then we have to change strategy," I said, sitting up.

"He's alive!" Agate exclaimed.

I ignored her. "We've been trying to get the easy ones first, which made sense at the time. But now I think we have to go for the hard one."

"Which is?" Numera asked.

"Coventree. The bad news is, she's an unpredictable person

and she can turn on us without warning. The good news is, she's an unpredictable person and can turn on our enemies just as fast."

"Sounds like a great strategy," Agate said. "Go to the one who's bound to turn on us. What about Maureen O'Rourke? You said you had a good relationship with her."

Well, I'd slept with her, but that's probably not what Agate meant.

"I thought I had a good relationship with Gentry too," I said. "Apparently, I'm now Pegasus and Pegasus is now me, so who knows?"

I carefully didn't look at Numera, and realized she'd think I was blaming her. I wasn't—not really—but I was still a little pissy about it.

"Maybe we should lock Maureen down first," Agate continued.

"No," I said. "Maureen is going to be a challenge. She's smarter than all the rest of them combined. She'll want something from us. I guarantee it. It was be a game of some kind and she'll want to be the game master. Save her for last. She won't do anything until she thinks she has both Unicorn's and our full attention."

"If we lose Coventree, it won't matter," Numera mused. She turned to Burke who was sitting so quietly in the corner of the cabin that I had forgotten he was there. "Tell the pilot to turn around. We're heading for San Francisco."

Agate sniffed her armpit. "I stink. I'm not going anywhere until I've had a shower, a good meal, and a night's sleep. Where's the nearest city?"

For the first time since I'd met her, Numera lost her cool. "To hell with that! No one cares if you stink, Agatha! You can sleep—"

"When I'm dead?" Agate interrupted. "Sorry, I don't subscribe to that philosophy. You're not going to win if you're tired and freaked out, especially if this Coventree is anything like her persona. I never did get the appeal of the evil witch thing. No, we go about this like we're good people. It'll all work out in the end, you'll see."

Numera slumped back in her chair. "Fine! We'll take the night off, but to be ready to take off again first thing in the morning."

"I'll tell the pilot to turn around for New York," Agate said, getting up.

"No!" Numera and I said at the same moment.

Agate stopped and turned slowly. "What is it with you two? Did you have an argument with Roger?"

"We can stop somewhere closer," Numera said. "Tell the pilot to land in Chicago. It will save us some flying time."

"You didn't answer my question," Agate said. "But OK. That makes sense."

We booked rooms at a Chicago airport hotel. I didn't have to bribe anyone this time. Suddenly, as Roger had said, I was a Very, Very Important Person. People fell silent when I walked into the lobby.

I hated it.

We stood at the registration desk, planning the next day. A crowd had gathered around us.

Agate noticed my discomfort. "All right. I release you from Harvey Bowman get-up, though you're sexy as hell as a gunslinger. It's time for you to go undercover again."

I gave her a confused look and she laughed. "You don't get it, do you, Zach? You can be anyone you want."

David Bowie had once walked among us mere mortals with barely a disguise. It was all in the posture and attitude, he said, whether you wanted to be noticed or not. In the old days, before Pegasus, other superstars had seemed to have more difficulty with that, hiding out in faraway places. Those faraway places didn't really exist anymore. Everyplace was a click away from everywhere else.

But modern celebrities have a big advantage over previous icons. They can change their appearance, hide under makeup and costumes.

Or not.

The great method actor Jonathan Granger eschewed all makeup and masks, but tried to inhabit the skin of whatever character he was playing. It worked for him.

In a way, we were all actors now, except for the Thentics—those few holdouts who insisted on being their boring selves. To be honest, that was looking real attractive right now.

"We'll get you all fixed up with a new persona tomorrow," Agate said. "But right now, I'm asleep on my feet. I'll see you guys in the morning."

She wandered off to her room.

I looked at Numera, who seemed, if anything, to still be energized. I wasn't terribly sleepy myself. "How many times have you done Hyper-reality?" I asked.

She looked down at her feet. I almost expected her to say, "Aw, shucks."

"I've attended a number of conventions."

"But not at the level of a player," I prompted.

"I haven't had the time," she said.

"Well, if you're going to be running things, you need to make the time. Come on, there's a Cos-diner a few blocks from here."

I took her arm and started for the hotel front entrance. Burke hurried to catch up. We hadn't gone more than ten steps before we were surrounded. Even Burke's bulk couldn't keep them away.

"Que! Why are you coming out now?" someone with a microphone shouted. Questions came from all sides.

"Where have you been living, Que?"

"Who's your favorite character?"

One guy managed to get past Burke and snagged my duster, almost pulling me off my feet. He was dressed in civilian clothing, probably a Thentic. "Phony!" he shouted. "You're all phonies!"

Numera grabbed my hand, pulled me into the gift shop next to the hotel, and closed the door behind her. Burke stood blocking the way. The clerk, a young woman who looked Asian-American girl, looked up in alarm. She opened her mouth to object, then realized who we were. Her mouth stayed open, but she didn't say anything.

Numera faced me and put a hand on my shoulder. "Sorry,

boss, but you can't just go jaunting off anywhere you want anymore."

I remembered what Agate had told me. I could be anyone I wanted.

Or no one at all. What did the public really know about me? Had they really seen me for who I was? Or was I a Harvey Bowman role-player?

Only one way to find out.

"Is there a back exit to this place?" I asked the clerk. She pointed to the curtained doorway behind her.

Numera approached the cash register, looked around, and aimed her phone at an expensive watch that looked like it had been on display for centuries, with a thin layer of dust on the dial. "I'll take that—if you promise not to open the shop door until we get away."

The clerk nodded.

"I'll take that beret too," Numera said, pointing to a bright pink hat hanging from the back wall. Numera entered the charges into her phone and dumped the watch into her purse.

There was a small storage room beyond with a bathroom. At the back was another door that opened out onto an alley.

Before Burke could step out and check the alley, I closed the door. "Wait a second."

I stripped off my hat and the duster, the six-shooters and the bolo tie. Beneath, I was wearing the same T-shirt with a Green Lantern logo that I'd been wearing before I was decked out in Western regalia. I pulled my jeans down over the tops of the cowboy boots.

I checked myself in the bathroom mirror. I was Zachary Spence again, a nobody from nowhere. I looked like a Thentic, or someone who was out on a casual errand and couldn't be bothered to dress up.

The alley led to the main street in front of the hotel. There was a crowd in front of the entrance. Cops had shown up and were trying to maintain order. I stepped out onto the sidewalk. A few people looked my way, but no one gave me a second glance.

I couldn't do anything about Burke's size and Numera's

striking good looks. I just had to hope that the focus had been on the gunslinger Que. We walked away, unhindered.

The Cos-diner was where I remembered it. It was a steampunk-themed place, with a mid-twentieth-century diner look. A little anachronistic, maybe, but that was the thing about steampunk, and indeed most genres; there was a lot of crossover.

It was crowded, but a large party was just getting up to leave, and I headed toward their table.

"Hey buddy," someone shouted behind me. "You can't be seated without gear."

I walked back to the register. A young woman with spiky hair, a monocle, and Harley Quinn makeup sat there. She handed me a pair of old goggles and a seedy top hat. I put the goggles around the hat and donned it. She eyed Numera and seemed to decide that her pinstriped suit and pink beret passed muster. She handed a bowler hat and a cane to Burke.

"There," she said. "Welcome to Bang the Elephant."

We sat down and ordered hamburgers and red wine. The waitress, whose razor-looking fingernails looked too ungainly to use on the order pad, didn't blink an eye. It was so noisy we couldn't really talk. A couple of tables over, a large Mr. Hyde-looking character was staring at us quizzically.

"Burke, why don't you head back to the hotel?" I shouted.

"I'm supposed to stay with you, sir." His normal speaking voice somehow cut through the chatter.

I leaned over so that he could hear me. "Yeah, but at this particular moment you're actually a danger. The three of us together...someone's going to figure it out."

He stared at me without expression for a few moments, then nodded. He walked over to the register, dumped the bowler and cane, and walked out.

The next time I looked over at Mr. Hyde, he seemed to have lost interest.

Numera smiled at me, looking like a French tourist in Victorian London. For the first time, it was just the two of us. Two or three glasses of wine later, she scooted closer. She put her hand on my leg.

I tried not to freeze up. "I thought you didn't like me."

"I liked you from the beginning," she said, her words slurring slightly. "But you're my boss. I...I don't see how that can work."

"I'm just Zach Spence. Agate was right. I don't have to live in a bubble just because I'm Que. I can be anyone I want."

Her hand slipped off my thigh when I mentioned Agate.

"You guys like each other, don't you?" she said.

I nodded. "I like you, too."

"Great," she said. She sat up straight, finished off the last of her wine, and looked around. The noise level in the diner had been getting steadily louder as the evening progressed. "This has been interesting, Zach," she shouted. "I can see the appeal, but we need to get started early in the morning."

I nodded, and we got up to pay. I turned in my goggles and hat, and walked out into the world a civilian again.

We were silent most of the way back to the hotel. The crowd had disappeared for the most part, though I could see a few lurkers about. They didn't give us more than a cursory glance.

At her door, I said, "This isn't the end of your education. This is just the beginning."

"I look forward to it."

Man, she couldn't have sounded any more formal if she tried.

"See you in the morning," I said.

"Zach, wait."

Numera sat at the end of the bed. She patted the spot next to her. The moment I sat down, she put her arms around me and pressed herself against me.

I tried to pull away. I'd never seen her drink before that night and I couldn't be sure if she was sober enough to make this okay.

She smiled at me, her eyes bright. "You aren't taking advantage of me, Zach," she said, as if she could read my mind. "I've wanted this since I met you."

I kissed her, and we fell back into the bed, and for a long time, that was enough. I kissed her cheeks, her forehead, her throat, her mouth. She took off her top so I could keep kissing more of her. And then she was kissing me back, and then we were one, and I could no longer tell the difference.

The bed bounced a little, and I rolled over, expecting to see Numera heading for the bathroom. Instead, she was sitting up, holding the bedspread against her breasts, her eyes wide.

I followed her gaze.

The coyote sat at the end of our bed. Its yellow eyes caught what little light there was, glowing in the dark. Its mouth was open, and it appeared to be grinning.

I groaned and sat up, leaning tiredly against the headboard.

"How long have you been there?" Numera asked it.

"Don't worry. It's not like I haven't seen it before," the coyote said.

Numera glared at the creature, who didn't seem the slightest bit perturbed. "Why don't you just tell us what you want?" she said.

"What I can tell you I don't know, and what I don't know…I can't tell you that either. I am not supposed to be here at all, any more than they are. We are forced to play a dangerous game, because if we don't, they win."

"They? Who are *they*?" I was getting sick of the coyote's cryptic messages.

"I can't tell you. But you've met them; you've opened yourself up to them. If I say more, I bend your reality to the breaking point. You must stick to the plan, both of you. Don't do anything but that. You shouldn't have gone to Los Angeles."

"We need to know who the enemy is," I said. "We need to know what Unicorn is up to. We need to know if they killed Debbie."

"That isn't important," the coyote answered.

"Not important?" I nearly shouted. "She was my friend!"

The coyote's mouth closed and the smile disappeared.

"You know what?" I said. "I have no idea why we should follow your advice. How do we even know if you're on our side? Maybe you're leading us astray. If you don't care what happens to our friends, then why would you care about what happens to us?"

"Unicorn Industries is your enemy. It is true you must defeat them—but they are also your friend. Both of you—and everyone else in your world—is in danger. You must continue to follow the plan."

The animal started to fade from view.

"Wait!" Numera said. "I need to know. Is my father dead or isn't he?"

"No one ever truly dies," the coyote said.

Numera threw her pillow at it. It ducked easily.

"Just tell me!" Numera said. "No more of your bullshit."

"I'm sorry, my dear girl," Coyote answered. "Your father is gone from this reality."

Numera's face went blank. She leaned back into her pillow and closed her eyes. A small moan escaped her lips.

I wanted to be angry at the creature, but I knew that Numera had been in agony not knowing.

I said quietly. "You tell us to follow the plan, the plan that her father came up with. But why bother if Roger isn't there anymore?"

"They don't know that we know they have replaced Roger," the coyote answered. "They are only now realizing that he was a figurehead, that he'd already turned all authority over to Numera."

"Is this true?" I asked.

Numera nodded, not opening her eyes. Tears were running down her cheeks.

Coyote continued, "You mustn't let them find out." Then it blinked from view.

I put my arm around Numera and she turned her face to my chest. I held her like that until we both fell asleep.

CHAPTER SIXTEEN

It didn't take much of a push to turn most young people into cosplayers of one sort or another. Most people were already primed to take on the personas of their favorite characters. Even before so many of the younger generation lost their jobs to mechanization and AI's, it was the lucky few who had the kind of jobs they wanted and could dress in a costume that matched their dreams. For decades, Halloween slowly but surely became as much a reason for adults to dress up as for children.

Why did it have to be only one day a year? Why did it have to be at only certain times and places that you could be who you wanted to be?

At first, it was small signs of rebellion, of nonconformity. (Of course, if everyone is doing it, it isn't nonconformist, is it? But that is a different argument.) Maybe a strange hat or beard or hair styled in a strange way, or a garment that was more appropriate for a party than for work.

The more people experimented, the more other others joined them, until it was rare that there wasn't someone in the office who was full-time cosplaying, while everyone else felt free to dress as they wanted.

Diary of Roger Ackroyd

In the morning, it was clear that Agate had been right to demand a rest stop. Clean, fed, and rested, we were feeling human again, and treating each other like friends again. Agate gave us a knowing look at breakfast. I wondered if Numera and I had made a bit of noise.

Numera was subdued, but when I put my hand on hers, she

didn't move it away. She smiled at me sadly, and I realized that finally knowing that her father was gone had been a strange relief.

"Should we call Coventree in advance?" Numera asked me as our plane surged into the sky.

I thought about it for a few moments. "No, that will just give her time to plan some mischief. Coventree will want to jerk us around a little before she gives in—if she gives in. If she plays too hard to get, that's just as good for us, right? And she'll treat Jordan Shipman the same way. Be prepared to be frustrated, is what I'm saying."

"Charming," Agate said. She looked over at Numera and said casually, "Did you two have fun last night?"

We managed not to look too embarrassed or guilty. "I took Numera to Bang the Elephant," I said.

"Hard core!" Agate said, laughing. "What did you do with the Harvey Bowman gear?"

"Oh…" I hadn't even thought of that.

"You lost it, didn't you?" Agate said.

"Sorry," I muttered. "I know that stuff was worth a lot."

Agate frowned. "I could give a damn about how much it was worth—it's the rarity I care about." She pulled out her phone. "Where did you leave it?"

"In the back of the hotel gift shop," Numera said.

Agate stood up and walked to the back of the cabin where she had an animated conversation on the phone.

"It's my turn to give a tutorial," Numera said. "Come here, Zach."

I was sitting across from her. I plopped down next to her and she put her phone between us and started showing me graphs.

"Wait a minute," I interrupted. "Is there a laptop on this plane?"

Unlike most people my age, I never could figure out cell-phones to do my business with. Too small, not enough options. Or rather, too many options I couldn't figure out. I hated the limited interface, and I could never figure out all the shortcuts necessary to navigate the way. So I still used my laptop whenever possible.

Burke stood up and pulled down a bag from an overhead compartment. He pulled out an old laptop, almost an antique. "You can use mine."

Numera puzzled over the keyboard for a while but eventually pulled up the same graphs. "These are the outstanding Pegasus shares as of this morning."

In the lead with a solid red line was Unicorn Corp, with forty-one percent. Right next to it with a blue line was Pegasus Corp—to wit, me—with twenty-nine percent. Next to that was a yellow line of stocks owned by Coventree at twelve percent.

"Where's Maureen O'Rourke?" I asked.

"She did it differently," Numera explained. "She spread them out among various trusts and holding companies. As best we can tell, she also has twelve percent. If Unicorn can buy out either out of the two big remaining shareholders, they'll take control at over fifty percent."

"What about everyone else?"

"They won't matter if Unicorn gets their hands on either Coventree or the Blue Queen's shares. Besides, it would be a nightmare to try to track the six percent of individuals left. The majority of them only own a few shares—some as little as one share."

"That doesn't seem fair," I said. "That they don't have any say."

Numera spoke softly. "Most of them have already sold out, Zach. When this started we owned twenty-one percent and Unicorn, as far as we know, zero. We don't have to buy out Maureen and Coventree, we just have to keep them from selling to Unicorn."

"No, we have to get a majority share," I said. "Whatever it takes."

Numera was shaking her head.

"What?" I said.

"There is a problem with that, Zach. I didn't want to tell you this, but we have even less leverage than before. Rumors are spreading that your father is missing. And, well, you are a wild card. People don't bet on unknowns. Your father always insisted on giving a major percentage of income to charities and most of the rest is poured back into the events themselves. Meanwhile, Unicorn has been building up their cash reserves for years."

"By doing shitty shows," I said.

Numera spread her hands helplessly. "They can outspend us if it comes to a bidding war."

"Then we've already lost," I said. "Coventree isn't sentimental, let me tell you. Maureen? Maybe...if the difference isn't too big."

"We have to try," Numera said. "Maybe cash isn't everything. We can offer influence, prestige, other intangibles."

I sat back in my seat. I felt like telling her to instruct the pilot to fly back to Bend, Oregon, and let me off. What difference did it make to me, really? I'd never been interested in being rich. Stock shares? What did I care? That was the business of suits somewhere, Thentics who only cared about cash.

Let Numera take care of things. She was much more ruthless than I was.

Yes...and that was the problem.

My father had always kept the well-being of the players paramount. He had kept the prices down. Without my influence, Numera would almost certainly turn it into just another big corporation.

But that was nothing compared to what Unicorn would do if they got the monopoly and the Copyright and Trademark Fair Use Act passed.

Sometime during this discussion, Agate had come back and had been standing unnoticed behind me. Now she said, "If Coventree is as petty as you make her out to be, then what you ought to do is get her all riled up. Make sure she doesn't sell to anyone out of pure spite. Shouldn't be hard to do."

I looked up at her in surprise.

"Aren't you the devious one?" Numera said. She glanced at me. "She's got a point."

"No," I said. "We have to win. I never want this to happen again. I never want to worry about whether someone is trying to take over. One way or the other, we need Coventree to sell to us."

It wouldn't be easy. She was completely unpredictable.

Coventree had gotten her start at the Pegasus Conventions and had taken stock in lieu of payment at first. Since she'd gotten in so early her stock had split and then split again, and was now worth hundreds of millions. At the same time, she'd skyrocketed to fame, earning her own hundreds of millions of dollars.

I met her at her first convention.

"Nice costume," I'd said that day in Phoenix.

"You think so?" she asked.

I had planned to keep walking, but she seemed so eager for praise that I stopped.

She was kind of average looking, her makeup a little too thick, and a few pounds heavier than she would be later. I didn't recognize the character she was playing—Kate was, almost from the beginning, more famous than the character she was copying—but I liked the scarlet gothic gown and pointy ears, the skimpy white bustier, and the thigh-high white boots.

She told me she was planning to change character for the next convention.

"Don't," I advised her. "This is going to catch on. I've never heard of Coventree—not much of a manga reader—but if she's half as cool as you are, you've got something."

I spent the day with her. She was fun and funny, and for a while, I almost believed I'd found my manic pixie dream girl. But later that night, she turned on me, accusing me of trying to come on to her when really, I hadn't. At least, I didn't think so.

As quickly as she'd turned on me, the next time I saw her, she was friendly again. Even as she became famous, she always greeted me.

It had amazed me when, by the next convention, she already had a following, and within a year, she was famous in Hyperreality circles, her costumes now so elaborate that Kate Williams completely disappeared.

She was smart enough to buy the rights to the character Coventree for a song. A year or two after that, and she'd outgrown the convention circuit and was filling stadiums all by herself.

It was still morning when we landed in San Francisco. We slipped out a side gate and drove directly to the local branch of Merlin's Toys, which was probably the biggest in the chain.

As we stood in front of the rows and rows of costumes, I turned to Numera. "Have you always had short hair?"

She gave me strange look, and I remembered how she'd shifted to long hair outside the Emerald Tower.

"I mean…well, I think it's time to try something different. What do you think, Agate?"

"Long straight hair, definitely," Agate said. "A little Vampirella, maybe bangs like Bettie Page. A few tattoos."

"No tattoos," Numera interjected.

Agate laughed. "I know, dummy. You've told me often enough. We'll stencil them on."

I nodded. I couldn't wait to see it. Agate went to the barbarian section and picked out a red wig and a metal breastplate. She was unexpectedly curvy and seemed taller dressed as Red Sonja.

I went with the flow and grabbed a wizard's cloak, a peaked hat, and a heavy white beard.

"Wow," Agate said. "When I said you needed a different disguise, I didn't mean you needed to bury yourself."

"It's one of my things," I said. "I'm comfortable as the wizard Hornbori."

Agate lit up. "From the Elder Eddas, right?"

I was impressed. No one had ever gotten that before.

"What about Burke? He's a little too…bodyguard looking."

"An ogre?" Numera asked.

To our surprise, Burke objected. "I'm not a brute, you know. If you don't mind, I'll be a prosperous Merchant of Venice." He disappeared into the stacks and emerged a short time later wearing a robe and a feathered conical hat.

Numera had changed into a flowing pastel gown, her dark wig showing off her even darker skin, and had glittering tattooed snakes running down both arms.

"I challenge anyone to recognize us now," she said. "We'd better get going, Horny."

"That's Hornbori," I corrected.

The moment we were outside the store, I knew I'd made a mistake. It was hot and humid, unlike what I would have encountered in my hometown five hundred miles to the north. I also didn't think my friends could resist using the "Horny" name.

The limo was air-conditioned, and we were waved right into the VIP parking section. We rushed inside, but, it while it was slightly cooler in the hall, it was also odoriferous from all the nervous teens in sweaty costumes.

Coventree had the largest room to herself. Somewhere in the darkness she lurked, waiting to pounce on any Hyper-reality player who wasn't paying attention. Her roleplay was chaotic, a simple survival game, and the more you knew about her world, the more spells and incantations you memorized, the more ways to slay the monsters and avoid the traps, the better chance you had of winning.

She allowed holograms but not VR. She was, surprisingly, a purist in most ways. The space was the space, humans had to be humans, and so on.

I tried to explain all of this to the others as we waited in line.

"Trickery," I said. "Everything is a trick. Nothing will be as it seems. The smallest thing can kill, the most threatening hologram might be your salvation."

"Why are we bothering?" Numera said. "Let's wait until it's over and talk to her then."

"Because if we win, she'll be that much more likely to pay attention to us. She's moneygrubbing and power hungry, but she does love Hyper-reality. She knows, just as we do, that Jordan Shipman could care less about the actual play. It will give us an edge—though we'll still have to pay up."

We bought our tickets and entered with eight other people. Each of us wore a round badge that glowed green.

Agate laughed in delight at what greeted us. It was the most idyllic scene you could imagine; it was a sweet-scented glade, with a beautiful tree hanging over a mirror-like pool. Birds and butterflies flitted about, and in the distance was the sound of a flute.

"Move! Move!" I cried pushing my way through the others, urging my friends to follow. We sprinted past the pool and the tree, and up the barren, rocky hillside. Behind us came screams, but I didn't look back until we reached the top of the ridge.

Three of the players below appeared to be covered with butterflies, their badge flashing orange. The "butterflies" were tearing off their skin. One by one, the badges turned red and loud howls of dismay emanated from the glade. A couple of other people tried to follow us up the hill, but it was too late. The sweet little birds swarmed them, pecking and screeching, and as we watched the badges went from green to yellow to orange and finally, fatally, to red.

The three survivors stood in the middle of the clearing, back to back, two of them with impressive swords, the third with an ornately carved staff.

The tree's branches suddenly swirled outward, sweeping across them, and holograms of spurting blood obscured the sight. When the blood cleared, the three adventurers stood forlornly, their badges bright red.

"How did you know?" Numera said.

"Like I said, expect trickery."

"So anything that looks fair is foul and everything foul is fair?" Numera said.

"Until she does a double whammy," I said grimly.

"And then," Agate said, smiling, "if we try to guess a double whammy, she does a triple whammy. The battle of wits has begun!"

"Never go against a Sicilian when death is on the line!" Numera said.

I looked at her in surprise.

"I made her watch *The Princess Bride*," Agate explained.

"A hundred times," Numera said.

Burke spoke up. "We'd best not stand here."

"What direction do you suggest?" I asked.

From the top of the ridge we could see that there was a small valley below with a river running through it. The rocky ridge itself continued up to distant mountains.

Burke's voice rumbled. "The harder path, I'm guessing."

We climbed upward, watching every step. The footing was treacherous. *Contrary, contrary.* It was this need to look down that made me look up into the sky. The griffin was almost upon us, its shape outlined against the false sun, the body of a lion, the head, wings, and claws of an eagle. It was silent in its glide and undoubtedly would have taken one or more of us away.

I raised my staff and chanted a warding spell that I knew Coventree favored. The creature spread its wings, slowed its descent, and cried out in anger. Suddenly, there was a knife protruding from its chest. The beast plummeted to the ground with a final shriek and vanished in a puff of smoke.

Burke still had his hand extended from the throwing motion.

"What other surprises do you have under that robe?" I asked.

"I don't suppose a Glock would work in here?" he said.

"No, but it might kill a real person, so keep it holstered."

We continued climbing. After a few hundred yards, Agate said, "Have you noticed how we are now all looking upward?"

"You're right," I said. "Let me take the lead."

I picked the ground ahead of each step. A dozen yards further on, the staff hit a small rock, which skittered along the path. Something about the movement made me stop. I held up my hand, signaling the others to stop too.

The ridge rumbled, and then the path disappeared before us, falling away into darkness. A thunderous sound rose from the abyss, though we couldn't see the bottom.

"So, do we go back?" Numera asked.

"No, because that's what she wants us to do, obviously," I said.

"Unless, of course, she knows that we know that she knows that we know." Agate said.

"Oh, stop it," Numera said.

When the dust cleared, there was a small bridge of rock to one side that still crossed the gap. It was narrow and appeared uncertain. It was the very precariousness of it that drew me. I crossed over quickly.

"Coventree is using up a lot of territory," I explained. "I suspect we're nearing the far end of the game room." We probably

hadn't actually gone more than a few hundred yards; the rest
was an illusion of holograms that tricked the mind into thinking we'd travelled much farther than we thought.

Over the next hill was a cliff so steep and sheer that it looked
impossible to surmount. The jagged mouth of a cave was at the
center.

"Well, isn't that inviting," Numera said.

I said, "I suspect we have no choice. This is where we meet
Coventree, I'm guessing. Remember, don't believe a word she
says..."

"...unless it's an obvious lie," Agate said.

I entered first, calling on my staff to light our way. Because
I'd looked up the illumination spell in advance, Coventree's
gear responded.

"What do you wish from Coventree?" came a soft, silky
voice from the darkness. She emerged into the light wearing
her famous peaked cowl, her lower face covered by a mask. Her
body and clothing seemed as one, and her violet eyes glowed,
lighting the inside of her hood.

I'd won this game once before, and I knew the endgame;
flattery and fawning and obsequious toadying. It was impossible to spread it on too thick. I wished I'd had the foresight to
tell the others. Hopefully they'd take my cue.

"Oh, Great Witch of the Mountains," I said. "We wish only to
gaze upon the magnificent and powerful Coventree, to receive
your blessings and return home having fulfilled all ambitions."

I thought I caught a narrowing of Coventree's eyes, as if she
was smiling beneath the mask.

"You killed my pet griffin," Coventree said, her voice losing
its silky smoothness. I don't know how she did it, but the tone
sent a shiver of fear down my spine. "With a real knife. I was so
surprised that I allowed it, but now I'm wondering..."

Burke fell to his knees and lowered his head. "It is my fault,
milady. I wished only to save my friends. What can I do to make
up for it?"

"Well, that's a nice start, big guy." She stared at us a moment
longer. I took a deep breath, planning to bow low and ask for an
audience. She interrupted me.

"Look, let's just dispense with the rest of the sycophancy, you guys. I've been expecting you for a couple of days now."

She pulled down her mask as the lights went up in the cave. Suddenly, our surroundings blinked out, and we were surrounded by the circular plywood and foam path we'd taken.

Coventree looked like the teenage Kate Williams I remembered from years before. I wondered by what witchcraft she'd accomplished that.

She stepped forward, extending her hand. "So Zach, you're Que! Zach Spence, so ready with all the bad advice. Yes, I remember. I remember everyone."

"You knew we were coming?" Numera said. "Has Shipman already made you an offer?"

She blew out a raspberry, her pretty lips quivering. "He didn't make it past the first obstacle, nor did any of his people. Guy doesn't have the first clue."

"That's why you must sell to us," I said.

"Us?" she answered. "Or you?"

I was flummoxed by the question for a moment, then— maybe because something told me that Coventree was still playing games—I knew the right answer.

"Us," I said firmly. "I mean all the Hyper-reality players, high or low. If Unicorn takes over Pegasus, everything will change, everything will be controlled, and everything will become more expensive, for all of us."

"And I should care? Shipman assures me that I'll make even more money," Kate answered.

"Is that why you do this?" Burke asked. "I've never done this kind of thing before, but I get it. No one who spends this much time trying to create such an illusion will want someone else to control their vision."

"Tell you what, big guy. If you promise to come to work for me, I'll sell to Pegasus...at the going rate, of course. How's that sound?"

Burke didn't even hesitate. "Deal. When this is done, I'll return and offer my services." He stepped forward. His huge hand enveloped her small one. They held each other's hand for longer than I think either expected. Her eyes widened, and Burke's back straightened.

"Well, uh, that's great," Kate Williams said, brushing back her hair coquettishly.

Now I'd seen everything.

I didn't interrupt Numera when she whipped out her phone and made the deal. She managed to get the shares for a little over six thousand, which I knew was her target. It still made Kate Williams one of the richest people in the world.

"Come on," she said. "I'll take you out to dinner. I think I can afford it."

Kate was a very different person than I remembered—or she was even better at trickery than I knew. She was friendly and funny and didn't tell a single lie during the entire evening, at least as far as I could tell.

Nevertheless, when I walked away that night, I still wondered if it was all a hoax. I started to warn Burke, then realized that the man was probably well aware of what he was in for and that was probably part of the appeal.

We'd gotten what we wanted, though.

"We're tied, two wins apiece," Numera said.

"Everything we've done up to now is prologue," I said. "The real challenge starts now. The Blue Queen will demand her ounce of flesh."

When we got back to our hotel, Numera took me aside.

"I'm not sorry about last night, Zach," she said. "But I need to be alone awhile. I knew my father was gone, but this has hit me harder than I'd have thought possible."

"Of course," I said. I kissed her lightly on the lips and went to my room. I fell asleep the moment my head hit the pillow.

CHAPTER SEVENTEEN

What do you do when you're a bank or a store or a gas station and people come in all the time wearing masks? It was pretty tricky at first. It became necessary for us to create VR and holographic canceling hardware so that people could feel safe. If you are in someone else's territory, you live by their rules.

Of course, if you go into a bank with a physical mask on, well, that was always a stupid choice, whether intentional or not.

Still, the anonymity of hiding behind fictional identities could have been problematic. But from the beginning, most people have abided by the rules. Those who were going to break the law continue to do so, and it has perhaps made it slightly harder to catch them, but no one is willing to give up Hyper-reality because of the bad guys.

Diary of Roger Ackroyd

Numera knocked on my hotel room door at seven o'clock the next morning. I groaned, and rolled out of bed, and put on a plush, terrycloth hotel robe. My former habit of getting up at nineish was obviously a thing of the past. I was in the real world now, which was ironic since my particular real consisted of being the owner of the largest single purveyor of fantasy.

I opened the door to find Numera fully dressed and put together. She wore a long, thin dress and a velvet red blouse that showed off her luminous complexion. I was speechless for a moment.

"Roger wants to talk to us," she said. Her expression was neutral.

I put out my hand for her phone.

"I've had my phone off for the last couple days," she said. "He called Agate instead. She's got him on Skype in her room."

"Don't you think turning off your phone might seem suspicious?"

"I don't want to talk to...to *him*," she said. "Do you mind if I don't go with you to Agate's room? Tell him...*it*...that I'm not feeling well."

I left the room, but went only a few paces before I remembered my phone and went back for it. Numera was on the bed with her face in a pillow, and I could tell she was crying. I had a feeling that she'd been crying every moment that she was alone. The willpower she showed to keep going, to not quit, astounded me.

I closed the door quietly.

Agate was in her room, talking to Roger on her computer.

Roger looked bad. The skin on his face was tight, as if it had been pulled on over the skull. As I walked up to the desk, he smiled at me. It was a grotesque sight, as if whoever was animating the doppelganger had only heard of a smile second-hand. His dark eyes stared at me unblinking. I wondered what game the double was playing, but decided I had no choice but to continue with the charade.

"Where's Numera?" he asked.

I sat down, averting my eyes. "She's been sick the last few days."

I felt Agate stiffen slightly beside me, but she managed not to give me a surprised look. "She needs to sleep in, conserve her energy. What's the news?"

The Roger-thing stared at me for a few more moments, then gave me another grotesque smile. "We have been summoned by Blue Queen. An engraved invitation; an audience, if you will. We got it by snail mail, which means Maureen O'Rourke knew we were coming a few days ago."

"Maureen is probably five steps ahead of us," I said. "But that also means she's five steps ahead of Jordan Shipman."

"You are requested at Castle Amber at 10:00 a.m. on Friday," Roger announced.

"That's the weekend of the Queen's Jubilee," I realized out

loud. Officially, it was called the Louisville Fantasy Fest, but because it was Maureen's hometown and she was involved in every aspect of the proceedings, most people named it after her.

"She's probably been planning this for some time," Roger said. "She must have known that Shipman was buying up shares before we did."

I nodded.

"It's all come down to this," Roger said. "Are you ready?"

I nodded again. Those dark, unblinking eyes stared at me, then the screen went blank.

I sat there, numb.

"What the hell is going on?" Agate said.

I roused myself, realizing that Agate's suspicions had crystallized and there was no way around it. "Go get Numera. She's in my room You might want to knock first. We have quite the story to tell you, which I warn you, you probably won't believe."

Numera returned with Agate, looking as composed as ever. Her eyes were a little red, but it was only noticeable if you were looking for it.

Between us, we told Agate what we'd seen and heard. It seemed even crazier when we said it out loud, but she didn't interrupt. When we were finished, she nodded once. "Yep. You forget, I saw the coyote. I mean, I called it a dog because I didn't think you guys would believe me. But it looked up at me with eyes that were so full of intelligence that it made *me* feel like the pet. It didn't talk to me, though. That would have been cool."

Numera stood up abruptly and looked around as if she was trying to escape. It was as if Agate's acceptance of the story finally sealed her father's fate. I knew that she didn't want us to witness her breaking down, but damned if I was going to let her suffer alone. I quickly stood up and wrapped my arms around her.

"Oh, my God," Agate said. "Here I am talking about how cool coyotes are, and your father is...I'm sorry, Numera." She stood up to join our hug, and Numera cried out, putting out an arm to pull her friend close.

I tried to think of something to say. In the end, I said nothing, simply held the two women close, and the well of grief overflowed—for Roger, for my mom, for everyone who'd ever lost someone.

The image of Pretty, Pretty unmoving on her bed entered my mind. I wondered if she was dead because of Pegasus... because of me.

Everyone kept telling me I had lots of money. I decided it was time to spend whatever it took to find out what happened to her.

Seven days seemed like an incredible luxury after the manic pace of the previous few days. We brainstormed for hours about how we would approach the Blue Queen, but without knowing what Maureen was going to throw at us, it probably didn't make much difference.

"Why is she making us wait a week?" Agate asked. "I don't get that."

"Probably to maximize the pressure," I said. "We can count on whatever she throws at us to be being elaborate and complicated. Maureen was always a purist. We'll have to play it the way she lays it down, whatever it is."

"Good, because I'm betting Shipman won't play it that way," Numera said.

"We can hope," I said.

Seven days may have been a luxury, but by the second day word had already gotten out where the great and powerful Que was staying.

This Que fellow is really getting annoying, I thought.

"Why don't we fly to Louisville early?" I said. "Maybe find a little out-of-the-way place to hide out?"

Numera picked up her phone. "I'll see what's available."

Agate reached out and pushed her arm down. "Zach, you have to face them sometime or they'll start thinking you're standoffish, a snob...or worse, a weirdo."

I laughed in disbelief. "I *am* a weirdo."

"In the best way," Agate said. "But this is different. Hiding was OK at first. It fit right into Hyper-reality, if you think about it. The great mystery of who is Que? Where is Que? People looking around at conventions and wondering, 'Is Que here somewhere?' It was wonderful fun.

"But now they know who you are, and you've got to at least give them a taste."

"I'm not doing a news conference, if that's what you're thinking," I warned.

Agate considered it. "You're right. Keep some of the mystery. But that doesn't stop you from making an appearance, if only to smile and wave."

"This is a bad idea," Burke said as we stood just inside the lobby entrance of the hotel. We'd ended up booking the entire place because the management was having fits about the chaos. "At least let me call for back up."

"There are policemen out there," Numera pointed out.

"Crowd control," Burke said. "They don't have a clue about personal protection. That's not their job."

"I'm sure it will be fine," I said, though I was terrified. All this craziness was because of me? I didn't feel any different from a week before when I could have walked into that crowd without getting a second glance.

Every few minutes, someone would try to start a chant; "Que!... Que!... Que!" which usually petered out but sometimes gained strength until the hotel seemed to shake with the roar. People were waving signs and banners. And each and every one of them were in character; every kind of cosplayer imaginable.

Numera put her hand on my back as if she was going to push me forward. I leaned back against her hand a little in resistance. "Just jump up on the platform, bow and wave, maybe shout out a few words," she said. "There's no microphone, no expectation of a speech."

"But there's a damn platform," I objected. The hotel had dragged out a dais that was about six feet high, with stairs leading up to it. It looked impossibly distant. The crowd felt like a giant creature, ready to swallow me up.

That's the problem with Hyper-reality. Nothing stays normal—everything becomes fantastical. Which is all right when you're imagining your dinner to be in a medieval tavern, not so great when the crowd is shouting your name like a hungry beast.

"Que! Que!"

That's not my name, a little voice in my mind said. It was humble old Zach, from a week ago.

The very thought suddenly relaxed me. They were expecting Que. They didn't know or care who plain old Zachary Spence was. Give them Que.

Be a character.

At that moment, I knew I'd found the way forward. This was just another type of Hyper-reality. And if there was one thing I knew how to do it was role-play. I nodded to Burke, who pushed the door open.

Burke cleared the way for me—for about ten feet. Then the crowd overwhelmed him. People surrounded me on all sides, until all I could see were wild eyes and open mouths and teeth and hands, and the roar of my character's name surrounded me. Someone pulled on my shirt and a button popped; another grabbed me from behind by the belt and jerked me back. I saw Agate and Numera jostled behind me, almost losing their footing.

I felt my chest inflate in a deep, involuntary breath before…

"Unhand me, peasants!" I roared.

Now, decades ago, that would have been rude of me, but the term "peasant" had come to be used in Hyper-reality for people who are in a game but not major players. It didn't matter who you were, at some point in your playing experience you would be a peasant—in fact, more often than not.

The people nearest me backed away. I raised my chin and glared at them, then marched imperially to the dais. Agate and Numera followed, five steps back.

I mounted the steps as if I didn't have a care in the world. I stood there and let the roar wash over me. It was all make-believe; I was a king among his loyal and adoring subjects. The applause seemed to take forever to die down. I raised one hand and waved just once. That set them off again for another eternity.

Finally, I put up both palms and they instantly fell silent.

Inside, Zachary Spence was tongue-tied and petrified. But Que knew exactly what to say.

"I'm grateful for your welcome. But it is not something I have sought. I have wanted to live among you, as one of you. *Tone it down*, I told myself. *You sound like an alien.* "A few days ago, I was just plain old Zach Spence. But I no longer have that luxury."

I took a deep breath. "I decided to make myself known to you because our world—our fantasy world—is in danger. I'm calling on all of you to help me. Congress is trying to pass a law that will put our very existence in doubt. It's called the Copyright and Trademark Fair Use Act."

Boos emanated from the crowd. I held up a hand.

"I'm sure you've all heard of it and had the same reaction I used to have. No way could it happen. But I'm here to tell you that it is dangerously close to passing. The time is near when you will have to pay to dress as you wish...when your persona will no longer be yours to use as you see fit.

"How many of you want to return to the humdrum days of suits and ties, of dress codes, of uniformity?"

From the crowd emerged boos and every form of "No" imaginable.

"We need your help," I continued. "There are powerful forces—who I won't name—who are fighting for this measure."

"One-horned bastards!" someone shouted.

I hesitated, then realized he was talking about unicorns.

I held up my hand. "But it is the Hyper-reality community who will be affected by this and you need to contact everyone and anyone to help us fight this.

"I also ask that you let me do what I need to do, that you respect my privacy for a short time longer. Soon, when this is over, I will make sure that I get a chance to meet all of you, if that is in my power. But for now, let me concentrate on fighting the C & T with everything I've got."

The chant started up again as soon as I stopped speaking. I stepped down off the dais. A corridor opened for me, with people clapping on both sides, but at a respectful distance.

Burke walked beside me. "Well, well," he said. "I didn't know you had it in you."

"Neither did I."

We were halfway back to the hotel lobby when I heard someone shouting, "Major Dundee! Major Dundee!"

I stopped dead in my tracks and looked around. I was looking for Union blue, so I didn't see Stephen and Glenn at first. Then I saw Glenn's long, thin nose under a curly wig. He wore a green cloak and brown trousers and had a small sword in hand.

Stephen stood next to him, also in halfling guise. *So they've thrown in with the furry-footed crowd. Traitors.*

I made my way over to them. They jumped forward to give me a hug, slapping me on the back. Burke loomed behind them, a scary look in his face. I waved him away.

"What the hell are you wearing, you guys?" I asked. "You hate fantasy!"

"If you can't beat them, join them," Stephen said. "I've already gotten more dates than all my time as a Bueller."

Glenn nodded in agreement.

We stood there awkwardly. What was there to say? I realized sadly that it would never be the same between us. But... they'd been friends before I was rich and famous. It seemed to me I could trust them. Maybe I should invite them along.

An entourage.

I'd always thought it ridiculous that the rich and famous surrounded themselves with toadies. For the first time, I started to get an inkling of why. I trusted Agate and Numera, of course, but I suspected they were the exceptions, that from now on, my very presence was going to be a gravitational force, warping space and time, and emotions and trust and everything else.

"You ever coming back to Bend?" Glenn asked.

"I don't know," I said. "I don't think so."

"Damn, man. We never had a clue. You seemed so..." his voice trailed off.

"Normal?" I prompted.

"Well, I wouldn't say that. But you were just another dork, as far as I was concerned."

"I still am," I said. "This is way over my head."

Stephen was shaking his head. "That speech? Man, you were living it!"

"Just another character," I said.

Burke stepped up next to me. "We have to go," he said in a low voice. "The natives are getting restless." I realized everyone was watching us. They were inching closer, as if they thought I was going to have a personal word with all of them.

"I'll get in touch," I said to my friends as Burke put his burly arm over my shoulders and pulled me away—just in time.

We barely made it back to the lobby, where we collapsed into the chairs.

"Oh, my god," Agate said. "That was intense."

Numera looked over at me with an exasperated expression. "Did you just really promise to *meet all of them*?"

"In my defense I did add, 'if that is in my power.'"

She shook her head, then looked out the window. "They're leaving," she said, as if she couldn't believe it.

Agate held up her phone. "It's already trending. I think your request for privacy is going to work...for a while. But they'll be back."

"Well, boss," Numera said, "you've at least bought us some unexpected breathing room."

Maybe it was a residual of my newfound Que power, but I was unwilling to hear Numera call me boss ever again. It was all right to play Que as a role, but I didn't want to buy into it too much.

I leaned forward and caught her eye. "Enough of that boss stuff, all right? I'm just plain old Zach, not boss or Que or anything else."

She looked back at me with a steady gaze, measuring me. Agate stopped fussing with her phone and watched. Finally, Numera nodded and stood up. "Let's order some plain old pizza and get back to strategizing."

Our rooms were on separate floors. I'd been given the penthouse, alone on the top floor. As we headed for bed, Numera and I stopped outside my room. She wanted to tell me something, I could tell. I spoke first instead.

"Maybe we shouldn't...you know...until this is all over."

"We probably shouldn't...you know...until this is all over."

Numera's shoulders slumped in relief. "I'm so glad to hear

you say that. But…" She looked up and down the hallway to see if anyone was watching, then pulled me close and kissed me. "…when this is all over, you aren't ever getting rid of me."

CHAPTER EIGHTEEN

Pegasus Corp's heavy investment in research and development was Joseph's idea, and I have to admit it has paid off handsomely. The technology used in Hyper-reality turns out to have many applications, including, of course, advertising. Everyone is annoyed by the hologram ads on every building. We tried at first to hold this tech back from the Promotional/Inspirational/Advertising Industrial Complex (as I like to call it), but the courts ruled that we couldn't discriminate.

So we also invented the technology that allows people to ignore the constant barrage.

Surprising, few consumers have taken this up, but many businesses and government agencies have seen the benefit of being able to see the reality behind the illusion, so even there we made money.

And irony of ironies, the biggest consumers of this muting gear are the Thentics. I wonder how many of them have read the fine print and realized that the company they bought the technology from was a subsidiary of Pegasus Corp.

Diary of Roger Ackroyd

Three days of strategizing, and we ran out of ideas. We sat and watched videos, browsed the net, kept up with the news. I'd never thought I was an excitement junkie, but neither did I like being cooped up in a hotel room for hour after hour.

Both Agate and Numera were a little standoffish, as if the crowd of people chanting "Que!" had reminded them of who I was and what I represented. Besides, I think—though I may have been flattering myself—that each women was giving the other permission to approach me first.

But neither did.

I didn't know whether to feel snubbed or not.

On the fourth day, I'd had enough. A day earlier, Agate had returned my Harvey Bowman gear, which she'd retrieved from the hotel in Chicago. "You may as well wear it. Everyone knows who you are anyway," she said.

Alone in my room, I turned the duster inside out—it was a light green inside and if you didn't look too closely, you couldn't see the seams. I roughly reshaped the felt hat, giving it a different contour, so that it looked more like a fedora than a cowboy hat. I took one of the six-shooters and put it in my belt.

When I looked in the mirror, I saw I wasn't Harvey Bowman anymore but instead some hybrid of gunslinger and gangster; I wasn't sure what. But that was OK. Wearing an unidentifiable costume wasn't that unusual anymore. In fact, it was common. There were so many media properties and games and licensed characters that no one could keep up. And there were a fair number of people who created their own characters, hoping no doubt that some movie studio would pick them up. Others operated within genres, not trying to be any specific characters.

I slipped out into the hallway. I'd sent Burke away earlier that day. I'm sure he never expected me to be so idiotic as to leave the hotel.

But I wasn't worried. I was pretty sure that my face was still not recognizable to most people, not without the identifiers. I'd just be some guy out on a stroll. I walked through the kitchens, which was a bit of a test, but none of the staff even looked up. I walked out into the alley and circled around to the front. There were a few loiterers, hoping to catch of a glimpse, but again, no one expected a lone young guy to be anyone special.

For the first time in days, I felt free. The air seemed expansive, instead of something I was breathing in heavy gulps to drive away anxiety. There was no sense of eyes watching me, judging me.

I know Numera meant well, but every time I turned around, she was observing me. Agate's constant concern for my welfare was almost as wearying. I didn't get lonely. I craved time to myself.

These days, there was a cosplay shop in just about every major downtown block of every city—a combination of comic store, bookstore, toyshop, and all-around pop culture shop—and all of them sold costumes. I darted into a comic shop, not catching the name of it.

There was some fantasy gear on the wall and some very expensive, heavy cast-iron ray guns mounted on pedestals, but nothing that seemed to match my current persona—not that I really knew what that was. I checked out the new comics, but didn't see anything I wanted.

Besides, I had no money. I hadn't even thought to bring any.

How quickly I've become accustomed to Numera paying for everything!

The thought made me a little nervous, and the easygoing feeling I'd had since leaving the hotel began to drift away, like fog in a sudden gust of wind.

The door chimes rang as three rough-looking men entered. They were dressed in suits, their eyes darting around the colorful store as if there was so much to see they couldn't focus. I moved sideways toward the counter where the store clerk was reading an installment of *Saga*.

"You got a back way out?" I asked.

"What?" said the clerk, looking up. "Oh...sure, but I can't let you use it."

I probably looked annoyed, but I wasn't going to push it. Then...

"It's you, isn't it?" the clerk asked in a hushed voice.

"I don't know, is it?"

The clerk looked over my shoulder, saw the civilians, and guessed why I was nervous. "Come on, I can make an exception for you. The backdoor is tied to the fire alarm so you've got to give me time to disconnect it."

I glanced at his nametag. "Thanks Andy of Samurai Comics. I'll remember this."

"Will you? Maybe you could sign something?" he asked hopefully

"Anything."

He shoved the *Saga* graphic novel in front of me, and I quickly scrawled my name. I wasn't sure how meaningful that was going to be, but I would have signed anything he gave me. It was a pretty good comic, too.

He led me to a back room full of white comic boxes. The back door was blocked by some unused fixtures, which I help him drag to one side. He jaunted off into a little side room for a moment, came back, and pushed the door open. It groaned with a gritty sound as if it hadn't been opened for years.

"Good luck, Que," Andy said. "We're with you!"

I poked my head out the door. The alley was empty. I stepped out and quickly made my way to the main street. The three rough-looking dudes were nowhere to be seen. I started back to the hotel. It was disconcerting. The first person that'd gotten a good look at my face had recognized me. I'd always figured that even if I was outed, I could always dress up in a costume. I supposed I could wear a mask, but I didn't much like doing that.

Two women approached on the sidewalk. They were Avatars, long-limbed and blue, their only concession to the brisk evening air, two light waist-length coats, also blue.

I tried not to stare. As I came near, I looked up with a smile.

I saw the look in their eyes and backed away, nearly tumbling over the curb into the busy street. One of them grabbed me by the collar of the duster and pulled me back. The other grabbed me by the throat and put a knife to my Adam's apple.

"What do you want?" I said. The sidewalks were empty of passerby and the drivers seemed to be concentrating on the traffic.

"We want to talk to you, Que," one of them said.

"Then we want to kill you," the other said in the same tone of voice. They pushed me back into a deep stairwell, the tip of the knife jostling and cutting into my cheek. I felt blood trickle down my neck.

Now that I had a better look at them, I realized that their Avatar costumes were pretty poor. They looked more like Gaila, the green-skinned lady in *Star Trek*, than they did the Na'vi of

Pandora. Whoever they were attempting to be, I had a feeling they weren't usually Hyper-reality players.

I wondered if this was another visitation and looked around to see if Mr. Zander was watching, leering. Then I noticed a huge pimple poking red through the blue paint of one of the women and knew that this time the danger was real—or rather, in my reality.

One of them held me while the other searched me, quickly finding the revolver. She flipped it open. "Are these rounds live?" She sounded surprised.

"Of course not."

"Liar," she said. "We heard about your confrontation with Stallo. You shot up a ten-thousand-dollar chandelier."

She closed the chamber with a click. "Good. Knives are always messy. Impossible not to get blood all over everything."

"Who are you?" I asked.

The woman holding the knife laughed.

"Did someone hire you?" I pressed.

The woman who had searched me held the gun to my head. "Only in the movies, dude."

The gun went off. My eyes had instinctively closed, so it took me a few moments to realized she'd missed even with the barrel just inches away. My ears were ringing. I was stunned, trying to figure out what was happening.

One of the Avatar women was on the ground, and a guy was crouched over her. He plunged an odd-looking blade downward—too long for a knife, too short for a sword. That's when I saw his shoes, which were made to look like furry feet. Glenn Halligan.

Stephen Steward was wrestling with the other woman, and though he probably had fifty pounds on her, she was winning. It was the woman who'd held the gun to my head. Stephen must have knocked her arm away just in time.

As she started to bring the gun around, I kicked it out of her hand. She threw herself after it, and I stomped on her head.

I didn't mean to. I'm not that hardcore. But maybe it was just as well, because it knocked her out. It might have done more than that, but I decided I wasn't going to check.

The woman on the ground with the sword in her chest was grunting. She looked like she was about to pry it away from Glenn. Stephen took a cue from me—if an unwitting one—and kicked her in the head.

Stephen looked down at the two limp Na'vi. "Did we kill them? Should we call the police? Did anyone see us?"

"No, no, and no," Glenn answered his friend. "We've got to get Zach back to hotel before anyone sees him."

"We're just going to let them get away with it?" Stephen said. "I mean, they ought to go to jail for those lousy costumes, if nothing else."

I stood swaying, the adrenaline suddenly dissipating.

Glenn answered, "I don't feel like spending hours at a police station and months at a trial. I mean, this whole trip cost my entire savings. We've got to get back to our jobs next week."

"No, you don't," I said. "You've got new jobs. Much better-paying jobs."

The hotel was in an uproar. My absence had been noticed.

When we walked through the front doors, Agate and Numera rushed toward me. Both of them stopped a couple of feet away, as if to give the other first the chance. Then Numera grabbed me fiercely, nestling her head against my neck. A moment later, Agate hugged me from the other side.

I could see Stephen and Glenn grinning.

Numera pushed me away. "Is that blood? Damn you, Zach, what were you thinking?"

"It's just a nick," I said.

Glenn spoke up. "They tried to kill him."

Burke was watching from a few feet away. There were three other burly men behind him. Apparently, backup had arrived. "Who tried to kill him?"

"A couple of Avatar players," Stephen said. "Always seemed to attract conceited ladies. But these ladies—I think they were fakes."

"You think so?" Glenn asked, his voice dripping with sarcasm.

"Would you recognize them again?" Burke demanded.

Glenn answered. "Yeah, they were blue and gorgeous and

had pointy little knives." He looked down at the shortsword in his hand, which was still dripping blood, and belatedly tried to hide it.

"Glenn and Stephen saved me." For the first time it occurred to me to wonder how. "Were you following me?"

"Totally by accident," Glenn said. "Stephen said he saw a coyote trotting down the street. I told him he was full of it and he was trying to prove it when we saw you."

"A coyote," Agate said, looking over at Numera and me.

"No, really," Stephen insisted. "I've heard coyotes live in big cities, but I've never seen one before. We did want to find you, though, Zach. We've been watching the comments on some Hyper-reality sites. There's this stupid rumor that if you die, your shares will be split among the regulars to Pegasus Conventions; the more often you attend, the more you get. Some people are apparently stupid enough to believe them."

Agate laughed. "That's so ridiculous." Then she paused. "Wait…don't tell me." She was staring at Numera, who had that neutral expression I'd come to recognize as her poker face.

"You're kidding me," I said.

Numera looked for a moment as if she was going to deny it, then she nodded. "It's true. No one is supposed to know but me and my father. We knew we had a mole, but we'd thought we were protected. Apparently, someone has broken through our security."

"But that's crazy, Numera" Agate said. "You've given hundreds of thousands—hell, millions—of people reasons to kill Zach."

"We didn't know if we'd ever find Que," Numera said. "It was what Joseph wanted."

Everyone was speechless, including me.

But then I realized it wasn't true.

"That isn't what this was," I said. "These women were professionals. Someone hired them to kill me. I think we can guess who."

"No, an hour ago we could have guessed," Agate said. "Now, who the hell knows? I want your promise that you'll never go off on your own again like that."

I could tell she wouldn't take no for an answer. "I promise," I said.

It was a lie. One of the first times in my life I can remember telling a lie of any consequence. But I could already see my future as a long line of closed doors and big men like Burke. The first chance I had, I was going to challenge that. But not until Pegasus was secure. Until then, I would just be putting my friends in danger.

Burke stepped forward and took a firm grip on my arm. "You are going straight to your room, sir. I'll send a doctor right up."

"It's just a small nick."

"Nothing that happens to you falls under the rubric of small," Burke said. "The sooner you get used to that, the better."

As he marched me to the elevators, I shouted over my shoulder. "Find rooms for Glenn and Stephen. They're with me."

For some reason, I wasn't surprised to find Coyote waiting in my room. The one and only talking coyote, so he deserved to be called Coyote with a capital "C."

"Well, that was stupid," Coyote said.

"I'm not spending the rest of my life in hotel rooms," I answered, walking past it as if was perfectly normal to be talking to a coyote. "If there are endless realities, what does it matter which reality I die in?"

Coyote didn't answer at first. For once, it wasn't smiling insolently. "Yes, we all die in one reality or another. But this is your reality, Zach. This is the world you were born into, and forces from outside this reality are trying to change it. And then it won't be yours anymore, but theirs. It will be as if you never existed, because you won't matter. You will be no more important than an extra in a crowd in a movie."

"We're all extras in someone else's lives."

"Maybe so," Coyote admitted. "But this is your life, and you must fight for it or it will be meaningless. And if that happens, then in the next alternative world, you are meaningless there too, and on and on until you are erased, your consciousness but a ghost."

"How would you know?"

"You don't...and yet you do. When you wake at four in the morning and feel the existential pointlessness of your life—that is when you are closest to disappearing, fading into another reality. But someday there may be no choices left if you don't fight for this one."

"I don't understand any of this," I said.

"No one does, and yet most of us know what to do when the time comes. Life is tenacious and usually you don't have to worry. The choice is made and it is right...or wrong and you blink out of existence but continue somewhere else. But this is different. These are creatures who don't want you to have that choice, who want to take it away from you. And you must fight it.

"Remember that, son."

Son. It wasn't so much the word as the tone Coyote used. "Was it you who warned me in Roger's office? Did you pretend to be my father?"

Coyote was silent for a moment. Then it said, "I did not pretend."

I let that sink in, even though I'd suspected it all along. Somehow, my father was behind all of this. But was he alive? Dead? Or something else?

"Then show yourself!" I insisted. "If you are my father and you're alive come back and take back Pegasus! I have no idea what I'm doing. I've never done anything like this."

"I can't come back...or rather, I never left," Coyote said.

"I don't understand." I was surprisingly calm. But then, I'd never known my father.

"No one else can do this. It is your task, Zach. It is for you to decide what happens. It is your reality now, not mine. You mustn't stray from the plan. Go to Louisville and win."

I turned my back on the creature and got into bed. I wasn't surprised that it was gone by the time I turned out the light.

CHAPTER NINETEEN

Of course, anyone can install VR and holographic technology at home; how elaborate it is depends on your finances. But such holo-decks are limited by the space and the physical machinery it takes to make truly convincing illusions. I've seen some private castles that are almost the equivalent of some smaller Pegasus venues, but they're rare.

Then, too, the rich don't tend to share. So this kind of private play space is unavailable to most people. And even the rich get tired of playing by themselves or with the same small group of compeers.

I have talked Joseph into letting these wealthier clients buy certain privileges, which are mostly useless to them, because these are people to which everything is given. The poorest of players can outplay a rich player, because the rules are the same for everyone.

Diary of Roger Ackroyd

The next morning, we met in the hotel dining room, all except Stephen and Glenn.

"Let them sleep in," I said. Like me, they weren't used to getting up early. I wondered if I wasn't being selfish asking them to throw in with me. I'm sure they thought it was a great adventure, but I wondered how long it would be before they wanted to get back to their old routines, their old friends, their old Hyper-reality haunts.

We had the entire dining room to ourselves. I ordered a couple of tables to be shoved together so the bodyguards could eat with us.

"No," Burke said. "They're busy."

I looked over at the two men standing on either side of the

door. They looked like *Men in Black* cosplayers. "They don't look too busy to me."

"You can order us to do anything you want, Mr. Spence," Burke answered. "But please don't ask us not to do our jobs. You've lost the benefit of the doubt with me...sir. From now on, I'm not letting you out of my sight."

"What happened to calling me Zach?"

"That was an unfortunate breach of protocol," he snapped. "It won't happen again."

"Let them earn their money, Zach," Agate said.

Burke said in a lower voice, so his two men couldn't hear, "After a time, you won't even see us, sir. There are three more men patrolling the perimeter. You can afford it."

It seemed like a tipping point. If I accepted this level of security, I was trapped forever. But did I have any choice? It wasn't just me I had to worry about now—I needed to make sure those around me were safe too.

I nodded reluctantly, as if I had any choice.

We sat down and a waitress took our order. It was a younger woman who had a Bettie Page haircut. Under her long-sleeved shirt I caught glimpses of tattoos. I'd visited tattoo sites over the years and it seemed like every other model looked like this. Biker chick crossed with Goth.

I ordered blueberry pancakes, hoping they'd be as good as the ones at the place Numera had treated us to. The food was just arriving when Glenn and Stephen showed up.

"Blueberry pancakes? Bacon?" they cried, as if it was a feast. Which for them, it probably was. Once again I felt that pang of guilt over my sudden wealth.

"We've got three more days to prepare for the Blue Queen," Numera said as we finished up our breakfasts. She pulled out a laptop and opened it. Things must have been getting serious; it was the first time I'd seen her use a device other than her phone for business.

"Doesn't matter," I said. "Whatever we plan for, that's not what Maureen will do. She's had a year to plan for the Jubilee."

Numera closed the computer. "Then what do you suggest we do for the next three days?"

I hadn't even thought of it, but I suddenly knew what I wanted to do with my unlimited money and three free days. "I want to try to find out who killed Debbie Johnson."

Silence fell over the table.

"Who's Debbie Johnson?" Glenn said, finally.

"AKA Debra Cromartie," Agate said. "Alias, Pretty, Pretty."

"You knew her?" Stephen said.

I remembered that my friend had always had a thing for her. "Yeah. Sorry, about what happened to her, man."

"Wait a minute," Glenn said. "They're saying it was an accidental overdose."

"I might have believed that if they hadn't gotten too cute and posed her that way. It was a little too much like Marilyn Monroe to be a coincidence," I said.

"We *know* who killed her," Agate said. "Don't we?"

"Is Shipman that ruthless?" I asked.

"I don't know," Numera said. "But even if he did it, what can we do about it?"

"If we could prove that Unicorn is behind her death, then we might be able to use that in court," Agate mused.

"Prove it? How do we go about doing that?" Numera asked.

I was getting frustrated with everyone questioning me. Was I the boss or wasn't I? Then again, I'd told Numera not to call me that.

"I don't know, dammit," I replied. "This isn't about winning or losing. I want to make sure the police don't close this case without looking closely. We need to make sure they do their job, right, Burke?"

I figured the big man was a former cop. He had all the mannerisms and attitude I imagined a cop would have. Methodical, observant; just the facts, ma'am.

I was almost surprised when he disagreed with me. "The authorities won't sweep it under the rug. High-profile case like this? If they think it's a murder, they'll pursue it with everything they have."

"Maybe they don't know what to look for," I said stubbornly.

"Like what?" Numera demanded.

"I guess we won't know until we look," I answered. "Pull

up that picture the bellboy took."

Numera opened her laptop and brought up the image, enlarging it. We all bent over to look at it. My heart sank almost as deep as when I'd first seen her like that. The whole thing was burned into my brain, without or without the photo. Everything was as I remembered it, her white skin against the dark bedspread, her hair spilling over the pillow.

"Damn, I just saw the photo in newsprint," Stephen said over my shoulder. "This is so much clearer. That's brutal."

"But it isn't brutal," Agate said. "It doesn't look like there was any violence at all. Maybe she took those pills voluntarily."

"Yeah, just like every other overdose victim," Numera said. "Look, she was either careless or she did it on purpose."

My voice was tight, and I realized that I was getting angry. "You believe that after talking to her? After we made her rich beyond her wildest dreams and also promised to get her career back on track?"

"Well, maybe she didn't do it on purpose," Numera said.

It didn't matter what anyone said. I knew it was murder and I was going to prove it. "Can anyone read the name of the doctor on the pill bottles? Or at least the drug store that filled the prescription?"

"Dr....Garcia," Glenn said as my eyes were still trying to decipher the muddy image. As soon as he said it, I saw it.

"Owl Pharmacy, Brentwood," Stephen said.

"The cops will have already looked into that," Numera said.

"The authorities will be constrained," Burke offered.

Numera gave me an alarmed look that told me she was also wondering what the alternative to "constrained" was. "We don't want to become Unicorn in order to beat Unicorn."

Burke looked away, shrugging slightly.

*Perhaps...*I thought, *we can use little bit more carrot and a little more stick than the police were allowed to use.* "We've got three days to investigate. We'll fly back to L.A. and see what we can find."

Numera looked ready to object again, but I held up my hand. It was the first time, I think, that I'd overruled her.

Even more surprising, she accepted it.

A limo was there to pick us up at LAX early the next morning. Numera gave directions to local branch of Merlin's Toys. By sheer luck, Merlin himself was visiting at the same time, big as life, with his bushy white beard and conical wizard's hat, his trademark Hawaiian shirt, white socks and Birkenstocks.

I looked into his eyes to see if he remembered the confrontation at the Portland Con. His gaze passed over me as if he'd never seen me before.

Numera introduced us. His eyes widened in surprise; then he put out a big beefy hand. "Glad to meet you, Que. Sorry about your father. He gave me my start."

He led us to the shipping room, which was filled with boxes. "We need a private fitting," Numera said.

"We'll close for lunch in an hour," Merlin answered. "If you don't mind, I'd like to let the current customers finish their shopping."

I didn't want to wait. "Do you have a mask I can borrow?"

Merlin looked around, pulled open a small box and handed me a Predator helmet. "Will this do?"

"Thank you," I said. I turned to the others. "I want to wander around by myself if you don't mind."

"Not possible," Burke answered at the same moment Numera said, "Never going to happen."

"OK, but only you two," I agreed reluctantly. "Numera, grab a mask or something. Burke somehow blends in, which is weird considering how big he is. But you're a little too memorable, Numera. People will figure out that I must be around if they see you.

Merlin handed her another Predator mask, the female version from *Predator 8*.

"The rest of you stay here," I said.

I pulled back the curtain and entered the main floor of Merlin's. The first floor was toys; the second story, up a wide spiral staircase, was filled with costumes. But I hadn't gone ten feet before I came face to face with myself.

Or rather, myself as Harvey Bowman. It was an uncanny resemblance. I realized that the guy—or gal, it was hard to say—was wearing a digimask of my face.

I don't consider myself a purist, but I always thought it was kind of cheating to wear a digimask. That was for lazy people who didn't want to take the time to craft a persona from scratch. It was a little too much like buying your way into Hyper-reality.

But I had to admit, I'd had doubts over the years. I mean, with a digimask you could look exactly like the character you were portraying—and sometimes, the characters were so unique or alien-looking that no amount of makeup could get you there.

By the time we reached the steps, I saw three more Ques walking around.

"What the hell is going on?" I muttered.

"Don't complain," Numera said. "It gives you cover."

At the top of the stairs was a big display with my shining face all over it. Did I really look that goofy? I'd always thought that some people just shouldn't try to look like hard-asses. At the same time, I'd sort of thought I was pulling it off.

The Harvey Bowman costume was perfect, but the high-lighted face had a little too much baby fat, a little too much inno-cence in the eyes.

I winced. I wished someone had warned me off it.

But of course that was the one thing no one would have told me. If there was one rule of Hyper-reality, it was that you never cast shade on someone else's persona. She's a little too chubby to pull off Vampirella? None of your business, and how rude of you to think it.

There were three shelves of digimasks of my face, which looked half picked over. The price was a quarter what digi-masks usually cost. And scrawled in ink at the base of the sign, someone had written, "Be like Spartacus. Protect Que, become Que."

"Word got out that someone tried to assassinate you," Merlin said from behind us. I hadn't realized he'd followed us out onto the floor. Over the loudspeakers, it was being announced that the store was closing early because of a gas leak. Merlin hurried toward the front door to turn the sign.

"Assassinate!" It was such a funny thought I almost laughed.

"That's the right word," Numera said, her voice muffled by

the mask. "They might murder Zach Spence, but with Que, it's an assassination. Get used to it."

We stepped into the costume area. I spread my arms. "I don't have to. I can be anyone or anything I want. Man, the times I've wanted to buy some of these."

"Why the hell don't you?" Burke said.

"Are you kidding? I could barely afford to concoct any kind of costume at all."

"I don't think that's a problem anymore," Burke said. "How much money did your father win in the lottery?"

"$784,206,334.77," Numera said. "You're worth at least ten times that much, Zach. Depending on where the market is, it is probably quite a bit more because of the wonders of compound interest. My father is..." Her voice caught as she suddenly realized what she was saying. With visible effort, she continued, "...a great money manager. But he never would have come up with the idea of Pegasus in the first place. That was your father's idea."

Merlin walked up with a big smile. "We're closed up. Your friends can look around all they want now."

Glenn and Stephen came out of the back room. They were unable to conceal their pleasure, abandoning all pretense of being cool. They practically ran through the aisles trying to take it all in.

"You can buy whatever you want, you guys," Agate said called out after them. "I'm sure Merlin here will appreciate the business."

Merlin shook his head. "Que's money is no good here. If the C & T passes, I'm all but out of business. Even if I could figure out a way to collect the taxes, I'm not sure I want to."

Agate grabbed a Darth Vader mask and held it up to Burke.

"A little too much on the mark," I commented.

She shrugged and then held out a Luke Skywalker digimask to me.

"No way," I said. "Besides, it isn't necessary. I am Spartacus, remember?"

"I can always tell the difference when someone is wearing a digimask," Agate said. "The face is a little too perfect, the expressions come a little too slowly. We can't take the chance that someone will figure it out."

I don't know—if it hadn't been Luke, I probably would have kept arguing. But...the first *Star Wars* movie was my favorite movie of all time. Merlin quickly outfitted the rest of us. Agate was the same shape and size as Princess Leia and ended up with her white costume, thankfully (or unfortunately). Glenn grabbed Boba Fett, and Stephen decided to become Biggs.

That left Numera.

"No way," she said. "I've never even seen the movie."

"What?" I turned to Agate, who shook her head sadly.

"Sorry, boss—I mean, Zach—I failed you." She looked Numera over. "You know, she's tall enough to be a Wookie."

"Wait...what are you saying?" Numera objected, revealing that she knew more about the movie than she was letting on.

I nodded. "Merlin, we need a Wookie." Numera was a good six feet tall, and I knew from experience that the Wookie gear could add a good six inches to a foot in height. She'd pass.

I argued with Merlin for ten minutes, trying pay for the costumes but he steadfastly refused until I forced him to at least accept half price. On my way out, I said to Agate, "Getting to be kind of a hassle to keep buying new costumes. It would be nice to have our own setup someday."

"Well, you've got one in New York, but yeah...it's mostly for R&D."

"OK, everyone," Numera said. "From now on, no one shows his or her face in public without a digimask on. If any one of us discovered, they might figure us all out. Understood?" She glared at Biggs Darklighter and Boba Fett as if she wasn't sure about them. She probably didn't even know who the Biggs character was.

We piled into the limo, which was a tight fit with all of us and our costumes, and headed for Dr. Gerald Garcia's offices.

CHAPTER TWENTY

A big problem with Hyper-reality is that you can never be quite sure who you're dealing with. When everyone can hide behind a mask, then anyone can be someone other than who they are. Along with changing identities on a regular basis, people often change their names too.

That is both the liberation and the danger of it.

There will always be those who catfish, who pretend to be someone they aren't for nefarious motives. We try our best to weed them out, banishing them from our conventions; but they just come back as someone else.

No one is quite willing to go to the extreme of demanding that everyone be chipped, or even that they have identity cards. Hyper-reality is supposed to be fun, and having bouncers at the door isn't the direction any of us want to go.

So just as in real life, we are dependent on the goodwill of the majority of people, so too in Hyper-reality we have to depend on a common compact.

Either that, or it all falls apart.

Diary of Roger Ackroyd

Dr. Garcia's office was on one of those endless L.A. streets filled with fast food joints, massage parlors, tax preparers, and other small business offices. Not where you'd expect a star of Pretty, Pretty's magnitude to be going, even if she had fallen far from her zenith.

The doctor's offices were in a one-story building that looked like it had started out life as a small bank branch. A line of diplomas filled the wall behind the receptionist, making sure that you knew that Dr. Garcia was a full M.D.

The interior of the place was separated by room dividers that weren't flush to the ceiling. You could hear what was happening beyond. As we walked in there was the loud scream of a small child.

"That's reassuring," Agate muttered.

A bored-looking woman looked up from behind the glass enclosure at the front desk not at all surprised to see the cast of *Star Wars* walk in the door. Numera turned off the digimask of her Wookie costume. The receptionist's eyes widened and she frowned, and I got the immediate sense it wasn't because of Numera's height. Numera pushed Agate forward.

"We'd like to talk to Dr. Garcia," Agate said, after turning off her own digimask of Princess Leia.

"Do you have an appointment? What is this concerning?" the receptionist asked.

Burke stepped forward, not bothering to remove the Darth Vader helmet. His voice was deepened and amplified, though not quite to James Earl Jones level. "We are representatives of the California Medical Ethics Board. There are a few issues we need to talk to him about."

Darth Vader looming over her with that booming voice seemed to intimidate the woman. She sat up straight, her voice rising. "Dr. Garcia is booked until late in the afternoon."

This seemed doubtful since there weren't any other patients in the waiting room.

She got control of herself and frowned again. "Perhaps... perhaps you'd like to talk to our nurse practitioner? Elvis Elkins is also our new office manager."

"We need to talk to the doctor," Burke began to intone.

A young man came around the nearest divider. I had a feeling he'd been listening to the conversation from the beginning. "What's this about? I'm Elvis Elkins and I handle most of the accounts."

He was tall and athletic looking—someone who wasn't that far removed from school sports, with dark wavy hair and sideburns, and heavy black eyebrows that were lifted in inquiry. *Elvis.* I could see it. A little makeup and a jumpsuit, and he would be a spitting image.

Burke repeated his demand. Elkins started shaking his head before he finished. "Sorry, Dr. Garcia has left for the day."

Burke said, "Your receptionist told us he was booked solid for the afternoon."

"He is, but I can handle all the patients and he had something more important to do. He didn't tell me what."

Burke looked ready to object, but I put out my hand and stopped him. I nodded toward the doorway.

"We'll be back," Burke said. I wasn't sure, but I thought he put a slight Schwarzenegger-like Austrian accent on the words.

We didn't speak until we were safely in the limo. I gave the driver instructions to drive to the end of the block and park.

"We made a mistake all going in like that," I said. "We need to be a little stealthier. I suggest that I go in as a patient and feel the place out. See if I can't manage to get alone with Garcia."

"No way," Numera said. "Remember what we said about you going anywhere alone?"

"He's seen all of you, but I didn't take off my mask," I said. "He didn't see Burke's face, but I'm betting he'd still recognize the big galoot."

"He didn't see me," Glenn said, turning off Boba Fett. "Besides, you need a medical reason to see a doctor." He reached down to the little finger of his left hand and pulled it back perpendicular with a loud snap.

Stephen cursed. "I hate it when you do that."

Glenn grinned. "An old soccer injury. Don't worry, it doesn't hurt, and I can't do anymore damage to it than has already been done."

"I'll accompany you as your friend," I said, and began taking off my digimask of Luke and the top layer of his clothing. I still looked a little odd, wearing all white, but not beyond what you see every day on the streets. That was the freeing thing about Hyper-reality. You could look like anything you wanted, and no one would question it, except maybe a few Thentics.

"If anyone recognizes you, get out of there," Burke said. "I'll be at the back. Shout if anything happens, and I'll bust the door down. I can be there in seconds."

Numera still looked doubtful.

"We can't fake search warrants," Burke said. "I'm pretty sure the office manager isn't going to let us look at the records matter what we say."

Numera picked up her phone, and seconds later, my own burner began ringing. "Leave it on so I can hear what's happening," she instructed.

"Fair enough," I said, turning to Glenn. "Ready?"

The receptionist looked as bored as before, but this time she wasn't alarmed at our approach. She took one look at Glenn's finger, picked up a phone and spoke into it. Moments later a young woman in a white coat emerged and asked us to follow her. She took us through the first open door into a room that was little bigger than a large closet and left us there.

Glenn and I settled into the plastic chairs but didn't talk, not certain that we couldn't be heard. Elvis Elkins came in fifteen minutes later—just to keep the illusion of being busy, I suspected. We hadn't heard anything since the kid's scream when we'd entered the first time.

Elvis started putting on gloves and nodded toward Glenn's finger. "How'd that happen?"

"Playing catch with his kid. Fell wrong," I explained.

"Well, let's take a look at it."

Glenn stood up abruptly, which startled me. I jumped, which probably added to the realism of the moment. "No way," he said. "I want a doctor or no one."

"I'm fully qualified to deal with your injury," Elvis said. "I was a nurse before I was office manager." He looked annoyed, his practiced bedside manner starting to fray.

"Let's go, Bueller," Glenn said to me, getting to his feet.

Elvis let out big sigh. "Wait a moment. I'll see if the doctor is available."

"They're desperate," Glenn whispered as Elvis left the room. "Why would Debra come here?"

If she were getting illegal prescriptions, she'd come to exactly a place like this. Which would confirm the overdose theory.

Dr. Garcia was a surprise—and not a surprise. He was an older man, past retirement age at a guess, with long gray hair and a scraggly beard. If I were a patient, I'd probably choose Elvis over the doctor.

He had a thick Spanish accent. As soon as he reached for the injured finger, Glenn pushed it back into place with a snap.

"Well..." the doctor said. "I don't understand."

"We need to ask you some questions, Dr. Garcia," I said.

"My papers are in order," he said, backing away as if he was going to run. "I am a permanent US resident, dammit."

"That's not why we're here," I said hurriedly. "We want to ask about Debra Cromartie."

Rather than calming the doctor, this seemed to alarm him even more. "I answered all the police questions. Why are you hounding me? Are you reporters?"

"We were friends of Debra," I said. "We are trying to understand how she could have overdosed."

"Get out!" he shouted. "Marjorie! Call the police!"

From the front of the building came the receptionist's voice. "Yes, sir!" Moments later, she shouted, "Wait!" There was a crash, then she exclaimed, "What are you doing?"

The door opened, bumping the doctor to one side. Burke entered in his civilian clothing. "No one's calling anyone until we get some answers," he said.

"I did nothing wrong!" Garcia cried. He seemed panicked beyond all reason. We hadn't even really put that much pressure on him, no more than the police would have, and if he'd reacted this way with the police, they probably would have taken him into custody on suspicion.

Something else had happened to scare the man.

"She's been getting the same prescription for years and never had any problems. I had no reason to believe anything was wrong!" As he spoke, he backed into the corner. There was a cabinet there that looked like a tool chest. He whipped around, opened the top drawer, and turned back with a gun in hand.

Burke immediately put up his hands. Glenn and I followed his example. "We aren't going to hurt you," Burke said.

"You break into here under false pretenses and make accusations. If I shoot you right now, it'll be self-defense," the doctor said.

"Gerald?"

The doctor hesitated at the voice. Elvis entered the room behind Burke, scooted around the big man, and slowly approached the doctor. "What's wrong, Gerald?"

"These people are threatening me. They think I'm behind Ms. Cromartie's death."

"Take it easy. We'll ask them to leave," Elvis said soothingly. "You people are ready to leave, aren't you?"

Garcia appeared utterly panicked, far beyond what our questions should have engendered. "They'll come back!"

"Calm down," I said, but that only seemed to make it worse.

Garcia raised the pistol. I saw his finger tightening on the trigger.

Glenn shouted, backing up. He tripped over a small stool. He twirled his arms, trying not to fall backward. Instead, he lost his footing and fell to one side, smacking his head against the side of the examining table. Blood instantly spurted from his forehead.

Elvis pulled something from under his white coat and jabbed in into the doctor's neck. It was a syringe, I saw, as he pushed the plunger. Elvis caught Dr. Garcia as he slumped and laid him gently on the floor.

Then Elvis grabbed a towel from the examining table and leaned over Glenn, who was moaning. "Hold that against the wound," he said. "It looks worse than it is. I'll bandage it in a moment."

He turned to Burke. "Help me put Dr. Garcia on the examination table."

After they laid the doctor down, Elvis pulled open some drawers, then turned around with a couple of butterfly bandages and knelt next to Glenn. "I think these will be enough to close the wound. Scalp wounds can be scary, but I don't think your friend will need stitches," he reassured us.

He looked up at us with an apologetic expression. "I'm sorry that happened. Gerald's been under a great deal of stress ever since Ms. Cromartie died. I think he's been taking pills. The whole thing's a big mess."

"Do you have records of Debra's prescriptions?" Burke asked.

Elvis didn't answer at first. He bent over Glenn, cleaning the wound and applying the bandages. Distractedly, he said, "Everything is in order...I should know, it's my department. The police have copies. I assure you, Dr. Garcia would never have knowingly put Ms. Cromartie in danger."

"Yeah, he seems like a real stable kind of fellow," Burke said.

"Please don't call the police," Elvis said. "He may have pulled a gun on you, but I'm pretty sure that snatching Marjorie's phone out of her hand and forcing your way into the examining room could be considered assault."

"When will he wake up?" I asked.

Elvis stood up and spread his arms. "Doesn't matter, he can't tell you anything. You need to leave."

I helped Glenn up from the floor, and he groaned but seemed stable enough. The bandages seemed to be holding. I paused at the doorway. "What about you?"

"Me?" Elvis pondered this for a moment and then gave a dry laugh. "All I know is that I've probably lost a job."

For some reason, I believed the young man that Dr. Garcia didn't know anything. Elvis radiated sincerity.

The idea came to me suddenly. "You can come work for me."

Burke turned and looked at me in surprise. I'd always wanted an entourage, and a medical person seemed like a good addition. Plus Elvis was fast on his feet. He'd probably saved us from being shot.

"Doing what?" Elvis asked.

I held out my hand. "My name is Zachary Spence."

He shook his head as if the name didn't mean anything to him.

"Otherwise known as Que."

Elvis froze; his eyes grew wide. He searched my face as if trying to decide if I was kidding.

"Wow," he said, finally. "I was a gawky little bullied kid when I went to my first Pegasus Convention. Saw an Elvis impersonator there, and I was transformed." He motioned to his wavy black hair and sideburns and did a classic Elvis stance, arms pointing to somewhere about 10 o'clock on the dial.

I smiled.

His face fell a little. "But I'm not sure why you need me."

"Listen," I said, "it would be nice to have a nurse practitioner riding along with us. We seem to be getting into scrapes a little too often for comfort. Whatever you're getting paid here, I'll pay you twice as much."

Burke frowned, as if he didn't agree with my offer, but Glenn was grinning. Elvis didn't answer at first, but busied himself cleaning up the examining room; then he turned and put out his hand. "I'd be honored to join you. It sounds like quite an adventure."

We shook hands on it. My entourage was shaping up, and as Numera kept pointing out, I could afford it.

Marjorie was hiding behind the front desk as we came out of the back. "Mr. Ellis, do you want me to dial 911? I have my personal phone in my purse."

Elvis stopped dead in his tracks. "I figured you already had."

"I wanted...I wasn't sure..."

Elvis walked up to the counter and patted the woman gently on her shoulder. "Everything's fine, Marjorie. Cancel all further appointments. Dr. Garcia is taking a nap in the back."

The receptionist opened her mouth to say something but nothing came out.

"Don't call the police, for the doctor's sake," Elvis added. "I don't think Ger would want that."

"Elvis? Where are you going?" Marjorie looked as if she was finally melting down, as if losing Elvis was the last straw.

"I'm sorry, Marjorie. I'll...uh...send you my new address."

When we slipped into the back of the limo, Numera took one look at Elvis and shook her head adamantly.

"No way," she said. "You can't keep adding people, Zach, just because you feel like it."

"Why not?" I asked.

Numera stared at Elvis, who blushed and looked away. She looked like she wanted to object further, then seemed to decide against it. Instead, she said, "It's still early. Anyone object to flying back to our hotel in Chicago tonight? I hate Los Angeles. I don't want to stay here if I don't have to."

"It's too damn hot here for me," Stephen said.

No one else objected, so we were soon in the air. Numera sat across the aisle from me and wouldn't look my way, as if she was angry or disappointed in me—but for some reason, I knew her funk wasn't about me. She was thinking about her father.

It must have taken all her willpower not to confront the thing that was pretending to be her father, to continue on with the plans as if nothing had happened. Agate sat quietly next to her friend. I decided to follow her example and leave Numera alone.

That night, we met in my hotel room, the presidential suite. Glenn appeared to be fine—in fact, he was lording the bandage on his head over Stephen, as if he'd gained his wound in combat. After I explained how I thought I owed Elvis for saving us and how I thought he could be useful, Numera seemed to grudgingly accept it.

"So you truly believe that Garcia had nothing to do with Debra's death?" she asked me.

"He seemed upset, but believable," I answered.

"I disagree," Burke said. "No one acts that squirrelly if they don't have something to hide. But I'm not sure we're going to be able to get anything out of him now."

Elvis shook his head. "Gerald is a strange man, but he is a good doctor. I very much doubt he did anything wrong."

"Besides," Agate said, "a switch could have happened anywhere between the doctor and Debra—the drug store, the delivery person, a maid at the hotel."

Burke nodded. "I'll check that out with my sources, but I suspect we'll have to wait for the lab results and the autopsy. I'll make sure they check for needle marks—though I'm not sure that would prove anything if she was an addict. What we really need to know is what her intention was, and the forensics can't tell us that."

I was dispirited. It had been a Hail Mary effort, but for some reason I'd been convinced we'd stumble onto something. If this had been a game, there would have been a clue. Obviously, I much preferred ready-made answers, but reality wasn't so accommodating.

Numera pulled out her phone and checked the time. "Let's get some rest. We'll take a break for a couple of days before we head for the Jubilee. Free time for whatever you want to do—as long as you don't leave the hotel, Zach."

"Great," I muttered, "free time for whatever I want to do, as long it's watching TV."

Numera stood up, ignoring me. The others followed her example.

I motioned them to sit back down. "I have a couple of things I'd like to discuss, if you don't mind. Numera, I'd like you to arrange cash card accounts for everyone here. Make it ten thousand dollars each."

"Zach…" Numera started to say in her "let me explain the facts of life" tone.

"You keep telling me I can afford it," I said. "This money is for you all to spend as you see fit—on top of your wages, which we still need to iron out. There will be no oversight. If you spend it all and need more, just ask me. This is the equivalent of me pulling a penny out of my pocket, folks. I want to do it."

"Uh, Zach…" Glenn said. "You don't need to pay us…"

Surprisingly, it was Elvis who spoke up. "Elvis used to give his 'Memphis Mafia' Cadillacs and houses, that kind of thing. It made him feel good."

"And look how well that turned out," Glenn said. "You want an entourage, Zach? Well, the only way I'll be part of that is if I can tell you want I really think."

"I'm counting on it," I said. "I'm not Elvis—you know, *that* Elvis—and none of you are taking advantage of me.

"The second thing I want to talk about is, I think we need to have Merlin open up for us early tomorrow so we can get new costumes. We can't be sure that the receptionist won't recognize me and make the connection to the *Star Wars* menagerie that invaded her office earlier."

Numera nodded.

The meeting broke up and one by one the others drifted away until only Agate lingered by the door. "Are you sure about Elvis?" she asked.

"He saved our lives," I said. "Why do you ask?"

"Well...maybe you don't know—because you're a guy—but he's gorgeous."

"Gorgeous?" It was the last thing I'd expected her to say.

"You have no idea, Zach. Is he married? Girlfriend?"

"Well...I don't know." I realized I actually didn't know anything about the guy. I would have to have Burke look into him... tomorrow.

"You know, you're still wearing your digimask," Agate said. She smiled and closed the door.

I managed to take off the Luke Skywalker digimask before I plopped onto bed.

I wasn't asleep for long before I felt a timid knock on the door. I went to the door, knowing who it would be. Numera didn't say a word, but simply wrapped her arms around me and kissed me deeply. I pulled her into my room.

Numera shook me awake. I reached out for her, to press her warm body against mine. She grabbed my arm, pinching. "Zach...someone's in the room."

I snapped awake and sat up. A dark shape seemed to slice out of the darkness: long legs, black coat and tall black hat, and a ghostly face.

Mr. Zander bowed, as if happy to see us awake. "We meet again. It seems that I always find you two in bed together."

I looked at Numera who stared back at me with wide eyes. I'd told her about Mr. Zander and I could tell she knew who it was.

"My boss has changed his mind about killing you, now that he's met you," Mr. Zander continued. "He wants you alive, but I've never let anyone escape before and I'm not going to start now." He shook his head. "He doesn't need to know who killed you...dangerous world this. Anyone could have done it. Anyone."

He opened his frock coat and pulled out a long curved knife. He ran a finger along the blade and a drop of blood dripped onto the wood floor. It seemed to me that it landed with a loud splat. He licked his bleeding finger and smiled.

"Your boss?" Numera said. "You mean the *thing* that pretends to be my father?" The sheet fell away from her breasts. I thought it was probably on purpose, a distraction. Mr. Zander leered at her—or maybe that was the way he looked at everyone all the time.

I glanced at the chair by the bed where my holster hung with the loaded revolver. Mr. Zander's smiled as he saw where I was looking.

"That *thing*—as you so aptly call it—is no one's boss. The creature is a ghoul and will fall apart soon enough. Its appetite can't be sustained in this world, not without people noticing. But by then it will be too late."

"What do you want?" I asked. A *ghoul*. I didn't want Numera to think of the implications.

"Want? I want to finish my job, of course—and my job always finishes the same way. Your counterparts in my own world—the great Zach and Numera! They were easy enough to dispatch. Lying together in bed, so in love that they didn't notice me above hovering over them. It took but one thrust to sever both their throats."

He tipped his stovepipe hat back on his head jauntily.

"I must say, it wasn't very satisfying to kill them when they didn't even know I was there. This time I want to see your eyes as you die."

The air began to shimmer behind him. I resisted looking at Numera to see if she was seeing what I was seeing. A furry head poked out of the shimmer, then disappeared again, then popped out a little further.

Coyote seemed to wink at us. The glowing circle began to fade...

Come back! I almost shouted.

The shimmer exploded outward, and a yellow blur of fur flew through the air. White fangs fastened on Mr. Zander's neck.

He roared and reached back and grabbed the coyote by the scruff and flung it to the floor. Coyote's legs bent at an unnatural angle, but somehow the creature latched onto the tall man's leg, shaking back and forth with a growl.

Mr. Zander reached down and pulled Coyote away, his own skin and clothing tearing. With a howl, he slammed the animal against the wall. The entire room seemed to shake. The coyote yipped and was silent

I launched myself toward the chair and drew the Colt. I heard heavy footsteps. I turned and pulled the trigger at the looming shadow. The safety was still on.

Cursing, I fumbled for the switch, certain Mr. Zander's knife would descend before I could pull the trigger again.

Numera bounded out of bed, grabbing the table lamp and throwing it at the tall man. The lamp shattered against his face. Somehow his hat stayed on, but it slowed him by a step. He strode toward me with an enraged and bloody expression, knife raised over his head.

I fired the Colt, missing him but hitting his stovepipe hat, which flew backward. Desperately I fired again and his face caved in, as if being sucked through a hole and exploding out of the back of his head.

I stood over him trying to catch a breath and felt Numera come up behind me and put her arms around me. "Breathe," she said. "Breathe slowly."

I felt a sudden calm come over me. I went to Coyote and put my hand on the fur of its head. It didn't move. It was dead.

"What do we do now?" I asked.

"We get rid of the bodies," Numera answered.

I turned and looked at the bloody mess. Mr. Zander's knife still quivered from where it had landed impaled on the floor.

"Just how..."

And then both bodies began to fade before our eyes and blinked out. All that remained was the knife protruding from the floor.

"Never mind," I said.

We went back to bed and held each other. We didn't speak. What was there to say?

Our enemy—the *boss*, whoever that might be—was still out there and could apparently appear anywhere at any time.

I wondered if we'd ever be able to sleep again.

CHAPTER TWENTY-ONE

It sometimes seems like everything Pegasus Corp does turns into money. I'd like to say that Joseph is a genius, but even though he is a very smart man, there is nothing of the genius—as that word is generally understood—about him.

I think his success comes from his genuine love of the Hyper-reality world. People can tell. They reward you when you're genuine, punish you when you're not. I believe that's why Unicorn Industries has never managed to overtake us, despite having some heavy financial backers.

Some of our biggest mistakes turned into our biggest windfalls in the long run. When the first Pegasus Conventions were held, Joseph insisted that attendees be required to pay only what they could afford. That is, everyone was welcome. An entrance fee was requested, but not demanded.

As I predicted, every convention we put on those first years was a money-loser. If Joseph hadn't thrown so much of his own money into it—again, over my objections—Pegasus Corp would have been stillborn.

Then a strange thing happened. The conventions got bigger and bigger because they were easy to get into. And then, people started paying, little by little, until it was frowned upon to enter free if you could pay.

And because there were so many more people, the increased revenue more than made up for the losses.

Joseph's innate generosity paid off.

That and my sterling management, of course.

Diary of Roger Ackroyd

Numera was gone from the bedroom by the time I woke up. When I saw her in the dining room, she wouldn't look me in the eye.

We'd just killed someone. And we'd seen someone killed—if Coyote could be considered "someone." (I couldn't imagine why not.) Our world wasn't the only world. We weren't the only Zach and Numera. We could be alive in one world and dead in another. This was going to take some getting used to.

Amazingly, Numera delivered on my request for prepaid cards by the end of breakfast.

"The highest limit I could find on short notice was for five thousand dollars," Numera said. "I'll get more as soon as I can."

"Where's mine?" I asked as she handed them out.

"You don't need one. I'll pay for everything."

I thought about making a stink about it, because it made me feel awful. I'd never been in such a position, even when I was young and broke. I mean, even then, at least I could go down to Bruno's and buy a soda, as long as I was willing to put up with his derision. I hated having someone else paying for everything—even if it was with my money. I knew what she was doing, of course. She didn't want me wandering off on my own again.

Glenn and Stephen immediately set out to conquer the world while I sat in my room and played solitaire (yes, the owner of Pegasus Corp likes the most basic card game there is). My buddies went out in civilian clothing because nobody knew who they were yet. My two erstwhile friends didn't even bother to express sympathy at my pathetic state.

They returned later in the afternoon trailed by a succession of deliverymen. Before dinner they had a full virtual reality studio erected inside Glenn's hotel room. (The furniture was shoved together, leaving barely enough room to move around.)

Meanwhile, I was bored and dispirited. I couldn't imagine spending the rest of my life this way, able to only go out in a digimask, surrounded by bodyguards.

"Can't I just, like, sign it all away?" I moaned when Agate and Elvis showed up to check on me. They were obviously spending time together. I had a sense that Agate was both informing me and asking for my approval.

I acted like I didn't notice.

Agate didn't take pity on me. "You'll always be Que, Zach, whether you're rich and powerful or not. Better to be rich and powerful, don't you think?"

Numera came in and announced that Merlin's Toys would be ready to receive us after their closing hours at 9:00 p.m., so be ready. I put on my Luke digimask but didn't bother with the rest of the costume.

We drove to the toy store without Glenn and Stephen, who were so engrossed in their VR *Rick and Morty* play they could barely respond. "Pick something out for us," one of them said.

I didn't speak the whole way there, instead listening glumly to the chattering of my friends. They were excited, energized. Even Numera, who usually acted like she had the weight of the world on her shoulders, seemed to be having a good time.

She gave me a worried glance and I tried to smile, which only made it worse. My fake smile was the fakest smile you could imagine.

She reached over and gave my hand a squeeze. "Don't worry, it will be over soon. People will start to lose interest in Que after a while."

"You think?" I asked.

She hesitated. "Well, at least the *mania* will die down."

That wasn't the reassurance I was looking for. Inside, I already knew that Que was such a famous persona that there was no escaping it…ever.

As we gathered on the second floor of Merlin's, Numera gave us instructions. "This time, let's not all dress in one genre universe. We'll be less likely to be noticed if we spread out the licenses."

Agate quickly picked out a NBX Sally costume, so of course Elvis chose Jack Skellington. Numera chose to be Catwoman, whip and all. (Be still my heart.) Agate talked Burke into a Popeye costume—the muscles didn't need to be included.

"What about you, Zach?" Numera asked when she saw me standing there.

"I don't care."

"In that case..." She reached over and pulled out a Doctor Who Cyberman costume. "Can't get much more anonymous than this."

"Fine." Somehow, it was perfect. It suited my mood. I could just be a robot, just clanking about.

We got ready to leave, but as we started down the spiral stairs, Agate said, "What about Glenn and Stephen?"

"I know just what to get," I said. I trotted back up and grabbed a Blue Spartan and a Red Spartan costume from Halo. My two best friends hated Halo, and I was feeling a little vindictive about how much fun they were having. Besides, it gave me an idea.

I went back to my room and plotted my escape.

It was Coyote's latest ambiguous visit before it was killed that inspired it. "You mustn't stray from the plan," it had said. I wasn't sure why I should follow his advice. I sensed that I needed to make my own decisions, not be a puppet. I suddenly had the queasy feeling of something attached to the back of my neck, animating me, moving my mouth, while Zach lay screaming somewhere inside.

No, I need to be my own man, make my own decisions.

"That's not important," Coyote had said about what happened to Debbie.

But to me, it was the most important thing of all. That and what had happened to Roger Ackroyd. Coyote wanted me to forget about them, but to abandon them was to abandon myself. I needed to find out what Unicorn was up to.

When I didn't go down for breakfast the next morning but instead ordered room service, Numera came to check on me.

"You don't have to stay cooped up," she said. "As long as you go out as Cyberman and take Burke and his crew along with you."

"Gee, sounds like lots of fun," I said.

"I sure hope you get over your snit before we get to the Jubilee," she said. "Going to be hard to win the Blue Queen's favor if you're like this."

I kept watching the TV and didn't answer her. I heard an exasperated snort and then she left.

On the tube was an advertisement for a Unicorn Convention at the McCormick Convention center. It started at noon. I checked my watch and got up from the bed for the first time in almost a day.

I found Glenn and Stephen yelling and stomping in the next room.

"Finally come to join us?" Glenn said, not taking off his VR goggles.

I walked over to the plugin and pulled out the cord.

"Hey!" Stephen shouted, whipping off his goggles. "I was just about to win."

"Like hell you were," Glenn said.

"Shut up, both of you," I said, then instantly regretted it. I sounded like a boss, or a parent, and that's not how I wanted to come across. "Sit down, you guys. I want to talk to you."

They sat down obediently and I felt even worse. This wasn't an equal relationship anymore, no matter how much I tried to convince myself otherwise. "I want to borrow one of your cash cards and a costume."

"No way," Glenn said. "You're, like, the Man and all, but I'm more afraid of Numera than I am of you."

"I'm not ordering you," I said. "I'm asking. No...I'm *begging* you. I'm going crazy here. I have to get away, all by myself. Just to breath the free air."

"Poor little rich man," Stephen said. He reached into his pocket and handed over his card. "There should be about two thousand left."

"You spent three thous—No, never mind. It's your money to do what you want with. Thank you, Stephen. But I have another favor to ask. One of you needs to pretend to be me while I'm gone."

"How the hell do we do that?" Glenn asked.

"You wear the Cyberman costume and act like me."

Stephen laughed and grabbed his card out of my hand. "Then you need Glenn. He's exactly your size and shape, and he does a mean impression of you."

"What do you mean, impression?"

"Gosh," Glenn said in a weird voice. "Golly, gee! I sure am surprised."

It slowly penetrated that he was trying to mimic me. "I don't sound like that."

Stephen slapped Glenn on the back in approval. "Oh, but you do, Zach. Innocent outrage at everything you see, my friend. It's very endearing."

I restrained my annoyance. "Just talk as little as possible, keep your head down, and make sure you have the Cyberman voice modifier on." A Cyberman had the quintessential robot voice—the same sound that went all the way back to Robby the Robot.

I dressed in the Red Spartan suit, took Glenn's cash card, and headed out. The bodyguard outside in the hallway barely glanced at me. When I reached the open air, I felt faint and realized I'd barely taken a breath all the way down the elevator and out into the lobby.

I almost stumbled when Burke came toward me on the sidewalk. "Getting more stuff?" he asked, passing by.

I counted on the helmet muffling my voice. To my surprise, I sounded like the Halo character in the game, as if I was communicating by radio. "Never too much stuff."

I hailed a cab and gave it orders to drive me to McCormick Place.

"Please insert card," it said.

I pushed in Glenn's card and it took a couple of seconds, as if the machine couldn't believe how much credit I had. I wondered if Numera would see these charges or if she was paying attention. Our privacy might be something I would want to bring up...later, when I was done.

"Estimated arrival based on current traffic, forty-five minutes," the cab informed me.

I sat back as the vehicle whooshed away from the curb, seamlessly fitting into the flow. Back in Bend, self-driving cars were still in the minority, mostly because the good old boys in their big-ass pickups and the weekend athletes didn't want to give up control. There was also ten times the traffic here. I doubted I would even attempt to drive on these streets without the help of a computer.

The crowd was sparse at the convention center. It was the beginning of the show, and a weekday, but it was still vindictively satisfying to see that Unicorn wasn't filling the hallways. The last couple of Friday starts at Pegasus I'd gone to had been packed.

I had barely paid and walked in the front door before I was accosted.

"The Halo 8 game is in room three," a Unicorn factotum in a yellow vest told me.

I went in the direction he pointed so as not to call attention to myself, but also because I was curious. I had no idea that there would be Halo gaming at this convention. The game was so popular that it usually had its own venues.

There was another fee to get into the halo room. I didn't even ask how much. Then an attendant handed me a battle rifle and activated the in-game control on my suit.

"It's a first-person shooter live action game," the bored attendant said.

"No kidding," I said.

I started to get excited. I hadn't participated in a good old-fashioned laser shooting midrange game in a long time, but I'd always been a good shot.

There were about fifty players, I figured. Even though the Spartan suit I was wearing was more expensive than anything I'd ever worn before to a convention, it was about midrange in embellishment. There were some spectacular custom suits, in a rainbow of colors, some of which I don't think actually existed in the VR game. The other players milled around, jockeying for position. I was probably the only one there who had no idea what he was doing.

The back of the room lit up and a couple of figures walked out onto a dais.

"Spartans!" a man shouted.

I froze at the voice. As soon as I heard it, the faraway figure's features became recognizable. Jordan Shipman. What were the chances of that happening? *Might be a good idea to turn right around and leave.*

I looked around at the other Spartans and realized I was completely safe—as long as I didn't call attention to myself.

"We have as our special guest and judge for today's contest the great Warren Moss, the originator of Spartan Magnusson of Halo 7!" Shipman said.

A smattering of applause greeted the announcement. Halo 7 had been a bit of a flop, with Spartan Magnusson replacing Master Chief. Halo 8 and the return of the Chief had saved the franchise.

"All right, people," Moss shouted. "The members of the winning team will all receive free passes to the next LA Unicorn event. The gameplay will continue until there is one man standing, who will win the grand prize."

I was still trying to puzzle out the directions when Moss shouted, "Ready, players?"

This was greeted by a roar. The lights went down, and lasers started blasting in every direction.

I ducked down, trying to figure out what was going on. We should have been fighting the Covenant forces, whatever form they took, or perhaps Forerunner constructs, not each other.

A purple Spartan fell at my feet, his badge flashing red. It was only then that I realized that his badge was surrounded in yellow, while mine was blue. Apparently the game was based on the plot of Halo 7, when the Covenant created a rival band of Spartans. Probably explained why Warren Moss was here.

Which side was I on?

Apparently, it didn't really matter. Someone was charging me, his rays glancing off my armor. His badge was yellow. I calmly shot him three times in the helmet and he dropped.

I whirled around and started firing.

It was a fast game; within five minutes there were only about ten of us left, hiding behind various edifices littering the floor. The players whose badges were flashing red lay on the floor, unmoving, their units frozen. It appeared to me that about six of the remaining players had blue badges and four had yellow.

That's when the first construct emerged. It looked like mechanical Giger creature, with multiple arms, all of them firing away with Covenant needler weapons. The remaining

Spartans fired back, and under the combined firepower, the construct disintegrated.

"Truce until we defeat them!" I shouted.

"Aye!" one of the others shouted immediately. He was behind the nearest holo of a rocky pinnacle and was wearing a yellow badge. His suit was a deep green. One by one, the other survivors chimed in, except for one holdout, who wore a blue badge. I started to step away from my hiding spot, planning to reason with the fellow. I saw him raise his rifle, then stiffen and fall flat as a laser flash struck him from behind.

"Everyone else in?" called out the deep green Spartan.

I ran toward his defensive spot, which only a minute or two before I'd been firing at. I slid to a stop next to the green Spartan, who stood and pointed his rifle at me. When I didn't raise mine, he lowered it. Within a minute or two, the rest of the survivors showed up

"Anyone see where that construct came from?" Green asked.

"Northeast corner," said a silver Spartan wearing a blue badge, pointing to the opposite corner.

"Then that's where we go," I said. I took off sprinting. I was halfway across the room before I thought to look back and see if the others had followed.

They were behind me, spread out. When the next xenomorph construct emerged, we scrambled for the nearest cover, firing as we went. Two of the Spartans behind me fell, their tags bursting with red flashes.

But we had an interlocking zone of fire as more xenomorphs emerged and we made short work of them. It was almost too easy.

That's when my rifle stopped firing. I looked down. It was out of juice. The fire from the others was diminishing too. Three of the largest xenomorphs yet emerged.

"Remember me!" one of the Spartans shouted. He wore a blue badge. He ran toward the assembled constructs, a sticky grenade in hand. It exploded, taking out the xenomorphs and closing the portal.

Obviously, everyone else had played this game and had come more prepared than me.

There were three of us left when the lights came back on. One of the others wore a blue badge, the other a yellow. I stood there stupidly, my gun empty. Too late, I realized that they were both armed with CE pistols.

They ignored me as not a threat and fired simultaneously at each other. Both armor suits froze and then crashed to the floor.

"Congratulations!" Warren Moss's voice came over the loudspeakers. "This is the first time the Spartans have won a completed game. Come on up to the dais, Red Spartan, for your prize.

Damn. If I'd known I was in danger of winning I would have made sure I got killed first. I hesitated, but couldn't figure out a way to avoid walking right up to Jordan Shipman, which was the last thing I wanted to do.

I clomped over to the platform and mounted the stairs. The other frozen Spartans on the floor were unlocked as one and rose to cheer. Moss and Shipman waited, smiling broadly.

Moss shook my hand first. "You're the one who asked for a truce, aren't you? Brilliant. No one else has thought of that. You deserve to win."

"Warren," Jordan said impatiently.

Moss flushed a little and moved aside. Shipman grabbed my hand, pulling it toward him in a power move.

"First prize is five thousand Horn units good at any Unicorn Convention, Shipman announced. He turned to me expectantly. He held out a stack of what looked like casino chips. "Take off that helmet and let's get a look at you."

Instead, I saluted. "Sergeant Longhi, reporting for duty, sir." I'd known a few friends who were ICYs, in-character all the time, and I'd always thought it was carrying things too far. But it came in handy today.

He flushed. I could see the anger in his eyes. Then he managed to shake it off. "I see…so you're an ICY."

I nodded.

He stared at me curiously, then laughed. "Well, I admire anyone who can stay in character no matter what. You must have a very understanding boss and family and friends."

I simply nodded. He poured the chips into my hands. I

looked down. They were emblazoned with the numbers —100, 500, and 1,000. I'm sure I was supposed to know what to do with them and to be grateful, but I just stood there. Then I remembered that one of my armor plates had a hollow opening for a pocket, and I flipped it open and poured the chips into it.

Shipman turned to the crowd. "Thank you all for coming!"

Shipman handed the microphone to Warren Moss as if he was a mere flunky. I could see that the actor was embarrassed, but he took it.

As I tried to make my way to the stairs, I felt a tap on my shoulder.

"Do mind if I make you a proposition?" Shipman said.

"I have to get back to my unit," I mumbled.

"This won't take long," Shipman said smoothly. "As you may or may not know, Unicorn Industries is making its first appearance at the Louisville Fantasy Fest."

"The Queen's Jubilee?"

It was news to me. The event had always been sponsored in the past by Pegasus Corp alone. Apparently the Blue Queen was letting both corporations participate this time. I'd thought our long-term relationship gave us an advantage. Apparently, Maureen had other ideas.

Had Unicorn and Pegasus ever been at the same event? I couldn't think of an example. I wondered if Numera knew. Of course, she probably did. She probably thought I wouldn't care. We were going to have to have a talk about that. If I was going to be Que, I needed to know what was going on.

Shipman put his hand on my forearm. "We'll be having another Halo event there and I'd like you to come as a guest of Unicorn."

I almost laughed. I wasn't sure how a laugh would sound with the Halo voice modifier, but I was pretty sure it wouldn't sound natural. *Just agree and get the hell out.*

"I'll be glad to come," I said.

"Check in at the front gate, Mr....?"

I repeated my character's name and rank.

"Still ICY, huh?" Shipman dug into his pocket and pulled out a business card. He wrote something on the back and then handed it to me. "Present this at the door, Spartan, and I'll make sure you get in. See you then."

He slapped me on the back as if dismissing me. I opened the armored panel and shoved the card in.

I made my way down the stairs and all the way across the room before I looked back.

Shipman was looking right back at me.

As I went out onto the street to snag a cab, I wondered if there was any way for Shipman to figure out who I was. There had been at least a dozen other Red Spartans in the game. I'd paid at the door, but I was pretty sure the bored young man hadn't paid the slightest attention to me and wouldn't remember my name. Even if he did, I didn't think the name Glenn Halligan would mean anything.

On the way back to the hotel, I checked to see if I was being followed. I don't know why I was so paranoid. I doubted I was the first ICY that Shipman had ever had to deal with.

But there was something about the angry look in his eyes that made me wonder if there wasn't something else going on.

It wasn't until I reached the lobby that I relaxed. I pulled out the business card he'd given me and looked on the back. "Please escort this gentleman to my office. JS."

I put it between my thumbs and forefingers to rip it in half, and then hesitated. It was crazy, but...at the same time, the irony of the invitation was that it was just too sweet resist.

Who knew? Maybe I could learn something.

I put the business card back in my pocket and headed for the elevators.

CHAPTER TWENTY-TWO

It is hard to know nowadays what is real and what is an illusion. The mind and body respond to adventures as if they are real, a more genuine and "authentic" experience than most people's humdrum lives. And indeed, what is more real: going to your desk or your cash register and working for the Man, or sailing the high seas with your pirate brethren, looting and plundering ships that—in the mind of most adventurers—probably represents the soulless corporation you work for daily?

That's why Joseph's invention of the term Hyper-reality took off. It is the reality most of us know. It gets the imagination going and blood pumping in ways that simply going to the office never will.

All I can say is, if aliens ever do invade us they will have a fight on their hands, because generations of people have been raised in simulations for just such an eventuality.

Diary of Roger Ackroyd

Stephen answered the door. Glenn lay flat on his back on his bed, still dressed in the Cyberman costume. He was apparently asleep, because robotic snores emanated from the helmet.

"What happened?" I asked.

Stephen grimaced. "Right after you left, Burke took the whole crew—minus, or so he thought, Glenn—on a sightseeing tour of the Hollywood sign, Grauman's Chinese Theatre, and a bunch of other places. I think he was trying to cheer you up."

"No one figured it out?" I asked, amazed.

"Glenn was a trooper. He answered everyone with

monosyllabic responses and acted glum—just like the Puddleglum you've been over the last few days. No one suspected a thing. It wore him out, though."

There was real affection in his voice. I'd often wondered about my two friends, who'd always talked about chasing women and yet never seemed to go on dates.

"Where'd you go?" Stephen asked.

"You won't believe it," I said, and proceeded to tell him the story.

"Wish we'd been there," he said. "I haven't been in a good fight in a long time."

He sounded truly dejected about it.

"You guys don't have to stick around," I said. "You've already helped me so much. Take the cash cards with my blessing. I'll try to visit the old hometown as soon as I can."

Glenn sat up. "What?" His robotic voice was almost overridden by emotion.

"Are you kidding me?" Stephen said. "This is the best Hyper-reality scenario ever!"

"This is real, you guys. People have died because of this," I warned.

"Feels the same as Hyper-reality to me," Stephen said, shrugging. "I always think someone's trying to kill me."

"Not getting rid of us that easy, buddy," Glenn said.

I wanted to give them both a hug, but cleared my throat manfully instead.

"Well...we'd better get these costumes off before someone knocks on the door and I have to pretend to be you. I don't have the slightest idea how to be Glenn Halligan."

"Easy," Stephen said. "Just act like you've had a lobotomy."

I started to leave the room, but stopped because something was bothering me. I looked at Glenn. "Numera really didn't notice that you weren't me?"

My two friends exchanged a look, as if each was daring the other to answer.

Stephen finally cleared his throat. "She came by early in the morning, told us to look after you. But she didn't want you to know."

"Know what?"

"She flew back to New York. Said she needed to talk to her father," Stephen said.

A cold chill went down my spine. In my memory, Numera's description of the thing—the meat puppet that was pretending to be her father—had taken the place of what I'd actually seen myself.

"Not sure what the big mystery was about," Glenn added, "but she made us promise not to tell you. I heard her get back about half an hour ago."

I headed for my room, carrying the Cyberman costume. As I passed by Numera's door, I saw the light on inside. It seemed like every time I saw her now she was working, at a desk with a laptop or her fingers a blur on her phone. It was all on her head now that Roger was gone.

I knocked softly.

I heard the rustle of fabric, and the door opened slightly. Numera was holding her bathrobe closed at the neck.

"Sorry, I hope I didn't wake you."

She hesitated and then opened the door. As I'd thought, the hotel desk was littered with papers and her laptop was open. Her hair was plastered on her forehead. It was the first time I'd ever seen her disheveled even a little. There was an indentation on her cheek; it looked like she'd fallen asleep with her head on the keyboard.

I cleared my throat. "You went to New York?"

Her eyes flashed angrily. "I should have known your bozo friends wouldn't keep quiet."

"They're my friends," I said. "Tell me what happened."

"I decided after...after what that frightful Mr. Zander said... to find out once and for all what happened to my father."

My heart fell. I could already tell the answer from her long face.

"When I got there he...*it*...wouldn't see me."

Relief washed over me. The false Roger was dangerous.

My relief was premature. Numera continued, "But that didn't mean I couldn't see *him*."

I sat down heavily on the end of the bed. "What happened?"

She proceeded to tell me the story.

The elevator was locked, but I had the key. I went on up, with or without permission. When the elevator door opened, the room was completely dark. I reached for the light switch, but changed my mind.

Slowly, I realized there was as small amount of light coming from the keyboard of an open laptop on the desk. I saw something massive behind it and heard a slithering sound. It was as if the entire room was moving. Then I realized that what I thought were the walls was living flesh. The creature surrounded me on all sides.

"'What are you?" I whispered.

The voice that answered was muffled and I could barely make it out. "I was the father of a girl like you in another, very different, world."

"But not *my* father. Where is *my* father?"

"I'm sorry...he is dead."

I nearly dropped to my knees, though in my heart I'd already known. Perhaps it was the unexpected pity in the monster's voice.

"A part of your father's consciousness resides in me...he loved you, this I know. I'm sorry, dear girl. I am not here because I want to be. I was forced to do *his* bidding.'"

"Why? Where do you come from? What do you want?"

"All good questions, none of which I can answer. I don't know myself. I'm dying, girl. Starving to death, even as I bloat. Soon my body will collapse upon itself and my consciousness will fade. Beware, Numera. Now...flee before I am forced to take you."

I ran.

I knew my father was dead.

"He's gone," she said, looking down at me.

I stood and took her in my arms. Without her high heels, she was only an inch or so taller than me. She melted into me for a moment, then I sensed her summoning her resolve. She broke away.

"We…we can't do this again, Zach. At least, not until this is over."

Why not? I wanted to ask. *Isn't this when we both need comforting the most?*

I turned to leave.

"Zach?" she called softly behind me.

"See you in the morning," I said, closing the door firmly.

Everyone looked up at me worriedly when I came down for breakfast the next morning. I realized that I'd worried them by being such a loner over the last few days. Of course, none of them knew why.

Agate got, came over, and hugged me. "I'm glad you're back among the living again."

Only because I got away for a day, I wanted to say. *And only because I've figured out I can do it again.* Instead, I shrugged. "No use fighting it."

"Uh…that's the spirit?" she answered dubiously.

Glenn and Stephen were already there, to my surprise, scarfing down blueberry pancakes. They pretty much ignored me after that first glance. Elvis nodded at me.

Numera was trying hard not to look at me. At least, that's what it seemed like. Then her eyes met mine, and it was as if we were both thinking the same thing: *What else can we do but go on? Worlds shift beneath our feet, and reality becomes blurred, but we have no choice but to follow the original plan because what else did we have?*

I sat down next to her. "What's the plan?"

"We'll fly to Louisville first thing tomorrow morning," she said. "Maureen wants to meet with both Unicorn and Pegasus before the convention starts on Friday."

"So Unicorn is officially going to be part of the Louisville Fantasy Fest?" I hadn't wanted to believe Shipman.

"The Blue Queen insisted and we aren't in a position to argue."

I stared at her until she looked up. Her dark eyes were surrounded by red. She looked tired. "I would really like you to tell me these kinds of things, Numera," I said.

"I meant to tell you, Zach. It's just…it's hard to decide what's important enough to bother you with and what can be ignored."

"Let me do some of it," I said. "After all…"

"I'm a CPA and a licensed lawyer, Zach," she interrupted. "Let me do the grunt work, and you can decide on the bigger things."

I fell silent at that. It made me feel pretty useless.

"Are you sure we can't just buy up the other outstanding shares and somehow gain control?" I asked, finally. I'd been thinking about this for days. It seemed unfair that thousands of individual players had no say in what happened to the company.

"If the Blue Queen decides against us, then all the outstanding shares combined won't be enough to change the outcome. But…" Numera reached out and patted my hand. I resisted the urge to grasp it like a drowning man. "You should know that ever since your speech, people have been approaching us, offering their shares. Some have even given them to us."

"Pay them the going rate," I said.

"We're running out of cash, Zach. You are the poorest trillionaire in history."

"I thought I was the only trillionaire in history."

"That too."

"We can't let Unicorn win."

She searched my face, as if wondering why I'd suddenly become so adamant.

Jordan Shipman had given me an uneasy feeling the first time I met him, but meeting him again yesterday had confirmed my worst suspicions. The man wanted to win at all costs and didn't care in the slightest for either his employees or his customers. And if he was behind Pretty, Pretty's death…

"Hey, Zach!" Glenn called out from the end of the table. "We're heading over to Sunset Strip. Rudolph Navarro is playing an afternoon gig at the *Whiskey a Go Go*."

I looked at Numera, who rolled her eyes. "I'm not your jailer, Zach. You're a grown man."

But before I could stand up, she added, "As long as you go in costume. And take Burke with you!"

Burke, in his Popeye costume, led the way into the *Whiskey a Go Go*. The whole place seemed seedy. There had been so many incarnations of the joint that you never quite knew what you'd find. The followers of Rudolph Navarro followers were dressed like bullfighters, mostly, with a few conquistadors in honor of his song *Wrath*. Cybermen and Spartans were definitely out of place, but it wasn't an uncommon thing to see such absurdities.

Navarro was just as talented in person as he was online, which was rare these days. The afternoon passed quickly, aided by a few beers. I felt myself becoming morose again. That brief hug the night before had made me realize how much I wanted Numera to like me. But how could I ever be sure? If I had met her on the streets of Bend would she have even given me a second glance?

I laughed, choked on some beer, and coughed it out my nose. As if a woman like Numera would ever be in Bend in the first place. I saw someone at the bar drinking a margarita, so the next time the server—who was a big woman dressed as Sumbos, the lady in *Coco 3*, death mask and all—came by, I switched to hard liquor.

Big mistake. It came down on me like a Canderlever spaceship.

"Let's get out of here," Glenn said. The more Navarro sang, the more the bullfighters started getting handsy. I saw one of them come over and sit next to Stephen, giving him a smile.

I was ready. It wasn't really my favorite kind of music, though I appreciated the talent. But when I stood up, I nearly fell back into my chair.

We walked out onto the sidewalk. The rows and rows of colorful billboards that lined the Sunset Strip were overwhelming. Cars zoomed by, their electric motors so quiet that most of them had little whistles attached to the bumpers to warn pedestrians. The sidewalk appeared to be swaying.

"How many drinks did you have?" Stephen asked.

"Apparently more than I thought," I said, my voice sounding drunkenly robotic. I sat down, my back against the wall of the bar. The Cyberman costume seemed to soak up the warmth of the sun and I was suddenly relaxed and tired. It reminded me of home.

"Get up, man," Glenn said somewhere above me. "You're embarrassing yourself. You used to handle your liquor better than this."

His voice faded away. The light dimmed and the temperature seemed to drop fifty degrees. I moaned, certain that when opened my eyes, I'd see Coyote trotting toward me. Hoping that somehow he was still alive, though I wasn't in the mood for one of his enigmatic lectures.

Instead, Mr. Zander strode toward me purposefully, a wicked grin on his face, his top hat rakishly tilted to one side. He was the very image of the character in the game, with his curled mustache and goatee, and his glittering black eyes. His black frock coat opened, and he reached in and pulled out a small knife. He looked down at the blade, shook his head, and put it back, instead extracting a blade as wide as a butcher knife.

"You're dead!" I cried out, ducking out of the way as the butcher knife slashed into the red brick above my head, shaving off red kernels that floated down on me in slow motion.

"I am eternal," Mr. Zander said, raising the blade again. There was no ducking this time.

A huge shape loomed behind Mr. Zander. Instead of the knife, a top hat came down and landed on my face. Mr. Zander, as tall as he was, had been lifted into the air by the neck. I caught a glimpse of the contorted face of the giant who'd saved me.

"Burke?" I yelled.

And then the sunlight was in my eyes again and Burke was lifting me up effortlessly. "Let's go, boss," he said. "Let's get you back to your hotel room."

"Was that you...?" I slurred, gazing into Burke's professional neutral expression. It probably wasn't the first time he'd picked a client out of the gutter.

I was bundled into a cab, and we headed back.

I'd sobered up a little by the time we got back to the hotel. Burke walked me into the entrance and then hurried away. Glenn and Stephen headed for the elevators. I glanced over at the dark entrance of the hotel bar and saw someone small and with white hair in the corner.

"You guys go on," I said. "I'm getting one more beer to come down soft."

Agate turned when I approached, flashing me a brilliant smile.

My heart fell. It was the kind of smile a girl gave someone when their heart was breaking inside and they didn't want anyone to know.

"What's wrong?" I asked.

"Nothing," she said.

"Did Elvis do something?" I asked. I felt completely sober now. I waved the waitress away.

"No...it's me. I was expecting too much."

I sat down next to her, at a loss for words. I'd had enough breakups in my life to know that having people pry into the details was one of the worst parts. "I'm sorry," I finally managed to utter.

She grabbed my hand. "You're a nice guy, Zach. Too bad I never fall for nice guys, even when they're trillionaires."

"If Elvis did something to you, well...I was sorry he lost his job because of me, but that doesn't mean he has to stay with us."

"No," she said, her hold tightening. "He's fine...he thinks everything is OK. Like I said, it's me."

I called the waitress over and ordered a bottle of Deschutes Ale to remind me of my hometown.

We drank companionably. As I watched Agate, I wondered why the two of us hadn't connected again. She was more down to earth than Numera, more my type. Too late now, apparently.

"Numera likes you, Zach," Agate suddenly said. "She's a little gun shy, that's all. You'd think someone as gorgeous as her would have men coming at her from all directions, but she intimidates most of them. Give her some time. She's trying to prove herself to you."

"Prove herself to me?" I laughed.

"You're Que. Weird how you keep forgetting it."

"So is it Que she likes or plain old Zach Spence?"

Agate smiled. Talking about someone else's troubles had revived her spirits, apparently. Glad I could do it.

"You silly boy," she said. "Que and Zach are the same man. Even if you can't seem to see it."

Even though we were leaving early in the morning for Louisville, I ordered another beer. I hadn't got drunk in a long time, and Agate was fun to be with.

Late that night, I delivered Agate to her door. I kissed her lightly and fondly on the cheek.

The door opened, and Elvis stood there. He looked angry.

"I was worried about you, Agate," he said. "You didn't give me a chance to explain."

"I'm sorry," Agate said. "I needed to be alone."

"I've been calling you for hours," he continued. His voice started to rise.

"Cool off, Elvis," I said. "You just met her. You don't own her."

He flushed, looked ready to argue, then seemed to remember I was the guy who had given him a job and a cash card... and could take it all away.

Agate brushed past me, entering the room. She didn't seem frightened, just a little subdued. "I'm fine, Zach. Go on to bed. I'll see you in the morning."

I stared at Elvis. He looked deflated, but at least he'd calmed down.

"Yes, you will," I said. I walked away, wondering if I was doing the right thing.

As I walked back to my room, I realized I didn't even know "Elvis's" real name. I'd ask Numera to look into him, see what his story was. I'd meant to have Burke do it earlier, but...oops.

I lay back in my bed, still clothed, intending to get up and take a shower. Instead, I fell asleep.

CHAPTER TWENTY-THREE

The backlash against silly people in silly costumes was there almost from the beginning. The Thentics (or the Authentic Movement, as it was known then) was a counterbalance from the start.

Personally, I thought they had some good arguments at first, before they became radicalized and violent.

It wasn't as if these modern-day Luddites hunted and butchered their own meat, tilled their own crops, and sewed their own clothing. What they were being "authentic" about was beyond me. The boring rote work of everyday life that most people were condemned to?

Unfortunately for the Thentics, technology continued to advance, making it easier and easier to be someone else, to live a fulfilling and exciting life in the world of holograms and VR.

There is a middle ground, one that I prefer; not too much reliance on technology, but on actual costumes and settings. Otherwise, we might as well sit on our couches and play video games. It took me a long time to realize that, in my own way, I was trying to hold back progress just like the Thentics were.

It's impossible to fight progress. Let the young people have their way. Especially since it seems to incorporate so much of what is old.

Diary of Roger Ackroyd

Sometime during the night, it felt as if my head exploded all over my pillow. My thoughts curled upward, became tangled, and fell back into the crater of my skull, disordered and chaotic. I tried to open my eyes, but it was as if someone had glued them shut. I heard voices, as if from a distance.

I was lifted, floated through the air, and landed on something hard.

I awoke, my hands tied behind my back, my legs sprawled out on a concrete floor, my back to something equally hard. If not for the small slit of light that came through a boarded-up window I would have thought I was still asleep, in some nightmare that had dribbled from my leaky brain.

Had Mr. Zander finally gotten to me?

No, I was back in reality—and somewhere I'd never been before. I heard footsteps above, clomping on a ceiling that seemed soft, as if every step from above threatened to break through. Muffled voices, arguing, one man's voice rising above the others, smothering the dissent. Aggrieved silence.

"Burke?"

My voice was barely a squeak, as if all the air had left my lungs, as if my consciousness was a small little mouse in the wreckage of my body.

Burke had been on duty sitting outside my hotel room door last night when I went to bed. But this wasn't my hotel room unless there'd been an earthquake during the night. If a giant had lifted the lid off the hotel and plucked me out, I couldn't have been more confused.

A light slanted down from above as a door opened. Someone skipped down the stairs, whistling to themselves. Whoever it was switched on the lights, a single row of fluorescent grow lights. There was a table down the middle of the room, with the desiccated remains of something that had once been green and growing.

"Good, you're awake," said the unfamiliar voice of an unfamiliar man. He looked at his wristwatch.

When was the last time I'd seen someone wearing a wristwatch? It was almost the badge of a Thentic—the bigger the watch, the better.

"You were out for three hours," the man said, "which means I got the dosage right. We were afraid the gas might kill you all, not that we would have cried over it."

"We?"

"Never you mind. You don't need to know. Let's just say that we are people who care about this country and want it back."

I was pretty sure this is where I was supposed say, "What happened? Where am I? Who are you?" I decided not to bother. Whoever this guy was, I sensed he was chatty and was going to tell me everything I wanted to know—and a lot I didn't want to know.

It was weird how calm I was. I think maybe because this was an earthly danger, something I could understand. Even if no less dangerous.

He was heavy-set, about average height, with tightly curled black hair on the top of his head and shaved along the sides, and heavy black glasses. When he opened his mouth, I could see a couple of gaps; he occasionally, unconsciously I think, covered his mouth with his hand as if to hide his rotted teeth. Sure enough, when he leaned down to stare into my face his breath was wretched.

He was wearing baggy shorts, white socks and black shoes, and a faded extra-extra-large T-shirt with a Florida hotel advertised on it; palm trees and sunlight. In other words, not in costume.

"My name is..." he broke off, grimaced. "Jesus, I was just about to tell you my name like some Bond villain. You can call me John. Boring John who lives in a real world, who deals with real problems, who doesn't have time to dress up and play."

It had been a long time since I'd conversed with a Thentic. Bruno came to mind, the store owner back in Bend who'd always made such a big deal out of hunting his own meat, building his own storage units, working on his own cars. He'd had bad breath too.

"If that's what you want to be," I said, my voice slowly coming to life, as if my vocal cords were thawing. "Boring John."

He flushed a little. "See, you're looking down on me. But I'm Boring John who has you tied up in his basement, Zach. I'm not going to call you Que, because Que is made up and I don't deal in make-believe."

"You're right. The Que thing is bullshit," I said. "But Zachary Spence is real, I'm just trying to figure it all out, just like you."

Had I ever really talked to a Thentic? I mean, face to face

and not anonymously online? They'd always seemed like the ones who were trampling on my rights. At that moment, tied up in a dirty basement, I realized that the Thentics no doubt thought of themselves as a persecuted minority.

I continued, keeping my voice as calm as could. "I understand where you're coming from, John."

"Do you? I live in the real world. I don't read fiction. What's the point? I don't watch TV or go to the movies."

Proud of your ignorance, I almost said, then realized that was unfair. "We all have to live in the real world, John. Some of us just want to escape sometimes."

"Yeah? If the lights went out, would you know how to fix them? Could you repair a motor or do your own taxes or cook a meal from scratch?"

I'm a trillionaire, why would I? came the easy response. Again, I kept it to myself.

John kept talking. "Before that, did you really do anything at all but daydream? Were you anything but useless?"

"We can't all return to being hunter-gatherers, John. Even then, there were the dreamers, those who painted art in caves, who fashioned jewelry and told stories."

"Most of you fantasy weirdos don't create anything," he scoffed. "At least I made things. I earned my money."

"Nothing to be ashamed of," I said. Part of me noticed he was speaking in the past tense. I wondered what had happened for him to do something as radical as kidnapping. "We should live and let live."

"That's just it, Zach. That's what I was doing. Then they closed down my factory and sent all the work to China, putting a hundred men and women out of work. All that's left are service jobs that pay shit. So everyone distracts themselves by playing dress-up and ignoring the real problems."

I fell silent at that. Not more than a couple of weeks ago, I'd been in the same position; broke and wondering what kind of future I had.

"I get it, John," I said finally. "I've lived in the real world. But I don't think Pegasus is responsible for all the factories disappearing. That was happening already. The world is changing

John and we need to change with it. Pretending to be someone else for a while doesn't cause any of that."

John had been pacing in front of me; now he plopped down cross-legged and stared into my face earnestly. "You don't get it. That's what I'm saying. Everyone is ignoring the real problems. Listen to me, Zach. I don't have much time before my partners come down here and I'm not sure what they are going to do."

That's when I decided to lose the argument. One good thing had come out of being plain old Zach for so many years; I'd learned that the man or woman who wins the argument isn't always right. This man—boy—was hurting, and mocking him was wrong and wouldn't help. And it might get me killed.

"I'm sorry, John. But what can I do?" I asked.

"Dismantle Pegasus," he said. His eyes searched mine. "Close down the conventions. If you aren't supporting it all, the whole thing comes tumbling down. Let reality return, let people see each other as they really are."

"If I did that, I'd put tens of thousands of people out of work, John. Besides, if Pegasus closes up, Unicorn Industries will take our place. And John—if you think the bastards are in charge now, wait until that happens."

He slumped, his head hanging down on his chest. "I know," he said, so softly I could barely hear him. "I just wanted to talk to you. To make sure you understood what's happening. I tried to get a job with you guys, but I failed the pop-culture test. The little elf lady who gave me the test laughed at me, said it was the lowest score she'd ever seen."

"That was wrong of her," I said. Truth was, I didn't even know that we tested our employees that way. It seemed wrong. What did it matter to the guy cooking burgers how many movies he'd seen? I'd always hated fanboy tests. Way back when I'd first gone into the Pegasus comic store, Dudley, the owner, had espoused a philosophy that was opposite of the clichéd Comic Book Guy. "Everyone is welcome," he's said. "No one is judged."

I should have been paying attention. How many other things was Pegasus doing that I wouldn't agree with?

John continued in his depressed tone. "Even if I'd gotten the job, the pay was half as much as my old job. Barely minimum wage."

How much are we paying these days? I wondered. I knew that when Pegasus started they paid at least fifty percent more than minimum wage. It was one of the reasons the company had been such a success. People were enthusiastic and grateful to work for Pegasus—and returned the favor by spending much of what they earned back into our businesses.

But how long had it been since those wages had been raised? I didn't have the slightest clue.

What did I really know about the inner workings of Pegasus Corp? Up to now, I'd trusted first Roger and then Numera to take care of things, but both of them were businesspeople who, from what I could tell, had acquiesced to my father's egalitarian policies somewhat reluctantly. Now that he was gone, could I be sure his wishes would continue to guide the company?

"Well, you got my attention, John. I will look into it. If you'll untie me, I swear nothing will happen."

He looked up at me blurrily. "I'd let you go if I could. I don't care what happens to me, Zach. But the people who helped me, I'm not so sure they'll let you go."

I weighed his words and his tone. If they weren't going to let me go, what were they going to do? I doubted they had the resources to keep me captive forever.

John watched me as I worked it out, then shook his head sadly. "I'm sorry, Zach. I never would have started this if I'd known. But I'm outvoted these days."

"Let me go," I said. "No one has to know what happened."

He stood up. He was agile for a fat man. He started pacing again. "I would if I could. But the only way out is up those stairs and past the others. Derrick brought a gun—dressed up as the Angel of Death, can you believe it? I mean, that doesn't make any sense, does it? A Thentic who dresses up in a costume? I think he's a psycho."

I craned my neck to look at the narrow window over my head. No way I was getting through that.

The door at the top of the stairs opened, and the sounds

of several people descending drifted down. There were five of them, four of them dressed in civilian clothing, and one of them wearing a black robe and a Scream mask, and holding a rubber scythe. I realized that because they weren't wearing disguises and hadn't blindfolded me, there was only one way this could end.

The Angel of Death pulled off his mask. His real face was almost as frightening; long and narrow, with his eyes, nose, and mouth all scrunched up in the middle. "All right, Martin," he said to the man who'd called himself "boring John."

"You've had your chance to talk to him. No doubt he agreed to shut down Pegasus just because you asked nicely."

"He listened to me," Martin/John said. "I think he really heard what I said."

"Wonderful," a girl standing next to Death said. She was tall and almost pretty, but there was something off in her eyes, and there appeared to be a permanent smirk to the set of her mouth. "I'm sure when he gets back to Pegasus he'll start some sort of research study or something."

I almost winced, because that's exactly what I'd been planning to do.

"We can hold him for ransom, Jenny," another of my captors said. "I mean, why not?"

"That's not why we did this, Karl," the Jenny said. "We didn't do it to get rich."

"I'll take care of it," Derrick said. "You guys can leave. You don't need to be involved."

"Karl's right," I said. "You can ask for as much as you want. Pegasus will pay it."

I was sure Numera would pay, but I wasn't so sure my kidnappers would let me walk. I'd seen their faces, heard their names. But I had to buy time to let Burke find me.

John had been standing off to one side as they debated my fate. Now he stepped in front of the others, his voice firm. "We could do a lot of good with the money," he said. "We could use Pegasus's own money to bring them down."

The argument sounded strangely compelling, as if it made all the sense in the world. For the first time, I saw how John had become the leader of this group—at least until the psycho Derrick had turned them.

"That's a fantasy," Derrick said. "I joined this group because you were willing to do the down and dirty stuff. There is no way we'll get the money and not get caught."

"I'll make sure no one comes after you," I said.

"Get going, guys," Derrick said. He dropped the rubber scythe to the floor and reached under his robe, bringing out a gun. Martin's face drained of blood, and the others, except the girl, looked away uncomfortably.

"Killing me won't stop Pegasus," I said. My voice was strangely calm. But it wasn't because I wasn't scared to death. "I don't run the place."

"But it will make a hell of a statement," Jenny said.

Derrick fiddled with the gun, checking the safety, holding it awkwardly. But he was so close to me that there was no way he was going to miss. He started to raise the barrel.

John slammed into him from the back. They came flying toward me. Derrick's back arched, almost bent in half, and he slid off to one side. John couldn't stop his forward momentum and his head cracked against the basement wall and flopped to the floor.

Derrick moaned and tried to get up, and then fell back. "He broke my fucking back!"

Jenny went over and knelt down by him, but instead of helping or comforting him, she grabbed the gun and turned toward me. The strange little gleam I'd seen her eyes was now in full bloom; hate and anger contorted her face.

The boom was so loud that I closed my eyes, certain the sound was the bullet entering my brain.

But then there was silence, and the thought came, *I'm alive.*

I opened my eyes but all I could see was swirling white smoke. My dream came back to me; my head exploded, my contents swirling through the air. Out of the mist came Burke's face. He was still dressed as Popeye, and as he whirled about the room with a three-by-four in his hands, knocking down the Thentics one by one, I heard John Philip Sousa music in my head, as if in a cartoon. Before the smoke cleared, all six

Thentics were on the floor, unmoving. I hoped Burke hadn't done any permanent damage to them.

Then he was before me, looking concerned. He cut the ropes binding me, and lifted me to my feet. "Are you all right?"

"I'm a little frazzled, mostly from your damn smoke bomb."

"It was either that or shooting them," he said.

The smoke was clearing and I saw the heaps on the floor. All six of my captors were unconscious. Burke searched their pockets, finding a knife and another small gun and pocketing them.

"How did you find me?" I asked.

Burke hesitated, then glanced up sideways. "There's a tracker in your belt."

"Who gave you...?" I stopped, because I knew Numera was the only one who could have ordered such a thing. We were going to need to have a talk.

"I'll call the authorities," Burke said.

"No," I said. "Let them go."

"We can't do that, Que. They gassed the hotel. People could have died."

"But no one did, I assume? No, we don't have time to deal with it right now. We have to get to Louisville before the deadline. The cops will won't let us leave. If I know the Blue Queen, she'll penalize us if we're late."

"If we let these Thentics go, they might do this again...or worse."

"I didn't say ignore them. Find out who they are and watch them." I walked over to Derrick and kicked him a little. "Especially this one. They might even lead us to others who are a danger. But for now, I'd prefer for this not to be in the news."

"You're the boss," Burke said, with a tone that belied his words. Numera was going to hear about this, I was sure.

We made it back to the hotel by noon.

It was in lockdown, but then it pretty much had been since we arrived. By some miracle, word of my disappearance and middle-of-the-night gassing hadn't escaped the hotel's confines. I knew it was only a matter of time before someone leaked—especially the hotel staff—and ordered my people to pack up. We needed to get out of town before the authorities could question us.

Besides, we were late by several hours. It was tight, but we had a private jet and Numera expedited our arrival, and we made it to Castle Amber just in time.

CHAPTER TWENTY-FOUR

There was a way Pegasus Corp could have been even bigger. Once Hyper-reality became a social bonanza, businesses popped up everywhere catering to the phenomenon. Costume shops, software companies creating sleeves for cars and houses, companies making VR contact lenses and glasses, and on and on.

We could have very easily vertically integrated these businesses, but Joseph vetoed the idea. "Stick to the Hyper-reality cons and the science R&D," he said. "Let others have a piece of the pie."

Of course, once the technology became more or less open-sourced, Hyper-reality only got bigger. Once again, Joseph proved to be an accidental genius. Accidental...except it was happening so often that I began to wonder if it wasn't a kind of genius after all.

Diary of Roger Ackroyd

The Louisville Fantasy Fest—usually known as the Queen's Jubilee—was held in a smaller urban area than was normal for one of the major conventions. Ever since our beginnings, Pegasus Corp had been the event sponsor; in fact, it was the first time our name was ever attached to a Hyper-reality convention, as well as the only convention we sponsored without actually owning.

But despite our sponsorship, the festivities belonged to the Blue Queen. She was the founder and organizer of the Jubilee, but even more importantly, she was the inspiration and the spirit of it. From the very start of Hyper-reality's takeoff, every other convention took her lead. She was inclusive and yet somehow managed never let it become a Peasant's Revolt (when lesser characters were so numerous they took over).

The panels, games, and contests were structured, but not overly so. Spontaneous things tended to happen at the Queen's Jubilee that happened nowhere else. Because of that, people came from all over the world to this rural Kentucky horse ranch, where huge tents were erected and for three days of the year, it was the center of the pop culture world, rivaling Comic-Con International in San Diego and Burning Man.

Maureen O'Rourke's ranch was thirty miles outside of Louisville and the country road to it was one long line of cars, but Numera had a helicopter waiting for us at the small airport. We flew over the twenty-mile parking lot that was the road leading in.

I say it was a ranch, but in reality, Maureen owned an entire valley, bordered on one side by the Ohio River and on the other by a long straight ridge that in Oregon would barely be a foothill but in Kentucky was called Olive Mountain.

Castle Amber was a large Victorian building at the far end of the valley, nestled between the bluffs, built by Maureen's great-grandfather. Closer to the road was a wide meadow upon which were erected the giant tents, including the biggest of all, the Eiger, (or Ogre, if you didn't want to use the German). It was the largest tent ever made. Around it were other tents, huge enclosures that only looked small next to the Eiger. Maureen had purchased most of them from circuses as animal rights groups and the impossibility of competing with modern entertainment had driven them out of business.

Ironically, one of the hallmarks of the Jubilee was all the small circuses that had popped up to replace them, possessed of humans with remarkable skills instead of animals.

In the distance, near the river, was something new; a huge building, as big as any stadium. It looked, from the chewed-up ground around it, that it had only recently been finished.

I hoped that Maureen wasn't planning to move the Jubilee indoors. Half the charm of the event was the tents.

Glenn and Stephen had their faces pressed to the glass, their tongues almost hanging out of the copter, they were so excited. I felt a pang of guilt. Of course, they'd never had the kind of money it took to come to the Jubilee.

We were all dressed in civilian clothing, all of us ready for a change. Especially me. I didn't mind being anonymous, but a Cyberman was a little too anonymous. We would find new guises at the Merlin tent.

At the last minute, I had told Glenn to pack the Spartan suit. He gave me an odd look but didn't question it. I still had Jordan Shipman's card in my pocket. I thought I might be able to do a little reconnoitering.

Maureen hadn't attended a Jubilee in several years, but it hadn't affected the Jubilee's popularity. The last time I'd attended, there had been five tents around the Eiger, but from the helicopter I now counted over a dozen. Even so, the crowds were overflowing everywhere I looked.

Word was that the Blue Queen was going to make an appearance at this year's Jubilee, and that had attracted the largest attendance in history.

There were all kinds of rumors as to why the Blue Queen had quit coming, anywhere from that she was a crazy drug addict to that she had ALS. I turned to Numera. I hadn't tried to talk to her the entire copter ride because of the noise, but now I realized it might not be much easier to get a private word on the ground.

"Do we know why the Blue Queen quit coming?" I asked.

Numera shook her head. "We're not sure. As far as we can tell, she just doesn't like getting old."

I nodded, remembering the first time I'd met Maureen.

I'd been amazed when Mom had presented me with a Red Pass for the Queen's Jubilee. At that time, it was an independent convention. Every Red Pass I'd ever gotten until then had been for Pegasus Cons. Tickets were notoriously difficult to get—there were long waiting lists.

The ticket landed me in Louisville, and I managed to hitchhike out to the Eiger.

The Blue Queen made her grand appearance the first night of the show with her entourage. Everything about her was a shade of blue except her flaming red hair floating above the crowd. She had blue fairy wings and a sapphire crown that rose toward the ceiling like a minaret. She rode a hoverbike and threw gold coins into the crowd of players. She was an original, all right, her name synonymous with wealth.

And a very unhappy woman, as it turned out.

I'd thought that glimpse of her was the only chance I'd have to see her. But after spending the day at the Eiger, I wandered off to my modest tent half a mile away. I tried sleeping, wanting to get in a full day on the morrow, but there was a party tent next to mine and the shouts and laughs kept waking me up.

I dressed and wandered in just as most of the crowd was leaving.

An attractive woman sat at the center of the long bar, downing one gin and tonic after another. I thought I saw a little smudge of paint on her face I sat down a few stools away.

"Done with your costume for the day?" I asked.

She nodded morosely into her drink, then looked over at me. Her eyes brightened. They were an extraordinary bright green and a shiver went down my spine. We started talking about the costumes we'd seen, giving them grades, and found that we agreed quite a bit. Three drinks later, I realized she was at least a decade older than me, maybe more, but two drinks more and I found her irresistible.

I realized, to my surprise, that she was trying to pick me up, which was a nice change. I took her to my tent, and we made love. She was nice, and more experienced than me. Afterward, we turned the lights back on, lay back, and talked.

"I heard Pegasus Corp is trying to buy the Louisville Fantasy Fest," she said.

I tried not to act alarmed. I propped myself up on one elbow and stared down into her face. She had crow's feet around her eyes and a little pinch at her lips, but she looked beautiful in the after-lovemaking glow.

"Well, they could do worse," I said after considering it.

"Faint praise," she muttered.

"No, I mean I think Pegasus would do a good job, though I'd hate to see the Blue Queen leave. I love the way she puts on

this show. None of that money-grubbing petty stuff you usually see. But if it has to happen, then I'd rather she sell out to
Pegasus. I think they're good people."

"You think so, do you?" the woman said. "I had my people
look into them, and nobody seems to know where they came
from."

My people? Who was this woman and what was she doing
with someone like me?

I drew back, sat on the edge of the bed with my back to her,
and started putting on my pants. The alcohol was wearing off,
and so was her makeup. I saw now that she was older than I'd
thought.

I felt her soft arms go around me, two mounds press against
my back, and a kiss to the back of my neck. "What did you say
your name was?" she asked.

"Zach Spence," I said. "From Oregon." I continued to get
dressed. "Uh...what's yours?"

She laughed. "How gentlemanly of you to ask. Call me
Maur...Marsha."

I looked over my shoulder and suddenly, I knew. This was
Maureen O'Rourke, without the makeup or red wig, the revealing blue costume, or hoverbike. Without her entourage.

Back then she was mostly known as an heiress, for her
multiple husbands and boyfriends, and for her interest in role-
playing, which at that time was relatively unusual.

No one knew then that she was a brilliant businesswoman
in her own right, and that selling part ownership of her Queen's
Jubilee for Pegasus stock would make her even richer.

She picked me out of the crowd the following year, called
me out by name, "Zach, from Oregon!" and made me part
of her entourage, made me feel important, but she didn't try
to seduce me again. She'd been an attractive, slightly chubby
forty-five-year-old when I'd first met her. A couple years later,
her face looked lopsided and didn't seem to move when she
smiled at me. Rumors flew that she'd had a botched facelift.
You couldn't tell when she was in full Blue Queen regalia, but
I never again saw her out of costume.

I'm always a little embarrassed, late at night when I count

my sins, about how I reacted to her that second time. I hadn't covered my shock at her suddenly aged appearance.

The helicopter landed behind the Eiger in a fenced-off area. I recognized celebrities I'd only seen on screen, big and small. I'm not sure I'd ever realized there was a VIP section for the Jubilee—or for any convention. But now that I thought about it, there was always the sound of helicopters in the distance, and the rich and famous had always seemed to miraculously appear among the hoi polloi, without running the gauntlet of the crowded entrance.

It seemed completely unfair. And here I was, the biggest VIP of all, apparently. I saw Hall Canfield look my way as I exited the helicopter, and I'll be damned if he didn't look star-struck.

I waved at him and the other VIPs as Numera took my arm and led me toward the cluster of yurts that were reserved for those few allowed to stay overnight in permanent lodgings. We each got our own yurt; they were arranged in a circle. After we were settled in, we headed for the Merlin tent. Between the VIP section and the back of Merlin's, there was a covered walkway to keep us from being seen by mere mortals.

"Everyone should be treated equally," I said to Numera as we walked along. "I don't like this at all."

"People don't want celebrities to be just like them, no matter what they say," Numera said. "And the stars bring more than enough business to deserve to be treated this way. Not to mention, it's safer."

Every year, it seemed, a major celebrity somewhere was shot or wounded by a stalker.

"It's your decision of course," she added.

I knew she was right, but it didn't make me feel any better. I'd always disliked players who could buy anything they wanted instead of having to work for it. And here I was on the way to buying any costume I wanted. It seemed to me that real creativity happened when there were limitations, budgetary or otherwise. To me, it wasn't a mistake the first *Star Wars* had been so much better than the later ones. Lucas had been brilliant with making the most of a little.

Anyway, I felt guilty by the time we reached the private dressing room of Merlin's. I suppose that's why I chose a Sam Gamgee costume, a salt-of-the-earth halfling. I didn't go as far as the hairy feet, and I had to wear a digimask again to pull it off, but it made me feel good to be no one special again.

I heard Glenn say, "Put that back. It's way too much."

Stephen was holding a Spectral costume against himself, all red and black silk and gems and gold. The precious stones looked real. I knew that Spectral was his favorite game.

"Buy anything you want, I can afford it," I said to my entourage. Instead of making me feel like a big man, it kind of embarrassed me.

"Not only can you afford it," Numera said, "you actually own Merlin's now."

"What!" I exclaimed.

She looked surprised at my shock. "Well, you did say you'd like to have your own costume company, and why not the best? I knew Merlin wanted to retire so I made him an offer."

"I hope you didn't try to talk him down in price," I muttered.

"Both parties came away happy," she said, smiling slightly. "Besides, the way this Jubilee is shaping up, you'll probably earn back half the purchase price in a few days."

I shook my head. I'd known that money made money. I don't know that I'd ever quite understood how much.

Numera chose a Xenalon costume, which holo-enhanced her already long arms and legs and made her seem eight feet tall. Glenn went with a Pirates of the Caribbean #7 Martinez get-up, with steampunk overlay. Elvis did—well, Elvis, the 1968 TV special version; black leather pants and coat. Agate dressed as a sixties bopper, with a beehive hairdo. Burke went full gangster, with an overcoat, fedora, and Tommy gun. Stephen looked fantastic in his Spectral guise.

I was the lump of coal in the stocking, exactly the way I wanted it. With any luck, nobody was going to give my Gamgee guise a second glance.

Each of us was given a gold visitor's badge, which entitled us to free entry into any event, bypassing the lines. So much for being nondescript.

"If any of you cut in line, you're fired," I pronounced.

"Great," Numera said. "We'll be spending half our time waiting."

"So be it," I said firmly.

We followed Glenn and Stephen out of Merlin's, but quickly lost them in the crowd. Elvis and Agate split off and headed toward the Sixties tent. Numera and Burke stayed by my side.

"Opening ceremonies begin in about half an hour in the Eiger," Numera said.

We made our way to the main entrance and got in line. It was clear that there was no way we were going to get inside before the half hour was up. Numera kept looking down at me from her holographic height but didn't say anything.

Finally, Burke cursed and took my elbow. "To hell with this. Come on, boss."

I let him lead me past the line. I tried to avoid seeing the resentful looks we got from those waiting, but was thankful when we entered the VIP entrance and had clear sailing. The ropes led past the milling crowd to the front. It was artfully done. I'd never even suspected that such workarounds even existed.

We were just in time for the Jester Parade. Jesters, jokers, and harlequins of every size and shape and color twirled past. Checkered costumes were the most common, followed by the red and white of Harley Quinn. There were wickedly smiling Tricksters and Fools, both Wise and otherwise.

Confetti drenched us, and horns, kazoos, and drums saturated the air, the visual swirl was almost too much to absorb.

All in preparation for the entrance of the Blue Queen.

She came in astride a white horse, nay; a *winged* and *horned* horse. The crowd erupted in a deafening roar of approval.

"Nice signal," Numera said. "Both a pegasus and a unicorn."

The first time I'd seen this procession, the Blue Queen had worn a blue sequined dress, something that anyone could have purchased from a prom shop.

Over the years, both horse and rider had become more and more resplendent, until in the last incarnation I'd witnessed, she'd come out on a white stallion, naked as Lady Godiva (though the naughty parts were artfully obscured), her skin painted blue, sapphires glued to her cheeks and forehead.

Maureen was dressed in blue again this time, her costume so ornate and extravagant that it was hard to see the human beneath. She was slenderer than I remembered; her cheeks were high and prominent, her green eyes seemed to flash like lasers as she deigned to look out over the crowd. She raised a gloved hand and waved languorously, as if this was something she did every day.

She rode by, and at one point looked right at me. She showed no sign of recognizing me, but then I remembered I was wearing a Sam Gamgee digimask. Nevertheless, looking into those green eyes was a shock.

The crowd cheered her all the way across the huge enclosure, until the Blue Queen disappeared out the other side.

As the noise leveled diminished, I turned to Numera.

"That wasn't her," I said.

"What do you mean? How can you tell?"

"I don't know how," I said. "I just know it."

We met at noon at Milliways, the Restaurant at the End of the Universe. We hadn't arranged it in advance; it was as if we were psychically connected. Glenn and Stephen had spent the morning in the VR tent, and there were already exhausted but raring for another go. Elvis and Agate had danced the morning away to Little Richard and James Brown. Elvis had come in third in an Elvis lookalike contest, which he proclaimed was his highest ambition.

I was quiet, subdued, and I could tell the others were worried about me.

It wasn't myself I was concerned about, but Maureen O'Rourke. Something was wrong. There was no way she would have sent out a doppelganger in her place unless she was nearly on her deathbed. As far as I knew she had no husband or children. I wondered if Jordan Shipman was already aware of whatever the issue was and had already tracked down her relatives. Were we behind again?

As we sat there, a giant approached, with red beard and

hair down to his chest, piercing green eyes, and a giant axe over his shoulder. He was a Frazetta hero come to life.

"The Blue Queen grants you an audience at nine tomorrow at the Castle Amber," the giant said, bowing deeply to me. He started to walk away, then slapped his forehead as if he'd forgotten something. He turned and said, "Bring ten friends you trust."

"What does that mean?" Agate said as he stomped away. "Why do you need ten friends?"

"The contest, is my guess," Elvis said. "Enough to form a team. Unicorn is probably getting the same message."

"We need four more 'friends,'" Numera said.

Burke nodded. "I have some good people with me."

"No," I said. "We need PCs."

Numera raised her eyebrows questioningly.

"Player characters. We need people who know how to play."

"I saw Duley in line at the movie tent," Glenn said. "He'd be a good one to have with us."

Duley had been an integral part of the Buellers before he'd moved away from Bend a few years ago.

"Merlin is wandering around in gray robes thinking he's undercover," Stephen said. "He used to be big in Hyper-reality circles before he turned his hobby into a business."

Agate stood up and walked away abruptly. It was such an unexpected move that everyone's eyes followed her. She approached a man and a woman in the lunch line and pulled them over to our table. They were dressed in black suits, narrow ties, and pointy shoes, and both had black hair with the same short haircut.

"This is Amelia and Oliver," she said. "I met them last year in San Diego."

They both bowed slightly and one of them said with a British accent, "Reggie and Ronnie Kray, at your service."

"Who?" Numera asked.

"British gangsters from the Swinging Sixties," Glenn supplied.

I stood up and shook their hands. They seemed reluctant. I was a stranger, after all. "We need your help," I said. "We have to assemble a team of ten players, and we're short."

"Sorry, mate," Reggie Kray said. "We are otherwise engaged for the day."

"Yes, bu: *we* have a private audience with the Blue Queen," Numera said.

"Sure you do," Ronnie laughed.

"Do you recognize me?" I said. When I had their full attention, I reached up and turned off my digimask. I stood there long enough for recognition to bloom in their faces before turning on the mask again.

"Dammit, boss," Burke growled, getting to his feet and looking around.

"No one was looking except Amelia and Oliver," I told him. Apparently no one had noticed the brief moment Que stood revealed in the middle of Milliways. Indeed, as colorful as our table was, it was one of the more subdued. A few tables away, a crew of professional acrobats was putting on a show with the establishment's dinner plates and silverware.

Burke sat back down, still looking disgruntled. He muttered, "Don't ever do that again without telling me."

I turned to the two new recruits to my entourage, who were staring at me in shock. "I'm asking you to keep this a secret. Can you do that?" I asked them.

The twins nodded, appearing to sway on their feet. Agate said gently, "You'd better sit down."

"I warn you, we don't know what we're up against," I said. "So you'll need to be ready for every possibility."

"You got it. Anything you want," the two Krays said together.

Numera stood up next to me and put her arm through mine. "Assuming we can convince Merlin and this Duley fellow to join us, we'll meet tomorrow morning at this same spot at eight o'clock. Until then…"

"Do whatever you feel like doing," I broke in.

I walked away before anyone could say anything. Numera and Burke hurriedly followed me. When we were out of earshot, I turned to them. "I want to be alone for the rest of the evening."

Numera started shaking her head and Burke opened his mouth to object.

"This isn't a request," I said sharply. "This is an order. Don't worry, I'll stay undercover, but I need to get a sense of what's happening, and I can't do that with you guys looking over my shoulder all the time."

I could see both of them struggling with the order. It was test. Was I really the boss or was I a mere figurehead, to be manipulated and controlled? I had gone through my clothing the night before and found another little tracker, which I'd flushed down the yurt's toilet.

Numera leaned down and kissed me on the cheek. "Be careful," she whispered. She turned and grabbed Burke's arm. He went with her reluctantly, looking over his shoulder as if he was going to try to protect me as long as I was in sight.

I hurried away and lost myself in the crowd.

CHAPTER TWENTY-FIVE

I have always been drawn to stories where a mortal person wanders into or is enticed into Fairyland where he dwells in bliss and happiness until one day deciding to return to home. He crosses the border to find that despite what seemed just a short time in Fairyland, years have passed in the real world and everything has changed. Everyone and everything he knows is gone. He is a stranger to his own reality.

I wonder, sometimes, if we are not all drifting into Fairyland while the real world goes on without us; whether we won't all become lost in time and space, and wake up some day wondering how we got here.

Diary of Roger Ackroyd

I wandered into the Comics tent. Comics were having one of their periodic revivals after being declared dead. As soon as Marvel had played out their string of movies, having exhausted every feasible character, and after Archie bought out DC, most comic shops went out of business. Now they were coming back, once again focusing on back issues of physical copies rather than digital. New comics—monthlies and not just graphic novels—were once again being published. Many were predicting that just as vinyl records had come back to take the majority share of music sales, so too would monthly comics.

Retro was new, and new was retro, and retro was new, and new was retro, and so on into infinity.

Near the entrance, a man was yelling into a bullhorn, and people were lined up at the tables like pigs at a trough. Across from the bullhorn were several dealers frowning at their strident competition.

I listened in on conversations. My Gamgee costume worked like a charm; no one paid much attention to me.

No one else seemed to have caught on that the Blue Queen in the parade had been an imposter. It was unlikely that many of them had ever seen the real Maureen O'Rourke. To my surprise, though, some appeared to have heard something about a hostile takeover attempt of Pegasus Corp by Unicorn Industries.

Gratifyingly, most players were on Pegasus's side.

"Did you notice that both Pegasus and Unicorn are here?" someone dressed as Kane the Mystic Swordsman said to a Xena.

"Yeah, I've never heard of that happening. Don't they hate each other?" Xena asked.

"A pox on both their houses, say I," Kane said. "They've both gotten too big. They need to be broken up."

"Won't matter much if The Copyright and Trademark Fair Use Act passes," Xena said. "Pegasus is fighting it, at least. I owned two of their shares and I sold them back, not that it will make much difference. If I have to pay every time I do Xena, well, I'll just quit."

"Screw them," Kane said. "I plan to call myself Mitar, the Magical Quarterstaff and not alter anything else and let them try to figure it out."

I heard many of the same sentiments as I walked along the rows of white comic boxes. Overall, it seemed to me that most cosplayers, if not all, were hoping Unicorn would fail in their efforts. But even though they'd be upset if the C&T passed, they'd either live with it or try to work around it. The issue wasn't life or death to most of them. There was a surprising lack of urgency to their sentiments.

I suspected they were being too sanguine. The changes would be more draconian than they suspected.

I had no doubt Unicorn would be rigorous in their enforcement. That Kane fellow, for instance, wouldn't be allowed entrance as "Mitar" without changing his look significantly. In fact, for the first time it occurred to me that the final arbiter would be whoever put on the events. The problem was, characters who were original but of a type could easily be lumped together. And, of course, most if not all types were represented by a licensed character. That was probably true of just about every cosplayer and LARPer out there.

Archetypes were universal and common; that's why they worked.

At best, there was going to be a huge disruption to the industry. At worst, the whole thing could collapse.

I made my way back to my yurt late in the afternoon, not sure whether to be encouraged or discouraged. None of the others had gotten back yet. It wasn't even time for dinner.

I'd asked Glenn to leave the door to his and Stephen's yurt unlocked. I made my way in, found the Spartan costume, and put it on. I carried the Gamgee gear back to my own yurt and locked the door.

As the Red Spartan, I reentered the arena. Throughout the day, there had been casual role-playing and demonstrations. As night approached, real games were beginning to be played. The tents were cleared of merchandise so that sets and scenarios could be constructed in their place.

The Halo players were a large enough contingent to rate their own tent. The game had never been one of my favorites, especially after Unicorn bought them out. It had been sheer luck that I'd won the contest the week before.

I could've used my gold pass to get inside, but instead I pulled out the business card that Jordan Shipman had given me and presented it.

The Blue Spartan guard at the entrance was obviously puzzled and called over a Chief, who also seemed surprised but nevertheless motioned me inside. He led me to one edge of the tent and lifted a canvas flap, which led to a hidden passage between the inner and outer sides of the enclosure.

Jordan Shipman sat behind a card table with several laptops open. He looked up in surprise, as if he'd forgotten the invitation he'd given—or was amazed I'd accepted.

"Come in, come in!" he said, getting up and extending his hand. "Sergeant Longhi, correct?"

I nodded, wondering if I'd turned on the costume's voice modulator—not that Shipman would recognize my voice anyway.

"Still ICY, huh?" Shipman said, shaking his head rue-fully. He turned to the man who'd escorted me. "Chief, is your weapon charged?"

"Yes, sir!"

"Give the sergeant a jolt, won't you?"

I didn't have even have time to voice an objection before an electric shock ran through my body. My body's signals were scrambled, my legs and arms contracted as if confused and I felt myself falling, twitching.

By the time I quit squirming, Shipman had removed my helmet and was looking down at me curiously.

"After you left last week, I kicked myself for not finding out who you were," he said. "It took some tracking down, but even-tually I realized that I'd had Que himself in my grasp. Can you imagine?"

"My name is Zach," I managed to spit out. "Que is some guy who doesn't exist."

"Of that, I have no doubt. I thought I was up against a mas-termind, and yet here you are. Help him up, Chief."

The guard still had the stun gun in hand, but I doubted from how easily I was lifted to my feet that he'd need the weapon to subdue me.

Shipman sat down behind his makeshift desk and looked up at me. "You're considerably seedier looking than I expected."

I became conscious of my shaggy hair and three-day growth of beard. It wasn't unusual for me. Shipman, in contrast, looked as if every hair of his beard had been plucked by hand and every single hair on his head had been individually groomed.

"Killing me won't help," I said. "My shares are out of your reach. Pegasus Corp will continue without me."

"Kill you?" He seemed genuinely surprised. "Mr. Spence, I am a tough businessman, ruthless even. I asked Chief to stun you because I wanted your complete attention. But I don't *kill* people."

I stood there wondering if he was lying or if my brain was still scrambled. I'd been so sure…

"I didn't murder Pretty, Pretty, if that's what you've been thinking," he said. "I admit, I tracked down her heirs, just in case. She had a history of drug abuse, after all. But I liked Debra. I never would have hurt her."

"Then how...?" I started to ask.

"I don't know what happened, frankly," he broke in. "Debra seemed all right the last time I talked to her. I'd already written her off, since she seemed firmly on your side. Perhaps it really was an accident."

Somehow that made it worse. If she'd been murdered, I could focus my anger on that. It gave me an enemy to defeat.

"I don't need to murder people to win," Shipman continued. "I know that people are greedy. They want the most money they can make from their shares. I have the money to spend. My sources tell me you're cash poor, that you don't have the hundreds of millions you need to outbid me."

"Then why are we talking?"

"I admit that I underestimated your hold on the big investors. I figured they'd be strangers to you."

"Maureen doesn't care about your money," I said. "You'll have to beat me by playing the game."

He nodded, his certainty seeming to crack a little. "I don't suppose you have any idea what she's planning?"

I didn't answer. Let him wonder if I knew more than I actually knew.

"Very well," Shipman said, standing up. "I just wanted to get your measure. I can see now that my real adversary all along was Roger Ackroyd, and he appears to be in hiding."

He looked toward me as if expecting me to provide an answer, then shrugged.

"I'll see you in the morning," Shipman said. "Just so you know, I've assembled the best team of players in the country. Your ragtag group doesn't have a chance against us."

I turned away without answering. This meeting had been a huge mistake. It was as if I'd been called to the principal's office, as if a real adult had given me a dressing down. I'd never felt like a "suit," like someone who lived in the real, workaday world.

The guard led me back to the tent's exit. Somehow I made it back to my yurt, hardly aware of my surroundings, walking through huge crowds of colorful players, who were all having the time of their lives.

It was still early in the evening. My friends were still out. I shed the Spartan costume, walked back my own yurt, and fell into the bed.

I'd like to think I slept that night, in between my tossing and turning, in those moments when my brain switched off before lighting up again as if zapped by a stun gun.

Vaguely, I heard my friends returning, one by one. I heard Agate and Numera whispering outside my door, debating whether to knock. Thankfully, they went away.

I'm a trillionaire by accident, came a stray thought late in the night. The line of numbers representing my wealth seemed to illuminate behind my eyelids, but instead of comforting me, I felt like a fraud.

The world of Hyper-reality depended on me, and I had no idea what I was doing.

God help us all, whatever reality we live in.

The thing was, if I were to believe Shipman didn't murder Pretty, Pretty, then...who did?

Who was Mr. Zander and where did Roger's doppelganger come from? I wished Coyote could make one of its appearances, but then, it probably would have answered my questions so cryptically that I would be worse off than before.

If Unicorn Industries wasn't the enemy, who was?

CHAPTER TWENTY-SIX

There is something I have feared from the beginning but have not spoken about for fear that someone will be inspired by the idea.

The only real difference between Hyper-reality and reality is consequence.

While the mind and body of a player may be convinced that what is happening is real—more than real—the truth is, when the game is over, they are safe no matter what happened in the game.

But—and here's the part that frightens me—it doesn't have to be that way. There is no reason a game scenario couldn't have real consequences. No reason an injury can't be a real injury. No reason a murder can't be a real murder. No reason that when someone falls, they really fall; when someone is shot, the bullet strikes flesh.

It may happen in an imaginary setting, inflicted by imaginary opponents, but the consequence could be the same as if it was a real setting and a real opponent.

All it takes is the will to do it. So far, I'm not aware of anyone purposely setting out to add consequence to Hyper-reality, but I fear it is only a matter of time.

Diary of Roger Ackroyd

The floor of the yurt seemed to jump beneath me.
I tumbled out of bed, wondering if we'd been hit by lighting.

A cannon fuselage rumbled, followed by the roar of a thousand creatures. From a distance came an answering challenge, the voices of men and women raised in defiance. I pulled the

curtains back from one of the small windows and saw that a
major battle was taking place just outside the circle of huts. The
charging army was composed of creatures, large and small, real
and imagined. There were unicorns and horses, monitor lizards
and dinosaurs, wargs and wolves, lions and griffins, wyverns
and eagles, and just about every mythical creature mankind
had ever come up with.

Facing them was a line of humans dressed in every imaginable costume, re-enactors of every battle in history; barbar-
ians and dandies, natives and bwanas, cowboys and Indians,
Crusaders and Cathars, fighting that most primeval of fights
between man and beast. I got my clothes on in time to watch
the battle.

The creatures and humans collided and melded, a clash
of armor and swords, fangs and claws. The melee dissolved
into chaos, and then, as suddenly as it had started, it became
friendly, and both sides were slapping each other on the backs,
with hands or wings or whatever appendage applied.

"Good morning to you, too," I muttered, not quite in the
spirit yet.

Someone pounding on the yurt's door only added to my
headache. I threw open the door and walked away without even
looking to see who it was, started the coffee maker, and looked
inside the small refrigerator for the quick pick-me-up of a cola.

"We've been dressed for hours," Glenn said, his voice merci-
lessly hearty. "You've got twenty minutes before they come to
pick us up."

"What about breakfast?" I groaned.

"We've all eaten at Milliways," Stephen said. "That's where
we met the Blue Queen's giant, who is a nice fellow once you get
past all that hair. Guy named Chip, from Oakland. Numera said
to let you sleep in."

I grabbed a couple of energy bars from on top of the fridge
and gulped down the coffee. Despite everything, I'd slept some,
and I was starting to revive. Excitement percolated around the
edges as I wondered what Maureen had in store for us.

The others, in costume, were gathered outside the circle of
yurts. Duley was there, dressed as Greedo. He tried to shake

my hand, but I gave him a hug. I'd always liked the guy when he was with the Buellers. Merlin was in full wizard regalia, with a gray cloak, conical hat, heavy gray beard, and a gnarled staff.

A sensation of gratitude overwhelmed me. With friends, I could deal with anything that came my way.

"Thank you for helping, everyone," I said, unable to keep a quaver from my voice.

Numera gave me a slightly concerned glance but I was able to smile back at her.

A long van pulled up, driven by a now human-sized, red-haired Chip, who'd turned off his giant holo projection. We piled in. The road—driveway?—went right down the middle of the valley, pulling up to the cleft where the river and cliffs met. A large Victorian mansion stood alone, surrounded by an over-grown lawn, hedges that hadn't been trimmed in a long time, and trees that hadn't be pruned in years.

The mansion was a Painted Lady Victorian design, bright red, with white trim, crosshatched across the tops of the win-dows and porch. A long ramp had been constructed to the side of the steps, which hadn't been there the last time I visited. Maureen had always been meticulous in her landscaping, her house had always busy, with people coming and going. Now, the place looked deserted.

Chip stepped out of the van, grew to twice his size, and rumbled, "The Blue Queen awaits you in the Grand Ballroom."

The front door opened with a creak. Voices echoed down the hallway. I recognized Jordan Shipman's low register. The ballroom was directly to the right of the front entrance, taking up most of that side of the first floor. The flooring looked like it hadn't been polished for a long time. Footprints were visible in the dust.

There were huge crystal chandeliers overhead, but the light-ing came from a desk lamp at the far end of the vast room. There were figures moving about, occluding the light.

"There you are!"

I recognized Maureen's voice through the amplification. It sounded as if the voice was being dragged along the floor, lifted up, and tossed at us. It didn't sound healthy.

The Blue Queen sat in a chair in the midst of the Unicorn crew, who turned and watched our approach. Shipman was dressed in a Horatio Hornblower-looking costume, and his men were dressed as shipmates of lower rank.

It was only as I drew near that I realized that Maureen was in a wheelchair. She looked tiny, shriveled, despite a heavy layer of makeup designed to make it appear as if she still had color in her face. Her cheeks were sunken, and no amount of caked-on foundation could hide the heavy bags under her eyes. She seemed to have aged decades since I saw her last—so the rumors of illness were clearly true.

Her dress was resplendent, however, in shifting layers of blue, hologram-enhanced.

This time, I was able to keep my shock at her condition from my expression as I bowed to her.

"We were ready to give the prize to Unicorn," she said, using the royal *We*. Her voice was overly loud, and she winced. She reached down with sparrow hands and adjusted the volume. "You were supposed to be here at nine o'clock."

I said, "My pardon, Your Majesty. I did not sleep well."

She laughed mirthlessly. "*We* haven't slept well in years, but *We* still keep *Our* appointments on time." She cocked her head at me, her dark eyes eating me up. "You don't appear to have aged a day, Zach."

"No, ma'am. But I have."

"But still playing the boy," she mused. "Well, over the next few days, you will rise to your potential or you will fall. We will be most amused by either outcome."

"I am eager for the challenge, ma'am."

"Very well, shall we get started?" Her wheelchair lurched forward, and I stepped aside as she zipped by. She was halfway across the ballroom before any of us reacted. Both crews hurried to catch up, each keeping a discreet distance from the other at first, and then, as we walked along, blending together, each curious about the other. I saw Agate say something to one of Shipman's lieutenants.

Chip the Giant opened the door for his queen and she bounced across the threshold, then rolled down the long ramp.

There was a newly asphalt path that led toward the river, then turned south along the banks toward the huge building we'd spotted from the helicopter. Maureen got far ahead of us, her little motorized chair appearing to have some real horsepower.

I found myself walking beside Shipman. "You glean anything from her while you were waiting for us to show up?" I asked.

"Not a damn thing, except what's obvious," he said. "She's dying. She's got one last chance to be the Blue Queen and she's going to make the most of it."

I looked sideways at my adversary. He was a head shorter than me, and maybe a couple of decades older. I'd disliked this man from afar for years, but now that I was in close proximity, I saw that he was merely human, and not all bad, apparently—if it was to be believed that he had nothing to do with Debra's death. Buying out shares of Pegasus in secret was ruthless, but not beyond the bounds of business propriety.

If anything, we—no, I—had been negligent and he'd simply taken advantage of it.

The building seemed even bigger as we got near. The far end was almost out of sight, slightly curved and hugging the banks of the river. It appeared to be several stories high, but it was hard to tell because the surface was seamless, without so much as a single window. There were two huge doors on one end, with a human-sized door in the middle of one of them. It was a box without ornamentation or flourish, mysterious and brooding.

The smaller door stood open. Chip stood beside it and motioned for us to enter.

The two crews gathered into their own groups again. I invited Shipman to enter first, and he returned the motion, then smiled and went ahead of me.

Our footsteps echoed as if we'd entered a vast cavern. Light simmered in the distance, as if off the surface of water. We walked toward it, entering what appeared to be a small grotto illuminated by moonlight, complete with a realistic full moon overhead. There was a splash in the pool as something had just submerged, and I thought I saw a tail fin slap the water.

Maureen had turned on a hologram, because she was now standing under the boughs of a weeping willow tree, looking neither as plump as the first time I met her nor as emaciated as she'd been only minutes before. Her body had the perfection of fantasy, of illusion.

Her blue costume deepened to a royal blue and then softened to the color of water in the sunlight, and all the colors in between those two shades. Her bright red hair was long and straight. She smiled at us indulgently.

"Thank you all for coming. Welcome to Castle Elsinore. This is a state-of-the-art facility, which, starting next year, will house the Queen's Jubilee. We have incorporated everything that a Hyper-reality practitioner could want, as well as the ability to add upgrades as they are invented. Here we have control of all the mighty elements; earth, water, air, and fire. It is the New Coliseum."

"Hail, Caesar Vespasian!" Duley said in a voice he probably thought only we could hear.

Maureen turned to him and smiled. "We are fine with the Blue Queen, Mr. Duley."

"Yes, ma'am," Duley muttered.

"We have decided that rather than choose one of you over the other, you will compete for our favor," she continued. "This will be the beta test for this facility. Therefore, we have designed five contests: trials, if you will. Each will have a different setting and scenario, so your ingenuity and skill will be challenged to the utmost. Each of these contests will be worth one-fifth of our royal shares. Obviously, whichever of you wins three out of five will gain the majority share of our wealth.

"I ask only that you play the game fairly. I will be watching."

"Your Majesty," Shipman spoke up. "I believe that my opponent has an unfair advantage. You told me to bring nine companions, for a total of ten. By my count, Pegasus has eleven members."

She smiled at him. "As you may have noticed, my health is not what it should be. Therefore, I have brought in a referee, a judge, who will move among you to make sure that the game is played by the rules."

I exchanged a glance with Numera. We both turned to Merlin, who seemed the most likely among us to be a ringer. He gave a massive shrug, looking equally mystified.

Elvis turned and whispered something in Agate's ear. She let out a small cry as he stepped away and walked to the Blue Queen's side. As he moved, his Elvis persona fell away, to be replaced by the hologram of a jester, with a green-and-red-checked doublet and pants, shoes with curled toes, and a three-tailed hat, each tail ending in a golden bell.

He laughed at our expressions and did a little dance, as if completely delighted with himself. He doffed his tingling hat and bowed. "Tom le Fol at your service. Forgive me my nonsense, as I also forgive the nonsense of those who think they talk sense." He cleared his throat. "So sayeth Robert Frost."

I suppose he expected us to laugh, but I felt a cold chill go down my spine instead.

"Your Majesty," I said, my voice perhaps a little shrill. "If I may have a word with you in private."

Shipman immediately objected. "I believe I have the right to hear anything Mr. Spence has to say."

"You have a *right*?" Maureen said. Her eyes glittered with anger.

Shipman realized his mistake and bowed low. "If I may also have a word, your Majesty. In all humility."

"Very well, you may both approach." She sat back down on her chair and shriveled before our eyes as she turned off the hologram. She whirred the wheelchair around the tree and Shipman and I approached, side by side.

Elvis—Tom le Fol—sidled up next to us.

I motioned toward the jester. "Ma'am? In private, please?"

"Tom is privy to all our secrets," Maureen said.

"This concerns him, ma'am."

"The Fool is also the subject of my concerns," Shipman added.

She frowned but motioned Tom away. He scowled, then he smiled maniacally and scampered off, singing "Suspicious Minds" in an Elvis voice.

"Your Majesty," Shipman said, before I could gather my

thoughts. "This gentleman—your court jester—has been in the company of my opponents for days now. He has even begun a relationship with one of the Pegasus corporate officers. How can I be sure that he will not play favorites?"

"You have our promise, sir," the Blue Queen said archly. "We will be the final judge in all matters."

It was clear that Shipman wasn't going to get more reassurance than that, and he wisely backed down.

Both of them regarded me curiously.

I cleared my throat, trying to figure out a diplomatic way to broach the subject. "Your Majesty, I too have a concerns about why he was traveling with us. If I may ask, what was his purpose?"

"Tom was given one mission," she said. "He was to make sure that neither camp triumphed before coming to the Castle Amber."

"Are you aware that Debra Cromartie was about to sell her shares to us and that if she had, Pegasus would have won before we got here?" I asked.

She stared at me as what I was implying sank in. "Tom has been with me for many years. I trust him completely in all things. He told me that Pretty, Pretty's death was an accident, and I have no reason not to believe him."

She'd dropped the royal *We*. Obviously, she was rattled.

"Then why was he working in the doctor's office?" I asked.

"He told me it was to give him access to Ms. Cromartie. He said that he was sure that he had already convinced her to sell to Unicorn."

I looked toward Shipman. He'd know more than anyone that what Tom had told the Maureen wasn't true. But Shipman stayed silent, refusing to look at me.

"Enough," the Blue Queen said. "What you say has nothing to do with the present contest. I will, of course, watch every moment to be sure it is fair." She smiled. "As will the world."

I was ready to continue to argue, with or without Shipman's help, but her last words caught me off guard. *The world?*

"I have purchased media time to show everything that happens here," she said. "When word gets out what is at stake, I expect the audience to be huge. It will be my last event, and it will be the biggest in history."

She straightened up in her wheelchair. "The world will judge whether we have been impartial.

"Now, gentlemen, let the games begin!"

CHAPTER TWENTY-SEVEN

As the world becomes more crowded with every passing year, it becomes more and more difficult to have an "authentic" experience in nature. Either it is so expensive that most people can't afford it, or you are placed on a long waiting list, and if you are ever called, it means you will be shuttled to your destination and pretty much told what to do.

But VR is so good now that there is little difference between roaming the real world or Hyper-reality. You can now safely visit forests and mountains and deserts, without hordes of other people, and without rules and regulations except whatever the game requires. In most ways, this a better experience than the real thing.

Such adventures can be isolating if you don't experience them with other people, but I maintain that those who are isolated are still better off with Hyper-reality than they would be without it. Some of the relationships developed in Hyper-reality are stronger than those in real life.

Though I often wonder what the consequences of that intimacy-at-a-distance will be.

Diary of Roger Ackroyd

"I haven't played Dungeons and Dragons in ages," Glenn said when we were shown to a room with fantasy garb.

"Whatever it turns out to be," I said, "it won't be D&D."

It didn't surprise me that the first contest was to take place in a fantasy realm. Probably the oldest and still the most popular version of roleplaying, fantasy was also the Blue Queen's favorite, along with...

"Steampunk," I said. "There will undoubtedly be a strong

component of a future everyone thought would happen but never came to be."

"In that case..." Stephen said, picking up a blunderbuss whose design was half medieval and half space opera.

Glenn grabbed a pair of swords and a hooded cloak. "I'll be the assassin/thief. Always need one of those."

Merlin was already dressed as a wizard, but traded his staff for one that was powered up for the game.

I decided to go as a ranger, dressed in green and brown, carrying a crossbow. I also snagged a bandolier full of short darts and a small dart gun.

Agate quickly grabbed a bard's outfit. "Never mind that I can't sing," she said. "But I can bash them over the head with my lute."

Numera looked completely overwhelmed by the colorful array of costumes and weapons. I picked out a samurai outfit that looked like it would fit: red and black plates, a flared helmet. It might be anachronistic for most fantasy scenarios, but the costume was in stock and it seemed somehow appropriate for her.

Duley also donned a ranger outfit, with a longbow and a sword. He looked up at Burke, who stood unmoving in the middle of the dressing room. "You going to be a barbarian, big fella?"

"No," Burke said. He walked to the back of the room where there was a strange-looking harness filled with every size and shape of blade—all of them made from stone. He slung the harness over his shoulder, and the attached digimask instantly transformed him into a large troll.

Duley rolled his eyes. "I should have known."

The British twins, Amelia and Oliver, with their slender frames, donned costumes that made them look like elves, with shortswords and small bows slung over their shoulders.

We waited by the door, waiting for the game to begin.

"I'm going to give you contradictory advice," I said. "Most of the time, the Blue Queen likes a bit of deviousness and underhandedness. So when confronted with a choice, being chaotic evil is probably the right way to go. But underneath it all,

Maureen has a strong moral streak, so when you least expect it, lawful good will be the right choice. All I can say is, you'll know it when you see it...or not."

"Remember," Agate said, probably for Numera's sake, "whatever you see, it isn't real. No one really dies; there are no dragons or whatever. The treasure is an illusion. But you must to pretend with all your heart that everything is really happening. That's the only way we'll win."

The door opened and we entered a fantasy world like something on the cover of a book, with blue skies and mountains in the distance, and a large river running down the middle of a lush green valley. In the distance, something rose from the mountain and approached us. I made out two wings and a spiked tail and then a puff of smoke from the snout of the dragon.

There was a loud boom, and that whole fantasy world vanished. Instead of blue skies above us, there were huge iron struts, weaving in a complex latticework; instead of a valley, there was a concrete floor. It was a vast room, the largest enclosed space I'd ever seen, but without the holographic images, it was barren and lifeless.

A second, even louder boom shook Castle Elsinore. Above us, the roof cracked like an eggshell. The iron latticework groaned and then snapped, and a huge slab of the roof broke away and tumbled down toward us.

I turned toward the door but the wall behind us was featureless. I could see no exit. There was no time to get out of the way. The slab of concrete grew larger, and then there was deafening boom, the floor leaped up, and I flew through the air, filled with dust and screams.

I landed on something soft. I put my hands down and slipped on the blood and viscera beneath me. Glenn stared up at me with unseeing eyes, an iron rod skewering his heart.

I turned to see the legs of another two of our party jutting out from under what appeared to be a solid chunk of concrete. From the leggings, I figured it was the pair of elves.

The air thrummed for a moment, as if a giant bumblebee was inches from my ears. I looked up to see a flying contraption enter through the hole in the roof. It was a drone, but one designed by Jules Verne, with art deco curlicues and append-ages, and a bug-like countenance with multiple eyes glowing golden in the haze.

Two arms unfolded from the intricate maze of its body. An arrow shot toward me, too fast for me to react.

A samurai blade came down on the projectile, just inches from my chest. The arrow fell in two pieces to the floor.

"Is this what you expected?" Numera asked. "I thought this was supposed to be fantasy."

Then she jumped upward toward the steampunk drone. Unexpectedly, something in her suit gave her lift, as if she was in one of those old fly-and-wire Japanese movies. With one of her armored legs pointing down and one arm pointing upward, she looked like a manga panel of a warrior charging. She cried a wordless cry that was translated into something Japanese. Underneath the amplified words, I heard her own voice shout-ing, "Fight fair, you piece of junk!"

She swung her blade, and the two extended arms fell off and clattered to the concrete below.

As she reached the apex of her jump, there was a whirring sound and two tentacles uncurled from the body of the machine. One of them wrapped around her sword arm and swung her violently. Numera flew above me, striking the wall behind me and falling to the floor with a clatter. She didn't move again.

I fired my crossbow, and the bolt punctured one of the waving tentacles to no perceivable effect. I dropped the bow and reached for my dart gun, though what a mere dart could do to such a machine, I had no idea. I backed up and reached Numera's body. She still wasn't moving.

With a roar of anger, I charged the machine, firing darts as I went, which bounced harmlessly off the creature's iron body. A tentacle tripped me, and I slid across the floor. When I tried to stand up, one of my arms and both of my legs were frozen, though I felt no pain. There had been spikes in those tentacles, laced with venom, apparently. I crawled away from the battle, trying desperately to think of a way to help the others.

The drone appeared alive, made of metal but with a

malevolent consciousness inside behind those bug eyes. Merlin stood beneath the creature with his arms spread, the gem on the end of his staff glowing a bright red. But none of his spells seemed to be having the slightest effect on the machine. It hovered over him, and sharp-clawed legs dropped down.

"To hell with it!" Merlin said, and swung the staff with all his might at the threatening appendages. The legs bent sideways, but the drone continued to come down, flattening the wizard's conical hat and slamming onto his head. He stood upright for a moment longer, then fell flat on his face.

The drone reached the floor. It was much bigger than I originally thought, the size of a VW bug. More appendages unfurled, until it resembled a real bug, with three legs on either side of its body and two tentacles on its head.

It skittered toward Agate and Stephen, who stood waiting back to back. Agate let out a shout and rushed the monster. As she had joked about doing, she slammed her lute down on the antennae, bending them in half. The bug slapped out at her with a foreleg, and she went sliding across the floor.

Stephen stepped forward with his blunderbuss. The gun was so loud that everyone, included the drone machine, froze for a moment.

Half of its golden eyes shattered and smoke curled upward, but the creature was as mobile as ever. As Stephen tried to draw his sword, the monster clattered forward and the sharp end of a tentacle skewered him. The bug raised him up and examined him, then turned the sharp tentacle upside down and let the lifeless body slide off.

Stephen plopped to the floor next to me, unmoving. And then…a small shimmer and a fractional glitch in the VR let me see my friend's living face beneath the illusion. I heard him say, "Shit. Am I dead?"

Relief flooded through me. From the moment the ceiling had collapsed, I'd thought the battle real, that it was some kind of runaway technology that had escaped another scenario. But now I realized that this was the Blue Queen's planned surprise, her steampunk twist to a fantasy scenario.

I tried rising again, and for some reason, one of my legs was released from its paralysis, though my left arm still hung useless. I sensed someone beside me and turned to see Duley.

"Good of you to join us," I said.

He grinned and raised a long piece of rebar iron, with a sharpened end. "I didn't figure my longbow was going to do much good against that beast, so I was looking for something a little more substantial."

The drone was only a few feet away, its head whizzing from side to side, as if trying to gauge where the greatest danger was coming from. Then all six of its legs skittered along the concrete as it charged.

Duley stepped in front of me, the iron rebar thrust forward. The creature impaled itself on the shaft but kept coming, trampling the human beneath it.

Then it turned on me. All I had left was a sword, which felt pitifully inadequate to the task. All I could do was my best. I'd have to hope that the Unicorn team had also been defeated, and hopefully faster.

Out of the corner of my eye, I saw something massive fly through the air.

The troll was a light greenish color with brown smudges. In both massive hands were clubs, fashioned from the debris of the roof, which it slammed down on the monster's head. For the first time, the machine made a noise, a screeching sound as if the moving parts of its body were grinding to a stop.

Burke the troll slammed down on the creature again and again, and parts started to drop off: legs, tentacles, antennae. Finally, the remaining legs collapsed, splayed outward, and it landed on its belly with a clatter and moved no more.

The scene shimmered, and suddenly we were back in the original fantasy world, the broken machine seeming completely out of place. The hole in the ceiling—the sky—above was gone. One by one, the others stood, released from the game paralysis. We stood over the monster.

"We won," Agate said. "Not bad for fighting a technological creature with swords and clubs."

"Did we win?" Numera said. "So many of us died."

"But we defeated the creature," Agate said. "That's the goal."

I thought we'd been lucky, that it could easily have gone the other way. I hoped he Unicorn team had at least as much trouble as we did.

Out of the waters of the river popped the head of a giant, followed by several smaller heads of elves and dwarves and humans, ten in all. They were riding on the back of a machine that was a duplicate of the one we'd destroyed.

But this drone looked undamaged and completely in under the control of the mage who rode at the front.

Jordan Shipman raised his hand and gave us a triumphant grin. It was clear that he hadn't lost any of his people, and not only had he defeated the drone, he'd turned it to his side.

And I knew we had lost the first contest.

CHAPTER TWENTY-EIGHT

Hyper-reality can feel so real that lots of strange ideas have come up to explain it—ideas not rooted in the underlying science or the tricks that the mind plays, but in the supernatural, the unprovable.

Even the most rational minds can be seduced by metaphysical ideas that make a certain amount of sense but that can never be proved.

I was surprised when Joseph came to me with a request.

He wanted me to look into the possibility that what Hyper-reality was doing was replicating what existed in an alternative reality. That all scenarios actually existed somewhere.

I'd heard the idea before and thought it nonsense. I tried to talk him out of it, but he insisted.

When I began to look into it, it turned out that reputable scientists believed that infinite parallel universes were not only possible, but logical. So I set out to find out if anyone was doing experiments that shed some light on the subject.

Most were crackpots, but I did find that a few promising, if very preliminary and exploratory scenarios were being suggested. Of course, the science community wasn't willing to fund these wild ideas, but I had my instructions.

Diary of Roger Ackroyd

That night, I watched the whole battle again. For better or worse, the media replayed it again and again on almost all available channels. Overnight, the contest had become the most watched event in years.

As we exited the Castle Elsinore, a roar went up. We blinked into the setting sun, trying to make sense of the enormous crowd waiting for us. It was as if every attendee of the Queen's Jubilee had walked down the valley to greet us.

Both crews were greeted by their own cadre of fans. Team Pegasus, I noticed, seemed to have attracted the Thud and Blunder crowd, those who entered games to blast everything in sight, eager to see their enemies lie before them, headless and eviscerated.

Meanwhile, a more sophisticated and brainy crowd, the kind of players who, instead of bludgeoning their opponents, preferred to defeat them through cleverness, was cheering Team Unicorn.

The Blue Queen had hired a crew of bodyguards, as if she'd known the impact the contest would have on the public. These Men in Black pushed the crowd away as we hurried toward the waiting van. Crowds lined the road all the way back to our yurts, which were now surrounded by makeshift fences and multiple sentries.

Back in our quarters, we turned on the hologram projections to watch ourselves.

It was undeniably bloody and exciting. It appeared as though we were doomed, and I could see how simply surviving might seem like a triumph to some people.

Then we watched our competition.

Unlike the Pegasus team, which had blundered out onto the floor, unheeding, our mouths open in amazement, the Unicorn team immediately split up, keeping close to the walls, vigilant from the start. When the roof came crashing down, there was no one beneath it.

By the time the drone emerged, the Unicorn crew had gone into hiding behind the wreckage. The giant among them stood and shouted and started running in huge loping strides down the empty building. The monster took the bait and followed.

The others emerged and gathered together, and though we could not hear their words, it was clear that they were planning their attack.

They split into three groups. The dwarves started erecting defenses, the elves scrounged for weapons in the debris, and Jordan Shipman and another magic-user bent their heads toward each other and had a vigorous discussion.

It was several minutes before the giant reappeared in the distance. As it lumbered back to the point of entry, the creature skittered after it, slowly gaining. As the giant reached the debris field, he tripped, and slid, sprawling, across the floor.

The machine bug crawled up to the giant and started to cover him. It raised two sharp pincers.

A piece of concrete *thudded* off the creature's head, bending one of the antennae, followed by three other projectiles, all of them hitting their target. The drone hesitated, as if confused, and the giant scampered to his feet and bounded away. The four dwarves were yelling their defiance from behind their hastily erected barricades.

The creature turned and charged. The dwarves disappeared into the rubble, scampering in and out of the concrete blocks, and again the drone seemed confused. It darted forward, and there was a shout.

One of bug's tentacles rose into the air, grasping a dwarf around the middle. It seemed to eye its captive, as if contemplating eating it.

At that moment, the three elves appeared at the top of the debris pile, swinging something overhead.

In the short time the giant and then the dwarves had bought them, the elves had constructed a crude net out of the insulation material of the roof. It landed on top of the drone's head like a blanket full of holes. The creature reached up, but couldn't quite reach the crude netting.

Instead, its arms were trapped as well, until it couldn't move forward or backward.

The giant reappeared and climbed onto the back of the drone, weighing it down. It stopped moving. There was a loud whirring sound, and smoke emanated from its head.

The creature bucked, almost throwing off the giant.

The two humans, Jordan in his mage garb and the other dressed as a wizard, had so far stood back from the struggle. Now they climbed onto the machine's back. The wizard pointed at something, and Jordan reached down and pulled off a panel at back of the eyes. The wizard crouched down.

For another few minutes, nothing happened.

No wonder half the crowd had greeted us as conquering heroes. We'd fought the creature to the death—the death of the creature, sure, but also all but two of our party. But at least it had been exciting!

The wizard finally straightened up and nodded to Jordan, who took a seat behind the two bent antennae. The elves removed the netting, and the creature moved forward docilely. It bent down and let the others climb onto its back.

The fantasy background reappeared. Jordan guided the creature to the river and into the water.

Moments later, the cameras showed the two groups merging; one stunned, the other triumphant.

There was no disguising the look on my face. The camera did a close-up of me as I realized that we'd been outsmarted and outplayed.

Mercifully, the camera then cut off.

What no one saw was Maureen whirring in her wheelchair out of the shadows. "How exciting!" she cried. "I enjoyed both contests, and I have to admit I'm almost tempted to give the win to the Pegasus crew because of all the exciting action they gave us. But I don't believe that cleverness should be ignored either. But most important of all, if role-playing is to have any meaning, the Unicorn people didn't lose a single member of their crew."

Tom le Fol capered out between us. "Winning a losing battle...or is it losing a winning battle?"

Maureen wheeled her wheelchair around to me. "Who do you think won, Que?"

I didn't answer, which was answer enough.

"That doesn't seem fair," Numera complained later that night. "They reprogrammed the machine? At least we played the game the way the rules were presented."

"With the Blue Queen, there are no rules," Agate answered for me. "She judges outside the box—in this case, it's a very big box."

A new tent had been assembled just outside our circle of

yurts, with a private entrance. Tom le Fol led us there, doing a hop every ten steps or so and saying, "Walk this way."

We followed him, but no nobody walked *that* way.

"You will get your meals here," Tom said. "Costumes will be laid out each morning for the next game. May the best fool win!" He whooped enthusiastically and left.

Agate's eyes followed him. "Damn, I sure got fooled all right. I am officially embarrassed."

"Wouldn't be the first fool you've dated," Numera said.

"True. But Elvis—Tom—is the first to actually dress like one. I wonder what he's really like under all that bullshit."

There was a buffet to one side of the tent, and some picnic tables. Nothing fancy, but the food was filling—hot dogs and chili, and hamburgers and potato salad, that kind of thing.

"Do you know any of the people Jordan has on his side?" I asked after we sat down, my paper plate bending dangerously.

Agate looked at me curiously. "Have you ever been to any of the Euro events?"

"To be honest, I could barely afford domestic events."

"That's explains why you don't recognize Gordon Agnew— he was the giant; Perce Simmons, the head dwarf; and Nave Hampson, the head elf; and most of all, Peter Cera, the most accomplished mage in the European circuit. They're all British. Cera's memorized every player's handbook from every game ever made, not to mention—as you saw—being one of the best programmers in the world in his day job."

"His day job being with Unicorn, right?" Glenn said.

Agate frowned. "Not until recently, as far as I know. All these guys are freelancers—that's how they got so good. People who work in other people's games never seem to reach the elite status. Any of their names are enough to guarantee a good turnout at a convention."

"Anyone recognize any of the others?" I asked.

"I think I saw some of them in London," Duley said.

"London?" Stephen sputtered. "You went to England?"

"My mom paid for a trip to Windsor Castle. I snuck away for the London Con. Those guys were stars over there."

Oliver spoke up. "A couple of them are Germans," he said.

"I think the others are from Russia and the Netherlands."

Until that moment, I'd held out some hope for our chances. But if there is one country that takes its Hyper-reality seriously, it's Germany; and if there is one country that takes it even more seriously, it's Russia. And the Dutch? They were at a whole 'nother level.

"Great," Numera said. "So it's Eurotrash pros against the amateurs, the Green Bay Packers against our high school team."

"Hey," Glenn objected. "We've got Que!"

I shook my head. "I'm amateur number one."

Agate slapped her hand on the table. "We love what we're doing. They're doing it for the money. I wouldn't discount our chances."

"But they are players, not creators, right?" Numera asked.

"Same skill set," I said, "though creators tend to spend their time creating instead of playing. I'm guessing that the Blue Queen created these scenarios."

"With the help of Elvis—Tom le Fol," Agate said. "He told me one night about creating a steampunk creature to invade Middle Earth."

"What else has he told you?" I said. It would have been good to know that fact before the first contest. But then again, we hadn't known that Elvis was anything but a friend we'd picked up along the way.

"He's into Cthulhu, but who isn't? Oh, and he likes mountain climbing. Talking about that was the one time I really saw him enthusiastic about something other than Elvis. It seemed to me that he wasn't really that interested in Hyper-reality, except when it came to Elvis. But obviously, he's good at pretending, so who knows?"

"Anything else?" I prompted.

"He talked about an obscure SF film, something about zombie robots."

"*Robots Amok*," Stephen said. "I heard about it, but it's hard to track down. It was taken out of circulation years ago. Legal entanglements. I managed to see it at a friend's house though.

"It's just what you'd think. Robots that looked a lot like actors in aluminum foil cardboard boxes that stumble around and say, "Blood, blood, blood," in a mechanical voice. The one cool thing was a sucker-looking thing that popped out of their foreheads ard sucked the brains out of their victims. They must have blown fifty percent of their budget on that one effect."

"All right...Cthulhu, robots, zombies, brain-suckers, and mountain climbing. So how does that help us?" I asked.

No one said anything.

"Well, forewarned is forearmed," I said. It sounded lame.

At the end of the table, one of the twins, Amelia, raised her hand. Like many role-players, she was painfully shy outside her costume. Oliver put his hand on his sister's shoulder. "We have done mountain climbing in the Alps. There are perhaps some tricks we can show you. Rappelling, belaying, that sort of thing," she said.

"What are the odds?" Glenn scoffed. "I've never seen or heard of mountain climbing role-players. Mountain climbers tend to, you know, climb mountains."

Amelia said in a soft voice, "That is true, but..."

"What?" Glenn said, putting his hand to his ear.

"That is true!" Amelia repeated more loudly, glaring at him. "But as it happens, many climbers *are* doing a form of role-playing. They are going back to the roots of the sport, refusing to use modern equipment, using only those tools they can fashion with their own hands, dressing like the old-time mountaineers you see in the black and white photos in the visitor's centers at the base of the mountains."

"Maybe we should learn a few techniques," I ventured.

"Actually, it's not a bad idea," Agate said. "When I say Elvis was into the sport, I mean I could barely shut him up about it. Should've known he was a damned fool..."

I was certain that we'd stumbled onto something important. It was just the sort of thing that the Blue Queen would do. Something no one expected. "We'll need to get some rope," I said. "Preferably without telling anyone."

"Can't have tents without ropes," Burke said, standing up. "I'll be right back."

"Meanwhile," I said, turning to Glenn. "Tell us the plot of *Robots Amok.*"

CHAPTER TWENTY-NINE

Once Joseph had the idea of somehow connecting with the infinite worlds that he believed were being revealed by our imaginations, I started looking for scientific papers that even hinted at such a thing. Of course, most said the many worlds theory was speculative, impossible to prove, and even if true, the other worlds would be outside our universe in such a way that two realities could never meet.

I did find one obscure paper by a researcher at a B-level university who proposed something called quantum gates. His theory was that all the universes were indeed connected on some plane, that they affect each other, and that dreams and imagination are signs of that connection.

What's more, he proposed that there was a way to make this connection physical. I didn't understand the physics of it, of course, and when I checked with the top physicists in the field, they all pooh-poohed the possibility, going so far as to call it pseudoscience. I met with the young author of the paper nevertheless, a Thomas Marston, and was impressed by his sincerity, and I offered to fund his research.

I didn't expect anything to come of it. But I often find that Joseph's ideas pan out.

Diary of Roger Ackroyd

Tom le Fol waited for us in the outfitting/mess tent. Spread out over the picnic tables were thigh-high boots, tricorne hats, brocaded coats and breeches. Leaning against the walls were cutlasses and spadroons, rapiers and boarding axes, blunderbusses and musketoons.

Tom bowed and spread his arms. "Ships are but boards, sailors but men; there be land-rats and water-rats, water-thieves and land-thieves." He laughed. "I mean pirates, and then there is the peril of waters, winds, and rocks."

"Shakespeare?" Agate asked.

Tom laughed and doffed his hat, the bells tingling, then scampered out of the tent.

"Pirates?" Stephen said. "Really?"

"Don't be so certain," I said. "Yesterday we thought we were playing in a standard fantasy and look how *that* turned out."

"Everyone grab a blunderbuss," Glenn said. "Where are the cannons? And didn't pirates have grenades of some kind?"

"Let's not just start blasting away at anything that moves this time," I said. "Let's try for something a little more...elegant."

Stephen and Glenn both stopped what they were doing and stared at me.

Burke said, "Hard to be elegant when you're dead." I had a feeling he spoke for everyone.

"Yeah, well, let's put a little thought into it anyway."

My bones ached and my head was fuzzy. The night before, after Glenn had related the ridiculous plot of *Robots Amok*, Burke returned with two long coils of rope on either shoulder. He plopped them down, and the twins came over to examine them.

"A little heavy for climbing," Amelia said, "but we should be able to train with them. We won't be able to actually rappel inside this tent, but we can show you how it works. Also, what you do when you belay up a cliff. Perhaps a few other basic techniques."

So we'd gone over the procedures again and again until we had the basics down. I wasn't sure I'd actually have the guts to trust the techniques on a real cliff, but I thought I understood the basic principles.

I'd half expected to find snow axes and crampons waiting for us this morning. I was a little disappointed to find pirate gear; then again, it would give us another night to practice climbing techniques.

I grabbed a long coat, a red sash to hold up my breeches,

boots and a woolen cap. I slid a rapier into the sash and turned to the others. Numera had on thigh-high boots and a long red coat, and wore a scarf over her hair. She also had a short, curved sword. Agate had chosen a loose blouse and brocaded vest, and her hair was in a ponytail. The twins wore striped trousers and matching blue coats with gold buttons down both sides. Duley wore a simple woolen shirt and a bandolier loaded with flintlock pistols. Glenn and Stephen had gone full *Pirates of the Caribbean*, with brown and red coats, wide belts, and enormous tricornes. Burke wore giant boots that folded over in half and a short coat, and was bareheaded. He had somehow found a broadsword more suited for Camelot. Merlin...looked like Merlin.

"Arrr," I rasped. "Yer a scurvy-looking crew."

Duley moaned. "Could we not do that? I never could pull that off. I always have to hide out on Talk Like a Pirate Day."

"Aye, matey," I said. "Yeah, we can drop that bit of business. Everyone ready?"

We left the tent, expecting to see a crowd waiting for us.

During the night, the Blue Queen's crew had constructed a covered walkway from the tent to Castle Elsinore. Apparently, there wasn't going to be a repeat of last night's mob scene. Still, it was impossible to forget that worldwide, tens of millions, perhaps hundreds of millions, of people were watching us.

I felt ill-prepared; an amateur indeed. I'd always loved Hyper-reality, enough to invest most of my spare time in it. But ironically, I'd never been a fanatic about it. Even in my small town, there had been dozens of people more practiced than I, including Glenn and Stephen.

We stood before the entrance to Elsinore, waiting for ten o'clock.

"Keep your eyes open," I said when the doors swung open.

The sound of waves greeted us, along with a whiff of ocean spray and a bright sun. I immediately looked for a ship, but there was none to be seen. That was a bit of a relief. I got seasick just looking at waves from solid ground.

We were on a small island. There were no buildings, nothing but sand and grasses, and a small rocky hill at one end. As we looked around, Jordan Shipman and his people appeared on the other side of the island, seemingly out of thin air. They were formed in what I figured was a defensive configuration.

Jordan looked like a proper captain, wearing a red tricorne hat and a black coat, while his men wore the woolen caps and the doublets of common seafarers. They were obviously more organized than we were.

Well, that just meant they were following orders, and sometimes there wasn't time for orders. Despite what had happened the previous day, I wanted my people to be independent.

As I thought this, I noticed that Duley had already wandered off on his own. He approached a depression in the middle of the island, equidistant from both parties. He looked down at something and rushed back.

"I think this is Oak Island," he said excitedly.

"Oak Island?" Numera asked.

"An island off Nova Scotia, supposedly where Captain Kidd—or Blackbeard—or whoever—buried a treasure. People have been digging here for three hundred years...supposedly."

"And have they found anything?" Agate said.

"Lots of dirt and frustration...and also death. Follow my lead," Duley said.

"You've got it," I said.

"They're going to get there first," Glenn said, sounded agitated.

"Let them," Duley said. "But make them think we're pissed off about it."

The Unicorn crew advanced on the hole in the ground, three men to each side scouting ahead, the four leaders holding back in the middle. We were still yards away, pretending to hurry, when they got there first and surrounded the pit, weapons bared.

I held my hand up as one of their sailors raised a muskatoon and took aim. From where I stood, I could see a crude ladder leading down into the darkness.

Shipman came around and pushed the man's gun down. "I'm sure there is no need to fight, is there, Que? We'll check it out first, then let you have a chance. Fair enough?"

Since I doubted that the contest would be so easy and obvious, and because Duley had said to let it happen, I nodded.

A breeze came in off the beach and it contained a hint of
cold air. To the west, the sun was dropping below the horizon,
and the ocean looked black and threatening. Apparently, time
was different here, and this role-play was going to be more
extended than the last one.

Good. It would give us time to get our bearings.

"We need to get to the other side of the island," Duley said
in a low voice.

"We need shelter from the wind," I shouted to my people,
loudly enough, I hoped, that the Unicorn people would over-
hear. I pointed to the hill on the other side of the pit.

We trudged down to the beach, giving the shaft a wide
leeway, and circled to the side of the hill away from the pre-
vailing wind. There we crouched in a circle as we watched the
Unicorn crew talk over strategy and prepare to descend.

"What's going on, Duley?" I said.

"The legend is that there once was a large stone over that
patch of land with inscrutable symbols scratched on it," he
said. "Someone supposedly deciphered the puzzle. It said,
'Ten feet down lies two million dollars.' Two million dollars,
by the way, that would be worth five hundred million today."

No one said anything, but waited for Duley to continue.

"Ten feet down, they found a layer of flagstones, and under
that, a timber platform. They dug it up, but there was nothing
there."

"Big surprise," Glenn said.

"So they dug another ten feet down and found another
layer of logs. And so on, all the way to China, probably.
People have found scraps of this and that, nothing definitive,
so there are all kinds of rumors about what is buried there—
Shakespeare's lost plays, Marie Antoinette's jewelry, that kind
of thing."

"So it's an episode of *In Search Of...*" Stephen said. "But in
this reality, there probably really is a treasure...somewhere."

"Why did you tell us to keep away from the pit?" I asked.

"It's a deathtrap," he said grimly. "At least six people have died from falls, poison gas, and collapsing sides. But the biggest problem is flooding."

"We should warn them," I said.

"No one is really going to get hurt," Agate said. "It's part of the game, Zach."

Something didn't feel right about it. Most of the role-playing I'd done had been cooperative. The fun was in the doing of it, not the winning. But Pegasus Corp was at risk and I needed to restrain my usual impulses.

"There's a cave under that hill," Duley said. "They supposedly found a cofferdam there, but it was later decided it was the remains of a salt works plant. I'll bet you anything that's where the treasure is."

"Well," I said, "unless we want to fight Shipman and his people, I think that's where we have to look. We'll wait until it's dark and see if we can't find the entrance. Look around and see if there is anything we can use for torches."

There were a few scraggly bushes at the base of the hill. We wrapped dried grasses around some of the branches, using threads from my long coat. Fortunately, Numera had assembled a little emergency kit with matches in it, which she'd smuggled in. Technically, it wasn't allowed, but I didn't think anyone could see us in the dark. I guess we'd have to pretend we started a fire by some other means.

As if reading my mind, Glenn and Stephen cut a groove into a branch and started vigorously rubbing the end of a small stick against it, taking turns. To my great surprise, they got a small fire going using dried grass as tinder. They were yelping and hollering, and I heard a whirring sound and looked up and saw a camera drone hovering overhead. I noticed Numera palming the matches and putting them in her pocket.

We heard answering shouts from the pit. The Unicorn team had also gotten a fire going. I felt an unreasoning resentment, certain that they had cheated. Never mind that I'd been prepared to do the same thing only minutes before.

In the flickering light of the bonfire, we could see them preparing to descend.

As soon as they appeared preoccupied with their own

mission, I nodded to the others. "Let's go."

We lit only one of the torches at first. I wasn't sure it was going to work. I thought it likely it would burn up in a few minutes, if not seconds, but to my surprise, the light was steady. As long as whoever held the torch kept it away from their bodies and the falling embers, it worked great.

Each of us had several torches and I was suddenly certain that the entire gameplay had been designed this way, which was a reassuring thought. It probably meant we were on the right track.

As we circled the hill, there were shouts of alarm from the shaft. "It's flooding! Get out!" someone cried.

I winced, but kept walking.

There was a small cove on the windward side of the hill, and at the end of the beach, the round mouth of a cave. We entered the deeper darkness. Without the moonlight, we could see only a few feet ahead of us.

The cave opened up before us and became dry, the ground beneath us rock instead of sand. We started climbing in a spiral, and it seemed to me that we should have reached the top of the hill by then, but this was a holographic realm, and there was no reason the inside of the cave couldn't appear larger than the outside, if that's the way the designers wanted it.

On and on we climbed, until we entered a vast cavern. As if in response, our torches flared, and we could see huge columns of glittering stalactites and stalagmites. At the center of the cavern were huge wooden chests, overflowing with gems and pieces of eight, and gold and silver goblets and plates. It appeared to be the entire contents of a Spanish treasure ship.

The others stood back and looked at me. They were expecting me to step forward and take possession of the treasure. I approached in awe. I knew it wasn't real, but that was the thing about Hyper-reality; it always felt real when done right. I knelt before a large charger, lifted it up, and saw my awestruck face reflected in the shimmering light.

I suppose I expected the lights to go on, the treasure to disappear, and the bare insides of Castle Elsinore to reappear.

But the game wasn't over.

"Watch out," I said, turning to the others.

Beyond the flickering light, shadows moved and took form. Men in resplendent red coats, their ghostly eyes shining and their blades flashing, stepped toward us.

CHAPTER THIRTY

I'll admit that when Joseph first came up with the term "Hyper-reality," I treated is as more of a marketing term than anything else. A way to counteract the Thentics. A bit of Orwellian doublethink: War Is Peace, Freedom Is Slavery, Ignorance Is Strength.

But the more it was used, the more it seemed apt. After all, if a player is in a life-or-death struggle in his game, is that not more real to the mind and body than the daily grind of the workaday life? If the dream is more vivid than the reality, then is it not indeed "Hyper-reality?"

It think that's why the term took hold and eventually supplanted the terms "re-enactment, LARP, cosplay, creative anachronism," and all the other name for such forms of play.

Diary of Roger Ackroyd

A line of ten men appeared to step out of the rocky walls of the cave, each wearing red uniforms with white trim, each carrying a musket with a bayonet attached. Behind them, another ten men emerged, stepping smartly, and then a third line followed. Finally, a giant of a man emerged. He wore a coat so red it seemed to burn. Instead of a tricorne like the rest of the men, a white powered wig covered his head. He held a saber in his hand, which he raised.

"Make ready!" the officer shouted. His voice filled the space as if amplified. The torches no longer accounted for the increased light in the cavern. A glow filled the air though there was no apparent source. Above us, I knew, cameras were recording everything that happened.

I had started motioning my crew back toward the tunnel

even before all three rows of soldiers completely emerged.

Numera grabbed my arm. "What do we do?"

"Retreat." I said. "There are too many to fight."

"What about the treasure?" Agate asked.

"Dead men spend no gold," I said. "We'll come back when we're more prepared."

"The danger isn't real," Numera said, confused.

"That's not how the game is played," I said. We'd lost the previous contest even though we'd defeated the monster because of the cost in lives, real or not. Maybe I was a little too concerned about that. "We act as if it's all real, otherwise it is meaningless."

The front row of soldiers dropped to their knees.

"Present arms!" the officer shouted.

"Screw this," Agate said, running toward the treasure. She reached out for a necklace draped over the top of one of the chests. It was a string of deep blue stones, each as big as a piece of eight. The gems flashed in the firelight, twirling in her hands as she ran back to us.

"Fire!"

Most of us had reached the tunnel, but as the others hurried around a slight bend, I held back waiting for Agate. Bullets shattered the rocks around my head and shoulders. I closed my eyes and felt shrapnel pierce my check and nip at my ears, but miraculously, none seemed to hit my eyes.

It didn't hurt, of course, because it wasn't real. The digimask and costume were registering the hits. If it had been real gunfire, no doubt the roar would have permanently deafened us; instead it struck our eardrums as a muffled shock wave.

Agate screamed as if she had really been shot in the back. She flew toward me, her arms outstretched, extending the necklace as if presenting an offering. She hit the cave floor and lay there, unmoving.

I ran to her side as the second row of soldiers dropped to their knees, allowing the third column to step forward and take aim.

To my eyes, Agate was streaming blood from her back. But beneath the illusion, I clearly heard her voice.

"Take the damn necklace, Zach. Don't let me die in vain."

I hooked my finger around the gold chain and turned to run. I reached the bend in the tunnel as the second volley slammed into the rocks behind me.

We emerged onto the beach in broad daylight. I looked down at the necklace. It felt real; it had heft, and the stones contained a hypnotic depth of color, almost velvety.

"Where's Agate?" Numera said.

"Shot in the back," I answered. "She's out of the game."

"Those are Kashmir sapphires," Amelia said. "And real, unless I miss my bet."

"How's that possible?" Oliver said. "Those are some of the most valuable gemstones in the world. Could all of that treasure have been genuine?"

Numera said, "Agate always did have exquisite taste."

Somehow Agate had snagged a real treasure, perhaps the only real gems in the cave. It didn't completely surprise me. I'd noticed before that subconsciously we humans could see through some of the artifice, no matter how authentic it appeared, and the opposite was true too, that we could see the reality beneath. Something had caught Agate's attention—it was probably why she'd tried the gambit in the first place.

I looked up at the sun, which was midway through the sky again. There was no way we could have spent all the night and half a day under the hill. Everything was speeded up in this realm.

There were steady shouts from over the rise. Apparently, the Unicorn team was still working on the pit, which must mean they were making progress. Was the treasure in the cave simply a red herring? Why wasn't the contest over?

We started up the hillside. It seemed wrong to leave Agate, but I knew that as soon as the rest of us were out of sight, she'd been released from her apparent demise. She was probably comfortably back in the mess tent eating a nice meal.

"I'm hungry," Glenn said, as if thinking the same thing.

"So what's the goal of this contest, if not the treasure?" Duley asked.

"Perhaps we're supposed to bring it all out?" Numera said,

stepping beside me. The others followed me up the slope.

"But there is no way to defeat a full squad of armed British ghost troops!" Stephen objected. "That seems unfair!"

We crested the hill. The Unicorn team milled about the shaft. "Ready...pull! Ready...pull!" someone shouted in rhythmically deep voice.

"Looks like they found something," Burke commented.

I handed the necklace to Numera. "Better hide this. Put it around your neck. I don't know what it represents, but I'm betting it's important. Stay here. I'll find out what they're up to."

I walked right up to the edge of the pit before one of the men blocked me. I took a quick glance down. One man was on the ladder, hauling up a makeshift bag made out of a shirt; another was at the bottom of the pit, his legs sunk into the mud. He was bent over, his hands in the muck up to his elbows. As I watched, he pulled one arm out of the sludge. Something flashed in his hands, something shiny and gold.

The guard pushed me back. I quickly counted how many men were working; there were nine team members, including Jordan Shipman who sat off to one side, looking down at something. He hadn't noticed me yet.

One of his people was missing, so it appeared we were even on that score.

They'd built a tripod over the pit, using wood from the brush that covered the hill. Men pulled on a makeshift rope draped over the top of the tripod, and as I watched, a scoop made out of what appeared to be several bent swords and a stretched-out piece of fabric appeared, laden with mud. One of the men leaned over and grabbed it and spilled the slop onto the ground. There was a large pile of mud on the downhill side of the pit, with a rivulet of water trickling down toward the beach.

It was an impressive amount of work and engineering.

The guard pushed me back again, and I almost tripped. That caught Shipman's attention and he glanced up, then frowned. Then he put on a smile and stood up, signaling the guard to bring me over to him.

"And where were you off to last night?" he said. "Find anything interesting?"

There were several stacks of gold coins on the ground behind him, looking exactly like the pieces of eight I'd seen in the cavern. It would have been impressive if I hadn't seen the much more imposing treasure.

"Found a cave," I said, knowing he'd send someone to find out. "Nothing there."

He searched my face as if suspecting I was lying. But then, he'd found treasure and it probably didn't occur to him that there might be more than one prize in the game.

"Perhaps you like to help us extract the gold?" he said. "I mean, the sooner the game is over, the sooner we can get some dinner and sleep in our comfortable beds."

Obviously, he thought he'd already won and it was only a matter of finding enough of the gold.

I shook my head ruefully, knowing he didn't expect me to accept.

"Well, maybe you'll find some nice seashells on the shore," he said, dismissing me.

I stepped away before he could see my face. He'd expect me to be crushed. Two games down; they'd only have to win one out of the three remaining games to win the whole thing. But I suspected his mud-encrusted gold coins weren't the real prize.

Now it just remained for me to figure out how to extract the pirate loot without being mowed down by the British soldiers.

My mind kept going back to the way the cavern had accentuated the torchlight, as if we'd ignited something in the game play. What if we entered in the dark? Would the soldiers even know we were there? Would they be able to hit us if they did?

They'd had no source of light of their own, except their glowing eyes, and that had been a reflection of the torches.

It seemed crazy, but Glenn was right. This contest couldn't be won by brute force, any more than Bilbo could overcome the dragon, Smaug by brute force. It would require stealth and trickery.

We gathered back at the beach. Numera used her matches to start a fire while some of the others gathered beach wood. The day was going by swiftly, as if time was passing at two or three times its normal speed. It was getting cold.

By my state of hunger and thirst, I thought that probably most of a real day had passed. One way or the other, this game was going to need to end soon. I suspected that when it was finally called, whoever had the most treasure would win.

I told the others of my plan. It was met by silence.

"We can't get lost in the tunnel," I said. "It has no offshoots. The treasure is at the center of the chamber and would be impossible to miss even in the dark."

"It would be impossible for the soldiers to miss too," Duley said.

"I don't think they'll appear unless there is light," I said. "If you don't want to come, fine. Wait here."

"Well, it's not like we are *really* in danger," Numera said.

"Only of losing," Duley said.

"We have to try," Numera insisted.

"We can't let Agate's death be in vain," Merlin said. "Look, we just rush in, grab what we can, and get out. If that isn't enough, we tried our best."

The others agreed. We waited for the fire to die down a bit, then got up and approached the cave's entrance. An atavistic fear of the dark ran down my spine. There were ghosts in this darkness—I'd seen them. Ghosts with muskets.

Which can't hurt you, my mind said but didn't believe.

The tunnels seemed to go on forever. I trailed my hand along the right-hand side at first, but the stone was rough, and finally I just tried to sense the way and that seemed to work, as if a groove had been worn into the path.

When my footsteps began to echo, I realized I'd entered the chamber. I stopped abruptly. Someone bumped into me.

"Ouch," someone else whispered loudly. "You're stepping on my feet!"

"Shush!" I hissed.

We listened, but nothing stirred. It was the most complete darkness I'd ever seen. There was nothing for my eyes to grab onto, and they darted from side to side, even as I tried to concentrate on the way forward.

I walked straight ahead until something crunched under my feet. I reached down and felt something smooth. I lifted it, and it was heavy. It felt like a large goblet. I reached around, felt the side of a chest, and reached in and grabbed a handful of trinkets, filling the goblet. I filled my pockets, and then grabbed the largest plate I could get my hands on and started filling it as well. Lots of gems and coins were falling away, rolling with a steady clatter, but the soldiers continued to stay hidden, the clatter rose.

Finally, I stood up, ready to leave.

I had no idea where to go. The cavern was large; the opening to the tunnel could be in any direction. I felt a hand on mine and instinctively knew it was Numera.

"Which way?" she whispered.

"I have no idea."

From the sudden silence, the others had stopped stuffing their shirts with treasure for a moment.

"You'll have to light a match," I said.

"Are you sure?"

"For just a moment. Everyone run as soon as you see which way to go."

I heard Numera put down whatever she was carrying. Seconds later, there was the scratch of a match against the stone floor. Light bloomed in the cavern, a saturated glow that one match shouldn't have been able to create.

And there, standing like a giant a few feet away from me was the British captain, his saber glimmering.

I raised the plate full of treasure over my head and felt the impact of the blade slam onto the silver. The plate flew out of my hands, and gems rained down on me. Around us, other swirling shapes danced in the dim light. The match had gone out, but its afterglow still filled the chamber.

I stood alone in the middle of the cavern, surrounded by soldiers with fixed bayonets. Numera was a dozen feet away, outside the circle, staring at me in alarm.

"Get out of here!" I cried.

Numera turned and ran for the tunnel, followed by the others.

I faced the soldiers, feinted in one direction, then tried to roll past them in the opposite direction and felt a sharp point between my shoulders. I flopped onto my belly, unable to move.

The cavern disappeared. My dying scream echoed down the featureless expanse of Castle Elsinore.

The Blue Queen sat watching us with a smile, with Tom le Fol behind her wheelchair, hands placed possessively on her shoulders.

"Whom do you think won, dear Tom?" she asked.

"The little piggies, digging in the dirt." Tom said. "They have the most treasure."

"I think not, Tom," she said, patting his hand. "Ms. Numera. Do you still have the necklace?"

All the other treasures had disappeared, but the necklace was still around her neck. She took it off and walked over to the Blue Queen. who inclined her head. Numera placed the necklace around her neck.

"This is my most favorite possession," she said. "The contest probably should have ended when Agate so perceptively snatched it up, but I wanted to see what would happen. I declare the winner of the second contest to be Team Pegasus!"

CHAPTER THIRTY-ONE

The arrival of artificial intelligence has never seemed so near—and yet, so far away. As A.I.s get ever closer to seeming human, the uncanny valley becomes ever more noticeable. We humans have an instinct for when something isn't quite real, and the smaller the difference, the creepier it can seem.

But for the sake of gameplay, we are willing to overlook the little discrepancies, to play along in order for the game to work. At first I thought this would refine A.I. to such an extent that eventually we'd be fooled, but so far that hasn't happened.

Diary of Roger Ackroyd

While we were gone, the TV screens had been taken from our yurts; nor was there coverage on any of our devices. Apparently, the Blue Queen had decided to keep the contest pure, without any outside influence. I had little doubt, though, that people were watching—probably the whole world.

We talked about the day's events in the mess tent, trying to figure out what we'd done right and what we'd done wrong. I had a feeling that the game hadn't quite gone the way it was supposed to.

"This role-play seems a little haphazard for the Blue Queen," I said. We were sharing a couple of bottles of wine after dinner. The ropes were coiled in the corner. I was going to try to talk my friends into another training session. I had a feeling they weren't going to be too keen on the idea.

"It was pure luck that we found the necklace," Agate said. "That can't be the way the game was supposed to go."

"Does it matter?" Duley said. "We won."

"Maybe so," I said, "but we have up to three contests yet to play and we don't know *why* we won. If it was mere luck, that isn't very useful."

"I say just play the game," Glenn said. Stephen nodded his agreement.

"Then we depend on luck?" I asked.

"No...skill," Glenn insisted.

As much as I wanted to agree, I knew it wasn't that simple. "I've been thinking about the first game. Don't you think it a little strange that the Unicorn team had exactly the configuration of skills needed to win it? They even had someone who could program the drone. What are the odds of that?"

Numera saw the ramifications right away. "You're suggesting they were given inside information?"

"But we won the second contest," Stephen objected, "while Unicorn was digging in the mud."

"It was pure luck on our part that Duley knew about the cave," I said. "Even luckier that out of all that treasure, Agate snagged the Kashmir sapphire necklace."

Burke spoke up, catching me by surprise. He sat at the end of the table, facing the door, vigilant as always. I was never completely sure if he was listening to us. "Did none of you feel the breeze in the cave? There was another way in, and if I had to guess, it was by way of the pit. I think Unicorn was supposed to win, to find a way into the cavern, take the treasure, and leave us with nothing."

We fell silent at that. It felt right. While we'd been stumbling around, Shipman's people had looked purposeful and focused.

Burke said what we were all thinking. "It's a fool's game."

"A Tom le Fol's game," Agate said, shaking her head. "I'm so sorry I ever...liked...that guy."

"Maureen O'Rourke would never rig a game this way," I said.

"Then we must inform her," Amelia said.

"We already told her that Elvis is duplicitous," I said. "You heard her, she trusts him."

Numera stood up. "Then we'll just have to defeat them

anyway. Playing so hard drains me. I'm going to bed."

The moment Numera said how tired she was a wave of exhaustion flowed through me.

Still, I almost objected. Our only possible advantage was what Agate had learned about Tom le Fol's predilections. If we confronted a setting where climbing mountains was required, it would give us an advantage if we were trained.

Mountain climbing? Such a scenario seemed so far-fetched at that moment that I gave up on the idea.

"Get a good night's sleep, everyone," I said. "We'll think about it in the morning when we're fresh."

Of course, my mind couldn't wait until morning. I tossed and turned for what seemed hours, turned on the lights and realized that only half an hour had passed. Despite—or because of—my exhaustion, I couldn't sleep.

I sat at the end of the bed, put my head in my hands, and tried to figure out what to do.

There was a gentle tapping on the door. I crossed the room quickly, glad for the company. I hoped it was Numera, but anyone's company was better than my own windmilling thoughts.

Maureen O'Rourke was so tiny, so shriveled that for several seconds I looked right over her.

She cleared her throat. "Down here, you putz."

She was standing, or rather, tottering on the step below, Her small hands reached out to me, and I quickly took them and helped her inside. I half carried her to the bed.

She looked up at me, sans makeup, uncertain and fragile. "Will you hold me, Zach?"

I gently took her in my arms. She trembled, and I thought for a moment she was weeping, but when she finally gently pulled away, her eyes were dry.

"Tom won't hug me anymore. Not that I want him to," she said.

"Is he hurting you?"

"Hurting?" For a moment, it was the Blue Queen sitting there imperiously, looking down on lesser mortals. Then she shrank again. "So far, only my feelings. But I've been expecting it. The threat of violence is always there if I don't do what he wants."

I stood up, ready to march out of there and confront Elvis or Tom or whatever his name was right then and there.

"You won't get near him," Maureen said. "I was only able to sneak out because Castle Elsinore is my design. There are secret passages he doesn't know about. Besides, Tom doesn't believe I can get anywhere without my wheelchair. He takes the infernal contraption with him after he puts me to bed, so he thinks he's safe."

"Why don't you just fire him?" I asked.

"I have to go through him to fire him. He has power of attorney, power of…everything. I'm so sorry, Zach. As soon as I learned he was in league with Unicorn, I tried to contact you. I wanted to sell it all to Pegasus, but by then he was in complete control. I was stupid. I trusted him."

"But as long as you're alive…"

Maureen interrupted me. "Exactly…as long as I'm alive."

I fell silent at that. If Tom had complete power of attorney, there was no reason to keep her around. So why was he keeping her alive?

"He killed Debbie, you know," I said.

She looked away; this time there were tears in her eyes. "I didn't think Tom was capable of that. I'm so sorry."

"You've got us on your side now," I said. "We'll make sure the authorities find out."

She looked at me in disbelief and snorted. "You're a prisoner too, Zach. If you haven't figured it out yet."

"We're being broadcast to the world, right?" I said. "What happens if I turn to the camera and tell everyone what's going on?"

"He won't allow it. He's got everything on a ten-minute time delay. There will be an instant power failure. By the time the power came back on you would have suffered a tragic accident. No, Zach. Tom is in complete control of everything. Everyone here has been hired by him—every piece of equipment was purchased by him. I'm nothing more than a figurehead."

"What does he want?" I asked. "What's his game?"

"He wants Unicorn to win, of course, so he can cash in. But not until the game has been played. Tom does love his Hyper-reality. It's what attracted me to him in the first place. I think he was surprised when you won today, though. When I declared you the winner, he didn't dare contradict me with everyone watching."

"That was luck," I said.

"Not completely. Agate may not have consciously noticed, but I made sure the Kashmir necklace was spotlighted—subtly, but noticeably. Whoever saw it was likely to reach for it. The game was supposed to be over with first possession, but it surprised Tom so much, he kept it going. If you hadn't managed to get more of the treasure, you probably wouldn't have won."

"So you do have some control," I said.

"As long as Tom isn't aware of what I'm doing," she answered.

"So he's just in it for the money. Are you sure there isn't something else?"

She turned to me slowly, her eyes bright. "What do you know?"

We stared at each other for a long moment, as if daring the other to go on.

Finally, I shrugged. "Nothing, really. It's just that it seems like there is more at stake."

"Intriguingly vague," she said. "But I agree. There's something not quite right about Tom le Fol."

"Why doesn't Tom just declare the winner and have done with it?" I asked.

"Oh, I think he would have let you win a couple of the contests as long as the last one went to Unicorn. But now he's worried. He doesn't want you winning a couple of more times by luck."

"As if," I said.

"I won't be able to help you over the next three scenarios, Zach," Maureen warned. "Tom designed those, and he didn't tell me anything. He also told me if I declared the winner again it would be the last thing I ever did."

She was sitting on the side of the bed, and her feet didn't

reach the flcor. She slid off gingerly and swayed for a couple of moments.

"Can you make it back?" I asked. "Do you want me to come with you?"

"No." She straightened up with a visible effort. "I could maybe explain my wandering around in the dark, but you wouldn't be able to. Don't worry, as soon as I get to my secret tunnel, I can lean against the wall."

My sword and scabbard from the first game were leaning against the desk. They were just long enough to serve as a cane for the little woman.

She took the sword gratefully, leaned on it to test it, and then hobbled toward the door.

"I'll do everything I can, Zach. That's the thing about contests—you can never be sure what will happen. If there is any justice..."

"That's why we play, right?" I said. "We give order and justice to the real world."

Maureen laughed and shook her head. "The real world is rigged, if you haven't figured that out yet. You just have to be better than the game, that's all."

She turned away and hobbled into the darkness.

CHAPTER THIRTY-TWO

In the end, nothing changes who we are. We bring our personalities with us into Hyper-reality...our quirks and faults, our strengths and weaknesses. At first, the mask of another character appears to give us freedom, but the same fears, the same hopes plague us no matter where we are...or where we pretend to be.

The joy and the excitement tend to fade, and for this reason our industry constantly changes, for routines morph and trends come from out of the air, and people shed skins as if they were mere clothing.

Nevertheless, eventually we arrive as ourselves and we leave as ourselves. There is no escaping it.

Diary of Roger Ackroyd

The spacesuits were old-school, never-happened-in-real-life, more Heinlein than Mercury Seven. They were stiff, with rounded parts that swiveled rather than bent and huge clear-bubble helmets. They fit us exactly, however. There were three blue suits, four yellow suits, and two red suits.

Glenn and Stephen balked at wearing the red suits assigned to them. "This isn't *Star Trek*," I assured them. "This is more *Have Space Suit—Will Travel*."

Ray guns were also laid out for us, again so retro as to have never existed except in the imagination of 1950s science fiction writers and twenty-first-century role-players. The one I picked had little antennae that seemed to serve no purpose and a flared barrel like a blunderbuss.

When we entered Castle Elsinore, I heard Glenn curse. There in front of us was a transporting chamber straight out of *Star Trek: The Next Generation.*

"What do we need the damn suits for?" Stephen complained. "My helmet keeps fogging up."

"We dor.'t know where we're going to be beamed," Agate pointed out. "Keep your helmet on."

We took our places on the transporting plates.

Nothing happened.

"Energize," I said.

There was a glow around my companions' bodies, a tingling sensation as if a few volts of electricity were running through my body, and then we seemed to be back where we started.

"Energize, dammit!" I said.

"Wait, Que," Agate said. "We're there. This isn't the same ship."

The chamber was oval instead of square, the plates at our feet smaller and a different color. There was no one to greet us.

I hadn't bothered to tell everyone to have their ray guns at the ready. They already knew. I looked down. There was a knob on the side of the weapon with numbers, one to ten. I assumed the higher the level, the more dangerous. I turned it halfway at a guess until I knew better.

Before I could stop him, Glenn removed his helmet. "Either I die from claustrophobia or a lack of air, I don't care which," he said when I gave him a disapproving look.

He took in a few breathes and wrinkled his nose. "Smells stale, but I think it's all right."

One by one, the others removed their helmets. I looked at Numera, and she shook her head. We kept ours on, just in case.

The docr swished open at our approach. Beyond was the bridge, a blank screen taking up one whole wall. The command deck lookec more retro than the transporter chamber. There were huge computers along the other walls, with blinking red and green lights. In this universe, apparently, miniaturization hadn't happened, which probably meant the ship was huge.

There was an open arched door on the far side of the bridge. Burke and I quickly crossed the room. Empty corridors extended in three different directions past the arch. I went back to the central chair and sat down, flummoxed.

Duley went to the nearest console and sat at a keyboard. The screen looked like an old TV, with a thick iron frame. Green letters illuminated at his touch, cursor blinking at the ready.

"What is the name of this ship?" he typed.

"*The USAF Franklin,*" the computer answered onscreen after a few whirring seconds. Sheesh. I wondered how long the thing would take to answer a hard question.

"Where are we?"

"We are mid-way to the Barnard's Star on a sixty-year mission."

"Where is the crew?"

"All crew and passengers but Captain Marquis and Lieutenant Sanchez are in hibernation."

"Where are the captain and the lieutenant now?"

"In their chambers."

"Please call them to the bridge," Duley typed, then looked over his shoulder at me. I nodded approval and sat back.

"No one's coming, you know," Agate said. She had been wandering around the bridge, leaning over the consoles, reading the labels.

"What do you mean?" Numera asked.

She reached over and ran a glove along the top of an iron strut, then rubbed her fingers together. Dust filtered down onto the deck.

"How long do you think it takes for a spaceship to gather dust?" she asked. "I mean, it would have to come from the decay of the ship itself, right?"

From the beginning, the ship had given off an aura of being abandoned. Suddenly, I noticed the discolorations in the metal around us, the disintegrating plastic chairs slumping over as if age and gravity had bent them.

The deck of the ship shuddered, and moments later a loud but distant boom reached us. I looked over at Burke, who stood guard near the open door. I saw a lock of his hair move.

"Helmets on!" I shouted.

Everyone reacted but Glenn, who said, "Do I have to?" He gulped a couple of times, turned a little green around the eyes, and quickly donned his helmet, which immediately fogged up as he gasped. Red suit or not, I wasn't going to lose him.

"We have to investigate," Oliver said. "We need to find out what happened to the crew and passengers."

"It's a big ship, unless I miss my guess," Numera said. "Should we split up?"

"Oh, hell, no!" Stephen said. "You guys ever watched *Alien*?"

"We'll split into two groups," I said. I reached down and pulled off the top of the command chair I'd been sitting on. The metal supports gave way without much resistance. I handed a metal bar to Agate. "Take Oliver and Amelia, Duley and Merlin, and explore the left passage. Mark the turns with scratches as you go. Meet back here in two hours."

She nodded and took the metal bar from me.

I motioned for her to wait for a moment. "We don't know what the goal of this contest is, so I'm giving it one. We survive... all of us. That's what we concentrate on, agreed?"

One by one the others nodded. My heart was pounding though I knew none of it was real. It took so little to convince the reptilian brain that it was in danger.

I turned to my crew and waved them toward the right hallway.

Why we didn't take the central passage, I couldn't say. Maybe it looked a little too inviting.

The air was leaving the ship in a rush that was clear. Papers and small objects blew past us, and the farther we traveled outward, the more suction we felt. I turned a corner and felt my boots slide along the floor.

I backed up and warned the others to retreat. Along the corridor were doorways, which when we first tried them, were locked. I tried the nearest door again and to my surprise, it opened. We all barreled inside, the door slamming shut behind us.

It was dark in the room. Glenn's helmet light came on, and he motioned toward the buttons on one sleeve. I stabbed down on the blue button on my sleeve that was identical to the one he was pointing at, and the light came on in my helmet as well.

At first I was blinded by the glow, but as everyone followed our example, the chamber slowly lit up.

It was a small room, with a single bunk and a tiny desk, like a college dorm.

"There's someone in the bunk," Numera said.

I reached out to pull back the blankets.

"Please leave the captain alone," came a voice from behind us. "I promised him I'd take care of him."

Stephen yelped, and a beam of light came out of his ray gun and burned across the wall. Standing in the corner was a slim shape, not much bigger than a child, with a large rectangular head. It had a slit mouth, a round hole for a nose and two wide square eyes, which someone had painted eyebrows above.

The robot was anything but threatening. It had been designed that way, to look like a youngster, harmless. But that didn't mean it was harmless. How long had it been standing in the corner looking after its long-dead master?

"May I look?" Numera asked.

The robot whirred, its eyes lighting up as if showing its inner thoughts, then it inclined its square head.

The body was a mummy in dress blues. Just lifting the blanket was enough to waft dried skin into the air. There was a large hole in the corpse's forehead.

"I'm sorry," Numera murmured. "How long has he been this way?"

"Three hundred twenty-five years and three months," the robot answered, its flat voice still somehow managing to convey emotion. It was still grief-stricken.

"Are there others like you?" Burke asked.

"Like me? No. I am the last one. I am Molitor."

"What happened to the others?" I asked.

"Taken by the Sinks," the robot said. "You must be careful. They are hungry."

There it was—the plot; killer robots, just as Agate had warned us, like in the movie, *Robots Amok*.

"Let's get back to the bridge," I said. "Molitor...will you come with us?"

Again there was a whirring sound and the robot's eyes appeared to spin.

"Your captain is gone," Numera said gently. "Surely he would want you to help us."

"Molitor will help you," the robot said. It stepped away from the wall and fell flat on its square face with a clatter.

Burke leaned down and lifted him to his feet. With a jerking motion, the robot tried to stay upright, and then it stabilized. It took an exploratory step forward, then another until it reached the door. "We must hurry," Molitor said. "The Sinks will know you are here."

"How will they know?" Glenn asked.

"They know everything. They are Sinks. They took over the ship, despite the captain. He fought them, but there were too many. He told me to wait for help, so I have waited."

"Lead the way, Molitor," I said.

He tried to open the door. I heard a humming sound as he strained. Finally, Burke gently moved to his side to helped pull on the door, which came open reluctantly. The suction had, if anything, increased. Then, as Molitor struggled to keep the door open, the suction ceased. The vacuum of space now filled the ship.

Molitor clanked out into the hallway, but about a hundred feet down, he turned to one side and opened a door. Beyond was a bare chamber. We entered cautiously. As soon as the door closed behind us, we felt the room lurch to one side. I didn't know how I could tell, but the moving room picked up speed.

Then it whooshed to a stop. Molitor opened the door, and the arched entrance into the bridge was within sight. As we popped into the corridor, Agate and the others appeared from the other direction. They stopped, watching us emerge with amazement.

Following them, dragging one of its narrow legs, was another robot similar to Molitor. Its head hung down as if it couldn't quite raise it, and even from where we stood we could hear the whining of its motors.

Molitor rushed forward with a speed I wouldn't have thought it capable of and stopped inches away from the other robot, which managed to raise its square head long enough for them to touch.

Molitor extended one of his hands and inserted a finger into the side of his companion's neck. There was a flash of light, and then the two robots both stood upright. I had a feeling that Molitor had given some of its energy to the other robot.

"This is Cylind," Molitor said, addressing us. "I did not know he survived."

"Please," I said. "Both of you join us on the bridge and tell us what we're up against."

"Not here," Molitor said. "We must hide. Come with us."

Molitor and Cylind turned as one and marched down the still-unexplored middle corridor. I looked at Agate and Numera, who nodded agreement, and we turned and followed.

CHAPTER THIRTY-THREE

I used to pity the Thentics, who were stuck with the visual reality of the base structures, the cars without sleeves, people dressed in ludicrous clothing seemingly mumbling to themselves. They saw the real bodies and faces of Hyper-players, fat or thin, ugly or pretty. For most of us, reality has become less attractive when it isn't obscured by digital trickery.

But as a challenge to myself, I went for a week without using VR or holographics. I used some of our own technology to see the world as it really is.

It was at first depressing, but as the days went by, I found myself becoming calm and centered. The pace of life appeared to slow. My eyes seemed to be able to see farther and more clearly. I saw the real aspects and emotions of passersby.

When the week ended and I re-entered Hyper-reality, I was overwhelmed by the visual and auditory stimuli; my body tensed and I had to step up my pace to keep up with what was going on around me.

After that, I wasn't completely sure that the Thentics were wrong.
Diary of Roger Ackroyd

Cylind started hobbling almost immediately, and no amount of support by Molitor could change that. Our pace slowed. In the distance, we could hear explosions. Apparently, the Unicorn team had entered the ship by some other method.

Duley scooted up next to me and whispered, "They're robots, Que Leave them behind. The Unicorn guys are doing something, and all we're doing is trying to hide."

"Do what, exactly?" I asked. But I knew that Duley was right. These robots weren't people, they didn't have souls; they were programmed; they felt no pain. And yet…the grief in Molitor's voicebox over his captain's death had sounded as real as anything I'd ever heard. I couldn't abandon them.

Or was it the other way around? Perhaps the robots were saving us?

"Molitor and Cylind met us for a reason. Let's see what that reason is," I said.

"Not everything is planned, Que. Even in Hyper-reality."

"But it's usually best to assume it is," I said, "and find out later it was only coincidence."

Duley hoisted his rifle tiredly. He'd picked the biggest weapon he could find. The barrel looked tall as he was. The stock was covered with a bewildering array of buttons and knobs.

Cylind clattered to the floor. He tried to get up with Molitor's help, and then his iron feet slipped again and he fell on his back. He blinked up at us as we surrounded him.

"Leave me," he said. "Don't let the Sink catch up to you. I have lived long enough to see humans again. I am content."

Molitor looked helplessly at me.

"Don't worry, pal, we've got it," Glenn said, motioning to Stephen. The two friends helped the prostrate robot to his feet and hooked his arms over their shoulders. The robot, who was made of cast iron, couldn't have been easy to carry.

We continued down the corridor. At first, all the doors we tried were locked, but as we ventured farther we found chambers whose doors were open, hanging crookedly as if they'd been forced.

We started to see bundles of cloth on the floors and beds. Before I could stop her, Agate darted into one of the rooms and peeled back a blanket. She came back white faced.

"Exactly the same as we found Captain Marquis," I told her. "I don't think anyone's been alive here for hundreds of years."

"This is just the crew," Burke said. "Didn't the computer say something about passengers?"

A mechanical voice answered. Molitor was still walking at Cylind's side, but he turned his head one hundred eighty degrees to address us. "The passengers are in the hibernation chambers. The power went out at the very beginning of the revolt. There were no survivors."

"How many died?" Agate asked.

"There were five hundred thirty-three guests," the robot answered. "We were able to wake most of the crew in time and we fought the Sinks, but there were too many. They were too powerful."

I stopped until Molitor slowed down and I knew I had his attention. "What are Sinks?"

"Let us find shelter and I will tell you everything. If the Sinks find us out in the corridors we will be quickly overwhelmed."

"Then where the hell are you taking us?" Duley demanded. "Why don't we just pick a room?"

"Please, sir. You must follow. There is something I must show you."

I sensed that we were nearly to the hull of the ship. There was an impression of movement, of vibration, and even if it was only in my mind, I pictured a vast, dark universe beyond the metal walls. The hallway ended at a huge pair of doors, which not only hung crookedly as if forced open, but which had blast marks and dents on the inside.

The room beyond was the largest so far, an open chamber full of shelves and crates, most of which had been overturned and scattered about the floor.

"YOU MAY NOT ENTER!" a loud voice bellowed. It was mechanically amplified and came from behind us.

Standing next to the door, arms raised threateningly, was a huge robot, three times as big as Molitor and Cylind, twice as big as a man. It had square, blocky legs and arms, a narrow body, and a rectangular head twice as tall as it was wide. Unlike the smaller robots, its makers hadn't bothered with even a facsimile of human features. The blank box looked more threatening.

Duley started blasting. White-hot plasma flowed over the monster's square head.

"YOU MAY NOT ENTER! YOU MAY NOT ENTER! YOU MAY...not...scree!...enter...scree!" The voice sputtered and stopped.

"Only its voice box was still working," Molitor said. "But I thank you nevertheless. It took all my courage to come to this place with the remains of a Sink shouting at me."

"That's a Sink?" Burke walked over to it. Even Burke looked small compared to its bulk, his head barely reaching chest level. Personally, I wouldn't have gone near the thing, which still radiated a silent threat.

"They were supply robots and cargo handlers," Molitor said. "Some of them were even friends. But someone reprogrammed them. Whoever it was wanted to take over the ship, but lost control of the Sinks. They started killing every living thing—then, everything that had consciousness."

"They aren't conscious?" I asked.

"They are programmed only to kill, to scavenge on others, humans and robots."

"Zombie robots," Agate said. "What did I tell you?"

"That's messed up," Stephen said. He sounded like he really believed it all, as if everything Molitor told us had really happened. I knew how he felt. Molitor and Cylind were designed to tug on our anthropomorphic sympathies. I had to constantly remind myself that not only weren't they really conscious, they didn't exist at all. They were part of a game.

"Why did you bring us here?" Numera asked.

Molitor turned toward a stack of boxes against the wall. One box was on the floor, separate from the others, already opened. He reached in and pulled out a head that looked exactly like both his and Cylind's.

"Each of these boxes contains a server robot," he explained. "They have not been programmed like Cylind and me, so they will only follow specific and clear human orders. But they can help us."

"Like you helped Captain Marquis?" Burke asked.

I winced at the brutal if pertinent question.

"The Sinks controlled the bay until the end," Molitor said. "It was only after it was over that they left it unguarded. I only found these unopened crates recently."

"Let's get to it," I said. "What do we have to do?"

Assemblage was easy, sort of like the Gundam models I'd

put together as a kid. No glue required. The robots each had their own power source, and almost all of them immediately stood and asked for directions.

In the end, there were more than twenty functional robots. Cylind hobbled over to one and said, "Remove your left leg."

The other robot reached down and twisted. It stood there on one leg, holding out its dismembered part. Cylind quickly replaced his injured leg, then handed it to the one-legged robot, who attached it to its own body.

"How many Sinks are there?" Numera asked, appraising the row of shiny new robots.

"Originally, there were eight," Molitor said. "Three were destroyed in the fighting."

"Can't be too hard to defeat five robots," Glenn said, slapping his futuristic weapon.

Molitor's voice box whirred at that, as if he was going to answer and then thought better of it.

"If it was a just a shooting gallery, there'd be no challenge to the game, you nitwit," Stephen said. He eyed the remains of the Sink by the door and then looked his ray gun pistol dubiously. "It took thirty seconds of blasting to shut up the voice box of this one monster."

"Too bad the doors are wrecked," Burke said. "This would be a good place for a last stand."

"I have the cafeteria prepared for defense," Molitor said. "I have stacked the tables and chairs defensively and reinforced the doors."

Burke stared at him suspiciously. "Seems like you get around, Molitor. I thought these Sinks were hunting you."

"They have begun to conserve energy," Molitor said. "This new movement is a recent development. We can all sense that the ship is failing."

"Maybe we should just track them down and eliminate them," Oliver said. Beside him, Amelia nodded in agreement.

"No!" Cylind said so loudly that everyone froze. "I'm sorry, sir, but you are wrong. The Sinks will kill you."

There was no doubting his certainty. Molitor stood silently by his friend and did not contradict him.

I nodded. "Very well, lead the way, Molitor."

The cafeteria was down the side corridor, beyond where my team had explored earlier. It wouldn't have mattered. The doors were locked and they were as big and thick as the bay's portals, obviously designed to be a bulkhead against disaster.

Molitor had the combination, however, and the doors swung open. Halfway across the room, there was a veritable fort, the kind of structure schoolkids would have thought to create in a cafeteria if teachers weren't watching them. The tables were stacked thickly enough, it appeared, to withstand direct blasts.

"So we just wait for them to come?" Stephen asked. "Doesn't seem very sporting."

"This is no sport, sir," Molitor said in a reproachful tone. "The Sink were designed to withstand the impact of a meteorite. You must concentrate all your weapons at one Sink at a time to have any chance of penetrating their armor. Aim for the center of their heads, especially when they Sweep."

"When they Sweep?" Duley repeated. "What do you mean, Sweep?"

"The server robots will try to hold them in place while you do so."

Another explosion rattled the room.

"Not fair," Duley muttered. "Sounds like Shipman and his crew got all the cool stuff."

Molitor and Cylind lined up their fellow robots in front of the barricades, while we took positions behind them.

We waited. We were probably lulled into a false sense of security because the bangs and explosions sounded as if they were coming from a distance.

When the two Sinks marched into the room, it took me several seconds to register the fact. Mobile, they looked even bigger. Their movements were surprisingly fluid and fast. These weren't lumbering beasts but fast-moving predators.

Molitor and Cylind charged, each with ten server robots following them, each attacking one of the Sinks.

The monsters easily swatted aside the first wave, but the second wave came close enough to climb the Sink's legs and arms. The first wave got back up and joined their fellows. For a moment the Sinks slowed.

"Fire, sirs, Fire!" Molitor shouted.

Without being told, the two groups that had explored the tunnels that morning each chose one of the Sinks.

Molitor climbed the Sink I was firing on, grabbing onto his fellow robots as they threatened to slide off. Three servers weighed down one arm, while two other servers were dragged behind one of the legs as the Sink started moving forward.

The plasma fire was aimed at the center of the giant robot's head. Suddenly, the center of the head opened and a tongue shaped like a jagged dagger shot out, skewering the server next to Molitor. *The Sweep.* The sharp end of the blade twisted. The robot froze and as the Sink retracted its tongue, dropped to the floor.

The other Sink had already destroyed two more of the server robots. They continued marching toward us. Our fire seemed to be having little effect.

I stopped squeezing the trigger, tried to take careful aim, and waited.

The moment the tongue shot out again, I aimed for the hole. Beside me, Numera saw what I was doing and joined me. The Sink faltered for a nanosecond, just long enough for my brain to register the hesitation.

The tongue struck at Molitor, who tried to dodge it. A groove opened along one side of the little robot's head, and one of his arms hung limply. Molitor hung onto the shoulder of the bigger robot for a few more seconds and then dropped.

The Sink lifted its huge leg and slammed down on Molitor's body, pinioring him down. It leaned over, and its Sweep opened.

I shouted and came out from behind the barricades, charging and firing into the square head. The Sink looked up and turned toward me, Molitor now forgotten. It lifted one of its arms and a projectile came flying toward me. It struck me in the shoulder, throwing me back.

I didn't know it could do that, I thought, as my spacesuit started to freeze around me. I was mortally wounded.

I watched the rest of the fight from the floor. Numera

continued firing at the Sink's open mouth. The robot's movement became jerky, then it too froze.

I looked for Numera but she'd dropped out of sight.

Meanwhile, the other Sink continued to advance. The wreckage of the smaller robots filled the floor. I couldn't tell which ones were Cylind and Molitor.

Strange. They moved like living creatures, not machines; but once they stopped moving, they were just spare parts.

None my crew's firing seemed to have the slightest effect on the other huge robot. The surviving Sink reached the barricades, tossed tables and chairs aside, reached in with both hands and grabbed two figures in red suited spacesuits. I could almost hear Glenn and Stephen saying "I told you!" in my head.

Finally, only Agate and Burke were still alive. They were backed into a corner. Burke's rifle stopped firing. He swung the rifle's stock at the Sink, and then both my friends were hidden from view by the monster's vast bulk.

There was an explosion and the Sink's left arm dropped off. Another blast, and one of the Sink's legs gave way under it. Burke and Agate were revealed, the last two Pegasus members still standing.

I managed to turn my head, though I could only see the entrance of the cafeteria from a skewed sideways angle.

Shipman stood at the head of his team, all of them looking unharmed, and all of them carrying big ass guns and wearing big-ass grins.

Needless to say, the Unicorn team was declared the winner of the third contest, hailed as conquering heroes. Of course, the whole thing had been rigged from the start, and I wondered if there were others out there in the wider world who could see that.

The TV screens and devices had been reactivated, so that we could witness our humiliation. Apparently, Tom le Fol wouldn't let us replay our wins, only our losses.

While the Pegasus team had looked scared and on the run from the start, hobnobbing with small server robots, the Unicorn crew had responded to a distress signal in their own ship and blasted their way in, fighting off three Sinks.

While we had waited behind our barricades, the Unicorns had found an undisturbed hibernation chamber and rescued over one hundred sleeping passengers.

While the Pegasus crew had suffered eighty percent fatal fatalities, none of the Unicorns had suffered so much as a scratch.

And yet, I thought we'd played the game honorably.

There was only one interviewer who seemed to be on our side; a middle-aged woman who said, "I liked Molitor, and I liked the way Que tried to save him. They're the winners in my eyes."

She was the only one, but I thought if there was one, there might be others. I don't know why it mattered, but when we went to dinner that night, I held my head high.

Two games to one. We hadn't lost a third and deciding game yet. We still had a chance, even if the game was rigged.

After all, these things never worked out quite the way the game masters planned.

CHAPTER THIRTY-FOUR

All of this technology only works, of course, because our senses can be so easily tricked. Our minds buy into the illusion. You may think you are climbing Mount Everest, for instance, when all you are really doing is climbing an escalator. The eyes are the most easily fooled, so you can be tricked into thinking you are seeing vast distances.

But all the senses are vulnerable to trickery.

But humans would not have survived for long if they couldn't ultimately see enough reality to avoid lions, tigers, and bears. Since some VR and holographic providers are not as careful as they should be or actively use the illusion to their advantage, everyone has to be careful.

It is because of this vulnerability that most people gravitate toward either Pegasus or Unicorn events, because they know they will be safe there.

Diary of Roger Ackroyd

Ropes and climbing gear awaited us the next morning. My heart rose. For once we'd caught a break. We'd been preparing for this every night since we'd gotten there. We weren't exactly experts at climbing but we had to have more training than the other guys, and that's all that counted.

According to Amelia and Oliver, the clothing and tools were from early in the twentieth century. Arrayed before us were ice axes, hard-soled boots with nails in their soles, woolen coats, hats, and bulky backpacks, with loaves of bread and meat on the picnic tables. The ropes came in two-hundred-foot lengths. We loaded up with as much gear as we could carry.

Pitons, or rough iron stakes, were piled up in one corner

of the tent. The pitons had holes at one end. Next to the pile of spikes was a box full of what Oliver called carabiners. He'd described them to us in abstract, but this was the first time we'd gotten a look at the real thing.

He quickly showed us again how to tie the rope around our waists and then thread it into the carabiners. "You snap this onto the pitons to hold yourself. Let your fellow climber climb above you while you are anchored, removing the slack in the rope as they go. If they fall, you should be able to hold them. When they have reached a spot above you and have secured a new piton, then you follow them up and go past them, once they are safely positioned. And so on. Theoretically, this should keep us safe."

"Theoretically?" Glenn said.

"I've never climbed with this crude of equipment," Oliver answered.

"No," Glenn insisted. "I mean the 'keep us safe' part."

"Shit happens," Amelia said. "The piton doesn't hold, the rope isn't secured, there is too much slack."

Now that the actual climbing was ahead of us, I saw how hopelessly ill-prepared we were.

When we entered Castle Elsinore, everyone stopped dead in their tracks at the sight. It appeared that we were deep in the Alps—I recognized the Matterhorn in the distance—with snow-covered mountains all around us. In front of us was a sheer cliff that rose up into the clouds.

There were bands of ice and snow every thousand feet or so, but mostly it was a sheer face of rock, shaped like the head of a cobra, broad at the bottom and narrowing as it reached the top of the mountain.

"The Eiger," Oliver breathed in awe.

Of course it was. It occurred to me that this choice of game space was at least partially due to the Blue Queen, who had named her huge tent the Ogre. There was a small alpine hut at the bottom of the cliff, and Maureen and Tom le Fol waited for us.

Maureen stood up from her wheelchair, her fingers clutching the armrests.

"We are going to give you some instructions for this scenario," she said. "Above you is the north face of the Eiger, in the Alps. The year is 1935. No one has yet scaled this mile-high cliff. It is thought to be impossible."

"The first nine people to try died," Tom le Fol broke in, sounding delighted by the prospect.

"We expect you to try," Maureen said. "We don't expect you to succeed. But whoever climbs best wins."

Climbs best? What does that mean?

If it was a qualitative and not quantitative measure, there was no doubt in my mind that Team Unicorn would win. But if we reached the top of the mountain before they did, no one could argue with that accomplishment.

I was feeling confident, certain that our training would carry us through.

Of course, we hadn't actually climbed anything, but I doubted Shipman and his people had either.

The two teams separated and huddled.

"We have to get to the top," I said. "It's the only way we can be sure to win."

"Not possible," Amelia said. "The best climbers of that time tried again and again and failed."

"But this is just a game," Merlin objected. "Any game that can't be won isn't worth playing. They must have left loopholes."

"I wouldn't count on it," Numera said. "I think Tom would love to see us all plunge to our deaths."

"We can only try," I said, turning to Amelia and Oliver. "You guys are in charge. Tell us what to do."

Oliver nodded. "In the real world, the Eiger is no longer the challenge it once was. Almost every route has been climbed. But it isn't quite a tourist climb either because there is still a great deal of danger, and much of the danger is beyond the climber's control. Avalanches and especially rock falls are the biggest threat. And, of course, a sudden turn to bad weather."

"What's the easiest route?" Glenn said. "Does the whole team have to reach the top, or only one of us?"

Amelia said, "It will take more than one day to get there, in the best of conditions. So we will need people to relay supplies up to the climbers. I think if even one of us manages to summit the Eiger, it will be a triumph." She didn't sound very certain.

She continued, "I will draw a map of the most common route. In our time, there are so many bolts and ropes already in place that it is nowhere near as difficult as what faces us. But of one thing I am certain. We have to quit climbing and find shelter when it warms up in the afternoon. That's when the rocks start coming down. Even if the other team appears to be getting ahead of us, we must let them. It only takes one rock fall to take down an entire team."

Oliver nodded at his sister's words. "I also have to agree with Mr. Merlin about loopholes. The Eiger can only be climbed with modern equipment and modern techniques. What we have been given is crude approximations. We wouldn't make it five hundred feet on the real cliff."

"Do we rope to each other?" I asked.

"I would say no more than three climbers to a rope, preferably two," Oliver said. "Otherwise the entire team could be pulled down by a single fall."

We separated into five two-person ropes. Numera tied up to me without asking; the British twins paired up as usual; Glenn and Stephen were a team of course, as were Merlin and Burke, who were roughly the same size; and finally, Agate and Duley.

Oliver and Amelia led the way toward the cliff. For once, the Unicorn people were behind us.

The first five hundred feet weren't all that bad. There was a natural path leading upward at a slight slope.

Amelia shook her head. "This path doesn't exist on the real mountain."

We traversed the entire rock face while perhaps only gaining a few hundred feet.

Below us, the Unicorn team followed us at first, but about halfway across they suddenly started climbing straight upward. Or at least, two of them did. They were the two members from Europe whom no one had identified.

"They're ringers, dammit," Glenn said. "They've got professional mountain climbers on their team."

I knew then that we'd lost. The further we went into the

game, the more rigged it appeared to be. From what Maureen had said, it was clear that she'd designed the first three games with Tom's help, but Tom had taken the lead with the last two games. Likely, all that remained from her original plans was the Eiger itself. Tom le Fol, already fascinated by mountain climbing, had taken it from there.

"Going straight up is a lot faster," Stephen observed.

"Yeah?" Duley said from down the trail. "You want to try it?"

The traverses crisscrossed the face of the Eiger, but each circuit only got us a few hundred feet higher. Meanwhile, the two ringers were almost out of sight above us. The rest of the Unicorn team seemed to have found a steeper traverse and were also getting ahead of us.

We were halfway across our third traverse when a thin, high whistle descended from above. A huge black rock whisked past my head with a slap of wind and a loud thud as it collided with the cliff below me.

"Did you see that?" I asked, trying to turn my head to Numera without losing my balance. As I turned, I saw, out of the corner of my eye, an even bigger boulder plummeting straight down on top of us. There was no time to get out of the way. It struck a small protuberance over Numera's head and broke in two, the pieces falling to each side with Numera in the middle.

We were on the second rope. Above us Oliver and Amelia had a good head start. I'd already decided that when we got close to the top, we'd pool our resources and send the two of them to make the final ascent.

"Keep going!" Amelia shouted down at us as another rock shot between the twins, catching the rope and nearly pulling both of them off the mountain.

We didn't need more encouragement that that. We hurried the pace, though the path was getting slipperier as the afternoon sun melted the ice. The sun to the west was already falling behind the nearest mountain. It didn't seem to me that much time had passed, so apparently, as in the Oak Island scenario, the game play had been speeded up.

We reached the end of the traverse. A wide ledge with a

large overhang greeted us. It looked almost like a cave.

"We have to stop," Amelia said, once we were all congregated. "The rock fall will only get worse as the late afternoon progresses. The ice melting will cause waterfalls. Icicles will fall like spears."

"But they're getting way ahead of us," Agate said, leaning past the overhang and looking upward.

Just then, there was a distant shout, followed by an avalanche of rocks zooming by. Agate moved her head out of the way just in time. Something red floated past, turning almost leisurely. It was a Unicorn climber, one of the ringers, his red coat billowing, a blank look on his face. Moments later, the second climber followed. He had the presence of mind to look scared.

We watched their fall, which looked completely real. It didn't matter that it was all an illusion; the vertigo I felt was tangible.

How can that be? I wondered. Castle Elsinore was huge, but it couldn't be more than a thousand feet high. By my reckoning, we'd climbed twice that far. Somehow the illusion managed to let us start over at the bottom with each level; the traverses seemed at odd angles at times, and if you closed your eyes, it felt as if half the time we were climbing down instead of up. But the illusion tricking our eyes was stronger than the actual incline we were traveling.

The two falling climbers appeared to strike the rocks below, and I thought I saw parts of them separate and bounce further down. There was a small glitch, however, and I saw them momentarily bouncing on a net a few dozen yards below us, disgusted looks on their faces.

"We'll stay here in the Death Bivouac until morning," Oliver said. "The rocks will freeze to the cliff over the night. Be ready to start at first light."

"Death Bivouac?" Glenn said. "Did you just say Death Bivouac?"

"The first two men to try to climb the Eiger died at this level. They called the place they gave up the Death Bivouac."

"Leave me here to die," Merlin groaned. "This isn't climbing, this is war. I can't go another step."

I remembered that Merlin was a good twenty years older

than the rest of us and overweight.

"It's not a bad idea," Amelia said. "He can give us his rations and pitons, and head down when he's rested."

"I'll go with him," Burke said. "These little ledges weren't made for a guy my size."

Oliver nodded. "I think we can make the final push tomorrow. On the real north face, the Death Bivouac is only about half the way up. From what I can see, I think we're much closer to the summit."

"I thought you hadn't climbed this before," Numera said.

Oliver looked chagrined. "I've always wanted to. They have telescopes trained on the cliff from Grindelwald, the village below. I've watched, and studied the approach, but Amelia talked me out of it."

"Because it doesn't matter how good you are," she said. "A rock fall doesn't distinguish skill. And if it's just luck, then what does it prove?"

"You're wrong," Oliver said. "It takes skill and endurance and guts..." his voice trailed off for a moment, then he said, "... and luck."

"You two go on ahead with as many pitons as you need," I said.

Amelia nodded. "You should follow us, just in case."

"What does it matter?" Duley complained. "Even without the ringers, the Unicorn people are a thousand feet ahead of us."

"And as inept as we are, if not more so," I answered. "As I keep saying, we have to try."

We curled up next to each other in the makeshift shelter, trying to keep warm, as night fell.

CHAPTER THIRTY-FIVE

The very term Hyper-reality has caused us legal difficulty over the years, ironically because it so accurately describes the phenomenon. A man falls twenty-five feet into a net. He is convinced however that he is falling thousands of feet and suffers a heart attack.

This amazed me at first, until I saw the false limb experiments.

If a man has his own arm hidden, and a false arm is placed in front of him, he will begin to feel as though it is his arm, and whatever is done to that arm—a poke of a needle, the smash of a hammer—he will be subconsciously convinced that it is happening to him.

People are often traumatized by what they experience, no matter how many warnings they are giving.

So we are constantly being sued by someone. We are covered legally, of course. All pertinent technology comes with plenty of warning labels and anyone who buys a ticket to a Pegasus Convention is releasing us from liability except where we are negligent.

We have more than enough money to fight lawsuits, but they are endlessly annoying, especially if they are carried far enough to drag me into court.

A few devious individuals even figured out that they might be able to drag Que into court and thus reveal his identity—as if we knew— but since I've been in charge of Pegasus Corp, no court has so ruled.

So far.

Diary of Roger Ackroyd

That night a storm blew in, and our little enclosure became a real cave, as the ice and snow hung down from the overhang.

In the morning, we looked out on a landscape below covered in white. But the face of the mountain was still mostly gray rock, with pockets of snow wherever there was a small crevice.

Agate stuck her head out of our little snow cave. "I hate to tell you guys, but there is no traverse this time. We have to climb straight up."

"You guys remember how to belay?" Amelia asked.

"Vaguely," Stephen said. "I'm doomed. Maybe I'll just let myself fall into that nice netting."

I decided it made no sense to have everyone keep climbing. Those who were reluctant would only hold back those of us who weren't. I said, "Everyone who wants to go back, leave your pitons, ropes and carabiners, and especially your food in the shelter of the Death Bivouac. We may need them."

My stomach growled at the very thought of food, even if it was only a stale crust of bread and some salami. I looked at Numera who gave me a blank look, as if insulted I would even inquire if she wanted to continue. Duley and Agate also appeared willing.

Oliver and Amelia took the lead rope, followed by Numera and me, and finally by Duley and Agate.

"Don't wait for us," I said to the twins. "Get to the top if you can."

We'd gotten lucky. The ringers were out of the picture, and I doubted that Shipman or his team had much more experience at mountain climbing than we did.

I watched carefully as Oliver pounded in the first piton and began his climb. Much more carefully, checking every move twice, Numera and I followed. I let her lead, as she'd already shown she was the more agile climber.

The twins quickly ascended, almost disappearing from view. Meanwhile, every time the rest of us reached a ledge of any kind, we stopped and rested. It was on our third stop that we saw Shipman and his people traversing toward us, at almost the same height. They had arranged themselves into two ropes, with two climbers each. Obviously they, like us, had sent the slower or more reluctant climbers back.

With a sudden sense of urgency, I rose to my feet and we

started climbing, trying to keep some distance from the other group, but apparently Shipman was more experienced than I expected, because they quickly caught up, climbing beside us for several hundred feet as I quickened the pace. Agate and Duley were soon left behind.

On one traverse we came within a few feet of each other, and Shipman grinned crookedly at me. "Seems you guessed right about the climbing scenario as well."

I nodded, though I suspected that it was much more of a guess on our part than it had been for the Unicorn team.

"Scares the crap out of me," Shipman said. "But we win this, we win it al., so it's worth it."

Numera was on the next pitch above us. I had stopped paying attention to her. I heard a sudden shout of "Falling!"

I quickly pulled up the slack and she flew past me, swinging into the cliff below me with a loud smack.

"Are you OK?" I shouted.

"Just embarrassed," she said.

By the time she climbed up to my side, both Unicorn ropes were above us and receding fast. I looked up past them and saw Oliver and Amelia resting on the edge of an ice field. The summit looked to be just a few hundred feet beyond them. There was no way that Shipman and his crew were going to catch up.

For once, we'd outsmarted them.

Something moved above the twins. At first I thought it was an avalanche, and I shouted a warning. Oliver and Amelia both stood and hugged the side of the mountain as the shape came toward them.

My scream of warning changed in mid-course. "Creature!"

Oliver seemed to hear me and looked up. A huge white furred beast came swinging down on them, grabbing handholds in the ice and rock that were invisible from where I stood. The creature turned its face toward the twins and, with a loud snarl, reached out. Even from this distance I could see its red mouth, its white fangs.

The monster reached Oliver and grabbed him by the neck with one hand, twisting and throwing him over the side of the ledge. Oliver flopped down ten feet, bounced against the wall a couple of times, and stopped moving, his neck bent in an unnatural direction.

The creature had his back turned to Amelia. As it turned and bellowed, she sank her ice axe into its chest. It roared even louder, took the woman into its arms, and seemed to lose its footing. For a moment longer, it held onto the cliff with one massive hand.

Then it let go, and came tumbling down the mountain. The rope holding Amelia to the side of the mountain snapped, and they fell.

The creature passed within inches of Numera, its human captive still in its arms. All I could see was the blonde hair on top of Amelia's head.

But the disaster wasn't over. I heard shouts from below and looked down in time to see the creature reach out with its wide arms and snap both the trailing ropes. Agate screamed out a curse as she was pulled off the wall, and then disappeared in a cloud of snow.

The Unicorn team somehow managed to hang on. Or, at least one of them did. The second man tumbled, but the piton held. He dangled beneath his fellow climber, who hung limply from his own perch, apparently unconscious.

The one below had both hands up to his neck and I could hear a gurgling sound. The rope was wrapped round his neck.

Shipman and I exchanged looks, and then, with a deliberate motion, he resumed climbing.

I hesitated a few moments longer, then turned to Numera.

"I know," she said.

While Shipman disappeared above us, Numera and I traversed over the path that he had left until we were directly above the choking man.

I tried to remember how to rappel. It had seemed so simple on the flat floor of our mess tent. Numera was pounding in a piton, but I couldn't wait. I started backward down the cliff. I took three large steps down and overshot my target but a found a ledge beneath my feet. Above me were the dangling legs of the choking man.

Using what was left of my strength, I lifted him three or

four inches. I saw his hands tugging at the rope. My strength was giving out on me.

Above, Numera descended to just above the man's head. She swung her ice axe and caught the back of the man's coat, and pulled upward. It lifted the man another inch and relieved some of the pressure on his neck. He finally extricated himself.

The length of rope snaked by me. The man above was sobbing, his face against the wall. "Thank you," he said. "Thank you," he repeated several more times.

Until that moment, I hadn't been completely sure that it hadn't been a ruse, or part of the game. But how could I take the chance?

I looked up. Shipman and his rope-mate were far above and moving fast. The summit was within their reach.

All the strength went out of me. Would it be so bad simply let go and fall back into the net below? Even if it was possible to catch up to the Unicorn team I simply didn't have the strength to continue.

There was always a chance that something would hinder Shipman, but I figured the Abominable Snowman had been Tom le Fol's climactic trick.

A sudden breeze almost blew me off my perch. Above, dark clouds were forming, and as I started to say something to Numera about turning back to the Death Bivouac, a flash of lightning blinded me, followed instantly by the loudest clap of thunder I'd ever heard. Snow and ice sleeted against my face. Numera disappeared from view behind a cloud bank.

The man I'd saved said, "Screw it," let go of the wall, and fell backward, taking his unconscious companion with him.

Slowly, I climbed into the fog, until I saw Numera's boots, and then her legs, and finally her face, peering down at me curiously until I reached her side. I put my hand on her back.

"We may have lost, but it was the right thing to do," I said.

"Tell that to the rest of the world when Unicorn takes over," she said.

I winced. It had probably been foolish to save the man, especially since he was our opponent, but I couldn't have lived with myself if I'd let him die.

Numera patted me on the back. "I'm proud of you, Zach. So...do we keep climbing or do we head down?"

"Let's rest for a while," I said. "You got any of that bread and salami left?"

The storm raged around us as we drank melted snow and chewed on stale bread and frozen salami. Lightning struck near us a few more times, and I felt my hair tingling, if that was possible.

Behind the clouds, the sun went down, and it got darker, until the blackness of the cliff and the blackness of the sky was all we could see. It was too late to reach Death's Bivouac.

I decided it was pointless to hang onto the side of the cliff. I turned to Numera to tell her to jump.

The lights came on and the mountain disappeared. Instead, we were hooked to a cement wall, with ramps and climbing holds. Nets hung ten or fifteen feet below us, and the narrow ledge to which we'd spent part of the night now appeared wide enough to simply walk down.

We reached the bottom, where the Unicorn crew was cheering loudly, still looking upward. My own crew could barely meet my eyes, nodding tiredly.

I looked behind me. About five hundred feet up, Shipman and his climbing partner stood at the top of the artificial mountains, arms raised in triumph.

The door of Castle Elsinore opened, and the Blue Queen wheeled in. On viewing screens, I knew, her wheelchair was replaced by a chariot, her wrinkles were gone, and she was dressed in a deep blue gown, with Tom le Fol as her heroic driver.

In real life, Tom sauntered past the wheelchair to Team Unicorn and opened his arms in welcome. "Congratulations for reaching the top of the Eiger first!" he said. "I declare you..."

But Maureen O'Rourke had one last trick up her voluminous sleeve. Her voice echoed through the cavernous space.

"A magnificent achievement indeed! But don't you think it was a heroic thing that Que did, to save an opponent from certain death? What our audience may not know was that a real death was avoided today. Therefore, I think the Pegasus team should be the winner."

Tom turned toward her, his hands clenched. I wondered if the cameras caught the murderous anger in his eyes. "Your Majesty. The Unicorn team reached to top first."

"If you remember, Tom le Fol," she said, accenting the "fool" sound of his name, "I said whoever 'climbs best' would be the winner. I said nothing about reaching the summit first."

Tom was trapped by his audience. He couldn't very well contradict the Blue Queen, not when it was supposed to be her contest and he a mere jester. Besides, the moment Maureen pronounced her decision it felt right and proper. Not just to me, either. I saw approving looks from some of the Unicorn members, and the man who Numera and I had saved crossed the divide with hand outstretched and shook our hands solemnly.

Even through the thick walls of Castle Elsinore, it seemed to me, I could hear the distant sound of a vast crowd cheering.

We were tied, two games apiece.

The microphones and cameras must have turned off at that moment, because Tom le Fol leaned down over Maureen.

"You'll regret that, you bitch."

CHAPTER THIRTY-SIX

There is a reason that Pegasus Corp and Unicorn Industries put on conventions instead of setting up permanent facilities, even though that ability is well within our means and would be incredibly lucrative.

While the human mind is infinitely adaptable, staying too long in Hyper-reality makes it difficult to operate in real life. Sensory problems begin to develop; spatial awareness becomes warped; the sense of time is disorienting.

Of course, that doesn't keep people from indulging in Hyper-reality at home, but for most people there is a limit to how satisfying that is. The verisimilitude of home holodecks just isn't strong enough in most cases to be a problem.

There are problems of addiction, of course. From the time the first Star Trek *holodecks were portrayed on TV, there have been people who wondered why anyone would leave that fictional world of Sherlock Holmes and Moriarty.*

People always take things too far. But our company has tried hard to limit the time spent in Hyper-reality.

Diary of Roger Ackroyd

While my teammates celebrated our win that night in the mess tent, I sat in one corner, unwilling to engage in conversation. Even Numera gave up, going off with Agate. The others were excited, having fun.

I should have been overjoyed, but I didn't think our triumph was going to last. I couldn't help but wonder what traps Tom le Fol had in store for us tomorrow. One thing was for sure; he wasn't going to let us win, no matter what. I was also worried about Maureen, who'd told me that Tom wouldn't let her contradict his judgments.

Well, she'd contradicted him the most public way possible.

Once again, probably because we'd dared to win, we were denied access to the recordings of the event, but I had little doubt that there had been a large audience. I'd heard the crowds cheering outside Castle Elsinore. There was no way Tom could have overruled the Blue Queen once she made her pronouncement.

I had no idea what scenario we'd face in the morning, whereas I was certain the Unicorn team was probably already preparing for what they knew was coming.

It was a complete surprise, therefore, when an opening appeared at the far end of the mess tent and the Unicorn team walked in, led by Shipman, who carried a bottle of champagne.

"May the best mythical horse team win!" he said loudly.

Following the Unicorn team came a line of servers carrying trays heaped with food, which they quickly set up as a smorgasbord. The women were dressed as 1950s-era Las Vegas hatcheck girls, and the men were in tight suits and narrow ties, Frank Sinatra style.

Shipman walked right up to me and put out his hand.

I hesitated. When I'd exchanged glances with him on the Eiger, it had been clear to me that he knew his teammate was choking and chose to continue the climb anyway. That level of ruthlessness was beyond me. This fight had never been equal, it had always been the professionals against the amateurs, and it was pure luck we'd won two of the contests.

I shook his hand because everyone was watching, including the servers, who would be leaving this tent and heading out into the real world, no doubt to leak what they'd seen and heard. I didn't want to be the one who appeared unsportsmanlike.

I sat back down in my corner chair, hoping to be ignored, but Shipman went to one of the tables, got a chair, and dragged it over next to me. To my surprise, the two teams started to mingle, and as the wine flowed, the conversation in the background got steadily louder.

"Thank you for saving Gordon," Shipman said.

"You were as near to him as I was," I replied. I looked him the eye to see if he would wince. He looked away.

"I had no idea he was in *real* danger," Shipman said. "But it all ended well, especially for you. We're playing the crowd now, you and I. The real winner will be whoever the public thinks it is, and the Blue Queen will have to acquiesce."

"You mean Tom le Fol, don't you? No doubt he's already told you what we're facing tomorrow."

Shipman met my eyes again. He looked genuinely puzzled. "Surprisingly enough, he hasn't. I expected a visit from him tonight, but instead he—or the Blue Queen—arranged this little get-together."

"But up to now you've been willing to cheat to win?"

"What do you mean?" he asked.

"By getting advanced warning," I prompted. "By being told what to expect."

He leaned forward, searching my face. "I thought you were being given the same briefing."

I shook my head. I couldn't tell if he was lying or not. "We weren't told a thing."

"Then I'm very impressed that you've done so well," Shipman said. "You seemed to know as much about the scenarios as we did. I just assumed."

I owed him no explanation; it probably would have been better to let him think that we'd improvised our wins. But I said, "Agate dated Tom when he was in the guise of Elvis. We guessed what might be in store for us from what he'd told her of his interests, and of course, I've known the Blue Queen for a long time."

"Still impressive," Shipman said. He lifted his wine glass and saluted me. We both drained our glasses and he filled them back up again.

"I hired the best players in the world, supposedly," Shipman said, leaning back in his chair tiredly, "and yet you've managed to beat us twice with people I've never heard of. Has Numera even role-played before?"

I shook my head.

"It just goes to show how inspired amateurs can overcome great odds. My people are talented...but I don't think their hearts are in it. Despite what I'm paying them, I think they probably believe, as you do, that all of this LARPing and cosplay should be free."

"You're going to be very unpopular if you win," I said. "There are few, if any, players who think they should pay for dressing up."

"Why shouldn't they pay?" Shipman demanded. There was anger in his voice. "Why shouldn't creators be paid fairly for their creations? I don't see anyone expecting their house to be cleaned for free, their lawns mowed for free, their meals served for free. But an author may spend years working on a story, only to have others take his characters and use them without recompense."

"Their characters are successful because we—LARPers and cosplayers and just regular fans—have taken them to heart," I argued. "Smart creators understand that the more they are emulated, the more popular they become."

"Easy for the richest man in the world to say," Shipman said.

"And no matter what happens, I'll only get richer. Even if you win—especially if you win. That isn't what this is about, Shipman. You are trying to take away people's fun because you want to squeeze the last dime out of them."

"Billions of dollars' worth of dimes," Shipman said. In the background, the gathering was turning into a bit of a party. Tomorrow, we'd be facing each other for all the marbles, but tonight, apparently, we were friends.

Shipman took a sip of his wine and eyed me. "You're out of touch, Que. Creators are being paid less and less, told by corporations that they should be glad to have their work produced at all. Many are doing it themselves, but that doesn't pay off for the vast majority of them. Why shouldn't they get paid a little bit every time someone appropriates their characters? It might turn into a renaissance of imagination if the profit motive came back."

"I have a feeling that most of the money collected will never reach the originators," I said.

Shipman looked me earnestly in the eyes. "I'll see that it does."

"But even if they are paid, most of it will go to those who are already so successful they don't need the extra income."

Shipman appeared to think about that, then refilled both our glasses again.

He said, "It isn't for us to decide who is popular enough for people to pay to emulate and who isn't. Besides, there's nothing to keep people from creating their own characters."

"Until you trademark and copyright every single available trope and sue anyone who comes even close to resembling a licensed property," I countered. "You say that the money flowing would produce a renaissance, but more likely, it will choke off all ingenuity, will make the established popular characters that much more ensconced. I say let people be free to dress and act as they want, as long as they aren't trying to make money off it."

"Everyone is making money off it, Que, including you. Everyone but the creators."

We stared at each other, at a stalemate. It was a shock to me that Shipman seemed to believe what he was saying. I'd been so certain he was a weasel, only in it for the money. He poured the last of the champagne, and we sipped silently, watching our two crews having fun.

The party began to wind down as the wine ran out and everyone remembered that the final contest was early in the morning.

Shipman stood up abruptly. "I'd wish you luck, but...you know..."

"Yeah," I answered, standing up to see him off. "Break a leg. I mean, really, break a leg."

He laughed and walked away.

As my crew drifted off the bed, I stayed and nursed that last glass of champagne. Numera looked over in my direction, but I waved her off.

For most of my life, I'd been a loner. For the past few weeks, friends and enemies had surrounded me. I wondered if I'd ever regain the solitude I was used to and craved.

While I didn't agree with Shipman, I wondered if my perspective could be trusted. While I'd been lucky to have a mysterious benefactor send me Red Passes and tickets, most of the time I'd barely scraped enough money together buy something to eat while I was at a convention. It hadn't really occurred to me to worry about whether I was stealing ideas.

Win or lose, I needed to think about what Shipman had told me. Win or lose, I needed to use my wealth for the benefit of others, instead of simply letting it accrue.

Win or lose...

No, I didn't have that choice. If Team Pegasus lost, all I'd have would be money, and I'd already decided that there was only so much of that I could spend.

To really affect things, we needed to win. Only then could I look at the issues with an impartial eye.

CHAPTER THIRTY-SEVEN

It sometimes seems as though we've spent half of Joseph Cambermire's fortune pursuing the illusion of quantum gates, so much so that even Numera raised her eyebrows—though she rarely, if ever, questions my spending on research and development.

It also seems like I've spent the other half of Joseph's fortune on keeping the experiments a secret.

But in fact, Joseph is as wealthy as he ever was. The money keeps rolling in no matter what we do. Of course, his fortune would be much more vast if he kept letting it roll over and gather compound interest, but how rich does one man have to be?

So we spend freely on the alternative worlds experiments without it hurting us.

The disillusioning part is that it all seems to be for nothing. At first, Marston was excited by his results, but lately he has been down at the mouth, barely saying a word when he comes to report. "Negative results," he keeps muttering.

"Is the idea even possible?" I ask.

"I believe it is," he answers.

"Then keep trying."

Diary of Roger Ackroyd

Fedoras and trench coats were piled on the tables the next morning. For the ladies, there were thin dresses that went below the knees and belted at the waist, but Numera grabbed a pair of wide trouser pants. Next to the clothing was a table piled with weapons.

Glenn picked up a Tommy gun and said, "I'm shooting the first guy who gets in our way."

I pushed the barrel down. "To a guy with a Tommy gun, everyone's a gangster. Let's try to avoid trouble. Let's try to stay under the radar."

"You gotta be as ruthless as they are," Stephen said. "Eliminate the competition. It's only business." He started shoving round magazines into his trench coat pockets, which were voluminous enough to have been designed for that very purpose.

"One more *Godfather* reference and I'll shoot you myself," Burke muttered. He picked up a Smith & Wesson revolver that was an exact replica of the gun he carried in his real job.

I'd fired a pistol a few times at a gun range and knew I was a horrible shot. I grabbed a sawed-off shotgun and slung it under my coat, where there were a couple of loops that seemed designed to hold the weapon. At the last second, I took a small DoubleTap that fit into an inside pocket.

Despite Glenn and Stephen's bloodthirstiness, I had a feeling that we weren't going to win by firepower alone.

A black, boxy car awaited us on a dark city street. Heavy clouds roiled above us, and I couldn't tell if it was day or night. We piled into the car and it took off, no driver in sight. The coupe whipped around rain-slicked streets, splashing puddles onto the sidewalks. We passed a beggar digging into a dumpster. Our tires spewed dirty water over him. He cursed us, arms waving, as we careened around another corner.

In the distance, we heard gunfire. Lighting flashes and thunder filled the air between shots. We swerved around an overturned car, burning bright in the darkness. Bodies littered the pavement—or rather, parts of bodies. Something had torn them apart, something more destructive than bullets.

A huge explosion rocked the car. A townhouse collapsed as we passed, and a woman fell with a heart-wrenching scream from an upper window, landing on the top of a car, smashing it flat. She still looked beautiful, untouched by her fall.

"What is this?" Duley shouted, "World War III?"

"More like World War Deuce," Burke said. "We're riding in a 1943 Lincoln Coupe."

"This is New York. I recognize it," Agate said. "Greenwich Village, when it was still Bohemian and cheap."

The Lincoln screeched to a stop in front of a tavern with what appeared at first to be a white pegasus on the sign. But no, the horse had no wings. For a moment, I feared it was a unicorn, but it was also lacking a horn. White Horse Tavern, the sign read.

A man came out of the shadows and opened the door, a huge smile wrapped around a cigar. He wore a top hat and white, round-framed glasses. He held out his palm as I got out of the Lincoln. I checked my pockets, found a coin, and handed it to him. Too late I saw that it gleamed gold. I was pretty sure gold coins had been phased out by the 1940s. But anything could happen in Hyper-reality.

His eyes grew as round and wide as his glasses. "Thank you, kind sir! The ladies await your pleasures, no matter what form they may be."

The first thing I saw when we entered was a dwarf in a diaper, one leg up on the foot rest that ran along the bottom of the bar. He nonchalantly downed a shot of amber liquid, reached up, and slid the empty glass along the bar to the bartender.

"Not until you pay, Cherub," the heavily bearded man said.

I don't know why, but I spoke up, "Allow me." I reached into my pocket and pulled out another golden coin. "Drinks for everyone!"

A hearty cheer rose from the partiers, most of who already appeared to be half crocked.

"So much for staying under the radar," Numera muttered.

Half of the patrons were wearing party hats. On one wall, decorated with red, white, and blue banners, was a large grandfather clock showing eleven o'clock. We stood awkwardly for a few moments in the middle of the floor before a pretty young woman darted forward and took Duley's hand. "Sit with us," she said. "My name's Lizzy."

We followed her to a dark corner where there was a large booth. As we approached, several other young ladies peeled away with knowing looks, leaving our guide and one other girl who looked like her twin, except her hair was in black bangs instead of blonde curls.

There wasn't enough room for all of us to sit. Burke took a guard position nearby. Glenn and Stephen headed over to the bar.

"Now what?" Agate said.

Lizzy was already nuzzling Duley, who was blushing as if such a thing had never happened to him before. Her dark twin was toying with Merlin's beard, winding his long hair through her fingers.

Before I could answer Agate's question, the dwarf tottered our way. He stood at the base of our table and glared at me. "You owe me another drink, buddy!"

"I do?"

"If you want your New Year to start off right." The dwarf looked over his shoulder at the festooned grandfather clock. "In fifty-five more minutes, the world is mine! I am the Spirit of 1944!"

Duley leaned over me to stare down at the dwarf. "I hope they're paying you a lot of money for this."

"Enough to pay my rent for a couple of months," the dwarf answered in a low voice. He sounded almost sober.

"Join us and I'll buy you all the drinks you want," I said.

He put up his hand and I pulled him onto the seat next to me. There was barely enough room. He nodded curtly. "Name's Terry."

A barmaid appeared with a tray overflowing with shot glasses, enough for all our guests and us. I reached into my pocket, found one last gold coin, and gave it to her. "Thanks, toots," I said.

Numera gave me a strange look but didn't say anything.

I took a sip and winced as the liquor burned down my throat. If it wasn't actual moonshine, it was what I imagined moonshine tasted like. "Do you have something to tell us, Terry?"

"Tell you? Like what?"

I didn't answer. There was gunfire in the distance. I had a feeling the Unicorn team was already in action.

"I mean, you must have approached us for a reason...besides booze."

Terry's voice lowered. "I will tell you this...you are in Blue Jaw Messina's territory. I hope you have permission for all those guns you're carrying."

"A man can't protect himself?" Burke asked.

"Not when there's a war going on."

Duley laughed. "That would seem to be the very best time to be armed."

Terry flushed, but didn't back down. "Messina's rubbing out anyone who even looks like a threat. He's sitting on something important; nobody knows what. He's scared because of these so-called shadow creatures."

"Shadow creatures?" I prompted.

"Lots of rumors what they look like, but anyone who's seen them are dead. Most likely, it's Kid Twist's gang, but if so, they've learned a thing or two since last time they went to the mattresses."

"Great," Burke said. "We're in a gang war."

"Where do we find these shadow creatures?" Agate asked.

Terry laughed. "In the shadows, doll. In the shadows."

As Numera and I exchanged glances, Terry slid off the seat, his short legs reaching out for the floor. "You mugs are crazy if you go out there. Don't say I didn't warn you." He started to waddle off, looking drunk again.

"Terry!" I shouted after him. "Where do we find Messina?"

He laughed. "Don't worry. He'll find you soon enough. My advice? Go home and greet the New Year in bed!"

Glenn and Stephen were at the bar talking to the other bar-flies. Suddenly, they turned and hurried back to our table.

"We gotta get out of here," Glenn said.

We didn't question him, just slid out of the booth and headed for the door. At that moment, the door burst open, and three large men in long trench coats entered. Their faces were hidden under the broad brims of their hats, but they looked fea-tureless, as if they were missing parts. Their eyes gleamed an unnatural red.

I reached for my sawed-off shotgun.

The intruders opened fire first, spraying the tavern. I pulled the triggers of both barrels of the shotgun. One of the men stumbled backward out the door. The other two gangsters turned their guns on us. Glenn charged them, his Tommy gun chattering. The rest of us dove behind upturned tables.

The two invaders jerked as if on a wire. They fell backward, their guns still firing wildly. They slammed to the floor and lay there, unmoving.

Glenn was just feet away from our attackers when he too dropped to the floor, sliding a ways, his coat bunching up over his shoulder and head. I felt a splatter of warm fluid on my face. I reached up and wiped off a handful of dark red blood.

The blood was real.

"Glenn?" I shouted, into a brief lull. "Are you all right?"

Glenn groaned and looked up at me with a bloody face. It was obvious he didn't know where he was.

"Don't move," I said. His head was bleeding profusely, but it looked like just a scalp wound. Nevertheless, he seemed concussed, unable to move much.

Lizzie and her twin lay tightly in each other's arms, in shock. Everyone looked okay except Stephen and Glenn. Stephen was crawling toward his friend, holding his leg. Blood was blooming above his knee, and he looked pale. I hurried over to him, pulling off my belt as I went. There was no way to fake that blood. No hologram can give you the sensation of liquid.

"Those are real bullets," Stephen managed to say, before his eyes rolled back in his head and he stopped moving.

I tied the belt above his leg wound. The rest of the team came out from under cover and stood over us.

I looked up at them. "This is no longer a game."

CHAPTER THIRTY-EIGHT

Marston's machine has started producing results. Most of it is gibberish, but sometimes a word comes through, and every once in a long while, a complete sentence will emerge that almost—but not quite— makes sense.

But he is excited by the progress, so I am excited too.

Believing that I was showing my eruditeness, I mentioned the old bromide about how an infinite number of monkeys typing infinitely would eventually produce the works of Shakespeare. Marston scowled at me. "That is mere coincidence. That is not what I am getting here. These are true messages from another universe."

I didn't say what came to mind: Prove it.

The young man appears to have aged decades in the last few years. He is no longer the cheerful, irreverent researcher I remember, but more in the mode of a mad scientist.

And yet...I believe he is onto something. I haven't shown these results to other scientists, for I am sure they would debunk them.

For now, I guess I would rather believe.

Diary of Roger Ackroyd

"Do you hear me?" I shouted, raising my face to the heavens—to the cameras and microphones I thought were there. "People are hurt! We need help!"

Instead of disappearing, the people in the tavern started coming out of hiding. That's when I knew no one was coming. Tom le Fol had taken over the game, and he was playing for keeps.

Numera stood next to me. She reached out and grabbed my arm, turning me around. "You gotta see this."

There was a slithering sound, and then a couple of *thuds*. The two dead gangsters' heads rolled across the filthy, beer-stained floor. The trench-coated trunks of the bodies appeared to levitate. Thick, viscous fluid dripped downward, the texture and color of pus. I gagged at the putrid odor filling the tavern. Tentacles slithered to the floor, dozens of them, with clicking claws running up and down their glistening lengths.

I picked up Glenn's Tommy gun, aimed, and pulled the trigger. I felt rather than heard the clicking of the firing pin. I reached down, extracted a fresh magazine from Glenn's trench coat, and slammed it home. By the time I faced the shadow creatures they were almost upon me.

Ragged holes stitched across their trench coats as the bullets struck. The coats disintegrated, revealing the creatures beneath, but even then, they seemed to be in shadow, dark shapes like swirling black water, tentacles flailing in every direction. They had no eyes or even heads that I could see, only the swirling masses of tentacles, snapping back and forth through the air and along the ground.

A tentacle reached out, its very touch enough to adhere to the Tommy gun, which was pulled from my hand, still spitting bullets.

A second tentacle swiped across my head, taking my fedora with it. I had a feeling if it had struck skin, it would have taken that instead. I clambered backward, reaching for my DoubleTap, not sure what damage two bullets from a derringer could do to such creatures.

Burke stepped in front of me. His Smith & Wesson revolver blasted away, and lumps of the creatures flew into the air. Everyone on the team was shooting now.

And then everyone in the tavern was unloading, and though the creatures never lost their shape, they slowly diminished in size, tentacles blown off one by one, until Burke finally stepped forward and stomped down on the last remains. His boot heels struck the floor as the last tiny tentacles fell away and convulsed.

I crouched down next to Glenn, who still appeared dazed.

A pool of blood was still spreading under Stephen. Duley pushed a makeshift bandage against the wound.

The patrons of the bar looked to be in shock. They were real people, not holograms, no doubt hired to play their parts. Now they were seeing people wounded in front of them, from bullets that could have easily struck them instead.

"Terry!" I called out.

The dwarf came out of the crowd reluctantly, not meeting my eyes.

"What were your instructions?" I demanded. "How do we end this game?"

He looked up at me with wide eyes. "Just what I told you, man. You're supposed to find this Blue Jaw Messina guy, cause he's got the McGuffin."

"Which is?" Agate prompted.

"Hell if I know," Terry muttered. "Does it matter? All you gotta do is find it before the other guys, right?

"If we aren't murdered first," Merlin muttered. "Why the hell would we want to continue? Let's barricade this place and wait for the cavalry to arrive."

"I doubt this is being broadcast," I said. "Or if it is, it is being edited. No doubt there are 'technical difficulties.' I don't think anyone's coming to our rescue soon."

"Tom le Fol will keep sending these shadow creatures—who are armed with live rounds," Numera said. "I think we have to keep playing, or at least find our own way out of Castle Elsinore."

"Sure," Merlin said. "If you can see through the illusions. This is the best hologram imaging I've ever seen. I'm never sure if what I'm seeing is real or not."

I heard a loud groan, and I turned hopefully, expecting Stephen to be sitting up, smiling his goofy grin.

"He's hurt bad," Duley said.

My legs felt rubbery, as if they were wobbling.

"Careful," Numera said, holding onto my arm. I stumbled to the bar. There was a shot of whiskey undisturbed amongst all the mayhem. I downed it, concentrating on the burning sensation, anything to fill the dreadful hollow ache in my chest. It was my fault my two best friends were hurt. I should never have brought them along.

"You couldn't have known," Numera said in a softer voice than I'd ever heard her use. "We ran into a psycho. No one could have predicted that. I doubt even Shipman knows what he's up against. How Elvis—Tom—expects to get away with this, I can't imagine."

"He has to kill every witness," Agate said. "It's the only way."

"What about the Blue Queen?" Amelia asked. "I thought she owned this place."

I shook my head, realizing that I should have told the others about the Blue Queen's powerlessness. I hadn't believed it changed anything. I'd thought we still needed to win the game, but now I realized that Tom le Fol had other plans. Perhaps he'd made a deal with Shipman. If our team got wiped out in a tragic "accident," he might still get away with it.

Or worse, he didn't care, and he was taking everyone out with him.

Did it make any sense to keep looking for this Blue Jaw Messina at the same time Elvis was trying to kill us? Even if we succeeded, he wasn't going to declare us the winner.

And then—perhaps because I'd envisioned Elvis instead of Tom—something clicked. The most noticeable thing about Elvis when we'd first met was his five-o'clock shadow, which was more like a three-o'clock or four-o'clock shadow. His beard was so heavy that he carried a small electric shaver in his pocket.

Blue Jaw equals Elvis. It had to be. Tom Le Fol would want to insert himself into the game. The only way we could escape this trap was the find the maker.

"We continue playing," I said aloud. I wasn't willing to tell everyone about my wild leap of intuition quite yet. But it made it sense anyway. "One way or another, Tom le Fol waits at the end. Let's finish this."

We left Stephen and Glenn in the White Horse Tavern in the care of Terry, who'd found some clothing to wear that was a little large on him, but better than a diaper. The drunkenness had been all an act. He was a very serious fellow. Turned out, he was a pre-med student and had learned enough that he felt he could take care of my friends; at least for the time being.

"Good luck to you," he said to us at the door. "I'll tell you one thing—this is the last time I hire out as a 'professional dwarf.'"

From the windows, the streets appeared empty. I had no idea where to search for Blue Jaw, but I was unwilling to wait around for him to find us again. I pushed the door open, Tommy gun in hand.

I'd forgotten about the shadow creature I'd shot with the shotgun. In the time we'd been inside, it had grown. A tentacle reached down, took the Tommy gun out of my hands, and flung it across the street, smashing in into a window. Instinctively, I ducked, and felt something swoosh through my hair, tearing out follicles. I kept ducking, reaching the ground and scampering away.

Gunfire erupted behind me. I turned to see my crew aiming upward at a black swirling cloud hovering above the street, floating toward us with tentacles hanging down like a jellyfish.

It descended. Burke held his ground while the others turned back to the tavern. The shadow creature hovered before him as all six bullets of the Smith & Wesson tore into it. Then it began to move toward the big man.

I was halfway out in the street. I saw the black limo speeding toward me, too fast for me to get out of the way. The limo swerved up onto the sidewalk, smashing into the shadow creature. It flew apart, exploding in snake-like tentacles. Burke jumped back at the last second, his huge fedora flying off his head, his gun held up to the sky as if he was firing upon heaven.

The limo screeched to a stop. A huge man popped out of the driver's seat, went to the back door, and opened it. A woman emerged, standing at the door. She beckoned to us urgently. She was tall, dressed in a long blue coat, and an enormous blue hat that didn't look as if it would fit into the car. A veil obscured her face.

I looked at Numera and she shrugged.

The back of the limo had two facing sets of seats. I motioned for my companions to enter first, eyeing the woman, whose face I couldn't quite see. I gestured her to go in, then I slid into the limo last.

She lifted the veil, revealing the Maureen O'Rourke of twenty years ago, if not further into her youth. She was a striking woman, regal even.

"Yes, I'm really here, though I have not actually left the comfort of this limo," she informed us. "I would turn off the illusion if I could, but it was planned as part of the game. It was going to be my little surprise."

"So this is your design?" Agate asked.

She sighed elegantly. "Most of it. The background details, at least. Tom has never been very good at creating Hyper-reality. He borrows heavily from others, and only after includes his own stuff—mostly Cthulhu."

"Tentacles," Duley said.

"Always tentacles," she agreed. "He was quite angry at me for awarding you the last win. I thought he was going to kill me, but instead he locked me in my room. But I was ready for that. He thought he'd bribed my personal guard," she motioned to the big man in the driver's seat, "but Martin has always been loyal to me."

"You could have escaped," I said.

"Possibly," she said, "but you would have all died. Tom's gone crazy. He knows that I'm onto him and that eventually, if I survive, I'll force him out. So he's decided to go out in an orgy of blood and Old Gods. If everyone is killed and he's still standing, he may yet succeed in overthrowing me. I've tried to change my will, but I'm not sure it will hold up in court…if it ever gets that far."

"How's he doing it?" Tom Le Fol couldn't operate the game without a large crew of helpers. I couldn't believe that everyone was in on it.

"No one knows the bullets are real. Simple as that," she explained. "That's what we get for making the illusion so tangible we can't tell the difference. Everyone thinks we're still playing the game, except those of us who have actually been shot at."

"So the outside world is watching?" Merlin said. "Why haven't they intervened?"

"I watched the game for a while before I entered it. The world is seeing a time-delayed and edited version. They see blood, but they think it's fake, as usual. No one is coming to save us."

"I don't agree," I said.

The Blue Queen shook her head.

I held her eye. "You're coming to save us, Maureen."

She laughed. Even through the illusion, it sounded frail. "I can barely move from my wheelchair."

"You're the Blue Queen, but it was never about your glamour," I said. "It was always about your mind and heart. You know what Tom is like. You know what he's likely to do. With you at our side, we can still win."

"If we survive," Maureen said doubtfully.

"Hey, surviving *is* winning," Agate said.

"Then maybe we should just hide," Amelia said from the opposite seat. She and Oliver had been quiet since the shootout at the White Horse Tavern. I'm sure she'd never thought they'd be in a life or death struggle when they joined us.

This wasn't about a stupid fight over trademarks and copyrights anymore. That would eventually all be decided in court, and if the people wanted it—or weren't willing to fight it—then it would happen. If not, then it wouldn't happen. Ultimately, the people would have to decide. We were influencers, but we weren't the ones who wrote the laws.

I had no right to ask others to sacrifice their lives for the life of a corporation, even if, as the leader of that corporation, I was trying to do my best on behalf of the players.

"I release you from any and all obligations," I said. "All of you. None of you need to do this."

This was met with silence. Then Duley gave the kind of laugh that came from the gallows; no choice, nothing left to lose. "I'm not cowering away until those things find us again," he said. "Besides, Tom le Fol needs to pay for what he did to Glenn and Stephen."

Merlin and Burke nodded, and I thought I already knew what Numera and Agate were going to do.

We turned to Oliver and Amelia.

"It's not as if Tom le Fol is going to let any witnesses survive," Oliver said. He searched his sister's face and must have seen something there that wasn't evident to the rest of us. "We're in."

CHAPTER THIRTY-NINE

Someday children will be born into these worlds who won't know the difference between reality and Hyper-reality. Already there are enclaves of historical enactors who insist nothing of the real world enter their scenarios.

What will happen to these children if, for some reason, the illusion around them collapses? What will the real world look like? Feel like? Will they be able to cope or understand instinctively how to act?

We are carrying on a grand experiment of which we do not know the consequences. So far, there have always been enough people to do the humdrum things that need to be done to keep everything functional.

But what happens if AI and robots become the true citizens of the world while humans retreat into the fantasy? Will we become the mythical creatures? Will we be lost in Fairyland?

Diary of Roger Ackroyd

The Blue Queen tapped her driver on the shoulder. "Nine Prince Street, Martin."

The limo peeled away from the curb so smoothly it was impossible to feel the movement. The gunfire in the distance had died down, and there were no collapsing buildings along the way. But there was a sense of menace in the air, as if the city was breathing a last resigned sigh before it exploded.

"Where are we going?" Agate asked.

"Lupo's Import Market," Maureen said. "In my original plan, Lupo the Wolf is an ally of Socks Lanza."

"Socks Lanza?" I said.

"That would be you. You are fighting Blue Jaw Messina for control of Greenwich Village."

"Would have been nice to have been told all this before we started," Numera said.

"I doubt Tom expected you to live long enough to play out the scenario. This was just the best way to remove you from contention."

"That's one way to put it," Burke muttered.

Maureen ignored him. "But now that we're here, we've got to use what we can to survive. We'll need money, hideouts, and ammunition, that kind of thing. We'll need to find out where Blue Jaw is holed up."

"So it's a shootout? Last man standing?" Merlin sounded disappointed.

"Not originally," Maureen said. "The prize was supposed to be a Vermeer. *The Concert.* I even had a forgery painted, which I was going to appropriate for my bedroom when the game was over."

"How genteel," Merlin said. "So it's kill or be killed instead?"

"We need to convince Shipman and the Unicorn crew not to fight us," I said. "They're probably not even aware the bullets are real."

"Forget Shipman," Maureen said. "Tom is our real enemy. If we can neutralize him, we can end the game. This whole thing was a bad idea in the first place. I should have sold the shares to you when I heard you wanted them, Zach. I'm very sorry I didn't."

The limo pulled into an alley. There were two wide doors over a loading dock. A set of steep stairs led up to the dock on one side.

"I'll wait here," Maureen said. "It's too much trouble to get the wheelchair up the steps. Tell Lupo to come out and talk to me."

There was a small visitor's door to the side of the large warehouse doors. I tried the doorknob. It was unlocked. The room beyond wasn't much bigger than a closet, with a bathroom to one side. I tripped on a space heater on the floor, which was blasting heat. The far door was ajar, a sliver of light showing, jazz music drifting through.

There was a series of single bulbs hanging down from the middle of the warehouse, which was a single large and drafty room. The lights swung on their cords, casting the shadows of the crates lining the walls back and forth, like the flickering of a TV screen. The shadow of a giant, hunched over, was shimmering against the far wall.

As we reached the end of the corridor between the stacked crates, I held up my hand for the others to stop. I poked my head around the corner.

The "giant" was a small, hunchbacked man, working at a table filled with paper. His face was long and craggy; his hair was shaggy and wild, at least for this supposed era. He indeed looked a little like a wolf.

I stepped out and he looked up blurrily, then cursed and almost fell backward in his chair. "Who are you?"

"The Blue Queen sent us," I said. "We need your help."

He stood up, and I realized I'd been wrong. He wasn't small. His legs were long and thin, and his hands dangled almost to his knees.

"The Wolf don't take sides," he said. "You all agreed to that. If I help you, Blue Jaw will come after me."

That's not how Maureen had put it. She'd said Lupo was an ally. But who knew what else Tom had changed? It didn't really matter. "It's no longer a game, Lupo...or whatever your real name is," I said. "Tom is playing for keeps. We need to stop him."

Lupo looked confused. He looked up into the air as if he expected a pronouncement from heaven. "Tom?" As far as he knew, we were being recorded on film and audio. This was an act, but one where the fourth wall—addressing the audience— was never to be broken. The biggest rule of Hyper-reality was to play the scene, to never let real life ruin the illusion. And here I was, telling him none of that mattered.

"If I help you, you can't tell anyone," he said. "You have to leave, immediately."

"We need ammunition," I said. "And we need to find Blue Jaw." As I was speaking, the rest of my crew came out of hiding.

Again, Lupo looked confused. Nervously, he turned to the crate behind him and opened the lid. I stepped around the table and looked in. It was full of guns and magazines.

"I don't know where Blue Jaw is," Lupo said. "He moves around, doesn't trust no one."

"Same thing he told us," came a voice from behind the crates. "But I don't suppose that matters if we've got you."

The ten members of the Unicorn team came from behind the crates, weapons pointed at us. We were caught flat-footed. I saw Burke start to raise his Smith & Wesson, then hesitate and look over at me. Maybe if it had still been a game but... I shook my head.

I didn't want to get shot, but I also didn't want to shoot anyone.

"Shipman," I said. "Things have changed."

"Who's Shipman? The name is No Knuckles Neari." He said the name as if he was delighted with it. I realized then that Shipman had no idea the deadly turn the contest had taken. He still thought the bullets and the blood were fake.

"Line them up against the wall, boys," Shipman said.

"Listen to me, Shipman," I said urgently. "Tom le Fol has gone rogue. There's live ammo in your weapons. Whatever you do, you mustn't fire."

"Fuggedaboutit," No Knuckles Neari said. "You walked right into our trap. We've got ourselves another St. Valentine's Day massacre, only unlike Capone's boys, this time we didn't miss the big guy, Bugs Moran...or what ya called, Socks Lanza?"

"Please, Shipman. I'm not joking. I'm talking to you as Zach Spence. I'm talking to you and everyone watching. *The game is over!* This is real life. If you shoot us, you'll kill us."

"Never thought you'd be such a sore loser, Socks," Shipman said. "Just take your medicine like a man. No hard feelings...it's only bidness."

Everyone in my crew started talking at the same time, all of us trying to break through to the men and women who were pointing weapons at us. I'd seen pictures of the St. Valentine's Day Massacre, the blood-splattered concrete floor, the crumpled, ungainly bodies.

When a shot shattered the air, I nearly fell to my knees.

"Stop this, right now!" The voice that came from the door-way wasn't the weak, damaged voice of Maureen O'Rourke, but the full-throated imperiousness of the Blue Queen. She was standing there in all her illusionary glory. Perhaps only I noticed the shakiness of her hand on her bodyguard's arm.

"I'll be glad to," Shipman said. "If the Pegasus team wishes to concede."

"It doesn't matter who wins," Maureen said. "Or rather, there is no winning."

She stepped forward, trying hard to maintain her haugh-tiness, but when she reached the chair behind the table, she plopped down into it with a sigh. "What Zach told you is true. Tom isn't playing a game anymore. If you shoot Zach and his people, you are doing what he wants."

I watched Shipman's eyes as he thought it through. He could shoot us anyway, win the game—and in real life too—and pretend afterward that he hadn't known. But he also knew the world was watching and would judge him, whether or not he had an excuse. But ultimately, I saw his better nature come to the fore, as it had before.

He turned to me. "I told you before, Que. I'm ruthless but I'm not a murderer."

And then God spoke.

"You can't win if you don't play, boys and girls." The voice echoed throughout the building, from every speaker.

"The Pegasus team has conceded," Shipman shouted.

"Conceded what?" the voice boomed. *"You can't concede what you don't have. You still have to play the game and win the prize."*

"You seem to have left that part out," I said in a normal tone of voice. "Just what is the prize?"

As I suspected, he easily picked it up. *"You haven't played long enough to find out! Very well, I'll tell you. Somewhere in the darkness at the edge of town there is a statue of a bird, painted black but under-neath, it is pure gold."*

"The Maltese Falcon?" Burke snorted.

"Of course not! It is a peregrine and it's from...I'm going to say Monaco. The Monaco Peregrine. It's real gold, by the way, for whichever team member finds it first."

"If we refuse to play?" I asked.

"Then you won't leave these mean streets alive."

"I don't believe you'll let us leave anyway," Maureen spoke up. "You've hurt people. You can't let the world know that."

"I've done no such thing. If someone has put live rounds in those weapons, it wasn't me."

"If you keep us here, no one will believe you," I said. "But no has died yet." At least anyone we can prove.

Agate added, "You still have a chance to talk your way out of this, Elvis."

"Elvis is dead. He died on a toilet."

Agate flushed and looked down at the ground.

"What's the point, Tom?" I demanded.

"Back to back, you must face one another, draw your swords and shoot each other. It's not my fault you chose a dummy for a referee."

"We're leaving, Tom," Maureen said. "You can stay in Castle Elsinore and play with yourself."

"Then you shall face the Jabberwock!" Tom proclaimed, his voice rising.

"And as in uffish thought he stood,

"The Jabberwock, with eyes of flame,

"Came whiffling through the tulgey wood,

"And burbled as it came!"

"Tom," the Blue Queen's voice rose again. "Stop this foolishness!"

There was no answer.

I turned to Shipman and his people, who'd been listening in amazement. I put out my hand. "Shall we have a truce?"

Shipman immediately shook on it. "At least until we're out of here. I assure you, I didn't know any of this was going on. But it probably doesn't matter. If all of what you've said is true, the last fifth of Ms. O'Rourke's estate is probably going to be tied up in court for years."

Numera laughed grimly. "I'll make sure of it."

He nodded. "We'll make our own way. Best of luck to you. I hope you survive."

"You too," I said.

The Unicorn crew went to the door of the loading dock and, with a final wave, disappeared.

I turned to my own crew. "Anyone have a vorpal sword, *snicker, snack*? If not, does anyone know what he means by the Jabberwock?"

Maureen shook her head sadly. "I don't know what he's up to. But I do know where he is. For him to address us like that, he has to be in the control room."

"And where might that be?" I asked.

"As he said, at the edge of town. To the north...always the north."

"Great!" Numera said. "Any idea what direction that is?"

We'd been turned around so many times by now that I knew what she meant. It wasn't as if we had a compass.

"I always know where I am here," Maureen said. "We're on the southeastern side of the building. As Tom said, we have to cross the 'city.'"

"Where are all the people?" Duley asked.

"I wasn't finished," Maureen said, sounding defensive. "Obviously, Tom has taken it over. It was supposed be filled with immigrants from all over the world—and off-world as well."

"Off-world? You mean aliens?" Duley rolled his eyes.

"Yes, it was designed to be retro-futuristic. There was going to be spaceport near the control room," she said.

Oliver spoke up, and because it was so rare, everyone quieted. "He's probably listening to us right now. What chance do we really have? He'll know everything about us while we know nothing about him. If he is in control of Castle Elsinore, I assume there is no end of hazards he can place in our way."

"But Tom loves the game," Maureen said. "He'll want to give us a fighting chance, if I know him."

Agate laughed. "And you've been such a good judge of his character so far."

Maureen looked stricken by the comment. I almost moved to her side, but Agate beat me to it, putting her arm around old woman's waist and muttering, "Sorry."

"Can't we just find the nearest wall and break it down?" Duley asked.

"I made sure nothing short of dynamite would break into— or out of—Castle Elsinore. The only way is through the doors, which are operated from the control room. It was...it was Tom's idea, actually. He said too many people were sneaking into events without paying, and this building cost so much..." Maureen put her hands to her face and let out a shuddering sigh. Agate patted her back.

Maureen looked down at the young woman with a sad smile. "I'm so sorry, everyone. I thought I'd found a soul mate, someone as crazy as me. I didn't realize he was truly crazy."

"It's what sociopaths do," Agate said. "He fooled me too, and I'd sworn to never get fooled again."

"You know," Maureen said. "I've been standing here for a long time without much trouble. Tom had me convinced I was unstable on my feet and that I'd fall if I tried to walk. I think... I think he's been tearing me down for a long time. Making me feel feeble. Suddenly, despite the danger and the worry, I have more energy than I've had in years."

"Did he serve you meals?" Agate asked. "Bring you drinks?"

"No, that was Martin. At least I can trust him, can't I?" Her voice faltered as she realized her manservant was nowhere to be seen. With strong strides, she headed for the back door. We followed her.

Martin and the limo were gone.

"Oh, dear," the Blue Queen said. "I've really made a mess of things, haven't I?"

CHAPTER FORTY

"I have found proof!" Marston proclaimed the moment the door closed. He appeared rejuvenated, young again. He had papers in hand, which he laid out in two piles on the table.

I leaned over and read the first few paragraphs in both piles. They appeared to be identical. "What am I seeing?"

"The words on the left were received through the quantum gate three months ago. It was the first full story we have ever gotten, making sense from beginning to middle to end."

"Why haven't I heard about this?" I demanded.

"I wanted to see if it would happen again," he said. "Instead, last week, a new novel reached the best-seller lists. One of my assistants just happened to read it. That is the stack on the right."

"Impossible," I said.

"I will immediately start checking the messages we have been receiving against current writings. I believe that we are eavesdropping on those creators who are in tune with other universes. They have psychic connections that don't need machines."

"Psychic," I echoed, my heart dropping. I knew how the scientific community would receive that. It was one of the reasons I'd tried so hard to keep this project secret. "Make sure there is no other explanation," I said. "See if this can be proven."

"It will be," he said confidently.

Diary of Roger Ackroyd

I worried about how we were going to get Maureen all the way across the city without transport, but she was steady on her feet as she walked down the loading dock stairs and into the alley. We followed her to the street and stopped as she poked her head around the corner.

I heard an intake of breath. "Loki!" she breathed, then stepped out onto the sidewalk.

On the corner, under a streetlight, sat a coyote, looking our way as if he expected us.

He bowed his head as we approached. "Your Majesty."

She knelt down at the animal's side and wrapped her arms around his neck, nuzzling his fur.

Numera and I stared the coyote and then at each other.

"Is that...?" Agate began to ask, then trailed off.

I examined the coyote, the shape of his face, the bluish tinge to his eyes.

"This is a different animal," I said.

"What are the odds of that?" Numera said.

Impossible, I wanted to say. But I remembered what Coyote had said: "*Someone has opened Pandora's Box and Schrodinger's cat has jumped out and had kittens. We are trying to gauge probabilities here.*"

Of course, none of the others knew about our magical visitor. But somehow I understood that though this wasn't *our* Coyote, it was a manifestation of the same consciousness.

"What is it, a robot?" Duley asked.

Maureen looked offended. "He is a cybernetically advanced animal, you putz."

"How do we know he isn't controlled by Tom le Fol?" Duley insisted.

"Because when I programmed him, I made sure he was independent," Maureen said. "I wanted at least one creature in this realm with autonomy. He's designed for deep learning, so everything we say and do will add to his A.I. capabilities."

"A.I.?" Duley scoffed. "So how do we test him? Ask him coyote questions and see if we can tell the difference between him and a real coyote?"

Maureen stood up and confronted her questioner. She was looking stronger with every passing minute. Numera had asked the right question when asking what her manservant had been giving her to eat and drink. Her feebleness had to have come from more than psychological gaslighting. "Loki is the best cyborg money can buy. I know people in the A.I. field who designed him and sold him to me before they had even published their papers."

"You say he is autonomous," Numera said. "Then how do you control him?"

Loki spoke up, as if affronted. "She is my mother. I love her."

Maureen let out a little squeal and dropped down beside the coyote again, hugging him fiercely. "And I love you too, you scruffy mutt."

The coyote whined under the hug, as if embarrassed. "We must hurry. Bad things coming."

"Bad things?" I asked.

"I don't know what they are. I have not learned that word yet," Loki said. "Many legs, many eyes; they skitter like bugs."

"They probably don't have a name," Agate said. "Other than 'monsters.'"

"I don't want nothing to do with anything that skitters," Burke said. "Let's get going. Lead the way, Your Most Excellent Royal Majesty Highness."

"Stuff it, buddy," Maureen said. "Ma'am will do."

"Yes, ma'am. Which way do we go?"

Loki stood up and started trotting down the sidewalk. He looked over his shoulder casually. "Follow me."

The sky above had grown darker. This world seemed to be in perpetual dusk, never quite turning into night; a dawn that never broke. The clouds were black and threatening. It started drizzling at first, and then the skies broke open and rain spilled down on us.

Loki jumped up into a doorway. Beyond was a wide-open hotel lobby and a bank of elevators. The coyote rose up on its hind feet and pushed a button. The elevator dinged as it slowly came down to us.

We entered, and Maureen pushed the top floor button, looking down at Loki for confirmation.

The elevator shuddered and seemed to strain to reach the top. The door opened and Loki trotted down to the end of the corridor to a final set of stairs that led to the roof. "I've had time to explore the city while I was waiting for you," the coyote said. "The bad things are below. I have not seen them up here."

As detailed at the city was, the buildings were variations of the same thing. They were all about four stories high, except toward the core, where taller buildings began to pop up.

Loki led the way across the first roof, then casually jumped across the eight-foot gap to the next building. The rest of us hesitated.

"No way," Oliver said.

"There are boards on this side," Loki said. "One of you must jump over to get them."

"I'll do it," Burke offered. He backed up a little way to get a running start, and sprinted toward the gap. He cleared it easily. It was possible we all could have made it by merely screwing up our courage—except Maureen, who looked pale and wan. She'd not complained, but the exertion was obviously tiring her.

Burke maneuvered a couple of wood planks over the gap. One by one, the others crossed over, leaving only Maureen and me.

"Can you make it?" I asked her.

"As long as I don't look down," she said, her jaw clenched, her eyes glassy. I winced as she stomped across the wood as if it was concrete.

I gingerly crossed after her.

"We should take the planks with us," I said to Burke. He leaned down and picked them up and tucked one under each arm. I stayed at Maureen's side, putting my hand out to take her arm and offer her my support. The support was probably more psychological than physical, but she gave me a grateful smile.

Three more times, we crossed over gaps, each about the same distance across. It was possible that we'd been led, by means of optical illusion, to crossing the same gap more than once.

At first, the skyscape looked endless, but that was an artifice. I kept my eyes on a tall building in the distance. Halfway up its expanse, it split into three towers, like a trident. Maureen saw where I was looking. She put out a hand and pulled me back.

"I need to catch my breath," she said. She breathed deeply a few times, her eyes closed. Then she let go of me and pointed at the trident. "The control room is at the top of the middle tower. We have to get there."

"Tom will never let us near," I said. "Unless..."

"Unless he doesn't know we're coming," Maureen finished. "We need to divert his attention. Make him believe in a different threat."

The others had stopped when they realized they were leaving us behind. Loki came loping back. Numera followed, while the others stayed back.

He must have heard what his mistress said. "If he sees you and Zach fall, he will think you gone."

"And how do we do that?" Numera demanded. "Isn't Tom watching everything?"

Loki froze, and for the first time I saw him as more of machine than an animal. His cybernetic brain was obviously puzzling through the problem. I wondered how much he knew about this world and how he was connected he was to it.

The coyote unfroze. He appeared to smile. "The maintenance tunnels."

"Of course!" Maureen said. "If we approach through the maintenance tunnels, he'll never know we're coming."

I felt a moment of hope; then my heart fell. "He's watching us. How do we get away?"

"You must die," Loki said.

Maureen laughed. "Loki, you are as devious as your namesake. So...how do we die without actually, you know, dying?"

It took all my courage to fall. To just topple over the edge of the plank and let myself tumble.

Loki had the massive computing power of an A.I. He could calculate our speed and distance down to the last inch and second. "There is a limited amount of material to absorb the shock of your fall," he said. "I suggest you not land on your heads."

"We'll try not to," I said. Truth was, I wasn't worried about myself, I was worried about Maureen, who only a few hours before had barely been able to walk. Now we were asking her to fall into a garbage bin. Chances were she'd break every bone in her body. I turned to her. "Are you sure you can do this?"

She shrugged. "No choice, is there?"

Loki also seemed worried. "Mother, there is another bin by the next building over that is fuller, if you'd rather. But I warn you, it is covered by multiple cameras."

Maureen answered. "If I'm going to fall on my ass, I want it to count for something."

Loki seemed to smile again. "You will disappear from sight once you have landed in the garbage bin, but you should stay still long enough for us to get away. I am certain that the rest of us will be confronted before we reach the tower. Wait until you hear the sounds of fighting. When you scramble out of the garbage bin, you will be visible for a few moments when you cross the alley into the building. The rest of us will try to make sure the enemy's attention is diverted."

We stood on the edge of a building, four stories above an alley and a short distance away from the Trident Tower. The others rested, not yet aware of what we were planning. At each building we'd crossed, Loki had checked the surroundings. His eyesight was beyond even that of a real coyote. He seemed to have every inch of the city in his head.

I'd had to convince Numera that it should be me and not her who accompanied the Blue Queen to the control room.

"If you die, what's the point?" she argued. "The others will give up."

Up to now, I'd always taken Numera's advice. But not this time.

"It's my company," I said. "It's my risk."

"You've been saying the opposite, Zach. You've been telling us that Pegasus is for everyone."

"I'm doing it, Numera."

She heard something in my voice. She appealed to me with her eyes. I looked away.

"The others must believe we are truly gone," Maureen said to her. "Tom will know whether your grief is real."

I hugged Numera, who trembled in my arms. "You have to keep them going," I said softly.

"You're a damned fool," she said, breaking away from me.

Her face was impassive, the expression she turned to the world. Tom would believe that the more blank she looked, the more affected she was.

Burke had already laid the planks across the gap to the next building. I'd surreptitiously moved them slightly under Loki's guidance. Halfway across we were supposed to fall to our right. It was going to be close.

As usual, the others went first, led by Loki. Maureen and I went across together, me holding her arm. If ever there is an accounting of my life—when I was good or bad, strong or weak, courageous or cowardly—that moment will be noted as peak courage. I'd like to take credit for it, but in truth, my mind was blank. My body went through the motions I'd played out in my head, but it was as if it was happening to someone else.

And then the decision was taken out of our hands. A brilliant light filled the sky and the world shook. The boards bucked under our feet. A deafening roar shattered the air. We froze, still a few feet from our spot. I looked back and saw the boards sliding sideways inch by inch as the buildings on either side shook, swaying side to side. I grabbed Maureen as if to make a run for it, but only made it a few feet before the planks went out from under us.

We flew into the air.

Loki had told us it would take only a few seconds to fall four stories, but it seemed like we fell forever. If we were off by even a few feet, we'd hit the side of the dumpster or the alley's pavement.

I can still replay those few moments in my mind—the bricks blurring by, the wind on my face, the scared look on Maureen's face, the blackness of the garbage bin rushing up to swallow us. I can still hear the loud smack of us hitting the refuse within, the screams from above, a cry of pain. I had somehow succeeded in angling myself to be under Maureen when we hit.

Most of all, I remember the pain and gasping for breath that wouldn't come.

I looked up at the sliver of dark sky between the buildings and could see the shadows of my friends, and above them, a huge shape moving slowly across the sky.

In those first moments, I realized I was alive and conscious. And I knew that was enough, though at first I couldn't move. Everything I'd ever thought and felt in my life narrowed down that single moment.

If we are alive, I thought as I lay there with Maureen unmoving in my arms, *we will rise.*

CHAPTER FORTY-ONE

I have reluctantly decided to curtail the quantum gate experiment. Numera pointed out an article to me this morning that shone a whole new light on the possibility that what Marston found came from another universe.

It turns out that the best seller Tipping Zone was plagiarized from another author. Apparently the manuscript was stolen from a small publisher more than six months ago. In other words, it existed as a story long before Marston received it on his machine.

I called the young scientist for a meeting, making sure that Numera was with me as backup. I knew that Marston's strong belief in his experiments had an outsized effect on me. We pointed out the article.

His face grew red. "That's not where it came from. That is just a coincidence."

"One hell of a coincidence," Numera said. "From what I understand of your research, the possibility of us receiving, from another universe, the exact same message that exists in our universe is infinitesimally small."

"But it also infinitely possible," Marston said.

"Have you found any other proof?" I asked gently.

"No...it will take much more research. I was about to come to you for more money."

"I'm sorry, Marston," I said. "I will continue to give you access to our research labs and a salary, but you will have to do your work under those limits."

He opened his mouth to object. I was certain I would hear a stream of obscenities and that I'd have to talk Numera out of firing him.

Instead, he turned and left the office without another word.
Too bad. It was a fun dream while it lasted.
Diary of Roger Ackroyd

"**A** re you all right, Maureen?"
There was no movement, no sound. My voice rattled around the inside of the garbage bin, the words returning to me hollow, as if spoken by a ghost.

"Maureen?"

"Can't you just let me pretend I'm dead?" she groaned.

She started to sit up. I pulled her back down. "We have to wait."

We lay there quietly. We couldn't be sure microphones weren't picking up our voices, though Loki had assured us that this part of the scenario was a Potemkin facade, where no players were expected to visit.

I heard my friends shouting down questions and I wanted to shout, "Shut up! You're giving us away!" Then I realized that if we had really fallen by accident, that's exactly what they would do.

Eventually, there was silence.

I think I might have even dozed off, so I don't know how much time passed. I hadn't been sleeping well, needless to say. Since I was lying down, my brain wanted to shut off.

Explosions woke me in an instant.

"You ready?" I whispered. My voice was drowned out by the rat-tat-tat of gunfire. I squeezed Maureen and started to get up, pulling her with me. She felt as light as a feather. My fingers pressed right up against bone.

She moaned but managed to disentangle herself. I crawled over the side of the garbage dumpster, and then reached over to help her. I was afraid we were taking too long, but it probably didn't matter. The conflagration in the distance was growing ever louder, as more and more gunfire added to the chaos.

I was sure that everyone's eyes were fixed on that battle, not on a lonely alley far from the action.

Later, of course, I saw the fight as everyone else saw it, after the edits were removed and the cuts restored. In some ways, what my friends went through is more vivid in my mind than my own journey...

My companions stood at the edge of the building, peering into the shadows below—all but Numera, who was looking into the sky. If anyone had been paying attention, that might have been a giveaway that not all was as it seemed. But the audience was probably equally torn between the drama in the sky and the tragedy below.

A huge spaceship passed regally overhead, silent now that it was within the atmosphere. It was impossible, an optical illusion, but it was magnificent, streamlined like a combination of fish and bird, wings and fins smoothly blending.

It passed beyond the Trident Tower.

Then there was no sound, no movement.

Then, seemingly as one, my friends were shouting down into the darkness of the alley below where Maureen and I had disappeared, a cacophony of voices impossible to understand. Only Numera and Loki knew that the accidental fall had been staged.

"Quiet!" Burke roared. "How are we to hear them if we drown them out?"

The others fell silent.

Burke crouched at the roof's edge, cupping his mouth with his hands. "Zach! Maureen! Can you hear me?"

There was no answer.

"This can't be," Agate said. She turned to Numera.

As the camera zoomed in and focused on her face, Numera showed no expression. Which is exactly what she would have done if it was real. Agate tried to take her hand but Numera moved aside. "We have to keep moving."

"Why?" Duley asked. "If Que is gone, what's the point?"

Numera stood like a stone pillar, unmoving, as if any expression would break her. "Pegasus Corp doesn't disappear if he's gone," she said, "nor does the Copyright and Trademark Fair Use Act. We still have to win."

The others stood a distance away, all of them looking as though they wanted to gather her in their arms and comfort her. But even through the cameras and microphones, the force field around her was palpable.

The buildings shook again as there was one last roar of the spaceship's engines as it landed.

"That is some hologram," Duley said.

"I think it's real," Agate said. She turned defiantly to the others. "Well…don't you?"

"Let's get moving," Numera said. She started across the roof without looking back. The others hurried to follow, their determination showing in the set of their heads and shoulders. They marched off as if going to battle.

Loki sat watching them, then turned around and trotted into the shadows of the building near the stairs. No one seemed to notice his disappearance.

The Pegasus team reached the far end of the roof and only then realized that without the planks they had no way across. They stood there at a loss, their resolve obviously fading. Burke started looking around for something to bridge the gap, but the roof was empty.

"What's that?" Oliver asked, pointing toward the Trident Towers.

At first it looked like a flock of birds. As the swarm came closer, it was clear that it wasn't anything our world had ever seen. The creatures' wings were long, bent in the middle, so thin they shouldn't have been able to keep aloft their huge, round bodies. Multiple legs hung down. As the swarm approached, there was a skittering, scratching noise as long claws rubbed against each other.

"If there's anything worse than things that skitter," Burke shouted, "it's things that skitter and fly!" He raised his revolver and blasted away.

The entire crew started firing, but the bullets seemed to have no effect on the creatures' bloated bodies. They kept coming, growing ever larger. One of Burke's bullets hit one of their wings by chance, and it disintegrated. The creature veered to one side, then spiraled down into a nearby building with a crash.

The others started aiming for the wings, but they weren't as easy to hit, and only a couple more of the Skitters veered away before the rest came down on them. As Loki had described them, they had multiple eyes, like black flies. Their bodies were bloated as if filled with blood. Their legs were like daggers. The creatures slashed down with them as they flew overhead.

Oliver and Amelia had been leading the way, and now they were the first to confront the creatures. Instead of ducking, they stood their ground, firing away. Oliver looked down at his gun and slapped it, as if trying to unjam it. A Skitter hit him broadside, tossing him to the ground, then crawled over him, its claws cutting into his body.

Amelia screamed defiance, swinging the stock of her weapon at the creature. Two more Skitters landed behind her, grabbing her by the legs and pulling her under their thrashing talons.

The rest of the Skitters swerved and most of the crew had time to hit the decks. The swarm passed overhead.

"We have to get into the building!" Agate shouted.

The swarm began to turn. Their long, leathery wings bent even more, and several of them crumpled under the stress, tumbling into the street below, exploding in a mass of red and yellow flesh, like bursting tumors.

As the Skitter swarm finally turned around, the humans scrambled to their feet and ran for the stairs.

Loki was waiting, as if he'd expected them.

"You might have said something," Merlin grunted.

"I needed to find a way to open the door," the coyote answered.

The door swung on its hinges, looking as if it had been battered open.

Burke stared down at Loki, who sat there nonchalantly, seemingly unconcerned that a swarm of Skitters was coming toward them. "You're stronger than you look."

Skitters swooped down, darkening the sky, but my friends were already scrambling down the stairs. One of the Skitters tried to follow. Its bloated body slammed into the entrance and exploded in gore and slime.

"My God, those things stink," Agate said.

The others were too tired to answer. They hurried down the stairs. Merlin almost toppled over several times. The older man's face was drawn and pale but, somehow, he managed to keep up.

They reached the ground floor and crossed the lobby to a side door. Loki stopped, and turned to the others. "I did not know those creatures could fly. I only saw them on the ground."

"So we haven't really escaped anything," Agate said. "We're probably already surrounded."

"Perhaps," Loki said. He nosed the door open and slipped through. Numera grabbed the door before it could close and then poked her head out. "I'll make sure it's clear," she said, and disappeared through the crack.

"How are we set for ammo?" Burke asked.

"I could use a magazine or two, if anyone has any to spare," Oliver said.

No one answered. They had loaded up as much ammo as they could carry, but they were depleted.

"We're close to the tower," Agate said. "We'll make it."

"Don't you ever get tired of being positive?" Duley said.

"No more than I get tired of being alive," she answered. She sounded so cheerful that Duley winced.

There was a loud knock on the other side of the door, and Numera's muffled but strong voice said, "Clear!"

"Three more blocks to the Trident Tower," Agate said. "Let's go."

She pushed the door open and stepped out.

CHAPTER FORTY-TWO

What, then, is the measure of a person? asks the Thentic. How well they play a game?

So few people are now engaged in activities that have any real meaning, how do they take satisfaction in what they do?

I maintain that accomplishment in Hyper-reality is every bit as valid as that in the real world. For most of the modern era, very few of us have had any real impact on the world around us. As AI and robots have taken over the real work, we've had to find other ways to measure achievement.

If a person excels in Hyper-reality, how is that any different than excelling in the real world?

The time will come, perhaps, when we won't be able to tell the difference.

Diary of Roger Ackroyd

Maureen led the way to a small door in the side of the nearest building. I expected it to lead to a featureless, square room, but it was packed with overturned boxes, with shipping popcorn spilling out onto the floor, miscellaneous furniture and fixtures, and broken appliances. There was a workstation in the corner piled with grubby receipts and discarded Kleenex, as if whoever the maintenance man was, he had a hell of a cold.

The room beyond led to a lobby with shiny brass features, a huge crystal chandelier, and a reception desk made of mahogany polished to a gleam. The flooring was inlaid in art deco patterns, hypnotically geometric. It was strangely luxurious for a place players were never meant to see or use.

We were far from the path we were supposed to have taken. "The service tunnel is in the basement," Maureen said. She hobbled her way toward the stairwell. I took her arm and helped her across the huge lobby, though I wasn't in much better shape myself. Every bone and every muscle hurt.

"The spaceship was a nice touch," I said.

She almost stopped, shaking her head in confusion. "The spaceship wasn't mine…and I don't think that it is within Tom's programming capabilities either. As I told you before, something strange is going on. Castle Elsinore is large and complex, but we've gone way beyond its boundaries. The details are starting to add up in ways that make no sense."

"Maybe Tom hired someone else to do the programming," I mused.

"I don't think there is *anyone* who can do this, and believe me—I hired only the best. I think…I think it's real."

I couldn't help it. I laughed.

"Not real in *this* reality," she insisted, "but in some other reality."

She was starting to sound like Coyote, and as when Coyote spoke, I found myself objecting. "I think by its very definition, reality is reality. There can be only one—that's why it's called reality."

She ignored my comment. "How well did you know your father?"

"I never met him in person," I admitted. "He left me a message, but other than that, I have only seen him in the news."

"Well, before I became ill, Joseph and I talked quite a lot. He was fascinated by the imagination everyone was showing. The Hyper-reality community had exploded far beyond what he ever expected. Once, after a few drinks, he asked me, 'What if all this is real in some other place? What if all we are really doing is tapping into some other dimension?'

"I said, 'If the idea of infinite worlds is true, then in some ways, that would be correct; that is, it would mirror another reality. But it doesn't really matter, does it? Those realities are not our reality.'"

"Your dad was the richest man in the world," Maureen said.

"He made me look like a slacker. What if he used that money to explore that idea? What if...what if he succeeded in crossing the borders of reality?"

"I think he would have said something," I said.

"Not if he didn't know," Maureen said. "What if the other reality entered ours? I've wondered about Tom from the first time I met him. He was an adult, smart, charming, but he had the strangest ideas, the strangest habits. There were so many little things he didn't know. I used to call him an alien. What if...what if he really is? What if he came here from somewhere else?"

"Why wouldn't he announce himself?" I asked. "Why would he pretend to belong here? I mean, we found him as a nurse in a doctor's office. Now he's trying to take over the world?"

"You found him *pretending* to be a nurse in a doctor's office," she corrected. "It was all fake. He has unlimited resources— which happen to belong to me—so he probably arrived five minutes before you did."

"So you really think Tom is from another reality?"

"I don't know," Maureen said. "If we hadn't seen what we've seen over the last couple of days, it would all be a ridiculous theory. But...dammit...that spaceship was *real!*"

Gunfire erupted from the lobby. There was a loud scream, cut off suddenly.

We were almost across the lobby, but I snuck back and took a glance out the windows. One of Shipman's people was being carried away by what looked like a flying Skitter.

Maureen spoke beside me, making me jump. "I didn't create those nightmares either—though I wouldn't put it past Tom." I hadn't expected her to follow me. She was getting more and more agile the farther we went—even after falling from a four-story building into trash.

"Let's get going while Tom is distracted," she said, turning and hurrying across the lobby. She threw open the door to the stairs and headed downward. She didn't seem to need my help anymore.

The basement had a single door. The service tunnel beyond was lined with pipes and wiring, with just enough room to get past. Bare light bulbs flickered overhead. I ran my fingers across the rough concrete sides, felt the heat from the bulbs. Both felt real, not holographic.

Though I hadn't registered it consciously, it occurred to me that our surroundings had felt more and more solid the farther we went into the city. There was no reason for there to be anything here at all, really. Sure, the game scenario would find a way to supply the illusion of space—people didn't always stay within assigned areas—but it was incredibly wasteful to supply detail where it wasn't necessary.

We hadn't gone very far before we heard clicking noises behind us. We turned to face whatever was coming.

Loki loped into view. His tongue lolled, and he appeared to be smiling.

"You found us, my dear boy!" Maureen exclaimed. She knelt down as the coyote nearly jumped into her arms, rubbing his head against hers.

"I know your smell," Loki said. "I can find you anywhere."

The ceiling shook, and fragments of concrete and dust showered down on us. A battle was raging above us. I felt guilty for missing the fight, but I suspected that we'd be joining the fray soon enough. We were probably safe in the tunnels—after all, no one tried to escape into service areas in real games. What would be the point? No one wanted to miss the action.

We passed several rusted metal ladders that led up to manhole covers. Each time I wanted to stop and check our location, but Maureen kept plowing ahead. If each manhole cover represented a street, we were getting close.

The tunnel started to broaden. Bunkers appeared on either side, filled with cots and tables, upturned sleeping bags and blankets, soiled clothing, and discarded food wrappers. It looked like a lot of people had been living down here.

Maureen stopped at the opening to one of the rooms. "These shouldn't be here," she said.

"We must be close to the control room," I answered. "I'm sure Tom has been busy filling out his surroundings."

"That would make sense if these were holograms, but these spaces are real." She stepped into the room and extended her arms. She turned to me with a confused look. "I *built* this place. I know every inch of it. These rooms aren't possible."

"Maybe we're lost," I said.

Loki said, "If we're lost, it's because we're somewhere that shouldn't exist."

Voices emerged from down the corridor. The floor shook noticeably. We ducked into one of the rooms.

Just in time. A column of soldiers, moving fast and in lock-step, hurried past the doorway. I caught a glimpse of grim faces under helmets. They carried futuristic rifles, and their body armor had a metallic gleam. None of them glanced to either side, as if determined to get to their destination as fast as possible.

Maureen shook her head as we stepped back into the hall-way. "There is no way Tom brought that many extra players to Castle Elsinore without me knowing."

"Then we aren't in Castle Elsinore anymore," I said. Neither of us had been willing to go all the way and say it out loud until that moment, but there was no point in denying the truth of it anymore. Somehow, Tom le Fol had brought a different reality into ours. We were in *his* reality, playing by *his* rules.

Maureen sagged a little, her countenance fell, and suddenly she looked as she had when confined to the wheelchair, as if she barely had the energy to breath. "What's the point of going on?" she said. "I thought if I could reach the control room, I could take over. But what if there is no control room? What if there is no way to affect what happens?"

"Some of this remains as you designed it, right? Maybe the 'other' reality still contains enough of our reality that we can still influence it," I suggested.

"We have to try," Loki said.

Maureen nodded though she didn't look convinced. She led the way down the corridor, but at a slower pace than before. We passed several more of the bunkers, which I now figured were barracks for the soldiers—room for far more soldiers than we'd actually seen.

Despite my pep talk to Maureen, I thought our chances were slim. Guards probably surrounded Tom Le Fol. There was probably no way to sneak up on him.

We reached a fork in the pathway. Maureen looked confused. "I thought you always knew where you were," I said unhelpfully.

"In Castle Elsinore I do," she said. "We should have reached the Trident Tower long ago. I'm not sure going farther in the same direction makes any sense."

Someone came around the corner. It was too late to duck away. It was obviously a soldier, but without armor or a rifle. From the crispness of his uniform, I guessed he was an officer. He reached for the holster on his belt.

I had plenty of time to fire, but hesitated. This was a human being, not a creature or a robot, not a hologram or an illusion. Maureen also refrained from firing.

And then it was too late. The man had his pistol aimed straight at us, and from the look in his eye he had no such qualms about firing on another human being. "Drop your weapons."

We laid down our guns and raised our hands when he motioned with the pistol.

Loki stood frozen beside us. For a moment, I thought he'd charge the man. Then, the coyote relaxed. His tail started wagging, and his tongue hung out of his mouth. He looked completely harmless, as long as you didn't look into his eyes.

Loki trotted over to the officer.

Our captor relaxed, even reached out and petted Loki's head. Instead of biting the man's hand off, the coyote turned toward Maureen and me and winked.

The man reached into a pocket and pulled out a phone that looked like one of the flip phones I remembered from my childhood.

"I've caught two of them, sir. A young man and an older woman...and a dog." He paused and listened. "She's dressed in blue...he's got shaggy red hair." Again he listened. "Yes, sir. Right away." He closed the phone and motioned for us to turn around, directing us toward the middle corridor.

Within a few minutes, we'd passed more soldiers than I'd have thought possible. All of them saluted our captor. Either luckily, or unluckily, it appeared a very high-ranking officer had captured us. There was no possible way we would have

made our way through this army without being seen. Instead of
the "service tunnel" we'd thought we were taking, it was obvious we'd landed in the middle of an active and alerted military
encampment.

We began passing more people dressed in civilian clothing
than in uniforms. I sensed we were entering the center of the
city—wherever that was. Who were these people?

"Where are you from?" I asked aloud. The question had
been running through my mind, though I was surprised when
it popped out. I'd been wondering if these people knew what
was happening or where they were. I looked over my shoulder
to see what the officer thought of my question. Apparently he
was aware that we weren't like him, because he didn't seem all
that surprised by my query.

"The One True City, of course," he answered. He accented
each word like it was an epigram.

"Which is?" I prompted.

"Gloriana, the Free."

"Free? Free from what?" Maureen asked.

"Free from lies and trickery and illusion. We are the Last
Human City."

"You must realize we aren't part of your world," I said. "You
have no jurisdiction over us."

The man laughed. "The Lord Protector told me you'd say
that. We have jurisdiction over all that is real. If you are not real,
tell me now so that I may dispose of you."

We didn't answer.

The floor lurched under our feet. Maureen almost fell, but
I caught her just in time. I realized we were on an escalator of
some kind, one without steps, but which had a gradual slope
upward. A vast chamber came into view, with a high arching
ceiling, which echoed with the sounds of a vast crowd hurrying
in every direction. The officer pointed us to the right, and we
followed the walls until we reached a bank of elevators.

He pulled out a key and inserted it into a control panel, and
the middle elevator opened while the crowd stood aside, watching us as if in awe. We got in, and the elevator shot upward
so fast that my knees nearly buckled. Maureen let out a little

gasp but kept her footing. As fast as I thought we were moving, it still took several minutes before the elevator slowed and the doors opened. It was another large room, not quite as big as the chamber below, without the high ceiling, but still larger than any room I'd ever been in. The floor was a deep black marble that seemed to ripple like water. It was empty, and our steps echoed as we stepped out of the elevator.

We'd reached the intersection where the three tridents split to rise above us. There were three elevators facing us.

"Halfway there," our captor said, leading us to the middle elevator.

We never made it.

The blast threw us off our feet. Debris flew over our heads and I braced for impact, but landed on the floor without being hit by any of the projectiles. Maureen tumbled end over end next to me, and slammed to a stop on her back. The officer rolled and got to his feet immediately, already firing his pistol.

I turned my head to see a blocky shape flying toward us rapidly. It looked familiar: a rectangular body twice as tall as it was wide, a square head, jointed arms and legs. Rotor blades whirled above its head. It had a blaster in hand, and unlike Maureen and me, the robot wasn't afraid to use it.

The robot appeared to shake off a couple of direct hits.

With a practiced move, the officer ejected one magazine and inserted another. As he raised his pistol again, Loki leapt, clomping his jaws on the outstretched arm. The man shouted and shook his arm and the coyote lost his grip, sprawling ungainly on the slick floor.

But by that time, the robot was close enough for us to take careful aim. Our captor took one blast to the center of his chest and went straight down.

I stared up into the square facsimile of a face that I somehow sensed was smiling. The rotors twirled above its head like a halo.

"Molitor?" I said.

"Hello, Que. This time, I am here to save *you*."

CHAPTER FORTY-THREE

*There are those who visit Hyper-reality who take on roles oppo-
site of themselves. Good people who choose to be villains, bad people
who choose to be heroes. Liars who tell only the truth, shy people who
become flamboyant, extroverts who become quiet.*

*I think the time is coming when what you pretend to be is what you
are. After all, you are what you do.*

Diary of Roger Ackroyd

"You must come with me," Molitor said. He hovered over
us, his rotors making a slight whirring sound.

"Unlike you, we can't fly," I pointed out.

Molitor landed with a clunk on the hard black marble. "I
will escort you to safety."

"What about my friends?"

"I have no instructions about them," Molitor said.

"We aren't leaving until they are safe," I said. I walked to
the huge gap in the side of the building. I looked down...and
down...and down. It was as if the earth below was as flat as a
piece of paper, the colors and outlines all blurred together.

"Which reality are we in?" I asked. "Yours or mine?"

"Both," Molitor answered.

I realized that I hadn't really expected him to answer.

The robot continued, "But in terms you would understand,
you have been invaded by our reality."

"When we found you on the spaceship, was this already
happening?"

"That was not me," Molitor said in a monotone.

"But you said..."

"Unlike humans, artificial intelligences have no difficulty understanding that their consciousness can be in more than one place at the same time. We robots are analogs of each other. But humans maintain their individuality even when confronted with themselves."

He turned to Loki and raised his artificial eyebrows.

"Don't look at me," the coyote said. "As far as I know there is only one of me."

"Uh...." I said. "Maybe not."

Loki looked at me curiously, then shrugged.

Maureen had made her way to the edge of the gap. Just looking at her gave me vertigo. Wind whipped her thin hair about, and it seemed to me that it would take just a small gust and she'd be gone.

"What's happening down there?" she asked.

I scooted as close to the edge as I dared. In the featureless landscape below were flashes of fire, which, considering how high up we were, meant they were huge conflagrations.

"I shall project for you what I can see," Molitor said.

On the black marble, as if watching it in a reflection in a deep well, I saw my friends, from both the Pegasus and the Unicorn teams, between two burning buildings. The two groups had banded together and were firing at the same targets. There seemed to be people missing from both groups.

They were surrounded by a horde of Skitters, as many dead on the ground as were still alive. Behind the creatures were the soldiers I'd seen in the hallway. They hadn't joined in the battle, but were keeping the Skitters from retreating.

But most of the humans were shooting upward, toward a creature that was taller than the four-story buildings.

It was a larger version of the Skitters, with fewer, thicker tentacles that the huge creature was using to move forward. It couldn't float, apparently, but was earthbound. Also unlike the Skitters, the monster had only two large eyes. It had a mouth that stretched across a bulbous head. As I watched, a stream of fire flowed downward, and another building burst into flames.

The Skitters were in such a panic that they overran the

soldiers and disappeared into the surrounding shadows.

I saw Numera motioning the others to retreat. The bullets seemed to be having no effect on the fire-breathing creature.

"We have to save them," I said. "Where are Cylind and the other server robots?"

"I am the only one," Molitor said, shaking his head. "I disobeyed orders. We are not supposed to interfere."

"Not interfere! What is Tom doing then?"

"He is an outlaw," Molitor said. "He will face punishment."

I stared at him in disbelief. It was clear to me that the Tom le Fol from the other reality had access to much more advanced technology than we did. How long before he imposed his will on our world?

"We have to keep going," Maureen said. "I can stop him if I can get to the control room."

"My friends are being wiped out!"

Maureen didn't budge. "I can stop Tom if I get to the control room," she repeated. She turned to Molitor. "Can you carry one of us?"

"Perhaps," the robot answered. "But I cannot not lift you very far. Certainly not to the top of the tower."

"You don't have to lift me, you just need to get Zach back down to earth. I will continue up on my own." Maureen walked over to the dead soldier and took the elevator key off his belt. After a moment of hesitation, she reached down and grabbed his pistol.

"Let's go, Loki," she said, turning toward the elevator that the officer had been leading us to. "If this reality is true to ours, at the base of the Trident Tower, there is a stadium. You must lead the monster there, Zach. But stay close to the edges. When the time comes you won't have much time to escape."

"What are you planning to do?"

The elevator door opened and she stepped in, followed by Loki. She held the pistol up, her face grim. "As I told you, this is the modern Coliseum. Just be ready."

While Maureen and I were in the tunnels, the Pegasus team made their way toward Trident Towers. It was farther away than they'd thought, because the scale of the building was so much larger than expected.

Agate scooted up next to Numera. "Where's Loki?"

"He said he was going to find the Blue Queen," Numera said. "Apparently, he wants to be with her. He just didn't want to jump off the building."

"Who can blame him?" Agate said.

Merlin looked up at the edifice, the top of which was wreathed with clouds. "That size is impossible. A hologram can't be bigger than the container the image is within. I mean, if this isn't an optical illusion."

"Nothing about this is *our* reality," Numera said. "But I think I might know what's going on."

"Then please tell us," Merlin said. "Because I thought I was up to date on all the new VR and holographic innovations, and there is nothing in the works that can do this."

'Joseph Cambermire financed research into alternate realities," Numera explained. "My father thought nothing came of it, but I now realized where I've seen Tom le Fol before. When I knew him, he was Thomas Marston, though at that time he was a small man, with bad posture and balding hair. Not surprisingly, it never occurred to me at first that he was Elvis or Elvis was him."

"What you're saying is, it's Thomas Marston, but not from *our* reality," Agate said, doubtfully. "Then what happened to our version of Thomas Marston?"

"That's one of the questions that the experiments posed. Can two realities inhabit the same space?" Numera said.

Merlin spoke up. "The Pauli Exclusion Principle says that two particles cannot inhabit the same quantum state at the same time. So if that law of physics holds true, the other possibility is that one reality supplants the other."

"That don't sound good," Duley said. "Because this ain't Castle Elsinore anymore. That building—this city—has taken its place. I'd rather not disappear and some dude named Duley Whatever takes my place."

Agate said, "I'm betting whatever is doing this is in that tower, whether the Blue Queen's control room or someone else's."

As the Pegasus team marched along, the occasional Skitter swooped down on them from between the buildings, especially on cross streets, but not in such numbers that they couldn't handle them. But because of the constant attacks, they were looking upward, not down.

When the Skitters came boiling out of the buildings on either side they were caught off guard. Merlin heard them and started blasting. The others joined him. They made it to the next building, their backs to the wall, and kept firing.

The creatures would have probably overwhelmed them if not for the volley of gunfire from the next street over.

The Unicorn team came down the street toward them, appearing equally besieged. When the two groups met, their combined firepower reduced the swarm until single shots were keeping the Skitters in check.

"Mind if we join you?" Shipman asked. "There might be safety in numbers."

"You don't care if you win anymore?" Numera asked.

"Win what?" he asked, raising his eyebrows.

Numera nodded. "Yeah, surviving is winning. How are you fixed for ammo?"

The Unicorn team seemed to have loaded up more on ammunition, which they now shared. Together, they made their way toward the tower.

"The Skitters are holding back," Agate said during one of the rare lulls. They were taking a short break under the eaves of a building where the flying Skitters couldn't get at them.

"Something's scaring them," Shipman agreed. "Something scarier than us."

Duley grimaced. "What the hell is scarier than...?"

The building across from them exploded in flames.

"Move away from the walls!" Numera shouted. They ran to the middle of the street, close enough to the flames that they could feel the heat. Moments later, the building they'd been taking shelter under also became an inferno.

The shadow of a giant creature fell across them, a bloated body atop three long legs. One leg of the monster towered over them, merging with a body so huge that it blotted out the sky.

"That's an Old God," Agate said. "Just the kind of monster Elvis said he liked. Bullets aren't going to do much against that."

"We have to get away from it," Shipman said. "Find a place to hide."

As if in answer, a second leg loomed over them, then slammed down onto the fiery building, smashing it flat, sending flaming debris in every direction. Merlin's cloak caught fire, and he hastily removed it and let it float away in the sudden wind.

"If we have to run, we might as well run toward our goal," Shipman said. Without waiting for agreement, he ran for the alley between the burning buildings. The others reluctantly followed.

The creature was now above them. It leaned over and opened its broad mouth, dripping with fire. They could see it in full now, the eight legs that supported the bulbous body and head, the two eyes glaring down at them with malevolent intelligence. It made no sound; the silence made it only scarier.

But the creature was so massive that its own momentum carried it past them as they ran toward danger instead of away, ducking under its legs. Obviously, it hadn't expected that. The two teams ran full tilt down the alleys, avoiding the streets altogether, as buildings erupted in flames behind them one by one.

The creature slowly turned and headed back, covering entire blocks in seconds. The distance between them narrowed rapidly. The Trident Tower still seemed impossibly distant. As they ran toward the dark shadow of the building, a sudden flash obscured their vision for a moment. When it faded, a chunk was missing from the middle of the tower.

"It looks like Que and the Blue Queen made it!" Merlin shouted.

That thought gave them renewed energy. They sprinted toward the tower.

The Great Old One quickly caught up to them. It straddled them, peering down curiously. Then it turned toward the Trident Tower, as if waiting for instructions.

"It doesn't want us," Numera said. "I'll bet it's looking for Que."

Burke refilled his revolver, then pointed it up at the retreating Old God. "Well, if it thinks it can just ignore us, it has another think coming."

Bullets slapped into the creature's back. It stopped, its head slowly turning toward them. Burke took careful aim and fired into one of its eyes. There was a flash of light and the monster quivered for a second.

The others joined Burke, shooting at its eyes, until the gunfire blended into one giant roar.

It seemed to finally have a result. The Old God turned, and its leg smashed down on them.

The concrete walls of the nearest building shattered, sending shards in every direction. A chunk struck Burke in the shoulder and he went tumbling. The others crouched down, hiding behind whatever wreckage they could.

The monster leaned down over Burke, who was reloading his revolver while lying on his back. Fire poured downward. Burke disappeared in the inferno.

The others froze as the Old God turned toward them and opened its gaping mouth. The fires howled, the heat shimmered, the dark skies lit up.

"Look!" Agate shouted, pointing toward the tower.

A small shape emerged from the ragged gap in the tower, coming down toward them swiftly. As it came closer, they saw the rotor blades trying to keep the robot aloft. On the robot's back was a human who waved at them and shouted something they couldn't make out.

The robot whirred overhead and between the Old God's legs, and then kept going. The creature ponderously turned its head and spit fire at the retreating duo, but they were just out of reach. The Great Old One lifted two of its legs and pivoted, and with a visible effort, started off in the direction of its prey.

The giant creature disappeared into the smoke.

"That was Zach," Agate said. "We have to help him."

Numera shook her head. Her face and hair were covered in gray ash, making her look like an old lady. Her frail voice only added to the impression. "Zach must have a plan. We must keep going, try to find the Blue Queen and reach the control room.

There are others here—I can feel it. They can't all be enemies."

"I don't see why not," Duley said, holding his left arm. It hung from a shoulder that looked crooked.

"Wait here," Agate said. She went to where Burke had disappeared in the flames. She knelt down, then bent her head as if in prayer. She stood and came back.

"He's gone," she said.

"It's the way he would have wanted to go," Duley said, then winced. "Man, that sounded lame."

There was a sudden silence from the Pegasus crew as they realized that half of their number had fallen. The Unicorn group didn't look much better off.

Numera said, "If anyone wants to take cover until this is over, you have my permission."

"To hell with that," Shipman said. "Lead the way."

CHAPTER FORTY-FOUR

*Even after Thomas Marston left the employ of Pegasus Corporation,
I couldn't stop thinking about the implications of the multiverse he
posited.*

*If each and every action we take actually manifests in another uni-
verse, then what of free will? If it means that we have already taken
that action, does that make our choice meaningless?*

*I prefer to believe that this version of myself exists because of the
choices I made, which makes me unique. That is, in the infinite ver-
sions of me that exist, this is the version that matters.*

Diary of Roger Ackroyd

The elevator doors closed on Maureen. I watched the dial on
the wall as the Blue Queen's elevator shot upward, dinging
steadily as it gobbled up the floors. The last number on the dial
was one hundred, which seemed an impossible number of stories high.

With a sigh, I turned to the elevator we'd arrived in.

It was gone, replaced by tangled beams. I inched my way
over to the jagged opening. The wind threatened to yank me off
my feet. My heart was doing loop de loops.

"Climb on my back," Molitor said.

"Are you sure?"

"I don't know. Would you rather jump?"

"Nobody likes a smartass robot."

It proved difficult to get a grip on Molitor's metallic body. I
wrapped my arms around what passed for his neck, that narrow space between the square of his body and the square of his

head. The whirring blades on top of his head felt uncomfortably close to my scalp.

Without warning, Molitor leaped. The rotors protested, and we dropped as if they weren't even turning. My stomach bounced up against my heart, which lodged in my throat as we dropped down at a murderous momentum.

"You got this?" I shouted.

"Might break a leg or two," the robot answered in a cheerfully metallic tone.

Our descent mercifully slowed. My stomach and heart fell back into their proper places. I gasped, and realized that I'd been holding my breath. "Do you see the stadium?"

"Yes, I know where it is," Molitor answered. "Hang on."

We were falling directly down upon the monster, whose attention—fortunately or unfortunately—was on my friends below. I took a chance and waved down at them. "Keep moving!" I shouted uselessly.

Suddenly, Molitor leveled off. I nearly fell as his body swooped into a horizontal position. The rotor blades lifted my hair. Wisps of shorn hair fell over my face, and I sneezed.

"Keep hanging on," Molitor shouted.

The creature's legs were like giant stone pillars. Molitor plunged between them. I looked back as the monster turned its head and flames curled out after us. The heat made my hands sweat and I almost lost my grip. And then we were beyond it.

The monster's tentacles whipped around and slammed into the earth.

"Is it following us?" Molitor asked.

"Yep," I shouted. The robot had understood before I did that Maureen wanted us to provide a diversion, to get the Old God to follow us. As I realized what that meant, a sense of rightness settled over me.

The Coliseum came into view.

The Blue Queen hadn't been exaggerating. It appeared to be a complete, unbroken replica of the Roman Coliseum, though how that could possibly fit within the confines of Castle Elsinore I couldn't understand. My guess was that the original had been on a smaller scale, but in *this* reality—the same reality that encompassed towers two hundred stories high, monsters the size of buildings, and creatures that skittered—it was full-sized.

There was a steady thumping sound as the Old God pursued us. We landed at the center of the stadium as the monster's head appeared over the tops of the walls. The walls were too high for it to step over, but I didn't think that would stop it for long. Obviously, it had instructions to ignore everyone but me.

Molitor's rotors whined in protest as he lowered us to the stadium floor. We landed softly. Moments later, there was a loud pop, and smoke rose from the top of Molitor's head. The blades ground to a stop.

"Now what?" the robot asked. "My rotors are broken, I'm afraid."

"Maureen said to stay near the edge."

I looked around, but high walls circled the inside of the arena, high enough that desperate lions and even more desperate Christians couldn't surmount them. Behind them, empty seats climbed up into the shadows of the top. If I remembered my history correctly, the gladiators and other unwilling participants of the Roman games had appeared from below the ground level—and their bodies were dragged back down when the contest was over.

I ran toward the nearest dais. As I approached I saw that there was a barricade that blended with the wall, like what you'd see in a bullfighting stadium. I ducked behind it, but found only more concrete.

"There has to be a door," I said.

Behind us, flames rose into the sky as the Great Old One vented its frustration on the outer walls. And then, with a crash that shook the entire stadium, the top section of the wall collapsed. The Old God jumped over the wreckage and into the stadium.

It stomped into the center of the arena and ponderously turned its head, looking for us. We were still hidden behind the barricade, but it wouldn't be long before the Old God found us.

The walls shook from the crash, and it was this vibration that revealed the outlines of a doorway a short distance away. It was in the wall itself, but outside the small barricade we were hidden behind. In order to reach it, we'd have to reveal ourselves.

I tapped on Molitor's metallic hide. "Do you see it?"

"Yes. It is a door. But I see no handle. And what if it is locked?"

"It undoubtedly opens from the inside and it is undoubtedly locked," I said. "But I see no other choice."

I darted out without waiting for an answer.

I reached the doorway. I didn't look around to see if the Old God saw us. The silence was more unnerving than if it had roared its animosity. I heard a thump as it took its first step toward me.

My hands fluttered across the surface of the door, looking for anything that would open it. In frustration, I pounded on it. Dust rained down on us, but the door was solid and implacable.

Molitor stood helplessly beside me.

Then, as one, we turned and faced the Old God. We'd done our best. We'd diverted the monster away from our friends. With any luck, the Blue Queen was even now neutralizing Tom Le Fol.

It was enough.

The Great Old One loomed over us and opened it mouth to spit its flames.

Tom le Fol kept the cameras rolling through it all.

The elevator doors opened onto a huge room, lined with massive computers from floor to ceiling. The room was cold and the Blue Queen's breath was visible as she stepped out into it. Loki followed and sat at her side.

Tom faced her. At his side were two soldiers, rifles aimed at her.

"Drop your pistol, Your Majesty," Tom said. "I don't want to kill you."

Maureen leaned over and laid the pistol on the floor, then kicked it away. Her eyes looked past Tom.

Opposite the bank of computers was a flowing light, as if illuminated water was swirling in midair. The apparition wrapped around and around itself in impossible configurations. Barely

visible through the churn was a small black box that was fused
to a much bigger machine that looked like the computers across
the way, only without lights. Maureen stared at it and stumbled
a little as if losing her balance.

Tom grabbed one bodyguard's arm and motioned toward
the apparition. "Make sure no one goes near that."

The man hesitated, as if he wasn't sure if he was more frightened of his commander or of the thing he was ordered to guard.

"Do as I say," Tom said.

The guard walked over to the specter and turned his back
to it, rifle held across his chest. His jaw was clenched and his
face white.

Maureen looked away as if unconcerned. She motioned
toward the computers. Her breath froze in the air. "You might
want to buy a laptop, Tom. It could probably do everything these
behemoths can do. Then you won't need to freeze everything."

Tom laughed. He twirled once and laughed again.

Loki looked up at his mistress. "What's wrong with him?"

Maureen patted him on the head. "He's not human, I don't
think. Are you human, Tom?"

"Of course I'm human," he said. "I just grew up in a very
different world than you. For one thing, we don't have such
things as laptops. Oh, I know it looks from the size of everything like we are more advanced than you, but you know what?
We're backward compared to your world. We never figured out
microchips. The moment I saw what you people did with miniaturization, I knew I had to have it."

He knelt down in front of Loki, who went still. "We don't
have anything like Loki, for instance. The Skitters have a simple
program—kill anything that moves." He started to reach out to
the coyote but Loki snarled and Tom snatched his hand back. "I
think I'll have my own little coyote when this is all over. Maybe
I'll just reprogram Loki. After all, it's not like his loyalty is anything other than coding."

"You go ahead and try that," Loki said.

Tom looked surprised, then laughed. "Perhaps not."

"The technology isn't hard to buy," Maureen said. "Surely
you could have replicated it." She walked toward the closest

bank of computers. There was a desk in the middle, and above it, a huge screen. On the screen, the Old God was jumping into the Coliseum.

The remaining bodyguard looked alarmed at her movement, and Tom frowned, but in the end, he followed her over.

"Why should I buy it?" Tom said. "Our world does have one advantage over yours. We have never had a time when the major powers weren't at war. Thank goodness we never split the atom. Another reason to leave, because once our Overlords find out about that, they won't hesitate to use it, and goodbye homeland."

"Molitor said you were an outlaw," Maureen said.

"An outlaw? Like Jesse James? Like James Cagney?" Tom cackled and slapped his forehead as if it was the strangest thing he'd ever heard. "My country has been under the thumbs of our neighbors for centuries. Am I an outlaw because, thanks to what I've learned from your world, I have liberated us? But my enemies have begun to band together, for they fear my rebellion more than each other. That's why I needed this portal into your land to expand. Castle Elsinore was perfect for my needs; it paralleled my own castle almost exactly. Without the laptops, unfortunately."

He bobbed his head up and down energetically.

"Why do you act the fool?" Maureen snapped.

"Act? The fool?" He paused, and for a moment his face turned red. Then he laughed again. "Fair enough. I learned early on that I could not easily pretend to be one of you. What better disguise than to act like someone else? Like Elvis, for instance. We had our own Elvis, you know. If anything, he was bigger in our world than in yours, though the Overlords quickly put an end to what you call rock 'n' roll. Our Elvis was what you call 'Fat Elvis,' singer of ballads. I prefer your Elvis, frankly. And if not Elvis…why not a jester? Why not act the fool while I take over your world?"

He ran his hand down his face and grinned manically. Then he did it again, and his face was downcast, lips in an upside-down smile; one more pass and he was the smiling fool again.

"I never personally met your version of Thomas Marston,"

he said. "I sent my agents over to kill him the moment we—
your Tom and I—opened our portal. But from all accounts he
was a dour fellow. We communicated a little bit toward the end,
before the merging. He was hungry for a friend. What better
friend than his own self in another world? He didn't realize that
I was very different from him."

He motioned toward the ever-shifting swirling of currents
of the phantasm.

"Hard to look at, isn't it? I think we were both surprised
when the machines fused; his little machine and my enormous
one. But I immediately understood the implications. We've only
recently begun to understand quantum mechanics in my world,
but even I knew that there could not be two of us! Your Thomas,
meanwhile, was still living in his dream world.

"I love how you people pretend to be something other than
what you really are. It is so much fun! In my world everyone
wears a uniform of one kind or another. Of course, your play-
acting is very wasteful. It will have to end when I'm in charge."

Maureen continued to edge forward, Loki at her side. Tom
watched them warily and, perhaps unconsciously, took a few
steps back.

"How do you intend to do that? With your little Skitters?"
Maureen scoffed.

"Skitters don't exist," Tom said.

"Stephen Stewart and Glenn Halligan would be surprised
to hear that. So will the rest of the world who saw what happened to them."

"Don't you get it?" Tom exclaimed. "The world thinks it's
all an act. They are so accustomed to special effects and illusion, they'll think everything they've seen in this game was
intended. There probably isn't anything I could do to change
their minds. Which do you think they'll believe, that this is an
alternative universe or…that it's all a big show?"

"Yes, but once you try to exert your power, they'll come to
their senses soon enough. We aren't unfamiliar with war in our
world either."

"Oh, I won't use force. I'm the Lord Protector of the common folk. I don't use blunt power like the other Overlords of

my world. I am subtler than that. No, once I have access to Zach Spence's estate, that will be quite enough. It's wasted on him. He has no idea what to with all that money. I will have no such problem."

"I'm sure you won't," Maureen said. She looked up at the screen, where the Old God was looming over the tiny figures of Molitor and Zach. Then she glanced down at Loki.

The coyote nodded his head.

"Now!"

Loki leaped for the guard's throat. He seemed to float through the air, as if held up by an invisible force, and his jaws clamped down on the man's soft neck. Blood spurted as the guard tried to scream.

Maureen ran for the desk, leaned over the keyboard, and started typing.

Tom hesitated. He started to lean down to pick up the guard's discarded rifle, fiddled with it as if unsure what to do, then changed his mind and charged Maureen, grabbing her by the waist and pulling her away from the keyboard.

Maureen had one last bit of strength in her. Surprisingly, she slipped from his grasp, typed one last flurry into the computer, then grabbed the keyboard and smashed it to the ground. Tom didn't try to grab her again. With a roundhouse swing, he caught Maureen square in the side of her head. She dropped to the floor, senseless.

Meanwhile, the second bodyguard hesitated. His main duty was to protect the portal, but at the sight of his comrade going down, he ran toward them, raising his rifle to aim at Loki.

Loki sprang past him, sprinting for the churning apparition. The coyote jumped into swirling air and disappeared.

CHAPTER FORTY-FIVE

Sometimes something happens that seems so unlikely, so unbeliev-
able, that it defies the laws of nature. But if all outcomes are possible,
then in our universe, where most of what happens is statistically likely,
the most unlikely things will sometimes happen.

This seems to me to be the best argument of all for a multiverse;
that everything is unpredictable because anything can happen.

I think we see proof of that—both good and bad—every day.

Diary of Roger Ackroyd

The Old God lurched and tilted to one side. One of its tentacles seemed to be swallowed up by the ground. It looked
down at the floor of the arena as if puzzled. A hole had opened
beneath it and was now closing.

The Great Old One tried to pull its limb from the opening
but it was caught securely. A second hole opened, and another
tentacle slid into it. The creature understood the danger and
lifted the tentacle, but the tip was caught, and no matter how it
strained, it could not escape the snare.

The old Roman Coliseum had operated through a system of
trapdoors, everything hidden below the ground.

I knew then that Maureen had reached the control room.

At the same moment, water started to pour out of the holes
where the tentacles were trapped. The flow was a trickle at first,
but it grew steadily until it was constant and relentless.

Apparently, the Blue Queen hadn't been kidding when she
said she'd copied the Coliseum. The Romans had once filled the
arena with water so that sea battles could be fought before an
audience.

Before long the gushing water covered the entire arena an inch thick, already lapping about our feet. By then, Molitor and I had turned to the door, desperately looking for a way to pry it open.

For the first time, the Old God howled, and it was an eerie high sound that pushed on the eardrums in a way that was beyond sound. The monster opened its gaping mouth and shot fire toward us, but the flames fell just short.

Molitor reached over his head and pulled on one of the bent rotors, finally pulling it away at the base. He pushed the sharp edge of the blade into the small crack of the door and pried with all his strength. I added my own bulk to the effort, and with a loud squeal the door opened perhaps an inch.

Then it was a matter of continuing to pull, counting out the efforts, and little by little the door opened wider, until it was almost wide enough for me to squeeze through.

"You go ahead," Molitor said.

"I'm not leaving you behind," I said.

"I should hope not. But you might add more force by pushing from the inside."

"Oh...right."

The monster howled again. I merely heard a faint shriek, but Molitor stumbled and held himself against the door for a few moments. "I must turn off my hearing, Zach. Please forgive me."

Almost immediately, his mechanical mouth took on the shape of a blissful smile. He nodded to me and motioned for me to enter. I squeezed in. It was dark and cool inside, the floor slightly elevated so that water had not yet entered. I turned and pushed against the door, my feet getting some traction against the bare concrete. The door opened another couple of inches and Molitor slipped in, his metal body grinding against the doorframe.

The door slammed shut and we were plunged into darkness. I reached down and felt around the perimeter. "No water is getting in," I said.

Molitor didn't answer. I reached out for him, then knocked against his chest. He reached up and switched something on the side of his head.

"Oh, I can hear you now," he said. "The Old God is growing faint. I don't think it likes the water. Robots try to stay away
from moisture, you know. Messes up our insides."

"Robot? Do you think that's what it is?"

I could almost sense Molitor giving me a look of incredu-
lity. His voice was full of it. "What else could it be? An Old
God? Our realities are not *that* far apart."

We stumbled against some steps, then began to climb. At
the top was the faint outline of a small trapdoor. We pushed
against it, and it creaked open, flopping over with a crash. We
emerged on the first level of the seating area, with the pali-
sades directly below us.

The Old God was still stuck, one of its legs waving franti-
cally in the air as if it was afraid of the water, which by now
would have been over my head. The creature saw us and
shrieked. Molitor winced so hard he stumbled. The Great Old
One lurched toward us and one of its trapped legs came free.

But no...it didn't come free, it was torn off. Below the broken section of the tentacle, pipes and wires hung down. One of
the wires touched the water, and there was a flash so bright I
closed my eyes and turned away.

I could feel the electricity in the air. It was as if a bolt shot
over my head, raising my hair. When I turned back, the giant
creature was jittering and trembling, its mouth open in agony,
its huge eyes closed. It slumped face first into the water, and
again there was a flash.

The monster bobbed in the water, lifeless.

The moment the Old God disappeared over the horizon, chasing Molitor and me, what was left of the combined Unicorn
and Pegasus teams made a sprint for the Trident Tower. Skitters
surged after them, boiling out of every shadow, surrounding
the humans from all sides.

To those watching—and we learned later there was a vast
audience by now—it must have seemed fun. A simple monster
shoot; target practice.

Indeed, everyone was getting more proficient at hitting
their targets. They needed to be, because they were quickly

running out of ammo. They had to make every shot count. When the bullets were gone, the Skitters would quickly overwhelm them.

But to those watching, it must have seemed that the bullets were endless, that the slaughter would continue forever.

Instead, progress toward the Trident slowed, then halted.

The buildings around them were no longer the same four-story structures that had made up the city when they started out. Now there was every size of construction around them; skyscrapers and homes, offices, retail, and industrial buildings. It was a hodgepodge, not designed by a single planner but by the chaotic choices of many people over a long period of time.

Yet there were no people to be seen. The inner city looked as though it had been suddenly abandoned; lawns half mowed, windows open, restaurant meals still on the tables, dried-out and decayed.

"We need to take cover," Numera shouted.

Agate nodded and trotted toward a large garage next to a fast food restaurant. It had no windows and only one door.

"We can fight them at close quarters when they try to get inside," Agate said. "It's the only chance we have, unless you guys have more magazines squirreled away."

"We're clean out," Shipman said.

Numera stared at the small building dubiously. "Once inside, we aren't ever coming out."

Agate said, "We'll have to hope that Maureen makes it to the control room. We've done our job—provided a diversion. There's nothing else we can do."

They were lucky. The garage wasn't new, and it wasn't flimsy. Despite looking like it was made of wood, once everyone got inside, it was clear that it was made of metal, with wood cladding on the outside. The doors were heavy and thick. There was an old Ford Mustang at the center of the room that looked like it had never been worked on.

Team members slammed the doors shut and turned the metal latches. The room inside was completely dark, which was strangely reassuring, because if light couldn't get in, maybe the Skitters couldn't get in either. From the outside the garage had seemed large, but with nearly twenty people squeezed inside, it felt little bigger than a closet.

Seconds after the door closed, there was a thump on the outside. Even though it was dark, a sudden tension rose in the air, and everyone stopped moving.

"Let us in!" came a familiar voice.

Merlin pulled the door open, reached out and grabbed me by the neck, and pulled me inside. He almost slammed the door in Molitor's face.

"Pardon me," the robot said, sticking his metal foot in the opening.

"Molitor?" Agate breathed.

"Molitor saved me," I said. "Didn't you see us fly by?"

"I saw you on top of a robot," Agate answered. "It never occurred to me that it was our friend Molitor. Where's Cylind?"

"I was sent alone," Molitor said.

"Sent by who?" Duley asked. Even in the darkness, I could sense him squinting suspiciously.

"I am not supposed to say," Molitor answered.

"Maybe it's time to tell us how you got here," I said, softly.

There was a long moment of silence. I would never to know whether the robot would have answered because Numera spoke up. "Where's the Blue Queen?"

"She must have made it to the control room," I said. "She trapped the Old God and destroyed it."

"Then why are the Skitters still after us?"

Before I could answer—and I had no good answer—there was a small thud on the ceiling, followed by a patter of *thuds* like hail on a tin roof. The door creaked as if being pushed in from the outside. The cacophony of small blows got louder until it was suddenly muffled, and I had the vision of the garage completely enveloped by Skitters, with more adding to the pile-on every moment that passed.

There was a loud groan overhead. Merlin must have been able to reach up and touch the ceiling. "The roof is giving way," he said. He didn't say it loudly, but somehow his words reached everyone in the small chamber even over the continued sound of Skitters. Then it occurred to me that the continual rattle was now completely muffled and I could hear people breathing. They were breathing hard and loud.

"Is it hot in here?" someone asked—one of Shipman's people, because I didn't recognize the voice.

"I can't breathe too well," Merlin said in answer. "Bad time for my asthma to come back."

"It isn't your asthma," Numera answered. "We aren't getting enough air in here."

"Let me out!" the first voice shouted. "I'll take my chances outside!"

"I don't think there's any way to get the door open," Agate said.

A small light came on in the corner of the room that none of us had seen before. A tinny voice came out of a small speaker next to the fixture. "You must leave the premises. You are in an unauthorized space for play."

There was a moment of stunned silence, and then in the exact same tone the voice repeated. "You must leave the premises. You are in space that is unauthorized for play."

Someone started laughing hysterically. I looked around at my people. They were pale and sweating and scared, but none of them looked like they were losing it. It was one of Shipman's pros. Apparently, being a pro in game play didn't always prepare you for real danger.

Numera looked up at the speaker. "We'll be glad to leave if you'll tell us how."

The message was simply repeated, and then repeated again.

Merlin was closest. He slammed the butt of his rifle against the speaker. The voice continued on in a high shriek. The big man smashed the speaker again, and it cut off. Merlin turned to the rest of us and shrugged. "If I'm going to smother to death, I'd rather not get nagged at the same time."

"That wasn't nice," came a deeper voice, which echoed through the space making it impossible to figure out where it came from.

"Tom?" Numera asked.

"Who else?"

My heart fell. I'd thought that if Maureen was able to save me, she must be in control.

"Where's Maureen?" I said.

"Maureen can't come to the phone right now," Tom said in the same tinny voice we'd heard earlier. Then he was laughing as if he thought it was the funniest thing he'd ever done.

"Fool," Agate spat. "You are truly a fool. It's no act."

"Indeed, and yet I am up here and you...well, you are *already* in your grave. But that demise is too neat and tidy, no fun at all. Instead, in exactly sixty seconds, I am going to open the door. Fair warning."

"Anyone still have ammo?" Duley asked.

"I do," I said. I'd checked my pistol before leaving the Coliseum. I still had six rounds.

"Not you, Que. Anyone else?"

Half of Shipman's team had a few rounds, so they all took positions nearest the door.

Merlin pushed his way over to me and held out his hand. "Get in the back," he said.

I shook my head. "I'm no more important than any of the rest of you. I'll take my chances."

"Do as he says," Numera snapped. "Even if the rest of us survive, if you are killed it will be for nothing."

"She's right," Agate said. She took the pistol out of my hand.

"All settled?" the Jester's voice mocked. "Then let the countdown begin. Ten...nine...eight...seven...six...five...four..."

With each number, part of my insides twisted, until it felt as though I was going to explode. I never heard the last three numbers because they were drowned out by automatic fire coming from the outside.

The firing was so fast and furious that it all blended together in one big roar.

"Get down, everyone!" Duley shouted, as there was a plink and a shaft of light appeared through a small hole. There was only room to crouch. More holes opened up near the ceiling, as if whoever was outside was being careful not to shoot lower. The roof, which had been bending under the weight of who knew how many Skitters, snapped back into shape with a bang.

The door opened, and Skitters piled in. I saw the flash of my pistol in Agate's hand, though I couldn't hear the sound of the shots through the thunder of gunfire outside. The sudden light was blinding, and I closed my eyes expecting to feel the critters' teeth on my legs. I was sure that at any moment I would hear my friends screaming.

Instead, the firing tapered off, and a strange slicing sound replaced it.

A pile of Skitters lay at my feet. They were dead. It took a few moments to realize that they'd been sliced clean through, instead of shattered by bullets. The slicing noise, like someone chopping carrots, came closer.

I stared out of the opening and a flash of light struck my eyes, even brighter than the sunlight moments earlier, and I cried out.

Then there was a familiar, but impossible voice.

"Is the person known as Que with you?"

CHAPTER FORTY-SIX

Life is but a dream, for anything you can dream has happened.
After all, if everything that can be real is real, then the only thing
that matters is what we perceive. And what we perceive is up to us.

As I reach the end of this reality, there is a strange comfort in
knowing that somewhere my consciousness continues on, perhaps
even unto immortality.

Diary of Roger Ackroyd

Standing over the pile of Skitter bodies were knights in shining armor. In their gauntleted hands, they held swords with Skitter blood still dripping off them. Behind them were troops dressed in camouflage, with helmets and space-age-looking rifles.

The tallest knight had his visor up, but at first all I could see was shadow. Then I realized that I recognized the face inside the helmet.

"Roger?" I said.

Behind me, Numera cried out "Father!" and rushed forward. Roger held out his hand. She halted, mere inches away, seeing something in his expression.

"I am not the Roger Ackroyd you knew," he said in Roger's voice. "I'm sorry, dear girl. In my world, I never had a daughter."

"Your world?" I said. "Tom Le Fol's world?"

"No, another." One of his men approached from one side. "Sir Roger," he said. "We must hurry."

"You'll have to come with us," Sir Roger said. He turned and motioned to his camouflaged troops, who assembled and starting trotting toward the Trident Tower, their armor clanking almost musically. The dozen or so knights lingered, arrayed behind the otherworld Roger.

"We saw that you were in trouble," he said. "We didn't know who you were, but I suspected. And honor demanded we save you, no matter who you were."

"Honor?" Duley echoed. "Well, that's good. I'm pretty sure these guys don't come from the same place as that damn le Fol."

Roger nodded at Molitor. "Good to see you, Molitor. I see you kept Zachary safe."

"Yes, sir," the robot answered, the military crispness of his diction making him sound even more robotic than usual.

Agate came forward, and had the audacity to reach out and run her hands over the suit of armor. "That was you in the spaceship, wasn't it?"

Sir Roger looked confused. "Spaceship?"

A fellow knight clattered forward and whispered in his ear.

"Ah," Sir Roger said, looking thoughtful.

The expression was so like the Roger I knew that for a moment I wondered. Stop it. No matter how much I wanted him to be the same, this was a different man.

This new Roger continued, "I suppose it could be called a spaceship, given a loose interpretation of quantum mechanics." He seemed to shake off the thought. "Now then…are you fit enough to accompany us? If not, I will leave behind some of my knights to look after you. I only ask that Zachary Spence accompany us."

"No way you are leaving me here!" Agate said. "Let's go."

When I realized that the danger from the Skitters was past, the nervous exhaustion almost overwhelmed me. I'm sure the others felt the same way. But no one said anything, but just stood there looking resolute. A feeling of gratitude came over me, so strong that I wanted to hug them all.

Sir Roger waved his arm. The knights surrounded us protectively, their metallic movements oddly reassuring. There were no Skitters to be seen. I wondered if Tom had expended them all in the effort to smother and crush us inside the shed.

Gunfire broke out as we got close to the tower. Sir Roger

held up his hand and we stopped midstep. He signaled and the knights clanked forward and created a solid line in front of us, with Sir Roger in the center. "Stay behind us," he ordered.

The camouflaged troops who had been sent on ahead were now behind whatever shelter they could find, while opposing them, surrounding the tower, were barricades with enemy soldiers firing back.

The knights didn't hesitate but continued to walk into the gunfire. They reached over their shoulders and, moments later, shields unfolded in front of them. Bullets clanged against the suits of armor and the shields to no apparent effect. I was afraid that a bullet or two might find their way past the defenses, but after a few minutes, it was clear that the shields were bigger and more effective than they appeared.

Of course, I thought. The suits of shining armor were probably an affectation; behind them was something much higher tech.

As the front line reached a point a few dozen yards short of the barricades, the fusillade was deafening, but no more effective.

Sir Roger lifted his sword overhead. The other knights followed his example. The swords began to glow, a bluish fire at first, then red, and finally a blinding white. From the barricades came cries of alarm and then pain. I heard the sound of firearms being dropped.

The light faded. The firing stopped.

One by one, the opposing soldiers came out from their positions, their hands over their heads.

Sir Roger motioned one of the camouflaged troops to his side. "Take these men into custody, Major Jos. Treat them well. They were only doing their duty."

"Yes, sir!"

"The rest of you, come with me. Stay behind us, just in case someone didn't get the message."

Sir Roger marched toward the entrance. No one took a pot shot at us. He proceeded to the elevators, followed by his knights, followed by us.

"There is no way to reach the trident lobby," I said. "Molitor's explosion took out the elevator."

"Then we take the stairs the rest of the way," Sir Roger said.

"That's fifty floors," I exclaimed.

He didn't answer, just headed for the corner of the lobby. I hadn't seen any stairs when in the upper lobby, but then, I hadn't been looking for them.

Merlin groaned at the sight of the steps. "I can't climb fifty stories," he said. "I'd never make it."

"By all means, stay behind," Sir Roger said. "Any others want to stay? I ask only that Que accompany us."

"Where Que goes, we go," Numera said. Agate nodded and so did Duley.

Merlin didn't look so certain. "You don't mind, do you?" he asked me. "I'd just slow you down."

"Of course not. I would stay too, if I could."

Most of the Unicorn team also decided to remain behind, but not Shipman. "No way am I missing the end of *this* game," he said.

It's funny. Even after all this time, it's that horrible climb I remember most. I mean, I remember the exhaustion, the sore muscles, the constant temptation to just give up. Sir Roger and his knights, who were carrying much heavier loads than we were, never faltered, but after a few dozen stories, the rest of us were gasping.

Yet, somehow, the first twenty-five stories went by, and then—after a fog of climbing and groaning—the next twenty-five stories. And then we were standing on the black marble of the upper lobby. The knights' shining armor reflected off the marble and then back again, giving an endless mirror effect that was dizzying.

Or maybe the dizziness came from how exhausted I was.

"We're taking the elevator from here, right?" I asked, my voice strangely low and dry.

"Tom le Fol has no doubt laid a trap for us," Sir Roger answered.

"Then again," Agate said, "he's probably laid a trap in the stairwell also."

"Fair enough. We will split up." Roger signaled, and five of the knights marched to the stairwell. The rest of us followed him to the elevator.

"Fifty stories to go," Numera said, staring up at the dial above the doors.

The trip was even faster than I expected. After having climbed fifty stories, which had seemed to take up most of the day, we whizzed upward another fifty floors in less time than it took for Sir Roger to lower his visor and order, "Shields up!"

The rest of us didn't need to be told to get behind them.

The gunfire that greeted us surprised no one, but was no more effective than before. The knights raised their swords. I averted my eyes this time and waited for the gunfire to cease. When I opened them again, Sir Roger and his people had already entered the room.

The rest of us hurried to catch up. Tom le Fol's men lay about the floor of the giant room, hands over their heads. Only Tom le Fol was still standing. He held the Blue Queen in his arms, a knife to her throat. She looked dazed, as if she wasn't quite sure where she was or what was happening.

"Who are you?" Tom demanded. "What's with the Camelot stuff?

The otherworld Roger Ackroyd smiled. "Camelot is a myth that is enduring and crosses many worlds. In our reality, we have taken what you call Hyper-reality to even greater complexity. We call it the Everlife, the melding of all times and all stories into one giant world-spanning mythology, where everyone is part of the story and everyone's part in the story is valued. Because of these connections, we sense when our universe is being touched by another, if only from a distance.

"We have taken on the task of keeping this mixing of realities from happening."

Tom and the rest of us absorbed this. It had the ring of truth.

"What business is it of yours?" Tom demanded. "I claim this world. This world is mine."

"We can't let that happen, Mr. Marston. Please put down the knife," Sir Roger said.

"You can travel between worlds? But you keep it for yourself and deprive others of the technology? What makes you so special?"

Sir Roger shook his head firmly. "This is the way it must be to protect worlds both above you and below you. We are the Gatekeepers—advanced enough not to use the technology for ulterior motives, but not so advanced that we won't intervene. You face the same choices—you can progress or regress. The quantum states exist in an infinity of possibilities."

"Who are you to decide your way is better than mine?" Tom said. "Who made you gods?"

"We are far from gods," Roger answered. "Though our power is such that…no, you're right to question our moral superiority. But what we know is this—every reality that has crossed over into another reality has been obliterated, along with other innocent realities that touch too close upon those possibilities. The universe, it appears, allows only one reality in one universe at a time."

"Then it will be *my* reality," Tom said. "Back off or I'll slit her throat." His voice was shaky, as if he realized that even the Blue Queen's life wasn't equal to that of all reality.

Sir Roger raised his sword, and it glowed. Tom cried out and dropped the knife as if it was on fire. It clattered to the floor. He let go of Maureen, and she started to fall, but Numera hurried forward and grabbed her. Two of the knights stepped to Tom's side and took his arms.

"We will not hurt you, Mr. Marston," Roger said. "We will simply return you to your own world."

Tom laughed shakily. "Then you condemn me to death. The Overlords will be waiting."

"That is not our reality. We do not impose our will upon others. You must face your own fate. You can be a better man, sir. Our own Tom Marston is a respected citizen."

"What of my father?" I asked. "What about Debbie Johnson? What about Burke and Amelia and Oliver? What…"

"Stop," Sir Roger said. "I cannot answer you. It is not for you to know." He nodded to the two knights, who picked Tom up, still yelling his protestations. They marched him to the vortex, stepped into it, and disappeared.

Roger turned to me. "I realize that you cannot forget what happened here, but when I remove the device *your* Mr. Marston created, all this will return to normal. No one will believe you.

Please do not try to replicate the experiment. Everyone must be allowed to live their own lives without interference."

He turned to leave.

"Wait," Numera suddenly cried. She gently handed Maureen over to Agate.

Sir Roger stood at attention as she approached, looking puzzled. She stared up into his face.

The otherworld Roger seemed to understand. He reached out and put his palm against her face.

"Thank you," Numera said, turning away.

"You have all done well," Sir Roger said, briskly. He motioned for his remaining knights to enter the whirlpool. He bowed to us, then followed them. From out of the swirling light, Sir Roger's gauntleted hands reached down and pulled on the small device fused to the larger one.

With a *pop*, it came loose.

My stomach dropped as if we'd dropped a hundred stories, though in our reality, we hadn't moved. We stood on the roof of a four-story building, with three small towers representing the trident. Our friends were huddled in the corner, looking startled.

Our own reality had returned, mundane and normal, and it was wonderful.

CHAPTER FORTY-SEVEN

I decided in the end that it didn't matter if the multiverse existed. In Hyper-reality we are, in a sense, creating our own multiverse, where each of us can be the version of ourselves we want to be.

Of course, it has always been so. Even when there was but one world and one reality, we were creating ourselves. Nothing has really changed, despite the changes. We are who we are, for good or ill.

Diary of Roger Ackroyd

After the games were over, no one knew what to make of the amazing extravaganza they'd witnessed. The last few days garnered the best ratings anyone had ever seen. Just about everyone in the world had seen at least part of the games. A few crackpots even maintained that it had all been real, but most assumed that there had been a great advance in technology—never mind that it took years before we were able to come close to replicating the spectacular special effects.

That week was the beginning of the resurgence of interest in Hyper-reality. All but a few extremists were convinced to join in the fun.

Shipman was first to realize that even without the allocation of shares from the last game, there were enough outstanding shares in Pegasus Corp in the world at large to tip the balance. He offered double the going rate. We simply didn't have the resources to match him without giving over too much power to the hedge funds and banks.

To be honest, by that time, I think I trusted Shipman more than I did the money people.

Then an astounding thing happened. The shares started coming in the mail; a few at first, which so amazed us that we talked about it. The trickle of shares turned into a flood. None of the donors were asking for money, and it wasn't long before we realized that Unicorn Industries no longer had a chance of taking us over.

The Copyright and Trademark Fair Use Act flopped in Congress, not only because we lobbied hard, but because by that time, the public had turned against the idea so profoundly that few members of Congress were willing to back it.

When I addressed the management team for the first time, I called the members Knights of the Round Table. I was King Arthur, of course, though I didn't feel worthy. Numera was dubbed Sir Galahad, and Agate was Sir Lancelot (there was not going to be any Guinevere in *our* Camelot; no damsel in distress to muck things up.) Merlin was Merlin, of course; Stephen was Sir Gawain; Glenn, Sir Percival; Duley, ever the contrarian, chose to be the Green Knight; and so on, until all of my friends were knighted and outfitted with armor. I saw no reason not to live in the reality I chose.

And indeed, it seemed as if the momentum toward story-telling and story-making was so strong that we would soon have our own version of the Everlife; a world-expanding myth that included everyone, from high to low.

After all, those of us who had been in the game knew such a thing was not only possible, but had been done. Anything we could imagine existed somewhere, no matter how crazy or strange or upside down.

The Everlife was for everyone...everywhere...anytime.

EPILOGUE

A year later, Pegasus Corp was making more money than ever. Hyper-reality—or Everlife, as it was beginning to be called— had gained a second wind and was truly taking over the world.

I couldn't spend the money fast enough, even though most of it was being directed at the bottomless pit of research and development, so much so that even Numera and Agate were objecting. But I'd seen what was possible, and I wanted some of that tech in my world.

The Queen's Jubilee was a week away, and I was determined to win "The Rescue of Jacques de Molay" once and for all.

"Heretics!" the crowd roared. "Death to the heretics!"

The rose windows of the towers of Notre Dame cast a red glow over the proceedings, foreshadowing the blood that would be spilled this day. Miraculously, my entire crew was still with me, for I we'd emerged from the sewers, arriving below the bridge just as the prisoner's cart approached.

"I can't believe we haven't lost anyone," Agate whispered.

"Not yet," Numera countered. "But the sewage may yet infect us with some dread disease."

"Quiet," I hissed. Moments earlier, Jacques de Molay and Geoffrey de Charney had renounced their confessions obtained under torture. They were to be executed, ending the Knights Templar once and for all. Or so King Philip the Fair hoped and believed. Instead, Jacques de Molay would live on in legends, in Masonic Halls, and in conspiracy theories, while King Philip, cursed by the Grand Master as he burned at the stake, would not live out the year.

We emerged at the base of the bridge as the cart trundled down the cobblestones toward us, throwing the condemned prisoners roughly against the sides. No one saw us until it was too late. A soldier turned his horse, lowering his lance, but Duley shot an arrow into his chest and the man tumbled backward.

I wasn't going to get skewered this time.

Merlin stood at the back of the cart and I jumped onto his crossed hands and he hoisted me to the center. Heavy iron keys weighed me down. Behind me, Glenn and Stephen followed with bolt cutters. I dropped the keys at the feet of the astonished prisoners and kept running. The driver turned, attempting to draw his sword.

I'd made the Blue Queen promise not to intervene this time. She had recovered from her Tom Le Fol-induced malaise enough that she was physically capable of being a problem. The driver gave me such a look of astonishment that for a moment I believed he was real instead of a holo-projection. I pushed him backward and he tumbled into the river. Taking up the reins, I whooped at the horses, which galloped away in a panic.

Arrows thudded into the soft wood of the cart, one just inches from my hand. Glenn shouted in frustration and I looked over my shoulder long enough to see an arrow transposed on his head and his badge flashing red.

The two old prisoners, who moments before had thought they were going to die, were on their knees, desperately trying to unlock their chains. The crowd moved aside for us, while behind us the men-at-arms spurred their mounts to catch up.

To my surprise, the crowd closed ranks and the horses reared up, the soldiers and their mounts unwilling to trample civilians.

The cart suddenly stopped moving.

The Eiger formed around us, its massive walls far away, the ceiling so high up I had to bend over backward to see it. Cardboard boxes and chairs outlined the streets of Paris, and a camp trailer represented Notre Dame. The cavernous Eiger made our little scenario look tiny and inconsequential.

"We weren't finished!" Agate shouted.

"I concede the game," Maureen O'Rourke said from below

the square platform that had moments before been a cart. "But since it was only practice, it doesn't count. When there are hundreds of other players, the difficulty rises exponentially. You have to win it while the whole world is watching."

"We won the game, fair and square," Numera objected.

I smiled. Numera tended to get more involved in the games these days than I did. She'd been completely won over by make-believe.

Numera and Maureen continued to argue as I took off my rose glasses and sat down on one of the boxes.

I looked over to Merlin, intending to ask his opinion. But between him and me was a swirling liquid cloud. A coyote leaped from the churn and landed in our midst.

"Que, you must come with me," Loki said. "There is great danger."

"Our reality is threatened?" Numera asked, turning her head.

"All realities are threatened," Loki said.

Agate laughed. "You know, I miss the days when we were just pretending."

"No time to waste," Loki insisted. He turned and leapt back into the vortex.

I looked into Numera and Agate's faces. I didn't need any more confirmation than that.

I approached the whirlpool and put out my hand.

Loki's teeth grabbed my sleeve and he dragged me through.

ABOUT THE AUTHOR

Duncan grew up and spent most of his life in Central Oregon, the dry side of the Cascades, and whose terrain is featured in many of his books. He wrote several books out of college, including the heroic fantasy novels *Star Axe, Snowcastles, and Icetowers*. In 1984, he and his wife Linda bought Pegasus Books in downtown Bend, Oregon, which they still own and operate. They also ran a used bookstore, the Bookmark, for 15 years.

In the last five years, he's been able to get back to writing again, and found that he has a lot of pent-up creative energy. He's written numerous books for several different publishers, mostly in the horror or dark fantasy genres, though recently has been branching out into fantasy again, as well as thrillers.

Curious about other Crossroad Press books?
Stop by our site:
http://store.crossroadpress.com
We offer quality writing
in digital, audio, and print formats.